Birthday Experience

Experiences: Book 4

*A Celebration of Openness and Submission
Among Adventurous Friends*

Simone Freier

OTK Publications
www.OTKPublications.com

Birthday Experience

EXPERIENCES: BOOK 4

By Simone Freier

Published by OTK Publications
http://otkpublications.com

Copyright © 2014-2018 OTK Publications
All rights reserved

ISBN: 978-1-942054-09-2
v1.5

Manufactured in the United States of America

COVER DESIGN BY OTK PUBLICATIONS

Table of Contents

CHAPTER 1: FANTASY FODDER

I watched Kelly drive off after our long weekend together. It had been an incredible experience – actually series of experiences – for both of us and, as I walked back inside and down to the playroom, I reminisced about some of the things that Kelly and I had done over the past 72 hours, including several new 'adventures': The violet wand, needle play, Kama Sutra positions, and Kelly's challenge with severe spanking implements.

And simple things like giving Kelly a full-body massage, the Italian dinner I served her wearing nothing but an apron, eating Chinese take-out while we watched one of the '*Indiana Jones*' movies, and spending Sunday afternoon at the pond.

Nearly all of these things conjured up additional memories, the most important among them being our first lovemaking experience. I could still smell the rose petals, and the wax – as the multitude of candles burned down to their bases; and the sensual beat of Bolero, as our bodies coupled.

We had probably overdone the alcohol, as I realized that we had gone to bed two nights without making love, our minds and bodies fully exhausted after the days' experiences ... and all the wine.

Kelly was now driving home with a new 'look', her pubes now nearly bare, with only a flame-shaped landing pad surrounded by smooth newly-waxed skin. She had submitted – to pain and to openness, with both her body and her mind. As I had deduced early on, Kelly was a very strong woman – again both in body and mind – and she was discovering what turned her on, and what didn't. So was I.

Although Kelly was great in the role of a submissive, or 'sub', her excitement had come mostly from her 'topping' me – taking almost any excuse to spank me, or do other things that had not been my preference.

It was clear that Kelly had been extremely turned-on by Julie's performance – if that's what it was. We both had. But I really wasn't sure if Kelly's thrill was due to Julie's shocking openness, alacritous submission, or something else.

There was a number of 'participants' of our long weekend, including Julie and Linda, two of Kelly's best friends, who had surprised her – both of us – with their acceptance of, and enthusiasm for, their spanking experiences. And Julie's masturbation scene, as she lay across my lap, observed closely by Kelly and Linda. There was also Barbara, the esthetician, who had done her job very professionally and with an obviously good result. And, finally, Fiona and Alex, whom we had met at the pond.

It was mind-boggling! There was fodder for a lifetime's worth of fantasies; for Kelly, and for me. Perhaps it had been too much, an overload? But there were still plenty of new experiences – and fetishes – to share with Kelly. And even more, if we included her friends.

That brought my mind back to Kelly's approaching birthday, and the party I was planning for her. It was a little over two weeks away, but I had a lot of preparations to complete: Costumes for Kelly's fantasy role-play; construction of the 'pirate ship' ... and the turntable on which I visualized Kelly and her friends, their bottoms in the air, as they played 'spank-poker'. If they would play with us.

I would need to get started immediately. Well, not quite 'immediately', I realized, as my manhood grew, just thinking about the possibilities. Lying on the playroom couch, I closed my eyes and masturbated, the fantasies still a jumble in my brain, the realities of the long weekend rising to the top of my consciousness.

My thoughts focused on Linda – probably the least outgoing and most conservative of Kelly's three best friends. Yet she had not only agreed to take a birthday spanking, she had obviously enjoyed it. I again visualized her walking to me, as I sat on the loveseat. Lying across my lap, as I flipped back her dress. Cooperatively helping me lower her underwear. Wordlessly accepting her spanking. Thanking and hugging me afterward.

My orgasm burst forth, as I looked into Linda's eyes, reached under her dress, and pulled-up her panties. I visualized every detail, including the enigmatic smile she had given me, as she rubbed her bottom through her dress. I had been wildly wrong about real-life experiences diminishing my fantasies; they only increased, with each new event, and every new participant.

Sitting down at my desk after a small lunch, I opened a browser and checked 'pirate costumes'. Up came some great images of pirates. I now realized that wearing such an outfit – and Kelly wearing hers – would be sweltering if the day were as hot as it was today. We would be dripping, if the humidity surged. But we would probably only be wearing it once – it would have to be re-tailored after Kelly's birthday scene.

As I scrolled through the images, and clicked to many of the websites, I realized that there was no need to visit a costume shop – I could get whatever I wanted here, so easily, and would get most of it by the weekend, with two weeks to spare!

I found the outfit I wanted. Trite, but acceptable for our private event: A 'Captain Jack Sparrow' – adult version – costume. It came with a billowy white shirt, faux leather vest, red sash, belt with buckle, cropped pants, cuffed boot covers, and a hat. It would work, if I added a few touches of my own: pirate wig with beaded bandana, eye patch, and pirate sword and sash. I went to another website and ordered some boots. The whole outfit cost under $100 and would be delivered by next week.

Then, I searched for an appropriate outfit for Kelly. I realized that the pirate era had been in the 17th to 18th centuries, while the Victorian era was in the 19th century, but I found some Victorian-style dresses that suited my vision of the event.

I clicked further, and learned about 'flounces', 'pagoda sleeves' and 'pelerine'. Then, I scrolled to the bottom of the page for one of these dresses, and saw the price: $6200. The site had dozens of beautiful Victorian dresses, but the cheapest (if I dared to use that phrase in this context) was more than two thousand dollars.

I clicked to other sites, and found some very reasonable dresses, as I had imagined them: Flowing outward, over crinolines or petticoats, layers of fabrics, a thin waist – undoubtedly created by a corset. I thought briefly of Kelly's needle play corset.

But having her put on a real corset for the pirate scene would require one of her friends helping her dress; I had been hoping I could send her downstairs, and all of the friends be surprised when she came back to the pool. I would need the help of her friends to get my contraption in place. And things would only go smoothly, if I had their cooperation, if not active help.

I thought about Julie going down to help Kelly change, and helping her with the corset, as they made small talk – Kelly only realizing what was happening when Julie mentioned the 'cruise ship' that they were on. We would all have our scripted parts. I felt sure that the girls – Julie and Linda, and most probably Kathy – would be happy to help. Especially as I had already made them aware of Kelly's fantasy.

Visualizing Kelly coming out to the patio (onto the pirate ship), I finally settled on an 'ensemble': A scooped-neckline top, buttoning in front (that would be important), with flounced sleeves; the skirt of calico and lace, with a bustle in back; it came with petticoat, but everything else was separate. That included boots, white gloves, a fan, and a parasol. Again, the price was reasonable, so I ordered the whole shebang, and ticked off that line on my 'to-do' list.

Getting out of the lukewarm shower, I dried off, and hung the towel on the back of the door. I gazed into the mirror over the sink, as I brushed my hair. After getting home from Sam's, I had called Julie, and thanked her for arranging my waxing with Barbara, and for providing moral support today.

We'd had a nice chat, but with no mention of the afternoon she and Linda had spent with Sam and I. There were so many questions that I could ask; I wondered if there would ever be a time and place appropriate for such a discussion.

I put the brush down, walked into my bedroom, and stood in front of the full-length mirror on the closet's sliding door. I looked at my now more-extended waxing. There was a lot of redness. I did a plié, as I examined my new look. Turning around, I bent over, looking between my legs. The area between my butt cheeks was smooth and glowing; I didn't see a single hair. It had hurt, but not that much; actually, I was more annoyed by the irritation now, than by the procedure, itself.

I took a hand mirror from the dresser, and lay on the bed, looking at my private parts. Well, they didn't seem to be that 'private', lately.

I closed my eyes, and tried to evaluate the weekend. It had been such a whirlwind – typical of Sam's style. If I were ... *when I am* in control, we will slow things down. The weekend had been an intoxicating jumble of seemingly unrelated events.

Of course, the 'main event' had been our first lovemaking – which I never would have thought a big deal, but Sam made it one. It was sweet, but unnecessary. For a moment, my mind recreated the event: Rose petals, candles, the pop of a champagne cork, and the unrelenting beat of *Bolero*. I had to admit, it *was* romantic.

The next thing that entered my mind was the scene with Julie. I was surprised it had ever been *out* of my mind. Out of my mind! It was the sexiest thing I had ever seen. Julie was the *hottest* 'thing' I had ever seen.

My mind snapped, and I realized that these thoughts were disturbing. Julie was an outgoing – I now realized, *exhibitionist* – teaser, actor. As the image of Julie approaching my dad by our pool re-entered my head, I might even call Julie a 'vixen'. Julie was never 'herself' – she was always playing a role.

The scene at Sam's house had been different. Or, maybe, she was a much better actor than I gave her credit for. The spanking was one thing; but her masturbation –

in front of all of us! – had been natural, unforced ... *real*. I remembered what I had thought at the time: She was feral, an untamed animal. Satisfying her own cravings and needs. I had never seen anything like it; this scene could not have entered my wildest imagination of Julie. The force of her passion in those moments seemed more powerful than any sex scene I'd seen in a movie. It was as if she had been in a different dimension, unseen by anyone in the mortal world.

I now realized that I was wet, but I wasn't going to touch myself. Barbara had given me a list of 'after-wax care' instructions, and I intended to follow them.

My next thought from the weekend was our time at the pond. It had been an idyllic setting to have a picnic. Alex and Fiona had been a surprise, but it had evolved into a nice one. I really liked Fiona – she was also natural, although very different from Julie.

Fiona was 'wild' in a quieter way, finding her own expression without worrying about what other people thought. I hoped that we could meet again, before she had to return to Toronto. I wasn't sure about Alex; she had been more reserved, mature ... *staid*. But, I guess I did have to give her credit for skinny-dipping with us at the pond; Fiona hadn't thought she would do it.

So much more had happened over the past three days, but I still saw everything in small fragments – Sam massaging me, and those crazy electrical sparks brushing my skin; sitting on the playroom bed, surrounded by take-out boxes, and overwhelmed by the huge video screen; a seemingly endless number of times in the pool and the shower. And Sam combing out the knots in my hair ... and weaving it into French braids.

Memories of Sam on the exam room table suddenly flooded my mind: Injecting saltwater enemas into his ass, and giving him huge shots in the butt. Sam, full of water, doing jumping jacks on my command. And me, sitting on his lap, as he expelled the enema. Not exactly normal dating activities. But we weren't dating. I wasn't entirely sure *what* we were doing ... except exploring things with each other. Sensual, sexual, and sometimes painful things. Dominance and submission. Top and bottom. Switch.

I thought again of the 'opposites' that Sam had mentioned. Everything was related; it was only a question of which order they had taken, and how they were perceived. All I knew is that I enjoyed being with Sam, submitting to him, and dominating him. Enjoying the lifestyle he had created, and the high standards that he held.

As I drifted off to sleep, I thought of Sam holding me, and my desperate grasping, as Sam let go of me. We were leaning towards each other, only our mouths touching, kissing passionately, lovingly. We were spinning, in candlelight, somewhere in the huge backyard ... or maybe the forest. We smiled at each other, as a multitude stars whirled above us. And then, Sam disappeared.

I woke Tuesday morning to a ringing telephone. It was Fiona. "Hi, Kelly! Sorry to call so early, but my aunt has the next couple of days planned, and we're leaving soon - to go horseback riding. It's some kind of outing with one of her clubs: Two days in the mountains, and spending the night at some cabin."

I yawned, and said, "That sounds nice."

Fiona said, "I guess; I feel like I'm in Brownies, or Girl Scouts. I was hoping that we could see each other again, before I fly home on Saturday. Would you have any time to get together?"

That didn't leave much time. I didn't know what my plans would be for Friday, but on Thursday I would be going over to Sam's house. And Fiona was in the neighborhood. I didn't think Sam would mind if Fiona came over for a while. As I thought this, an electric current shot through me, and I clenched my pelvic muscles. That was strange. I collected my thoughts and suggested, "Why don't we meet at Sam's house at Noon on Thursday? I'll pick up something for lunch." Fiona agreed, and I gave her the address.

By Wednesday afternoon, I felt that I was making good progress in preparing for Kelly's birthday party: The turntable had been built, and the pirate ship was well underway, although I was currently stuck trying to figure out how to make the 'sails'. I had returned to the hardware store twice more in the last couple of days, and had visited a nautical antique store, where I picked up some wooden 'blocks' – pulleys to landlubbers – and several other small items that would lend realism to the 'set'.

I had mounted tiki torches around the backyard, and even thought about finding some fireworks; but we weren't allowed to shoot off rockets in this area during the summer, due to the fire potential in the neighboring forest.

Kelly had called yesterday to let me know that Fiona would be joining us tomorrow (not in a manner of speaking, as far as I knew), which sounded like fun. Kelly had also offered to bring lunch for the three of us. The photo shoot would have to be delayed until next week.

Nevertheless, I spent time gathering, cleaning, and testing all of my photo equipment. I initialized memory cards, and charged the batteries for the cameras and flash units. As I cleaned the filters that protected all of my lenses, I considered the possibility of shooting Kelly and Fiona together. The more I thought about this, the more 'together' the girls were, in my imaginary images. We would just have to see ...

CHAPTER 2: FIONA'S PIERCINGS

Kelly arrived a little before Noon, carrying a bag of food; through the plastic, I could see several wrapped items. We stood at the kitchen counter, and I watched as Kelly demonstrated her culinary skills – unwrapping the containers, cleaning and cutting tomatoes, lettuce and avocados, and setting-up a self-serve line – with a choice of honeyberry bread to make a sandwich, or large pitas to make a wrap.

Kelly had bought a container of chicken salad, and some sliced roast beef from the deli in the market. She had also bought containers of coleslaw and macaroni salad. I put out jars of mayonnaise, mustards, and some hummus that I happened to have in the fridge. I opened a small can of large olives, which I drained and put into a bowl to put on the patio table.

The doorbell rang, and as Kelly opened the door, I set out heavy-duty paper plates, silverware and napkins, and took out a pitcher of iced tea and a stack of plastic cups. I didn't want to take the chance of having broken glass all over the patio before Kelly's party. I had assumed that we would be eating outside again today, as it was beautiful summer weather.

Kelly led Fiona into the kitchen, and we smiled at each other, then hugged. "Hello, Fiona. How have you been, since Sunday at the pond?"

Fiona smiled, "I'm fine. My aunt took me on a horseback adventure into the mountains, with a group of mostly-older women," she looked up at me and frowned, but continued, "all led by a couple of so-called ranch-hands, who were probably the main entertainment for the women. I like horses, but it was pretty boring." Then she looked at Kelly brightly, "I'm really glad we could get together again, before I leave for home on Saturday."

We all helped ourselves to the food, and went out to the patio, sitting down around the glass table. I hadn't put a tablecloth on it, this time. Fiona looked around at the pool and yard, and said, "This is awesome! My aunt has a similar-size yard, but no pool, and not so many large trees."

Between munches of her wrap, Kelly told Fiona, "We're going to have my birthday party back here ... skinny-dipping style."

Fiona nodded, "Sorry I can't be here. Sounds like it will be fun."

I thought, 'if only she knew'! My arrangements for Kelly's party were coming along nicely; it would be fun to get the costumes, and I had also ordered the party favors for each of the guests – one practical, and the other more 'fun'.

I looked over at Fiona, who seemed to be enjoying her sandwich. She was wearing short shorts, and a crop top that was tied just above her navel. Her hair still looked bright orange to me, although Kelly had called it 'ginger'. With freckles on her nose and cheeks, she looked like a pixie. Fiona would have been a good addition to the birthday party group.

Fiona asked Kelly, "How are your waxed areas doing?"

Kelly smiled, and glanced down, "I'm doing fine. There's still some redness, but not much pain anymore.

I'm just not sure I want to go through that on a monthly basis."

Fiona laughed, "I guess we're all into pain, in some way; or at least we accept pain for minor reasons. Getting my tattoo wasn't bad, and my genital piercing was done in an instant – but hurt for a few weeks. The nipple ring was a breeze, in comparison. My boyfriend wants me to get a navel piercing – which should also be relatively easy. None of these things are that painful, and the pain only lasts a short time – so it's no big deal."

I had to ask. "How do you like having a genital piercing?" Kelly gave me a 'look', but I could tell she was also curious.

Fiona looked at us seriously, "It's a VCH – 'vertical clit hood' – piercing. So it's 'out of the way' for most things, and I don't normally feel it. But it can also be a turn-on – with only a small amount of pressure applied."

The girls had finished their lunch, and it was getting hot in the backyard. Kelly looked at me and said, "Well, my waxed areas have healed pretty well – I'm supposed to be able to go in the pool by now. It will feel good in this heat."

I shrugged, "You'll have to make that call, based on how it's feeling. I haven't seen it since Monday. But you guys are welcome to go in the pool, if you want."

Fiona brightened, "That sounds good to me." She smiled at Kelly.

At that, Kelly stood, undoing her belt and unzipping her shorts. She removed her shorts and underwear, and walked over to where I was sitting. I took a look at her waxed areas: She was completely bare and smooth, except for a flame-shaped patch of short hair. "I think it looks great! There's not much redness. Turn around and bend over for a moment, please." Kelly did as I instructed, and I briefly separated her buttocks to examine the rest of her waxing. "It looks like Barbara did a great job. You look very nice."

Kelly stood and turned to me, bending enough to give me a quick kiss. Then she walked back to her chair, and continued undressing, taking off her t-shirt and bra. In the meantime, Fiona had also nearly undressed – now standing in a cute pair of low-cut bikini underwear; she had not needed, nor wore, a bra.

The girls finished undressing and walked over to the pool, where Kelly slowly lowered herself into the cool water, and then pushed off the edge. As she glided across the pool, Fiona slipped into the water and side-stroked over to Kelly. It was nice to have a couple of mermaids gracing the pool.

I got up and started bringing the remains of our lunches inside, where I dumped the paper plates, wrapped the unused vegetables, and put the leftover salads in the fridge. Then I went downstairs to grab some large towels, which I brought out to the patio, leaving one on each of the chairs. I sat down and sipped iced tea, as I watched the girls frolic in the water. They swam to where a boulder formed the edge of the pool near the deep end, and seemed to be engaged in a lively discussion. After several minutes, Kelly looked up and called to me, "Are you going to join us?"

What a great line! I suppressed the thoughts and images that flew through my head, and replied, "Do you want me to?" Kelly looked at Fiona, who just shrugged. Kelly gave me a nod, and I quickly got out of my shorts and shirt, then walked over to the pool, where I sat on the edge, dangling my legs in glassy water that reflected the blue sky. Kelly gave me a 'come here' signal, and I slipped into the pool and swam a few strokes over to her.

"Would you want me to get a piercing?" Kelly asked, giving me a seductive smile.

I laughed, "That's not a bad idea. I think it would be neat. But it's really up to you: You're the one who will have to live with it." Then, on further reflection, I asked, "Did you mean a genital piercing?"

Kelly nodded, "That's what I was thinking. But if you'd rather me get nipple rings, I would consider that, too." My mind was whirling again. I envisioned leading Kelly around by a small gold chain attached to a nipple – or genital – ring. I looked at Fiona, but her nipple ring was under the water.

Kelly surprised me when she said, "Fiona and I have been talking about needles." I had no doubt that there was a shocked expression on my face.

Fiona said, "I don't mind showing you my piercings. Kelly told me that you have an 'exam' room," she chuckled, "where you stick her with big needles." Now, I was even more shocked, but Fiona didn't seem to be.

I looked at Kelly; she just smiled at me sweetly. I guess we were going to be as open with Fiona as she was with us. "I view needle insertions as a form of submission. As you said, there isn't much pain, and it doesn't last that long, so it's more of a psychological experience than the physical experience that most people expect." Fiona was nodding.

"And, actually, we usually use very small needles." Kelly gave me a look, and was about to object, when I clarified, "They are 1 ½" long, but only 25 gauge – tiny, compared to the 12- or 14-gauge needles used for piercings."

Fiona laughed, "Yeah, my nipple jewelry is only 16-gauge, but my clit hood barbell is 12-gauge. It's not unusual to get pierced with a 10-gauge needle; that's pretty big." I nodded, thinking that I had never even seen a needle that big; the biggest needles used for medical procedures are usually 18-gauge ... and I thought *that* was big. The needles that Fiona was talking about would *definitely* produce a very physical experience.

Kelly said, "I was telling Fiona that you like to stick needles in my butt, and give me injections." I winced, but Fiona seemed OK with the discussion. Kelly continued, "And I was just explaining 'needle play' to her. We'll have to show her the picture we took of your 'artwork' on my bottom."

Fiona interjected, "My boyfriend would be interested in that – he'd probably have me stick the needles in him. He has quite a few piercings ... I guess I'll have to show you a photo of his frenum rings. He has a 'ladder' of 8 or 10 of them; and I think they are 10- or maybe 12-gauge."

That hurt, just thinking about it. "Don't they get in the way, when you're making love? I would think that would hurt, if they're pulled."

Fiona looked at me seriously, "Actually, he likes the feel of them during sex. At least vaginal sex; I don't think he would leave them in if we did anal."

I just shook my head. Here was another whole area of experiences that I hadn't considered. For me, or Kelly. I had read about various piercings on the web, but never really considered getting one; certainly not a Prince Albert or Ampallang!

And, a frenum piercing – like Fiona's boyfriend has – would only get me more turned on, which is – I guess – the point. But I get turned-on easily enough as it is, and wouldn't want to be walking around with an erection, all the time.

Fiona added, "It's possible to wear a condom over the piercings, and that might allow them to be used more easily during anal sex. But anal is challenging enough without adding jewelry." Fiona laughed easily, evidently quite comfortable with the conversation.

"And, before you ask, Kelly, his rings feel good to me, also, but I wouldn't say they give me much extra 'turn-on'. But if he decides to get more, I might suggest he try a pubic piercing – just at the base of the penis, on top – which might provide some clitoral stimulation. It's something we have to research further."

Kelly beamed, "Fiona said she might let me insert a needle or two in her bottom – just for the experience of it. She can let us know if the endorphin rush is more or less than getting a piercing." This was an interesting development. I would have to concentrate in order to not get an erection here in the pool, as we discussed all of this.

Fiona responded, "I don't think those small needles will compare to the piercing needles, in terms of either pain or endorphins." Then she looked at me, "But I'm not sure that I like the idea of you injecting anything."

I nodded, "We can do whatever you want. The injections use sterile saline, so they're safe, and don't hurt that much, given in the butt."

Then, I thought of other possibilities ... "For more endorphins, we could try sticking them through the labia. Something else we haven't tried is injecting saline into the labia." I looked at Kelly, and her face was scrunched. "That's another body modification technique; it's supposed to feel interesting, and it lasts only a few hours."

Fiona looked a bit more uncomfortable. "Well, I would be OK with needles in my butt ... and maybe even through my labia. But I don't think I would let you or Kelly inject me there." Then, Fiona looked thoughtful, "I'll tell my boyfriend about our discussion. He might be interested in some of these things."

I didn't want to give Kelly any ideas, but thought I should mention something to Fiona. "Another 'popular' saline injection – or infusion – is into the scrotum. Perhaps your boyfriend would find that interesting."

At that point, Kelly suggested that we get out of the pool. We walked over to the patio table, and retrieved our towels. I dried off and folded the towel lengthwise, wrapping it around my waist. As I was about to sit down, Kelly told Fiona, in a bubbly voice, "Sam also has a sauna downstairs. Why don't we get in there, and then we can take a quick shower before we go into the exam room?"

Now, it seemed like Kelly was pushing Fiona a bit too hard. But Fiona just shrugged, and said, "OK." So we all went downstairs, the girls carrying their towels, as they walked nude through the house. When we got to the bathroom, Fiona said, "I better use the toilet first."

Kelly and I continued through the shower room and proceeded directly into the sauna. The temperature wasn't really high enough for a 'traditional' sauna, but it seemed too hot outside to crank up the sauna to full intensity. A minute later, the smoked glass sauna door opened, and Fiona came in, carrying her towel. We all sat on the top bench, spreading our towels, and sitting cross-legged.

Fiona looked around in the dim red light, and commented, "My aunt doesn't have one of these, either. Even if she did, I doubt that she would invite anyone to take a sauna with her – even other women. But, remembering our afternoon at the pond, maybe she can get over some of her hang-ups; at least, if I'm there pushing her." She laughed.

I suggested, "Well, maybe Kelly and I will invite her over sometime ... and see if she'll join us in here."

Fiona was still laughing, "Good luck. Let me know, if she actually does it. You've all been nude together already, so it shouldn't really be that much of a challenge."

We all sat quietly in the sauna, beads of sweat dotting our bodies, the heat seeping into us. Kelly leaned over, and kissed me gently on the lips. She looked deeply into my eyes, and I felt that somehow I was gazing into my future; a future with love and caring ... and, yes, strength. There was a determination in Kelly's eyes that I could not miss. I wondered whether she was getting turned-on by the exam room experience that she had suggested – and to which Fiona had responded with amusement, if not enthusiasm.

As we sat a few more minutes in the heat, I looked at Fiona. The glistening globules of water now jumbled with her facial freckles, dripping off her chin and streaming down her chest, over her small breasts. While Fiona seemed very young, given her pixie orange hair, freckles, and small physique, her demeanor was mature, composed, comfortable.

Although she was sitting cross-legged in the corner, facing us, it was too dark to see her genital jewelry. Kelly seemed enthusiastic about the idea of getting a piercing, or two. But I winced again, as I thought of the images I had seen of male piercings. I wasn't sure I would ever be up for that.

Kelly suddenly sighed, "Are we done in here?" We looked at Fiona, who looked up at us and smiled, nodding her head once, in agreement. We got up, and stepped down onto the lower bench, and then down to the tile floor. I held the door open, and we all exited the sauna. I took everyone's towels, and walked to the hamper in the bathroom, as Kelly got the rain shower and leg jets going. When I re-entered the shower room, I saw Fiona smile and nod her head. Then she turned to face the wall, as Kelly soaped her body.

I stepped under the rain shower next to Kelly, and washed myself, turning around and around slowly, allowing the jets to cover my entire lower body. I felt a bump, and turned to see Kelly wink at me, and then push against Fiona, the contours of Kelly's front and Fiona's back merging, Kelly's arms around Fiona's waist, and leaning forward to whisper something in Fiona's ear.

But with the noise of the shower, Kelly's voice was no more than a whisper, as she asked if Fiona would like a 4-hand shower. Initially, I didn't understand, and thought she was talking about tennis; but when Fiona nodded and Kelly looked back at me, I suddenly realized that we would be having a shower ménage with Fiona.

Kelly walked around in front of Fiona, and soaped her shoulders, chest, and breasts, as I began washing Fiona's back. I also started at her shoulders, with Kelly's and my hands alternately and simultaneously caressing Fiona's neck, over her shoulders and down in front and back, as Kelly and I coordinated our efforts.

She then concentrated on Fiona's breasts, as I massaged her back, from shoulder blades down to her waist. I used some of the techniques that Liz had taught me, moving vertebra-to-vertebra, outward to cover all muscle groups, and finally down to her hips, where my hands joined with Kelly's once again.

Our hands did an erotic dance across Fiona's slim body, up and over her hips, then down in front, as Kelly soaped Fiona's stomach, moving down over her bare mons. My hands came up and over her hips, then down in back, taking one of Fiona's buttocks in each of my hands, kneading, and moving over her hips again.

My right hand soaped her butt crack, slowly making its way down, and over her anus. I stroked slowly up and down, again grazing her anus at the bottom of each stroke. Kelly was washing Fiona underneath, and I saw Fiona tense, as Kelly put two fingers into her.

Trying for synchronous perfection, my hand slid down, and my middle finger entered her rear, sliding nearly all the way in, and then – as quickly – back out. I continued bathing Fiona, moving down her hips, the back of her legs, and down to her feet.

Kelly leaned forward, took Fiona's cheeks in her hands, and kissed her on the lips. Fiona smiled, but didn't react, otherwise. Kelly frowned, "I'm sorry, Fiona. I'm not sure what's gotten into me. Everything seems to be more of a turn-on, these days." Kelly looked down at the water jets hitting her legs. "I was about to ask if I ... we ... could get you off." I think Kelly realized, at that point, what an isolated world we were living in – a world of openness and sex, which most other people didn't inhabit.

Fiona graciously said, "No worries, Kelly. I'm not sure if you knew that I'm bi; so, I might have taken you up on your offer. But I'm not comfortable with Sam being here, while we do that." Fiona looked down, and then back into Kelly's eyes. "Maybe he can get his 'exam' room ready, while we play in here. I'll let him give me one shot; and I'll let you insert as many needles as you want into my bottom."

I had heard Fiona, so stood, and walked out from under the rain shower. "Have fun!" I meant it. I grabbed a fresh towel, quickly dried off, then walked across the hall to the exam room. After punching in the combination, the door opened, and the bright light shined through; equipment was gleaming on the counter, and the exam table had a fresh paper covering.

I made up two 6cc shots – just in case. Maybe Kelly would like to demonstrate, first; then I realized what this meant – I hoped that I would be giving *her* a demonstration injection to make Fiona more comfortable. But I knew that Kelly's preference would be to demonstrate on *me*.

I also prepared the rectal thermometer, and a couple of butt plugs – the smaller ones; again, 'just in case'. As Kelly and Fiona were still not out of the shower, I walked to the desk and made a few additional preparations. There was still a slim possibility that I could turn this into a photo session with the girls, but I doubted that would actually happen. I lowered the screen – thereby hiding the bed at the far end of the room – and put on an underwater video of coral reefs.

Kelly and Fiona came out of the bathroom, and waved to me to come over. Kelly wore one of the spa robes that were hung between the shower room and the bathroom in the narrow closet. Fiona had a towel wrapped around her waist. They disappeared into the exam room, and I got up from the desk and put on my doctor's coat – wearing nothing underneath – and walked across the playroom to the exam room door – which was mostly closed. I knocked twice, and heard Fiona say, "Come in."

When I entered, Fiona was sitting on the exam table, wearing one of our hospital gowns, her hands clutching the edge of the table, and her feet swinging from it. "Hello, Doctor." Fiona couldn't help but laugh, as did Kelly.

I looked at Kelly, and sternly said, "Nurse Kelly! What are you doing out of your uniform? This may require a punishment."

Kelly cracked up uncontrollably, stamping her feet, and generally carrying-on. "No, Sir. You're correct, but I was helping Ms. Fiona with her sitz bath, and am just delivering her for her exam."

Then Kelly looked down – I thought maybe I had spilled something on my lab coat – and she said, "Umm, Sir? Would you need a little 'exam', also?" I glanced at Fiona, who now had a huge grin on her face, and then looked down at my lab coat – now tented by a structural 'member'. I knew I should have put on running shorts under the lab coat!

I looked at Kelly, and smiled softly, "OK, Nurse Kelly, point taken. I'm not dressed properly, either. Shall we get on with the exam?"

Kelly nodded, and helped Fiona swing her legs onto the table, and lie back, positioning the pillow under her head. Kelly took over, incredibly focused, with an air of authority that could not be ignored. "Fiona, what would you like to show us, first?"

Fiona turned her head toward Kelly, "You can take a look at my nipple piercing." Kelly folded back the hospital gown from Fiona's shoulder, exposing her left breast. I opened one of the drawers and pulled out a hand magnifying loupe, and Kelly examined Fiona's nipple.

Then she handed the loupe to me, and I examined her. The piercing had healed beautifully, and through the magnifier the ring looked huge, disappearing into a tissue tunnel.

I asked, "Do you take this out, often? Or have other jewelry you wear? And, how long can it be out, before it will start closing?"

Fiona smiled, "I take it out sometimes. I don't have any other rings, but I'm looking at some. I haven't left it out for very long – a few days at most. But it could probably be left out for a week or two ... I think" Fiona looked at Kelly, then me. "Do you want to see my VCH piercing, now?"

Kelly nodded, and put the gown back over Fiona's shoulder. I wasn't sure whether Kelly would have Fiona let her legs fall into the 'butterfly' position, but my curiosity was satisfied when she went to the foot of the table, raised the stirrups, and asked Fiona to scoot down.

I saw surprise, then resignation, in Fiona's face, as she positioned herself for our viewing pleasure. I stood next to Kelly at the foot of the bed, and we watched as Fiona explained. She reached down and pulled back her hood, exposing one end of the barbell.

"This is a VCH – vertical clit hood – piercing. It goes through the hood, *not* the clit, starting under the hood and coming out, as you can see, near the top of the hood."

I briefly wondered whether Kelly had masturbated her, but assumed she had. Maybe it had gone both ways. We looked closely, as Fiona explained that the bar had internal threads, making it less traumatic to insert, and the bells had portions that screwed onto the bar. She listed the pros and cons of various barbell materials – including gold and platinum, and said that the healing period was usually one to two months.

Finally, she asked, "Do you guys have any questions?"

Kelly shrugged her shoulders. "How much did it hurt?"

Fiona smiled, and put her head back on the pillow, "I don't know ... maybe a 4 out of 10? But only for a few seconds. It's not that bad."

I asked, "Did you consider other genital piercings, such as labial rings?"

Fiona said, "I've looked at the options. Outer labial rings look nice – as a fashion or style – but I'm not sure they would turn me on ... or my boyfriend. There are other clit-area piercings, such as the triangle piercing or horizontal clit hood piercing. The triangle piercing goes *under* the clit, and can be very stimulating; but I didn't have enough tissue to pull the clit up and get a needle under it.

"Not every woman is suited to every type of piercing. Another piercing is the fourchette – on the perineum, just below the vagina; actually, my boyfriend's next piercing is going to be a 'guiche' – the male equivalent of the fourchette, horizontal on the perineum, just under the balls. I've had this piercing for about a year, and I'm happy with it, so far."

Kelly turned to me, "Do you want to see anything else, doctor?"

I replied, "No, nurse. I think we've seen enough. Now it's time for the patient's shot."

Kelly helped Fiona get her legs back on the table, and put down the stirrups. "You can roll over onto your stomach now, Fiona." We helped Fiona roll over, her gown falling to each side of the table before we re-tied the bow at her neck. Kelly pulled the gown apart at the waist, and let it drop over the table, so that Fiona was bare from the waist down.

I picked up the already-lubed thermometer from the counter and showed Kelly, lifting my eyebrows. Then, she raised hers. "Fiona," she said, "I'm going to take your temperature while Sam gives you the shot." Fiona turned her head toward Kelly, and looked at the thermometer. Kelly nodded, and Fiona sighed and turned her head the other way.

I had planned to insert the thermometer – if we got this far – but Kelly was in control. She held Fiona's buttocks apart, as she slid the thermometer into her. Kelly continued to separate Fiona's globes, as she slowly moved the thermometer around. Again, I thought, 'what a monster I've unleashed in Kelly'. After a minute or so, Kelly left the thermometer sticking an inch out of Fiona, and let go of her buttocks. Kelly said, "Doctor, she's all yours." I smiled at Kelly. This was fun!

"Fiona, would you like to see a demonstration, before you get your shot?" I glanced at Kelly, and her eyes lit up; I knew that she would want to give *me* the shot. Fortunately, Fiona answered, "Not really. You can just do it."

"OK. Which side would you like it on?"

Fiona answered, "It doesn't matter. I guess the right side is OK."

Good girl! I found an injection site high on her right hip, and swabbed it with alcohol. Kelly handed me one of the syringes. I uncapped the needle, and held Fiona's tissues taut between the fingers of my left hand, as I positioned the needle a couple of inches above her bottom.

"Fiona, we'll take this slowly, so that you can give us some feedback at every stage. I'm first going to insert the needle." I said, "Here it is ..." and I inserted the 22-gauge needle quickly into Fiona's hip. Fiona didn't make a sound. I let go of the syringe, leaving it protruding from her bottom, being held in place by the needle.

"OK, Fiona, the needle is in you now. It's a 22-gauge needle, which is bigger than the needles Kelly will use to demonstrate needle play. How does it feel? How would you rate the pain or discomfort of this needle being in you?"

Fiona sighed again, and said, "It doesn't really hurt much – maybe a 1 out of 10. This is nothing like the big piercing needles going through a sensitive part of my body."

I said, "Now, I'll begin the injection. At a few points, I'll ask you to 'rate' the pain." I injected the first cc of sterile saline, and asked Fiona, "How about now?"

Fiona shrugged, and said, "It's still about a 1."

I then injected a second cc, and asked her again. "I guess it's about a 2, now."

After the third cc, Fiona commented, "It's between 2 and 3. It feels like I'm being pinched. It's not a great feeling, but it's not that bad."

I then said, "Tell me, if the pain changes." I then began injecting the last 3cc. I wasn't sure we would be giving the whole shot, but Fiona was doing OK, and not complaining. About the time I had injected 6cc, Fiona said, "It's probably a 3, now. Is it almost over?"

Kelly handed me a 2x2" gauze pad, which I held on Fiona as I withdrew the needle. I then applied some pressure, and massaged her hip. I informed Fiona, "It's over. You didn't seem to be too bothered by getting a big shot."

Fiona turned her head to us, and replied, "It's not a big deal. But it's certainly not something I would do to get turned on."

I disposed of the shot in the wall-mounted sharps container, and went around the table to the other side, giving Kelly full access on her side. She leaned over, stroking Fiona's hair, and asked, "Fiona, do you still want to try some needles?"

Fiona said, "I'm pretty relaxed now. You can do what you like, and I'll let you know if it's too much."

I realized that the thermometer was still in Fiona's rear, and she probably didn't even feel it anymore. I picked up the small black butt plug and asked Kelly with my eyes. Her eyes went to the ceiling, and then she shrugged, and nodded. She said, "Fiona, we're going to do a slightly bigger rectal insertion while you get the needles."

I thought 'we're'? Kelly nodded, and I separated Fiona's buttocks. Kelly pulled the thermometer out, and handed me the butt plug. I put the tip against Fiona's anus, and pushed gently, until the whole device slid into her, captured by the thin neck. I didn't move it around or play with it – I thought Fiona was being very open to allow us to do these things. I was surprised that Fiona hadn't reacted to the 'we're', and insist that Kelly do it. But, as she said, she was getting pretty relaxed.

Kelly handed me a 5-pack of 25-gauge needles, and I started unpackaging them, and handing Kelly the capped needles. Kelly took an alcohol swab, and swabbed Fiona's entire bottom; then she took another one, and repeated the process. "Fiona, I'm going to start with two needles, and then ask you if you want to continue; if so, then I'll insert two more. You can stop at any time. OK?"

Fiona shrugged, "I guess. If they're no worse than the needle that Sam inserted, then I should be OK with it."

Kelly chuckled, "Actually, these are much thinner needles. I'll try to insert them quickly, so they won't hurt. If one hurts a lot, just let me know, and I'll take it out." Kelly uncapped one of the needles. "Are you ready now, Fiona?"

All we heard was an 'Uh huh'. Fiona's head was in the pillow, and her body looked very relaxed. Kelly inserted the first needle on Fiona's left side; then the second needle on her right side. The little blue hubs sat on her skin symmetrically, about even with the top of Fiona's butt crack, but to the sides. Again, Fiona didn't make a sound.

Kelly asked, "Are you OK, Fiona?"

Fiona nodded into the pillow, and mumbled, "I can barely feel them. You can keep going. I'll let you know if they hurt."

Kelly shrugged, and uncapped another needle. Each of the needles glided through Fiona's skin atraumatically, like a diver barely making a splash when she enters the water. Kelly alternated sides, inserting two needles, and then waiting half a minute or so before inserting two more. Fiona was silent.

When she had inserted 10 needles in Fiona's bottom, Kelly bent down to talk to her, running fingers through her hair, and whispering quietly, "Fiona, this is all I'm going to insert. You have 10 needles in you now. You can let me know when you want them taken out."

Fiona turned her head and, for the first time I had noticed since we came into the exam room, she smiled. "Those thin needles hurt less than a mosquito bite. I could probably fall asleep with them in me. More annoying is that stupid butt plug."

Kelly laughed, and said, "OK, I'll take it out, now." I thought Kelly might give me the dubious honor, but she separated Fiona's buttocks, and pulled it out quickly. She then handed it to me, giving me the indubitably indubious 'honor' of cleaning it. I washed it in the exam room sink, as Kelly stroked Fiona's hair. Then, Kelly began pulling the needles out, and depositing them in the sharps container.

I thought we were done, but Kelly opened another needle and uncapped it. "Fiona, I'm going to show you what needle play feels like – with needles going through a pinch of skin and coming back out." Kelly turned to me, "Sam, could you please bring the camera, so Fiona can see your needle play art?" I nodded and dashed off to my office area to collect the camera. When I returned, Fiona was sitting on the edge of the table, swinging her legs again.

"Are you guys done, already?" I inquired.

Kelly said, "We decided it might be better on Fiona's thigh, like you did with me the first time, so she can see what's happening." Kelly pushed the hospital gown up Fiona's legs, and Fiona held it gathered at her waist. Kelly then swabbed Fiona's left thigh, and uncapped a needle.

She pinched Fiona's skin, and positioned the needle, telling Fiona, "It's going to go through this pinch of skin and back out." Then, she quickly pushed it through the skin. Fiona grunted, as she watched the needle come out the other side, and now laying parallel to her skin. Kelly must have been on a roll, as she decided to insert two more needles in Fiona's thigh.

Fiona said, "This hurts more than the needles in my butt. But it's still not that bad." Then she glanced at the camera I was holding and asked, "What do you mean by 'art'?" I cued up one of the images and handed the camera to Fiona, showing her how to zoom the camera's playback.

Fiona's eyes got large for a moment, and she nodded, as she zoomed in and out, and advanced to the next few images. She handed me the camera, and said, "Yeah, I think my boyfriend might like this – on *him*. He's into pain more than I am. And I can understand this much easier than just sticking needles in your butt; or giving injections."

Kelly pulled the needles out of Fiona's thigh, and swabbed the area again. She addressed Fiona, "Anyway, that's one of the things we do. In addition to spanking. When we're not in the pool or sauna, or eating ... or making love."

Fiona hopped down from the exam table. Her gown was falling off, so I handed her the towel she had been wrapped in. She smiled, "I don't need that. You guys have seen just about everything there is to see." We laughed, as Fiona led us upstairs, walking nude – with Kelly in a robe, and me in my lab coat, which no longer was 'tented'.

I asked Fiona, "Can you stay a while longer? I can open some wine ... And, I would really like to snap a few pictures of you and Kelly." Fiona untied the sash of Kelly's robe, and took the robe off her. Then the two women posed, holding each other around the waist ... thinking that I was talking about 'snapshots' with the small camera I was still holding.

I took a couple of snaps, but then explained, "Actually, I was hoping to get out my pro equipment and spend a couple of hours photographing you two together. Maybe intimately."

Fiona laughed, "That sounds like fun, but I need to get going. Alex is expecting me back soon, as she wanted to take me shopping one last time." Then she looked at Kelly, "Is this something that you want to do?"

Kelly was not sure how to respond, as I hadn't discussed the photo shoot with her. "It does sound like fun. And I'd love to spend more time with you before you fly home."

Fiona reached over and grabbed her top, putting it on, and tying it at the bottom. She then picked up her underwear, fumbled to get them oriented correctly, and slipped them on, pulling them up her legs, and adjusting them.

She looked at me, "I could come over tomorrow morning for a couple of hours. Let me know what clothes to bring." Then she looked at Kelly, "I'll come ... on one condition." Kelly cocked her head, and Fiona smiled, "No more shots and nothing shoved up my butt!" We all laughed. At least she hadn't said 'no needles'. It would be fun, no matter what we did.

Fiona put on her shorts, and we walked her to the front door. She turned and said, "Well, that was interesting!" She addressed Kelly, "Thank you for the needle experience. And the nice shower." She hugged Kelly, and then hugged me.

Kelly said with a smirk, "The pleasure was mostly mine."

After Fiona left, Kelly and I walked back out to the patio and sat down at the table. I looked at Kelly, "As Fiona said, 'that was interesting!'" Again, it was mind-boggling to me how open – and I guess you would have to say 'adventurous' – some people were. I added, "Although she could have let me assist, or at least watch, when you guys made out."

Kelly laughed, "We weren't 'making out'. And it wouldn't have been the same with you there. I thought Fiona was very open, as you said. Until I started to get horny, Fiona was allowing you to bathe her. But being open with sex is different than being open with your body. She certainly didn't have any qualms about letting you see her genital piercing."

Kelly continued, "And, she let you give her a shot; she really wasn't too happy about it, but offered that in lieu of staying in the shower with us. But she took it well ... and I couldn't believe that she was comfortable letting me stick 10 needles in her bottom." Kelly shook her head, realizing how much we had just done with Fiona.

Laughing again, Kelly said, "It's too bad she didn't want a demonstration. You had made up the shot, and I would have been happy to show her how nicely the needle goes into your butt, and how well you hold still, while I'm injecting you."

Now, I was shaking my head. "You're really getting into this, aren't you?"

Kelly thought a moment, and nodded, "As you said, it's surprising how open some people are to trying things – even perverted things like we did today. I hadn't planned on using the thermometer or butt plug, but Fiona didn't react badly to those, either."

"So what turned you on the most today with Fiona?"

It didn't take Kelly long to respond, "Our shower together." I waited. Then, I raised my eyebrows. Kelly nodded, "Ever since watching Julie masturbate, I've been fantasizing about doing it with a woman. I had a feeling that Fiona would be receptive. We kissed, and hugged ... and then went down on each other. It didn't take long for either of us."

I smiled, "You'll have to educate me, if she showed you some good techniques."

Kelly laughed, "Now don't get jealous, Sam. You have good technique, too. But it's different with a woman."

"Maybe you've been a closet bisexual? I hope you don't turn gay, and leave me for a woman."

Kelly laughed again, "I don't think that's likely. But, maybe I do have some bi tendencies. Both women and men turn me on. As I told Fiona, everything seems to be a turn-on these days." Kelly looked at me, and her eyes went to my lap. "Do you still have an erection, Mister? We're going to have to do something about that."

Then Kelly smiled sweetly at me, "And we can't let that shot go to waste." Now my erection grew, and Kelly took me by the hand and led me downstairs. We carried our clothes down to the playroom, and dropped them in a pile on the couch.

"If you're still not allowed to make love, I wouldn't mind some oral sex."

Kelly said, "I think it's OK now, it's been three full days, and I'm not sore. But if you would prefer oral, I'm happy to oblige. Sir."

"That's a great offer ... but I'd prefer to make love to you, if that would be OK. Maybe from behind would minimize the contact with your waxed areas?" Then, I knew what we would be doing. "Kelly, please bring that last shot, and an alcohol swab in here." Kelly smiled, and went to the exam room. I turned off the video and raised the screen. Kelly came back, shot in hand, and we walked over to the bed. I pulled a pillow to the foot of the bed, positioning it at one of the corners.

Kelly sighed, realizing that it would be her getting the shot. She handed me the syringe and alcohol swab, and bent over the corner of the bed, her legs straddling it, and her chest and head down on the pillow. I set the shot down next to her, and picked up the swab.

Kelly reached under and guided me into her; it felt wonderful. After a couple of minutes, I stopped thrusting, and opened the swab; Kelly held still while I swabbed an area on each side of her bottom. I picked up the syringe, and uncapped the needle.

I continued thrusting into her, as I gazed upon Kelly's bottom; it was perfectly shaped, perfectly proportioned to her body, and perfectly suited for spanking. I slowed my movements, and whispered, "Which side shall I do first?"

Kelly quickly replied, "Left side, Sir."

After a few more thrusts, I entered her deeply, and held my position. I then reached over, and inserted the needle into Kelly's bottom. I checked for blood, then pushed the plunger of the syringe, slowly emptying 3cc of saline into her. With the needle still in her, I re-started my movements, with long, slow plunges into the depths of Kelly's moistness. I held the syringe, and withdrew the needle after a half-dozen thrusts, as I continued our rhythmic coupling.

Only after a dozen more thrusts did I stop briefly on the in-stroke and quickly plunge the needle into her right hip. I moved very slowly inside Kelly, as I injected the rest of the saline into her. Kelly's vaginal muscles were completely relaxed. I pulled the needle out of Kelly's bottom, and stuck it into the bed. Within moments, I found my release, exploding into her, and slamming my hips repeatedly against Kelly's backside.

I pulled out of Kelly, and she relaxed onto the corner of the bed. I dumped the syringe and swab in the exam room, and used a cloth with warm water to clean myself. I brought a fresh dampened washcloth to Kelly. Afterward, we lay together on the bed, quietly stroking each other. Kelly crawled on top of me, and we kissed deeply. Eventually, she slid off of me, and lay on her side facing me. As she twirled my hair, she asked, "So what is your plan for photographing us?"

That was a good question. I had envisioned many things – like Fiona and Kelly butt-to-butt in knee-chest positions, needles sticking out of each of their bottoms; or having them joined by a large double-dildo – each end in one of them.

I also thought about Fiona's offer to bring clothes over, and envisioned Kelly and Fiona doing an underwear fashion show, modeling together. We could even go back to the pond, which would be a beautiful backdrop for photographing the two women. I wasn't really sure of the best plan, given that we would only have a couple of hours.

"Kelly, I had envisioned photographing *you* ... actually it was supposed to be today, but we can put it off until

Thursday next week. I am hoping to shoot a variety of images – some fashion shots, semi-nudes and nudes, and then a few related to spanking, rectal insertions, or shots and needles.

"I know you'll have your period, so we can limit the session to fashion, semi-nudes, and perhaps a few nudes. And tomorrow, we won't have much time, so I'm not sure we can organize a formal photo shoot; and, I'm mainly interested in photographing you two together – perhaps some set poses, but mainly candids."

Kelly's eyes lit up. "Then let's not do anything formal at all." I looked at her, awaiting her suggestion. "I don't know if Fiona will go for it, but my idea would be to let us play around together, and you can 'shoot' whatever happens."

Kelly looked at me with a strange expression, "And my plan will be to seduce her. Would you be interested in capturing some girl-on-girl play?" Kelly smiled at me, knowing full well the answer I would give her.

"Of course! That sounds like fun. We can still ask her to bring a few different sexy things to wear, and you guys can undress each other and do whatever you want. I'll try to stay quiet and mostly out of the way."

Kelly nodded, "That would be good. I think Fiona will do best if I distract her, and you keep quiet, so she's not reminded that you're photographing everything. I'll give her a call this evening, and we'll discuss *our* plan for the photo session."

I offered to take Kelly to dinner, and have her stay over, but she suddenly was more interested in getting home and working out her wardrobe and the plans for tomorrow. Kelly took off her robe, and dressed in the clothes that were next to the desk. I walked her out to her car, and I held her tight as we kissed deeply. As she drove off, I shook my head ... again: Our experiences – now incorporating her friends and Fiona – just got better and better.

As I walked back into the house, I realized that there would be a lot of set-up needed before Fiona and Kelly arrived tomorrow morning. I unpacked the studio strobes and their heavy power supplies, along with my cameras and lenses. Using a strobe would obviate the need to use a tripod, so I could take hand-held candid shots and reposition myself as needed, while the girls played.

I wondered what they would actually be doing, then realized that Kelly would be most interested in satisfying her evolving fantasy of having sex with another woman. That would be fine with me, and could make some great sensual photos ... assuming both Kelly and Fiona were open enough to 'play' with each other in front of me.

As I assembled the strobes and reflectors, and wired-up everything, I began to fantasize about what would happen in less than 16 hours. I finished the wiring and made a few test shots before my mind got the best of me, and I lay down on the playroom couch to resolve a little of my 'tension'.

Although much of my time with Kelly still seemed surreal, our experiences – including with other people – were becoming increasingly 'real'. And they were more exciting than any of my fantasies had ever been.

CHAPTER 3: PHOTO SHOOT

Kelly arrived around 9:30AM, carrying her tote bag filled with items of clothing. As she walked into the house and I glanced down into the bag, I thought I saw her 'Nurse Kelly' outfit. That was a surprise. I wondered what other surprises I would be in store for today. "Good morning, Kelly!" I kissed her, and led her downstairs to the playroom.

"Hi, Sam." Kelly saw me glancing into her tote, and smiled cryptically at me. "I spoke with Fiona last night, and we have the photo shoot planned."

I thought of it as *my* photo shoot, but the girls obviously had already agreed on *their* plan for the morning. "That's great. What's the plan?"

"First we'll model some things for you; you can shoot us together or separately. We thought we could spend some time in the backyard, first. And then, we can come down here for the rest of the photo session."

Kelly gave me a simpering look, and continued, "I can put on the nurse outfit, and Fiona agreed to let me take her rectal temperature, and play with some needles. She still doesn't want any shots, but I can insert a needle, and have the saline-loaded syringe sticking out of her, without injecting anything."

I thought that was an accomplishment, as Fiona had seemed adamant about no more rectal insertions or shots.

I realized that these pictures would have to be taken in the exam room. Then, Kelly explained the rest of the 'plan'. "Then, we'll come in here, and you can shoot us on the bed." I arched my brows, and Kelly arched hers back at me. "We will undress and 'seduce' each other." That sounded good! Then Kelly explained, "But there's are some conditions." Uh oh ... the girls had thought this out, and I wondered what 'strings' would now be attached.

Kelly listed the conditions. "You may take all the photos you want of us ... but will have to follow our rules. First, you may not get on the bed with us. Second, you must not say a word."

Kelly looked at me seriously, "I know you probably would want to direct us and arrange each shot, but our idea is just to play with each other, and let you take candid pics of us ... without disturbing us. Fiona and I have some kind of connection, and we both want to 'experience' each other before she leaves for Toronto. So you might get some really sexy images, if you can just let us do our thing, and stay out of the way."

That sounded pretty good, although I did have a lot of ideas for set-up shots of the two of them. I guess that would need to wait until Fiona came back for her next visit. "That sounds fine, Kelly. I agree to the conditions."

Kelly smiled, and started pulling clothing out of her tote. She quickly changed into the sexy red bathing suit she had worn for me during our long weekend together, and then put on a pair of cut-off shorts and a cropped blouse that was tied at the front.

She draped the nurse outfit, and a couple of dresses over the back of one of the desk chairs, and proceeded to pull out a few bras and some underwear. She looked up at me, smiling, and said, "Of course, I can stay after Fiona leaves, and you can get a few more pics of me, if you're interested." Of *course* I was interested!

The doorbell rang, and Kelly ran upstairs to greet Fiona. I stayed in the playroom, putting some camera bodies, lenses, and strobes in a small camera bag to take upstairs. The girls came down to the playroom, Fiona carrying her own tote, stuffed with clothes. "Hi, Fiona."

She put her tote down next to Kelly's, and I gave her a welcoming hug. Then I turned to Kelly, "Kelly, I know you guys have the morning planned, but could I please suggest one more possibility? How about if you and Fiona let me take some pictures of you in the sauna, between the pool shoot and the playroom shoot?"

Kelly looked at Fiona, who shrugged. "I guess that will be OK. Can your camera equipment stand the heat?"

I laughed, "I hope so! I'll use only one of the camera bodies ... just in case. I wouldn't want my equipment to be incapacitated, just as you guys are getting it on."

Kelly turned to Fiona, "Do you already have your bathing suit on?" Fiona was also in a pair of shorts, with a similar tied blouse; obviously, the girls had coordinated their outfits for the photo shoot.

Fiona reached into her tote, and pulled out a lime green bikini. Then she held up the bikini top, and gave it a strange look. "I can't remember the last time I wore this top. I usually go topless, whenever I can." Fiona was small on top, and didn't need any structural support.

She untied her blouse, and took it off, donning the bikini top. Then, she unbuttoned her shorts, and pushed them down, along with her underwear. She disentangled the underwear from her shorts, and dropped them into the tote. Then she pulled on the bikini bottoms, and put back on her shorts and her blouse.

Kelly smiled, "Shall we go out to the pool?" Fiona nodded.

I asked, "Would either of you like something to drink?"

Kelly nodded, and turned to Fiona, "Diet Coke OK? I think Sam also has juice or water, if you prefer."

Fiona confirmed, "Diet Coke is fine."

Then, the girls headed for the stairs, while I called, "I'll be up with the drinks in a minute." I grabbed cans for each of us, and carried them and the now-heavy camera bag upstairs, setting everything on the patio table.

The girls were standing at the edge of the pool, dipping their toes in, and having a quiet conversation. I took out the camera and put on a portrait lens; I would hold the strobe in my hand for fill-flash, as needed, to reduce the shadows from the bright sunny day. An overcast day would have provided better lighting for the shoot, but it would have been less conducive to the girls enjoying the pool.

I walked over to the girls, and suggested, "How about if we start by the boulders and plants over there?" I pointed to an area of the backyard that would provide an interesting 'natural' background for the images. We walked across the yard, and the two girls faced each other and smiled.

Kelly turned towards me, spread her feet, and put her hands on her hips, and Fiona did the same. As I snapped the first few images, I realized that this would be an epic photo shoot. I kept my distance (at least ten feet), and allowed the girls to 'do their thing'.

Kelly turned to Fiona, put her arms over Fiona's shoulders, and leaned towards her; the two women kissed and, after the kiss continued for more than a few seconds, I realized that they were not acting. Kelly gathered her long hair, put it over her left shoulder and draped it over Fiona's right shoulder, making a nice backdrop to their faces.

Kelly stood back and took the ties of Fiona's blouse in her hands and held them out. Another great shot. Slowly, Kelly untied and unbuttoned Fiona's blouse. Then, Fiona did the same for Kelly. Next, they both unbuttoned and unzipped their shorts, folding them back to expose the red and green bikini suits underneath.

Kelly decided that they would take off their blouses and their bikini tops, then put back on the blouses for the next photos. They stood facing each other, their blouses loosely open, exposing portions of their breasts. Then, they hugged, and kissed again. Kelly held Fiona's top open, and kissed her nipples. I changed lenses.

I quickly changed to a macro lens and got closer, as Kelly slipped the tip of her tongue through Fiona's nipple ring. Then, her mouth went to Fiona's other breast, and Kelly bit Fiona's nipple, pulling it out with her teeth. The girls then opened their blouses fully, and stood a few inches from each other, their nipples touching. Another great shot.

They took their blouses off again, and Fiona leaned over to suck Kelly's right nipple, with her eyes looking up into Kelly's. Fiona then arranged Kelly's hair, with half falling over each shoulder and covering most of Kelly's breasts. Kelly put the back of her hand against her forehead and gave a pained expression; I knew this would become one of my favorite images of Kelly.

Kelly turned Fiona to face away from me, and began to pull Fiona's shorts down from the back. Fortunately, Kelly kept an eye on me, and stood to the side, so that I could get the shot. Both girls then took off their shorts, and again stood facing each other, hands running through hair, lips grazing off each other's cheeks, and another intimate kiss.

Kelly put her hand down Fiona's bikini bottom, and gave Fiona a smile that was full of sensuality and desire. The girls then hugged each other and kissed again.

I would have stepped up to them, and arranged Kelly's hair, but didn't want to interfere, especially at the beginning of the shoot. The girls weren't models, but they were doing great: They were very natural, not paying any attention the camera, and adjusting their positions in fluid motions. I kept shooting, glad to have a digital camera with essentially infinite storage, rather than only 36 exposures of 35mm film, as in the 'old' days.

I pointed to the boulders bordering the lawn and flower beds, and Kelly nodded. The two girls climbed up onto the flat-topped boulder, and faced each other on their hands and knees, then moved so that they provided a ¾ view for the camera. Like animals kissing, they licked each other's tongues, closing their eyes and showing obvious passion.

Then, Kelly giggled, and she stood up on the boulder, and took off her bikini bottom. Fiona shrugged, and did the same; they both threw their bikinis to me, and I set them down next to the camera bag. Fiona got back on all fours, while Kelly stepped behind her, and bent over Fiona's backside, taking her by the hips, and pushing against her – in an animalistic sex position. Really great shots!

Kelly's firm breasts grazed Fiona's back, and slid along her buttocks. I quickly got a shot of Kelly's nipples against Fiona's bottom. Some studio lighting would help, and maybe a black-and-white image would be more sensual, but I could work on the image in Photoshop after the shoot. Kelly and Fiona then squatted on top of the boulder, in a casual position facing each other in a ¾ view pose. Their labia were protruding below them.

Then, Kelly must have telepathically received my mental pleading, and both girls got on their hands and knees, facing away from me, looking back over their shoulders (heads together) at me. Their genitals were on display, their anuses relaxed. Without moving their bodies, the girls turned their heads to face each other, and kissed.

Finally, they both stood up, and I suggested they jump down from the boulder together; as they did so, I captured the sequence in multiple stop-motion frames. As they had taken that suggestion, I asked if they could hold hands and swing around each other. They liked this idea, too, and I got some great shots of the girls leaning back, as they swirled around each other, Kelly's hair flying out behind her.

Kelly and Fiona picked up their bikinis and put them back on, then walked to the jacuzzi and hopped in. Fiona held Kelly's cheeks and kissed her deeply, as streams of water flowed from their hair, and drops dripped from their noses and chins. They stood up in the jacuzzi, close together, facing each other, but not touching. Another nice shot.

Then, they took off each other's bikini tops, tossing them onto the deck, and again hugging and kissing, oblivious to the camera. Fiona squeezed both of Kelly's nipples, as the girls gazed into each other's eyes.

"It's getting too hot in here; let's go in the pool!" Kelly announced to Fiona. They climbed out of the jacuzzi, and slipped into the cool water of the pool. I pointed to the rock waterfall, and Kelly nodded. They swam over to it, climbing onto the lowest rock, and sitting side-by-side. The contrast – in their hair, their breasts, and their overall style – was amazing, and made for some interesting images. They held each other and kissed, as the waterfall flowed around them and into the pool.

I realized that we had not brought towels up, so I ran downstairs and grabbed three of them. Walking back out to the pool, I called to Kelly, "I'm getting hot, too. I think I'll take a short break, and join you guys in the pool."

No, I didn't mean 'join' in that way, and the girls paid no attention as I slipped off my shorts and shirt, then dived into the pool. The water felt great. We were still having our hot summer weather, and I again flashed on Kelly's upcoming birthday party, hoping that we would have a blue-sky day, like today.

Kelly and Fiona swam past me to the edge of the pool, and took off their bikini bottoms again. This pool had never seen as much use – and nudity – as in the past few weeks, since Kelly had come over for her 'first experience' in spanking and submission.

I got out of the pool and dried off, not bothering to dress. Grabbing the camera, I stood at the edge of the pool, while Kelly and Fiona floated on the water's surface below me. I snapped some images of the girls head-to-head, the frame extending to below both sets of breasts.

The girls played around, and I took a few more candid shots. The reflective surface of the water sparkled in the sunlight, and would make it difficult to get good photos. So, I put the camera back in the equipment bag, and once again got into the pool, floating around with the girls, for a while.

We all got out of the pool, wrapped towels around us, and sat at the patio table. The Cokes were no longer ice cold, but were refreshing anyway. After we were rehydrated, we walked downstairs, the girls carrying their bathing suits. I put the camera on one of the chaises in the shower room, and we all got under a cool shower to rinse off before getting in the sauna.

After a quick rinse, I got out from under the rain jet, dried off, and picked up my camera; I guess the girls got the message, as they moved into various intimate positions: Kelly's breasts squished against Fiona's back; Fiona and Kelly facing each other, their foreheads touching, and breasts not quite touching; a full hug, with water streaming down both their bodies; and Fiona going down on Kelly, as Kelly held Fiona's ginger-color hair in both fists. They were two very sensual women.

Kelly turned the shower off, and the girls grabbed their towels off the hooks and dried off. I told them, "I'm going to let you guys go in and start warming up, and I'll join you in a few minutes. I don't want the camera to get heated up waiting for the beads of sweat to come out on your skin."

I had always wanted to photograph a beautiful woman nude in the sauna, her body glistening with sweat. Now, I would get the chance with two beautiful, but very different, women.

I don't know exactly why, but I found Fiona to be an incredibly sexy person. As she pretended to go down on me in the shower, I could only hope that this would turn real when we got into the bed.

Fiona was being very nonchalant posing and even kissing me, in front of Sam; I had to remember that although she was small, and her freckled face made her look much younger, she was nearly a decade older than me. She was obviously a very 'open' person, and Sam had seen her usually-private parts yesterday.

I turned off the shower, and we dried off, as Sam fiddled with his camera equipment, suggesting that we get in the sauna for a while before him. That sounded like a good plan. Sam had not turned up the temperature in the sauna, but it was still quite warm, at around 160 degrees. It would be even hotter, when Fiona and I got in there.

Sam went into the playroom to find another lens, while Fiona and I opened the smoked glass door, and entered the warm, cedar-scented room, illuminated only by a single red bulb. I wondered whether Sam would use a flash, which might disrupt the sensual atmosphere.

After arranging our towels, and sitting down on the upper bench, I turned to Fiona, and told her, honestly, "You are one hot lady! I think you know this is very unusual for me – I've never really been 'with' another woman, although I've fantasized about it."

Fiona chuckled, "I thought every woman had experimented at least a few times with another female. I consider myself 'bi', because I can get off being with another woman ... but I'm mostly straight: I do like men, and my boyfriend satisfies most of my needs. But you're an interesting person, Kelly – sexually open and free – and I've wanted to hook-up with you since we met at the pond."

I leaned over and kissed Fiona, our tongues swirling around each other, lips sealed together. I was already getting wet down below. As the beads of sweat popped out all over our bodies, Fiona looked even more sensuous, mysterious. As I was thinking this, I heard a soft 'Ow' come from Fiona. "What's the matter?"

Fiona smiled, and said, "I'm glad the sauna isn't any hotter. My body jewelry is heating up, and I'll have to be careful to not be burned. My VCH barbell is somewhat protected, between my legs, but I'm feeling the heat of my nipple ring. I'll know to take them off before I get in a sauna again."

I leaned over and took Fiona's nipple and ring in my mouth, and gently sucked on them. I flicked my tongue against the ring, hopefully giving Fiona a good sensation. It was at this point that Sam came into the sauna – nude, but carrying his camera and a strobe. He set his towel on the lower bench, and put the strobe down.

"I'll try a few shots with natural light; but there isn't much in here." Sam snapped a few pictures of us, as I sucked Fiona's nipple, then kissed her again. We turned to face each other, and sat cross-legged on the bench.

Fiona smiled at me, reached over, and played with my breasts, squeezing them, fondling them, and finally biting my nipples ... but all very gently and sensually. Very different from being touched by a man. It was nice.

Sam attached the strobe, and took a few more shots. Then he commented, "I tried turning the power down to the lowest setting on the strobe, but it's still too much. And, without it, it's too dark in here. I'll wait for you guys outside." And with that, Sam exited the sauna, carrying his camera in one hand and towel in the other. We watched through the smoked glass door, as Sam set his camera down and took a shower.

Fiona said, "It's getting hot in here. If Sam's finished, maybe we can get out of the sauna?"

I agreed, "Yeah, let's get a quick shower, and play around for a while in the bed." I couldn't remember whether Fiona had seen the king size bed at the end of the playroom or not, as the screen had been down when we were changing for the pool.

When I first arrived this morning, I had noticed that Sam had taken the spread, blanket and top sheet off the bed, leaving only a stretched bottom sheet for us to play on. I still wasn't sure exactly what Fiona and I were going to do, but I was excited to find out.

We got up and carried our towels out of the sauna, dumping them in the hamper, and taking a couple of fresh towels for our shower. Sam was not in the bathroom – he was probably fiddling with his camera equipment in the playroom.

Sam was a bit of a geek, with all his high-tech computer, camera, and video gear. I briefly wondered whether he would be recording a video our 'scene' on the bed; I decided to put it out of my mind: If Fiona knew about it, she might not go through with our planned romp in the bed. I'd rather not know.

We took our time soaping each other, and I was surprised that Sam hadn't come back in to photograph us – or at least watch us – as we frolicked under the rain shower.

After we had washed our fronts, I turned Fiona around, and soaped her rear; and, with plenty of lather, I inserted a finger deeply into her rectum. I heard a sharp intake of breath, but Fiona relaxed her anal muscles, and allowed me to move my finder in and out of her – much as Sam had done with me.

Then, I finished washing her back, and turned her around to face me. Fiona looked deep into my eyes, and we held each other tight, as soapy water streamed down our bodies. We kissed ardently, and I could feel a stirring again down below.

I turned off the shower, and gave Fiona a little 'pop' on her bottom. As we dried off, Fiona announced, "Kelly, I'll let you spank me, if that would turn you on." Then, after a second thought, Fiona added, "But only with your hand. And maybe you'll let me spank you, too." We laughed, as we wrapped our towels around our waists and walked into the playroom.

Sam, sitting at his desk, looked up at us, and asked, "Are you girls having fun, yet?" We laughed again, as we sat in the two chairs facing the desk. Sam got up and brought a tray with glasses, ice, and a pitcher of water from the bar, setting it on the desk in front of us. It was a good idea: We had been getting dehydrated sitting in the sauna. Fiona and I poured the waters, and quickly emptied our glasses.

Sam asked, "Can I get either of you anything else to drink? Some wine, maybe?"

"Fiona laughed, and said, "No, water is fine. If I have wine this early, I won't be doing much the rest of the day ... and my aunt is supposed to take me shopping again this afternoon. And I haven't even started packing for the trip home tomorrow."

I turned to Fiona and asked, "Are you still OK with us doing the medical scene?" The nurse costume was over the back of my chair. I hoped Fiona would play along, as I was excited to be Nurse Kelly again – this time with a female patient. Of course, we had already inserted needles and given some shots to Fiona yesterday; but now, I was in a more sexual frame of mind. And the nurse costume would help complete the fantasy.

Fiona shrugged her shoulders, "I guess so. I brought a dress, as you requested. Should I put it on?"

I smiled, and nodded, as my inner core glowed white hot. I squeezed my legs together, but knew that nothing would satisfy my needs now except a serious romp in the bed, culminating with a nice orgasm.

Now I realized that Sam and I hadn't discussed this: Could I have oral sex with someone else, and still meet the spirit of Sam's definition of 'sex'? He had already said that we would need to redefine sex to not exclude oral sex.

I thought that was a good idea, as I knew now that we would both probably want to broaden our sexual possibilities, and unbridle our restraint. I decided not to ask his permission, but just do whatever felt natural ... which would probably include going down on Fiona.

Fiona and I got up and rummaged through our totes, each of us pulling out the clothes we needed. Fiona dropped her towel, and put on a cute pair of bikini underwear: They were pink, with white and gray hearts, and had frilly leg openings. I put on plain white Jockeys and a white bra.

Fiona, with no need for a bra, slipped the dress over her head, and let if fall to below her knees. It was a simple, black cocktail dress, with spaghetti straps, and a slit along each side at the bottom hem.

I was sitting on the chair, struggling to put on my white stockings, so Fiona walked around to Sam, who zipped the back of her dress. I turned down the tops of the stockings, and stood, taking the nurse outfit and putting my arms through the sleeve holes. Then, I zipped it, from the bottom hem up to the top of my bra.

I realized that my hair would need some attention before our photo session was started, so pulled a brush from my tote, and held it up, looking questioningly at Sam. He nodded, and rolled his executive chair around the desk and over to my chair, which he spun around, so that he would have access to my hair, which fell well below the back of the chair.

Sam took his time brushing the knots out, and Fiona excused herself to use the toilet, and fix her hair. I realized that she was even carrying some makeup to the bathroom; I wondered what Fiona would look like, fixed-up for a party, or a night out at some clubs.

I didn't have to wait long: As Sam finished brushing my hair, Fiona walked back into the playroom, and stood next to her chair, in front of both Sam and I.

It was an amazing transformation: Fiona was beautiful, and now looked more sophisticated than I could have imagined, wearing the cocktail dress, and only a little makeup – which included eye liner, and a bronze-tinted lip gloss that coordinated with her ginger hair. She was stunning. I felt a stirring again, looking now at my partner as a sexy woman, rather than tom-boyish little girl. "You're beautiful, Fiona!"

Fiona smiled at me, "I don't get dressed-up very often. I guess I do look a little different with some makeup." Fiona sat in the chair, and watched Sam finish brushing my hair. Sam didn't bother with French braids, but rolled his chair back around the desk, and watched, as I put on the nurse's hat.

Then, I asked Sam for the combination to the exam room door lock; I held my breath, wondering whether Sam would share this with me. But Sam immediately gave me the numbers that would open the electronic lock, and I left Fiona and Sam sitting at the desk, as I excused myself to finish the preparations.

As Kelly headed for the exam room, I turned to Fiona, "You really look great, Fiona! Maybe I should take some shots of you, while Kelly gets everything ready?" The word 'shots' caused a flash through my mind of Kelly, now in the exam room, undoubtedly preparing shots to give Fiona; well, at least as props, as Fiona didn't want to be injected. I reached into my shorts and adjusted myself.

Fiona responded, "Sure. Just let me know where you want me, and what you want me to do." What a great offer! I would have to control myself, as today was supposed to be an experience between the two girls. Women.

I got up and signaled Fiona to follow me, as I walked over to the bed. There were several strobes set-up on tripods, and a couple of silver-metallic reflectors also set-up, to provide shadow-free illumination of the bed, where the action would be. I told Fiona to stand by the bed, and give me a 'come hither' signal with her pointer finger.

As I snapped some initial shots, I realized that Fiona looked entirely different now: She really *was* sexy, in that dress, and with a little makeup. Her orange hair contrasted with the black dress, making an exquisite image.

Then, I suggested that Fiona get on the bed on her knees, facing me, and again signaling me (or someone) to come over. We took a few more shots, and I asked Fiona to lift the hem of her dress very slowly. As she did this, I moved around the bed, photographing her, ending-up directly in front of her again, as the dress was lifted above her underwear.

Although I had seen Fiona in these underwear – and, of course, totally nude – I still found her pose very sensual. She gazed directly into the lens, with an inscrutable expression. I realized that she was a natural model, her poses and expressions evolving naturally, without any direction from me.

I asked Fiona to stand at the foot of the bed, and turn around, as she held her dress up around her waist. I took a few more snaps, and then, putting my camera down on the bed, I asked Fiona, "May I?", then lowered Fiona's underwear to just below her bottom. I took a few more snaps from behind her, and then told Fiona that we were done for now.

As Fiona pulled up her underwear and let her dress drop, Kelly walked into the playroom, a stethoscope around her neck, and a clipboard in her hands. She looked blankly around the room, and called out "Miss Fiona?"

Fiona and I laughed, and I said, "I guess it's time for your medical appointment, now." Fiona wouldn't be getting an exam, and I wasn't sure what Kelly had told her to expect. I carried my camera, as we all walked to the exam room.

Fiona stood in the doorway, and asked Kelly, "What would you like me to do?"

Kelly first told her to sit on the exam table. With Fiona sitting on the edge of the table, I snapped a few pictures of the anxious patient, waiting for the nurse. Then Kelly suggested that Fiona lie face down on the exam table. When Fiona was settled, Kelly lifted her dress, flipping the back hem onto her back, and exposing her up to her waist. I snapped a few more shots. Then, as I had done a few minutes before, Kelly lowered Fiona's underwear to mid-thigh. I snapped a few more pictures.

Kelly picked up the 10cc syringe with its 1.5" long needle and showed it to Fiona. Kelly told Fiona, "I've loaded it with saline, but won't inject you – I'll just insert the needle, and we'll pretend to be giving you a shot."

Fiona nodded slightly, "I guess that will be OK. I had a feeling that you would be sticking me with some needles today." We laughed, although I didn't think Fiona was too happy about it. But she had experienced this yesterday and done very well, so I knew she wouldn't have a problem with a couple of quick needle insertions.

Kelly pointed to the fattest part of Fiona's butt – which wasn't that plump – and I nodded; it would be the best place to insert the needle for the photos. Kelly swabbed Fiona with alcohol, and uncapped the needle. She held the skin on Fiona's right buttock taut, and positioned the needle about an inch above the skin. I took a few more snapshots. Then, I nodded, and Kelly inserted the needle fully into Fiona's bottom. Fiona was silent.

I had Kelly hold the syringe with one hand, and then with the other, pretend to inject Fiona, as I photographed her from the side, and then from the foot of the exam table.

I signaled to Kelly, and she pulled the needle about ½" out of Fiona, so that the stainless steel was showing – as if the needle was going in – and I took a few more pictures. Then I asked Fiona to raise her head and look back at Kelly; she did so, giving Kelly several different 'looks', as the syringe was held in her bottom.

We told Fiona to put her head down again, and Kelly pushed the needle back into Fiona's butt all the way. Again, Fiona was silent.

Kelly picked up the other shot, and repeated the process on Fiona's left side. I snapped photos, as the needle went in, and then some pictures showing the two shots in Fiona's bottom, as Kelly stood back out of the way. Again, I asked Fiona to look back at Kelly, and again she gave Kelly a number of expressions.

Fiona put her head back down, and asked, "Are you guys done, yet?

Kelly laughed, and looked at me. I nodded. Kelly told Fiona, "Yes, Sam got his pictures. Are you sure you don't wantme to inject the saline? It will just be wasted, otherwise."

Fiona 'harrumphed', and said, "No thanks. It won't be much to waste."

Kelly smiled, and pulled the needles out, disposing of the shots in the sharps container on the exam room wall. Kelly surprised me by picking up an already-lubed rectal thermometer, and telling Fiona, "I'm going to take your temperature, now. It will only take another few minutes."

Fiona groaned, as Kelly separated her buttocks. I stood at the foot of the bed, snapping away, as Kelly touched the tip of the thermometer to Fiona's anus, then slowly inserted it. The thermometer was only left in for a couple of minutes, and then Kelly pulled it out, and told Fiona that she could get up.

Fiona slid off the side of the exam table, then put her hands under her dress and pulled up her underwear. There hadn't been much to this part of our photo session, but Fiona had taken it well. Kelly stepped into the bathroom, as Fiona and I walked back into the playroom.

A couple of minutes later, Kelly walked over and sat down at the foot of the bed. She pulled her nurses outfit up above the tops of her stockings, and unzipped the front a few inches. She then gave Fiona the 'come here' signal, which I snapped before Fiona had walked over to Kelly. I continued taking pictures, as Kelly helped Fiona get over her lap, with her head on the bed. I wasn't sure what was going to happen; perhaps they were just getting into a spanking 'pose' for me?

Kelly rubbed Fiona's bottom, and whispered "Just relax." Then, Kelly began spanking Fiona. It was harder and faster than I would have expected, and Fiona held her position as Kelly reddened her bottom. I continued to photograph the scene, from a variety of perspectives, including from over Kelly's shoulder.

Kelly stopped spanking Fiona and rubbed her bottom. I didn't count the number of spanks, but it had to be more than 50. Kelly helped Fiona off the bed, and both women stood and hugged each other.

Then, Kelly had Fiona sit on the bed, and raised her nurse outfit, as she lay across Fiona's lap. Fiona lowered

Kelly's underwear, nearly down to her knees. Kelly put her hair over her right shoulder, and looked back at Fiona, "You may spank me now. Please give me at least 100 spanks, as hard as you want; I might get turned on more, if you spank me harder." This was another surprise; I hadn't expected Nurse Kelly to get spanked today.

Fiona rubbed Kelly's bottom, and then asked, "Are you ready, nurse?"

Kelly chuckled, and said, "Yes, ma'am." And, Fiona began spanking Kelly, tentatively at first, then harder and faster. It looked like Fiona was having a good time being the 'top'. As Kelly's spanking continued, I watched Fiona closely; I couldn't tell if she was actually enjoying this, or just doing it at Kelly's request. Kelly jostled about and whimpered a little, but held her position nicely. I wondered whether she had expected such an energetic response from Fiona.

Fiona suddenly stopped − I was certain she had given Kelly more than 100 spanks. Kelly was still sniveling, but had relaxed her body across Fiona's lap. I was surprised again, as Fiona asked, "Kelly, is that enough, or would you like more spanking?" I coughed.

Kelly kept her head down, and promptly said, "I'll take a little more, ma'am."

I was astounded! It had looked like a very hard spanking, probably a 'level-10', as we rated punishments. Kelly could certainly take more than that; but I was very surprised that she was actually *asking* for it. I think Fiona was surprised, also. She looked up at me, and I just shrugged; the girls would have to work it out.

Fiona rubbed Kelly's bottom, squeezing it roughly a few times. Fiona leaned toward Kelly's head, and whispered, "Kelly, I'll stop anytime you tell me to." Then, without delay, Fiona began spanking Kelly again − this time, even harder, if that was possible. Perhaps Fiona was testing Kelly's limits; or, again, just doing as Kelly had asked, assuming that's what would turn her on.

I heard one or two "Mmmm's" from Kelly, but that was about it. I snapped several photos along the way – of Kelly's red bottom, Fiona's expression, as her hand came down rapidly, impacting Kelly's buttocks, and of the entire scene before me: Kelly across Fiona's lap, Fiona wearing her cocktail dress, and Kelly with her nurse outfit pulled up to her waist. Kelly's red butt contrasted well with her white stockings.

It was a very surreal, but exciting scene; no, it was more than that: It was electrifying, breathtaking, ... *stimulating*.

And the girls hadn't begun what I assumed was the 'main course' of their activity: Having 'sex' with each other. Well, I would have called it sex a month ago; now, maybe it was just 'eating' each other? I realized that my frame of reference had changed dramatically over the past few weeks with Kelly. I felt younger, more purposeful, more *wanted* than I had in five years.

I also realized that perhaps *I* had been the one to have the most inhibitions – about sex and about certain bodily functions. Kelly was good for me; we seemed to always be on the same wavelength. I hoped that Kelly was as happy with our relationship as I was.

Fiona finally stopped spanking Kelly, and rubbed her bottom softly. I was very impressed how Kelly had held her position, without restraints, and taken her spanking. Kelly was a very strong woman, as was Fiona.

Fiona helped Kelly stand up, her nurse outfit still up around her waist, and her panties down around her knees. I snapped a few more pictures. The small flash in the camera triggered all the strobes in the room, and they combined with the reflectors to make a very 'soft' light for the images that would result from this photo shoot.

I had no plans to actually do anything with the photos. This thought led to a rapid train of ideas ... that I quickly put out of my mind.

Now, Fiona was stroking Kelly's genitals, her other hand around Kelly, holding her bottom. Kelly's eyes were damp, but her breathing was finally slowing. Fiona lowered Kelly's underwear, and Kelly stepped out of them. Then, Fiona pulled the hem of the nurse outfit down, and began unzipping it from the top, starting just below Kelly's bra. As Fiona pulled the zipper at an excruciatingly leisurely pace, she stared up into Kelly's eyes.

I was transfixed: It was several minutes before I realized that I hadn't taken any more photos. My mouth was dry. I picked up the camera, and tried to focus both the camera and myself. I wouldn't know what images I got, until I downloaded them to the computer and was in a more focused frame of mind.

As Fiona pulled down the zipper, I felt an electric energy pass through my body. My skin was tingling – perhaps a result of the endorphins released by the spanking. I was surprised at how enthusiastic Fiona had been, but I had asked for it; and now, I was in the afterglow of one experience, and beginning another.

My butt was stinging, and I was vaguely aware of Sam, somewhere in the room. But Fiona's gaze into my eyes had mesmerized me, absorbed me, until there was nothing else in existence. Fiona was still pulling down the zipper, finally reaching the end, where the coat-like outfit came apart at the bottom, and I could slide my arms out of it. The nurse outfit fell to the floor.

Fiona stood, pressing against me and kissed me roughly, softly biting my upper lip. Then she turned my head to the side, and began nibbling on my ear. I seemed to be in a hypnotic trance, as Fiona slid her tongue into my ear, bit the earlobe, and then lowered her head and bit my neck – perhaps fantasizing herself as a vampiress.

Her hands circled me, and I realized she had unclipped my bra. She slipped it off me, and it dropped to the floor. Now, Fiona began consuming my breasts, taking one, then the other, into her mouth, sucking hard, and biting my nipples.

I bent down, and pulled the hem of her dress up, and finally over her head, as she held her arms high. Then, I 'went down' on Fiona's small breasts. I lapped them, like a dog kissing them, then sucked and bit her nipples, taking the nipple ring into my mouth, and biting closer to her chest.

My tongue swirled around her nipples, which were now hard buttons, and then progressed downward, pausing briefly at her navel. Then, I lowered and removed her underwear, before continuing to her waxed pubes, and her clit. My tongue lashed out, finding its way under the hood, as it teased each side of the third hard button now adorning Fiona's body.

Fiona pulled me back up to a standing position, and when I looked quizzically at her, she shoved me, and I fell backwards onto the bed. Then, Fiona jumped onto the bed and, snarling, climbed on top of me; we seemed to suddenly be in a wrestling match.

Fiona pinned me down, bent over and bit my nipples, then ferociously attacked my mouth, her snakelike tongue extending into the warm, wet space, and entwining with mine. Sucking, biting, and finally taking my head in her hands, she changed pace – giving me a slow, languorous kiss, her entire weight holding me down to the bed. A vision flashed through my mind of my masturbation on top of Sam, with him face down, wearing a blindfold.

Fiona looked at me and smiled, then crawled around, facing the other direction, and positioning herself in the classic '69' position. Then she went down on me. I didn't know exactly what she was doing with my clit, but it felt incredible.

I pushed her legs slightly apart, so that her hips lowered enough for me to 'eat' her from where I lay. It was a little claustrophobic, but I closed my eyes, enjoying both the feeling of what Fiona was doing down below, and my tongue caressing Fiona's clit, moving against her VCH barbell, lapping, swirling, and flicking under her hood.

We were in a state of suspended animation: Oblivious to the world around us, time seemingly standing still, and our perceptions focused only on a couple specific parts of our anatomy. In fact, only one part: My tongue seemed numb, but the feeling in my core was building in an incredible crescendo.

I realized that Fiona had been 'playing' me – licking my clit, then along my labia, and repeating, keeping me at the edge, and taking me beyond where I had ever been before. Finally, my orgasm exploded. I heard myself scream, as if from another dimension. My head became light, and I thought I would pass out.

Fiona bucked a little, and I realized that I had forgotten her. My tongue had been on autopilot, but that was not enough: True focus and dedication to the job was needed. My head cleared, and I realized that my body was alive – suddenly hypersensitive to every feeling, everything touching me.

I worked on Fiona, alternating between licking under her hood, and pressing down on her hood, forcing the barbell into her clit. This apparently was working, as I heard her gasping, and finally letting go of her tensions, as I flicked my tongue very quickly across her swollen button.

Fiona relaxed on top of me, and I thought I would be suffocated ... but then she rolled off of me, and we lay heads-to-feet on the bed, both of us panting from our efforts and from our release. A few minutes later, she crawled over and lay down next to me, with her arm under my breast. I closed my eyes, and felt as contented as I have ever been.

"Are you OK, Kelly?" Fiona asked. Had I been sleeping? Suddenly, I was back in the 'real' world. Where was Sam? Fiona was looking at me with an enigmatic smile. "I hate to 'eat and run', but I need to get going." Fiona leaned over and gave me a peck on the lips, as she played with my breasts.

Then she continued, "This was fun. You're a hot lady! I hope we can spend more time together when I come for my next visit to see Alex." Fiona sat up, cross-legged, and watched, as I clumsily rolled off the bed.

I walked around to the foot of the bed, and picked up the nurse outfit, and my bra and underwear. Sam was sitting at his desk, and I walked over to him, as Fiona headed toward the bathroom. Sam looked up at me, and smiled. "So, how was it?" I pulled a light robe from my tote, and put it on, then sat down in one of the desk chairs facing Sam.

"Oh, it was OK," I casually told Sam. I tried not to laugh, but it was impossible. There was no hiding how much I had enjoyed the experience with Fiona. Sam was laughing, too. Then, he turned serious.

"Am I going to lose you to another woman?" he asked, only half jokingly.

I looked down to my lap. It had been thrilling ... and I still felt quivers when I remembered Julie's masturbation scene ... but I wasn't sure I wanted to give up men, quite yet. In fact, I wasn't sure what I wanted, at all. Sam had opened my eyes to new sexual possibilities, and they all seemed exciting right now. And I loved Sam.

I looked into his eyes, across the desk. Maybe I *was* bi? Right now, I realized that having my sexual freedom would be important to me, moving into the future. Sam and I would need to have another discussion about the definition of 'sex'. The lines now seemed much more blurry.

"I love you, Sam. Thank you for letting Fiona and I play together. And, for staying out of the way. I didn't even know you were there." I could barely re-imagine my state of mind while I had been with Fiona.

"Kelly, I can't *let* you, or *not* let you do anything. As much as I love you, I'm going to try not to be possessive ... especially, if something like this can excite you, like I saw today. And you *did* allow me to photograph the event." I suddenly remembered, and now tried to picture what shots Sam would have gotten of us. It paused me, for a moment.

Fiona walked back into the playroom. She picked up her dress and underwear by the bed, and stood next to me in front of the desk as she put her dress down, and stepped into her bikini panties. As she did this, she looked up at Sam, pointed to the camera, and asked, "Did you get what you wanted?"

Sam smirked at Fiona, "Did you get what *you* wanted?"

I broke in, "Touché!"

Fiona stood in her underwear, bent over to me, and gave me a deep kiss, her hand around the back of my head, pulling me to her. Then she suddenly ended the kiss, stepped back, smiled at me, spun around, and picked up her dress. She faced Sam as she put the dress over her head, and let it fall, once again transforming herself into a more sophisticated looking woman.

She said to Sam, "Yes. I got everything I wanted, today. As I'm sure you know, Kelly is one hot chick. I can't wait 'till we can hook up, again. Maybe, I'll have to come out here more often!"

Fiona picked up her tote and her shoes, and we followed her to the front door. I gave her a light kiss on her nose, and said, "Thank you, Fiona. That was really nice. You're pretty hot, yourself."

Fiona, with ultimate self-control, stepped back, and said, "Bye, Kelly." Then she looked over my shoulder, and yelled, "Thank you, Sam." Sam waved from the porch, as I walked out with Fiona, and opened her car door. She only had a few blocks to drive, but then there would be a whirlwind of shopping, packing, and getting on her flight to Toronto, all in the next 24 hours.

As she got into the car, I said, "Thanks again, Fiona. You really were a good sport over the last couple of days with Sam. And me. But I'm not going to apologize; I hope you felt what I did when we were on the bed. It was an incredible experience for me."

Fiona responded, "It was great. You're an awesome chick." She started her car, and I stepped back from the door. We gave each other a quick wave, and she was gone. It was going to take me a long time to process what had happened this morning. And I was sure it would be the source of many more fantasies.

CHAPTER 4: BIRTHDAY PREPARATIONS

Kelly and I had a very nice afternoon together, relaxing and finally being able to make love in a more normal position. Kelly's waxing didn't hurt her; it was looking nice – not nearly as red as it had been.

I took her to dinner at a local Italian restaurant, not fancy, but with very good home-style cooking. We had a bottle of wine – I guess we had also drunk some that afternoon – and Kelly slept over. Despite our inebriation, we managed to get ourselves upstairs and ready for bed, and make love twice. Then, we fell into a sound sleep.

We awoke together nearly 10 hours later, and enjoyed a Saturday morning in bed. I was tempted to suggest another session with the Kama Sutra, but didn't think Kelly's waxing would be quite ready for that. I offered Kelly a real 'breakfast in bed', but she declined; she was scheduled to have lunch with Julie.

I had asked Kelly to be entirely open – with me, and our friends. And she had been; extremely. We were beyond that, now, but Kelly had found that *I* still had some inhibitions; and I knew that she would eventually 'help me' overcome them. I decided to be proactive, and invited her into the bathroom with me.

She sat on the edge of the tub, as I pooped, and we discussed our day with Fiona. Then she had her turn. It wasn't as difficult – as embarrassing – as I had expected, primarily due to Kelly being so relaxed about it.

Kelly and I went down to the playroom so she could pack her tote, and we discussed the plans for the coming week. I really needed to get some serious work done over the next few days, and conveyed this to Kelly, without providing any specific details.

We agreed that she would come over on Thursday, for another photo shoot. This time, we would do portraits, fashion, and semi-nudes ... and perhaps a few nudes; but I would not be making the erotic images that I still planned to do, at some point, with Kelly. And maybe her friends ...

I was again sad to see Kelly go home, but hoped my birthday preparations would compensate for the few days we would be apart. I remembered to order the cake – a decadent combination of multi-layer chocolate cake, separated by chocolate ganache and fresh whipped cream, with a thick fudge frosting, a decoration of whipped cream, and dark chocolate shavings. Perhaps I should have made a cake myself, but I felt pressed for time, with a lot of projects to finish.

I found the 5th chair for the patio table, washed it, and set-up the patio for the party. That would give Kelly something to see, when she was here on Thursday, to show that I was working on her birthday. Hopefully, without her suspecting my other projects – mainly the spanking turntable (that I now called a 'Lazy Sam'), and the pirate ship to role-play Kelly's fantasy.

Kelly and I spoke every night on the phone. She offered to try 'phone sex' with me, but somehow that just didn't substitute for Kelly not being with me in-person. During the day, I was mostly pre-occupied with the birthday projects.

And, I realized, I had to add a few more things to the list – my menu and shopping list for the barbeque I was planning; purchasing 5 'AeroBeds', which we could inflate to make the sleepover more comfortable (if we decided to all sleep in the playroom); and, of course, Kelly's birthday presents – which included a very nice slave collar, but also a satin negligee, and a pearl necklace that I thought she would like.

I completed the 'Lazy Sam', an eight-foot round turntable, with rollerblade-style knee pads that I attached to the wood, and Velcro straps that were strategically placed for ankles; and arms, if needed. I found the cards and poker chips, and worked out a couple of 'games' that we might play using the Lazy Sam.

One of these was something I called 'Spank Poker', and the other was a version of Truth or Dare. I hoped the girls would be open enough to do these things, and maybe even get excited by them. I managed to tilt the Lazy Sam up against the pool room wall, and attach it by straps that I had bolted to the wall. It was out of the way, but could be lowered into position almost instantly.

And, I worked on the biggest project: The pirate ship. Basically, it was a 'mast' and two 'booms', with unfurling canvas 'sails', and a number of blocks and lines that could 'lower the boom' (and raise the skirts), and hold the mast up – using a block (pulley) and cleat I mounted on the eve of the house, and another two that I had mounted on nearby trees.

I would certainly need the girls' help to erect this (in a manner of speaking), while Kelly was changing into her Victorian outfit downstairs. And, hopefully, there wouldn't be any wind, or I would not be able to leave the sails down.

I cut canvas sails, and put grommets in them, with small lines to lash them to the booms. I ran a halyard to the top of the mast and back down, to control the lower boom, which was connected to the mast only by a loose lashing of rope; and another halyard that ended in a V of thin rope with a clip at each end. I put cleats in strategic positions, to which I would lash Kelly in place.

Near the edge of the pool, I dug a narrow but deep hole, into which I dropped a metal pipe, in which the mast would sit. I considered a 'walking-the-plank' scenario, with the diving board as the plank ... but wondered whether it would be too dangerous, with Kelly wearing all those clothes – if she accidentally fell in the pool. Of course, I would jump in to 'save' her, but then both her dress and my pirate outfit would be soaked.

I put a bunch of miscellaneous, but important, items in a canvas bag that I strapped to the mast, including the punishment implements, a nice, padded blindfold, a tube of KY (just in case), and a couple of butt plugs (although I wasn't planning to use them).

I left everything behind the garage, where Kelly wouldn't see it, and from where the girls and I could carry it to the pool, and erect the mast. I hoped it would work, as there would be no way to practice, ahead of the big event.

On Tuesday afternoon, both Fed Ex and UPS stopped by to deliver loads of packages. They included the party favors for the girls, both the pirate outfit and Victorian dress outfit, the gift bags, labels and tissue paper, a variety of sex toys, and Kelly's 'slave' collar.

I unpacked and inspected everything: This was going to be fun! I wrapped each of the party favors in very thin colored tissue paper, and put them in the party bags that were decorated with colorful balloons and small stars. There were four of them, one for each of the girls (including Kelly), and I labeled each of the bags with their names on a tag. I wrapped Kelly's collar in wrapping paper that also had a balloon pattern.

Then, I tried-on the pirate costume. It was pretty cheesy, but would do for the one-time event. From a distance (I was thinking of Julie, Linda and Kathy sitting in the spa) it would probably look pretty realistic. A real pirate sword would have been nice ... I could have used it to cut the rope tying Kelly to the mast.

It would take several minutes for me to put on the costume, and I could probably use help from the girls for that, also. I took the costume off, gathered all the accessories, and put everything in a large box that I concealed 'in open sight' in the pool room closet.

I unpacked Kelly's Victorian dress outfit. It was a bit tawdry, but would work fine for our pirate role-play. I hung the dress in the downstairs bathroom, next to the robes ... hoping I would remember, in case we used the sauna. The rest of the ensemble went into a medium-size cardboard box that I put under the sink in the exam room.

I unwrapped the 'sex toy' package, and took out nearly two dozen butt plugs of various sizes, colors and materials; a few were beautiful glass designs. I had four so-called 'triple threat' vibrators, in various colors, which I wrapped in colored tissue, and put into the party favor bags.

The rest, I rinsed, dried, and divided up into four small baskets. I also put a few more supplies and implements in the baskets, and brought them up to the pool room, where I put them in a box in the closet, next to the box with the pirate costume.

On Wednesday, I cleaned the smoker/barbeque, and made sure I had charcoal and hickory. I finished the grocery list, and bought some of the ingredients we would need for the birthday lunch and dinner. I stocked up on soft drinks, beers, and various juices, including mango and other exotic flavors. And I put a couple of bottles of white and rosé wines in the fridge. I was finally making progress, and it seemed that things were mostly ready for Kelly's birthday party.

It was around noon, and I was eating a slice of baguette with brown butter, when Kelly called. "Sam, I don't know what to pack for the photo shoot tomorrow; I'm not a model, and not even sure what makeup to bring. Or how you want me to be dressed. I don't have very many outfits you would consider 'sexy'."

"Don't sweat it, Kelly, it's not that big a deal. I just thought it would be fun, and I'd love to have some nice photos of you. In addition to the ones with you and Fiona. Just a minute ..."

I brought the phone down to the playroom, and checked a list in my files. "Kelly, if we want to get fancy, you can use a face primer, then foundation, and then bring a translucent powder, and brush that I can use here. An eyelash brush and eye liner, and maybe some rouge."

I chuckled, "But if you want to be simple, why don't you just get ready like you normally would going out on a date, or to a job interview? That should be fine for what we're going to do tomorrow."

Kelly whined, "And what clothes should I bring? I have a lot of stuff, but none of it seems right for modeling." I heard a certain tone of Kelly's voice that told me she was up to something; she shouldn't be whining, and her clothes were not that big of a decision. She also sounded a little 'turned on', but I was deducing all this from the way she had said a few words.

Then, Kelly came out with it: "Sam, I think you should come over here. You can help me pick some outfits – I can model them for you." Kelly was almost giggling.

I did miss Kelly, and would love to see her. And most of the birthday preparations had been completed. Spending an afternoon with Kelly would be fun. And it would be interesting to visit her lair, see how she lived. "Kelly, let me get some things together here, and I'll call you back when I'm ready to leave." I heard a squeal of delight over the phone.

I took the last bite of baguette, and sat back in the breakfast room chair. I remembered seeing the separated garage/apartment at Dave's house when I drove there for the party. I put my head back, and closed my eyes.

I was parking, climbing the stairs to Kelly's apartment, seeing her beautiful, smiling face, as she greeted me. Her sparkling hazel eyes, and her gleaming teeth, all framed by long, dark-auburn hair. I visualized walking into Kelly's apartment, and seeing clothes strewn all over; I really didn't know how neat or messy she was.

I pictured myself sitting on her bed, watching Kelly change into one outfit after another. And then, when she was in-between changes, in her bra and underwear, I pulled her onto the bed, and our bodies wrapped around each other. Holding. Kissing.

Then ... a knocking on the door. 'Oh, my God! My father's home early. And he must have seen your car!' Kelly hopped up, and grabbed a dress that she threw over her head, letting fall and smoothing it down as she walked to the door. I stood up and, seeing a notebook on her desk, picked it up, and walked toward the door as it opened.

My mind's eye saw her father smile, then look past Kelly to me, with confusion. 'I thought I saw a strange car parked over here. Is that you, Sam?'

Kelly withered as I shook Dave's hand – his grip almost breaking mine. I held up the notebook and said, 'I'm helping Kelly with her biomed, but she forgot her notebook when I visited her at the college ... so she suggested that I pick it up on my way home.'

It helped that Dave's house really was between the college and my house.

I snapped out of my daydream, and realized: It just wasn't worth it, to chance being seen by Dave or Darlene, and having to explain my relationship with Kelly; or make up some lame excuse. I didn't want to get into a dishonest situation with them, or put Kelly at risk with her family. Kelly would be coming over here less than 24 hours from now, and I could wait.

Then, I had an idea – it was obvious: Set-up a video link, and have Kelly model for me over the 'net. I knew that wasn't what Kelly wanted, but it would be a safe alternative. And, maybe we could try some video sex, rather than phone sex.

I now visualized Kelly as a cam-girl, sitting on her bed in her underwear, teasing me, and asking if I would like a private show. This could have some potential ...

I called Kelly back, and described the vision I'd had. She said that I could have driven around behind the garage, where nobody would see my car, and that it was very unlikely anybody would be home before 5PM. Still, she understood, and we agreed to do a video chat. I walked her through the set-up over the phone, and it was ready to connect in less than 10 minutes.

We hung up our phones, and used our laptops for the video, using the built-in cameras in the screens. Kelly was standing in her bra and panties, as I had envisioned, her laptop on the dresser, and my display showing a view of the entire room. There were some clothes in piles on the bed, but otherwise the room looked neat and clean.

Kelly picked up one dress after another, putting each one on, and modeling it for me. She also had a few pants outfits, a formal jacket, and a lot of casual clothes. Especially interesting was a pair of off-white designer jeans that really showed off her body – the long legs, nice hips, and narrow waist; and the bottom that I loved. We decided on the clothes she would bring over tomorrow, including several dresses, those incredible jeans and a classy blouse to go with it, several pairs of underwear, and even a pair of stockings. I'd never seen Kelly wearing pantyhose.

Then I decided to have a little fun with Kelly, over our private video link. "I was thinking, Kelly, that you could perform for me – like a cam-girl. See if I'll buy you some trinkets, if you give me a good show."

Kelly snorted, "Maybe you should give *me* the show?"

"Well, we could put on shows for each other. That would be fair. I'm already 'up' for some action ..." I briefly turned the computer screen to face down to my tented shorts, "so maybe we could masturbate for each other? We can set the laptops on the bed, and watch our 'porn' video of each other." As I said this, I was figuring out how to activate the screen recording function.

Kelly was walking and carrying the computer, the image on my screen gyrating wildly, until it was set down, and I had a view of Kelly sitting on the toilet. She looked up at me and said, "I'm soaked. I need to change this tampon, before I do anything else." She looked down, then up at me and smiled, "I hope you're not squeamish." Then, she attended to her needs.

I told her, "I'm not afraid to see blood ... unless it's my own."

She laughed, "You're such a baby!" That may be, but the scene on my display looked like it could easily be part of a horror film. Finally, she was finished. She closed and flushed the toilet, and then reached over to pick something up, put one foot up on the toilet seat, and proceeded to insert a new tampon. She went out of the field of the camera's view, and then the laptop took another whirling and tilting ride back into the bedroom.

Kelly lay back on her pillow, and faced the laptop so that I could see her head. I brought my laptop to the playroom bed, and positioned myself and the laptop similarly. I was not turned on anymore, but was sure we could both take care of that in a minute or two. Then I heard Kelly, and looked at the screen.

"Sam, as long as we have this great video link, maybe we should do some 'video training'?" I had no idea what she was talking about. She asked, "Do you remember? You were going to give me more formal instruction on giving intramuscular injections. And you said the goal was to be comfortable enough to give myself a shot." I was nodding, but already knew where this was heading.

"So why don't you demonstrate that to me by video. You can give me a little lesson, and then we can masturbate for each other." I sighed. Kelly was a 'monster' alright ... just one that I happened to love. And it was all my own fault; I had all-along hoped that Kelly would get into some aspect of my fantasies. Well, she had.

"OK, I guess I can do that for you." Kelly knew it wouldn't be for me; although it could be part of my turn-on afterward. But there was no free lunch. "Kelly, I do want to have that needle and shot session with you; and you know that you'll have to give yourself a shot. You can consider today the demonstration for that."

Then, I told her to wait, and I hopped off the bed, then went into the exam room to assemble the shot. I guess I was the one paying for the video idea, instead of going over to Kelly's place.

I attached a 25-gauge 1.5" long needle to a 10cc syringe; Kelly wouldn't be able to see the needle very well, and I decided a smaller needle would make it a little easier for me. I didn't mind the longer injection time that the smaller needle would require.

I loaded 6cc into the syringe. This amount made a very big shot – about as big as can be given in one injection. But I was going to ask Kelly to do this, so felt I should play by the same rules.

I brought the shot and some supplies into the playroom, and I got back up on the bed – which was still covered by only a sheet; the one on which Kelly and Fiona had made what appeared to be passionate love. I lay down on my stomach, put all the supplies next to me, and put the laptop on a pillow a couple of feet from my hip, the camera aimed slightly down onto my bottom.

When I asked Kelly if she was ready for her lesson, she nodded, and I could tell that her hands were already busy down below. Kelly was really getting into this. 'This' not having specifically to do with shots, or such, but focused on asking me to do something that I didn't like.

I guess it was no different from how I explain my own fantasies. Unfortunately, Kelly had found several things that I didn't like, so it was easy for her to pick one of those, whenever she wanted me to 'submit' to her.

I explained how to find the injection site on your own hip, reviewed how to swab the area, and finally uncapped the needle, held it over my skin, and did a nice smooth insertion into my hip. It wasn't necessary to 'plunge' or 'dart' the needle in; modern needles are very sharp, and easily go through the skin quickly and atraumatically.

I let go of the syringe, it being held in place by the needle in me, and asked Kelly if she had any questions. I could see by the picture-in-picture window on the screen that she was getting a good view of the shot.

Kelly replied, "No. I think I understand. You can inject the saline, now."

I pulled back on the plunger of the syringe to make sure I wasn't in a blood vessel, and proceeded to inject myself, the full 6cc taking about 30 seconds. I looked at the screen, and Kelly nodded, "You may take the needle out, now." And I did.

Kelly said, "That didn't look too difficult. I'm pretty sure I can do that." Although her laptop camera was aimed toward her face, I could still see the motion of her arm, as she continued to get off on my video presentation.

"I'm sure you can, Kelly. You've already received enough shots and needle sticks to know what it feels like, and be comfortable with it; and you've already given enough shots to know how to get the needle in comfortably for your 'patient'.

"It's mainly a matter of deciding that it's not going to hurt that much, taking your time, and doing exactly what you would do if you were giving me the shot. Try to look at the skin under the needle as someone else's, not your own. It's not that hard." Although, now that it was over, I was getting hard again, thinking about it.

Kelly said, "I think I'm way ahead of you in the masturbation department." She slid her laptop along the bed, and I saw her side, her hip, and then I was flying over her leg, as she set the laptop between her legs, the camera aimed at her genitals – which nearly filled my laptop screen. She laughed, "Well, at least I can see the top-half of the screen."

I lay back on the pillow, and moved the pillow and laptop into position for her see me – my manhood already hard, laying on my stomach, pointing towards my head. I made sure that the 'action' would be centered in the top half of Kelly's display.

Then, we both masturbated. Kelly spread her labia, and then lifted her hood; she made a circular rubbing motion of her fingers over her hood, as she moved her hips rhythmically. I realized that I was 'almost there'. "I love you, Kelly." I held myself back for one more long moment, and then my orgasm detonated, ripples of waves traveling across my body, through my mind.

I glanced at the screen, and it looked like Kelly was about to come – her fingers pressing on her hood, massaging in a small circular motion. Then, I heard Kelly cry out, "I love *you*, Sam." Kelly's body took over, thrusting and bucking, her hand never stopping its motion, as deep contractions racked her lower body.

When Kelly had calmed, the screen went blank, and then I saw her face from below – she must have put the laptop in her lap with the screen bent back. Kelly smiled at me, and said, "I guess that wasn't a bad substitute for you coming over. At least we got the 'coming' part. Just too bad it's 'over'." We laughed, as I reached for some tissues to clean the line of semen that had jetted up to my neck.

Kelly said she would start packing now, so we signed off of the video link, both of us looking forward to her coming over to my house tomorrow.

The Fed Ex guy delivered the remainder of Kelly's birthday presents that afternoon, and I wrapped them in the festive balloon-covered paper.

The video with Sam had been helpful – I now had an idea of what I would wear for the photo shoot, so I started packing. I couldn't see the pictures he would take as being anything more than some snapshots that Sam could put in his 'scrapbook'. I was not a model, and didn't have a very exciting wardrobe; I packed my sexiest dresses and a few lingerie items that Sam had not yet seen.

I also packed a suitcase for spending the weekend with Sam, and for my birthday party. As it would be a 'skinny-dipping' party, not much clothing would be needed. I decided to bring the red thong bathing suit that I had modeled for Sam, and a peach-colored strapless dress for the birthday barbeque dinner, my PJs, a jeans outfit, and assorted bras and underwear.

Sam had suggested that my friends and I plan to spend Saturday night at his house, a 'slumber party' – something we had not done in a decade; it sounded like fun. Sam also invited me to spend Friday night at his house. But I was intent on going over there tomorrow, and staying through the weekend. I didn't care if Sam still had more 'work' to do for the party – he would just have to let me help him with it.

I drove to Sam's house mid-morning on Thursday, with two suitcases plus my tote bag stuffed with clothes for modeling. It was the fourth day of my period, and I was relying on tampons; however, I decided to bring several boxes of 'female' supplies, including pads and tampons, to leave at Sam's house for future use.

I brought the makeup supplies that we had discussed, and decided that I would leave most of them at Sam's house, also. I wondered whether Sam would get the 'hint' that I was ready to move in with him?

Sam greeted me at the door, and helped me carry everything inside. He joked, "It looks like you've brought enough stuff to move in with me!" I guess he had gotten the hint.

I laughed, and said, "Do you want me to?"

Sam looked more serious, but then hugged me, and kissed my nose. "Kelly, I'd love you to stay here with me. But I don't want there to be any pressure on you, and it might be better that you stay in your apartment during the school year, as I think you'll get more homework done there than here."

I pointed out that there wouldn't be much 'homework' in the traditional sense; I would mainly be researching and writing my dissertation ... which was something on which Sam could provide useful input. We decided to hold-off the discussion of our living situation. However, I wanted to make clear my intentions for the weekend.

"Sam, I've brought everything I need for the birthday party and the weekend; I'm planning to stay over tonight." When I saw his frown, I added, "I can help with last-minute preparations for the party ... if there are any."

Sam nodded, "Almost everything is ready. But we'll need to do some marketing tomorrow, and you can help me get some of the food items ready."

Rather than taking me downstairs, Sam helped me carry everything into the pool room. The sliding doors were open to the outside and, against the wall, were two very tall tripods, a cross-bar, and a roll of background paper that had been pulled down hiding the back wall and covering nearly ten feet of the carpeted floor.

Sam had several large photographic lights set up, as well as a professional tripod. A small table held his cameras and a collection of lenses. We put my cases on the massage table, that had been slid to one side of room, and I started unpacking my modeling clothes. I realized that I would need some hanging space, and knew there was a closet in the room, but it was behind the background paper. Sam had anticipated my needs, and rolled over a portable stand from which I could hang my dresses.

When everything had been unpacked from the tote and one of the suitcases, I turned to Sam, "So what would you like me to do?"

Sam looked at me with a strange grin; I could *imagine* what he was thinking, with my open-ended offer. He chuckled, and picked up one of the cameras. "Let's start with some portraits. Take off your top, and sit on the stool that's positioned on the background paper." When I had done so, Sam stood next to me, brushing out my hair, and pulling my bra straps off my shoulders. He then mounted the camera on the tripod, and adjusted the settings.

"Close your eyes, and relax. When I call out a word, please open your eyes and smile." I closed my eyes, and got ready. Sam called out "Spanking!" I opened my eyes and smiled at the camera, the shutter clicking. We tried several more variations of this approach, with me looking off into space, looking at the camera, ¾- views, and some other simple poses.

After a few shots, Sam suggested that I put some powder on my face to eliminate the glare. I went into the bathroom and spent some time applying the powder, some eye liner, and lip gloss. Sam put my hair into French braids, and we took another series of shots, this time with me wearing a blouse.

Over the next couple of hours, Sam photographed me in several of my outfits, either in the pool room 'studio', or in the backyard. I noticed that he had arranged the patio furniture, set out additional chaises, and had streamers and other birthday decorations already up. A huge smoker-type barbeque sat near the house, just outside the door to the kitchen.

Sam had me climb on the boulders, swing from a branch of one of the trees, and twirl around in a loose dress, until it was flying up and my hair was flying out. We took a short lunch break, and then Sam and I carried all of my cases and clothes downstairs to the playroom.

Sam spent some time carrying the strobe lights from the pool room to the playroom, and setting them up around the bed. We threw another sheet and a couple of pillows on the bed, and I modeled some of my lingerie in sexy positions on the bed. Sam told me he would need to buy me some more sexy lingerie. It would be mostly his present: I told him that he could buy those things for me on *his* birthday.

Wrapping up the shoot, we did some semi-nudes, with me wearing a thong or bikini underwear, and nothing else. Holding the sheet up over my breasts; on all-fours, giving the camera an animal growl; and in a fetal position, sucking my thumb. He took some handheld close-ups of me, looking sultry, my head peaking out from over a pillow that I clutched to my chest.

I offered to take off my underwear, so we could do some nude shots, but we were both getting tired, and Sam suggested that we put that off for another session. It was mid-afternoon before Sam had put away the camera equipment, and I had organized and re-packed a pile of clothes.

Relaxing with some iced tea out on the patio, Sam wanted to talk about the plans for my birthday party. It looked like Sam had taken care of everything, so I didn't think much more had to be 'planned'. But Sam had some very definite ideas for birthday party activities that he wanted to discuss.

"Kelly, two of your friends have been very open with us, and I'm hoping that you are willing to be open with them, also." I nodded; of course, I was prepared to be open with my friends, and knew that Sam would be 'testing' me – with us doing things that a month ago I would never have considered doing in front of anyone else.

"For one thing, you'll of course be getting your 'birthday spanking'." I smiled, wondering how much different it would be than the spanking Linda had taken; but I knew that Sam wouldn't let me off that easily.

Sam continued, "Second, I would like to make a needle play 'corset' for you." Of course, he meant '*on* me'. That wouldn't be a big deal, as Julie and Linda had already seen pictures of Sam's needle play 'art' on my backside. I wondered what Kathy would think about this stuff, as she hadn't had the benefit of the 'introduction' that Julie and Linda had experienced.

Sam told me that I should expect to participate in at least one 'role play'; I wasn't sure what he meant, but assumed I would be either Nurse Kelly, or a schoolgirl, again. I frowned, as I realized that I hadn't brought the nurse outfit.

And then, Sam told me that he had planned a few 'games' that we would all play – that would provide a further introduction to spanking and openness for my friends. I had no idea whether my friends would be 'game' for Sam's games.

Sam suggested that we have a 'four-on-one group massage' session – perhaps in the jacuzzi. It sounded like fun ... if my friends would go for it; which I assumed they would. That led into a discussion about openness with my friends, and our re-definition of 'sex'.

Sam was first concerned that some of our activities – such as the group massage – could end-up with him getting turned-on ... and he asked what I thought about my friends seeing him with an erection. I was not bothered by the 'openness' of that, but felt that Sam getting sexually excited might be uncomfortable for everyone, and turn our casual, skinny-dipping day into a sex-focused experience that may not be appropriate.

"We'll just have to see how comfortable everyone is, as we go through the day, Sam. If we're all giving you a massage, it won't be surprising to anyone if you get turned on. I think if we all take it in stride as something natural, there won't be an issue."

Sam had told me his idea about playing a version of 'pin the tail on the donkey', where the 'pins' would be hypodermic needles, with paper 'tails' hung on them. That was a funny thought, but I told him I didn't think that would be such a good idea.

I realized now that there was no way my friends would be leaving the birthday party without being convinced that Sam really was perverted.

My train of thought went from everyone 'pinning the tail' on me ... to thinking about all of us pinning the tail on *Sam*. Then, I thought of Sam with an erection, and started laughing, now coming up with my own ideas of what games we could play.

When Sam asked what was so funny, I explained that if he got an erection, we would have him stand at the edge of the pool, hands on his head, and my friends and I would play 'ring toss'; with punishment being given to Sam, if he 'dropped' any of the rings.

Sam laughed hysterically. When he could choke out a few words, he said, "And I thought I had come up with of all the interesting games we could play!"

Then, we had a slightly more serious discussion – about sex. It had already become obvious that Sam's narrow definition – 'sharing of body fluids' – was much too strict, as this would not even allow someone to taste wine from his glass. Julie had already kissed Sam on the mouth. And, Fiona and I had gone down on each other. Should we relax just oral-oral contact, or extend that to oral-genital contact, also?

In his 'researcher' style, Sam pulled out some printouts he had made from Internet sources, detailing the incidence of STDs with oral sex. He found that every STD has a different safety profile, and that – yes – some can be transmitted by tongue-clitoral contact; human papillomavirus (HPV), herpes, and hepatitis are potential worries.

We decided to not include oral-oral contact in our definition of 'sex'. Regarding oral-genital contact, I told Sam that the issue probably wouldn't arise (not in a manner of speaking); I really doubted that any of my friends would give Sam 'head', even Julie.

Sam told me that in the event he was invited to go down on one of my friends, he could use a barrier of Saran wrap. This was still not entirely safe, and I now had a plan with Julie that I hoped would materialize sometime during the party.

I assured Sam that I would not be jealous, and would be comfortable with each of us having oral sex – at least with my friends; he had not been bothered by Fiona and I 'eating' each other. There were always risks in life. I told Sam I didn't think much of the Saran wrap idea; and, as far as I knew, my friends were perfectly healthy.

Sam informed me that didn't mean anything, as many people are not aware they have an STD. Then he softened, and said he would be OK if we agreed to limit oral sex to my friends; he was willing to accept the health risk, in the unlikely event that any of my friends were interested.

I told Sam that there was one thing I had been fantasizing about: Making out with Julie. I didn't know if there would be a feasible 'time and place' for this during my party, but Julie and I had talked about it during our lunch last Saturday, and I suggested to Sam that perhaps he think of a way this could be orchestrated. He smiled, and said he would have no problem making it happen. I thought this would be a nice 'birthday present' from Sam, even if he hadn't bought any other presents for me.

In the late afternoon, Sam's doorbell rang, and we found several large boxes that had been delivered, sitting by the front door. We carried these in, and down to the playroom. Sam opened all the boxes: Five Aero beds – inflatable mattresses that we could use for the slumber party. I informed Sam that he was going overboard (which he did often), and that we all could have slept in real beds upstairs. Or on the floor in the playroom.

Sam looked at me, "We can do that, if everyone wants ... but it won't be as much fun!" I think perhaps Sam had always wanted to join a girls' slumber party, and this would be his chance. I told him that if we wanted to talk openly – for example, about *him* – then I might make him sleep upstairs. He wasn't too happy about this, but I thought it unlikely that we would banish him from our slumber party, if he behaved himself.

Sam took me to dinner at a local Mexican dive, where we ate fish tacos and drank corona beers with lime. I suggested doing Tequila shots, but Sam was reluctant to get soused tonight; he said he wanted to have a clear head tomorrow for the final party preparations ... and he was also looking forward to making love to me.

So we kept the evening sane, and Sam drove us back to his house only slightly inebriated – less than we would have been had we shared a bottle of wine. We watched some TV on Sam's gigantic screen, and then decided to take a shower together before retiring to the master bedroom.

I undressed down to my underwear in the playroom, and walked into the bathroom, where I took off the panties and disposed of the last tampon I hoped would be needed for this-month's period. As I sat on the toilet, Sam got the shower started, and washed his hair. When I joined Sam in the shower, we took our time bathing each other. Sam asked me, "Kelly, I know it's a bit late to ask, but is there anything special you would like for your birthday present?"

Yeah, it was late to ask such a question, but I knew what I wanted – in addition to playing around with Julie. "Sam, all I want is you. I can't think of anything that you could buy me that would make me any happier than spending time with you."

Sam smiled, "Well, you have me." Then, he thought, and added, "I've hinted that I'm going to ask a few things of you during your birthday party – the corset, your birthday spanking, and being open in front of your friends."

He looked down, and said, "But, I'll also let you ask a few things of me, too, if there's anything that you would like to do with me – or *to* me – in front of your friends. I've already thought a little about this, and realize that you might put me in an 'embarrassing situation', but I'm willing to submit to you, as a partial 'birthday present', while your friends are here."

That was a good offer. I told Sam, "Well, I haven't thought about it, so I don't have any ideas at the moment ... but if I think of anything, I'll let you know."

And then, I started thinking of things: Putting Sam in the chair position, my friends watching, Sam's 'package' hanging down, as I spanked him, or stuck him with needles. Maybe doing the 'ring toss' would challenge his remaining modesty? Maybe, I should offer my friends the chance to spank Sam? I decided to push these thoughts to the back of my mind, until Saturday. I had no doubt that I would be thinking of things spontaneously during the party that might be interesting for Sam ... and the rest of us.

We climbed the stairs to Sam's bedroom, not bothering to put on robes, then we climbed into bed. We held each other, taking our time, kissing each other, as we allowed our sexual attraction to work its magic with our minds and our bodies. I climbed on top of Sam.

Although I was dry, and it took some effort for Sam to enter me, our combined secretions provided plenty of lubrication, once he was inside me. I lowered myself onto him, and we held each other and kissed deeply, as each of us thrust our pelvis toward the other. Thinking about the Kama Sutra, I stopped moving; Sam opened an eye to look at me, and I told him, "Let's try to make love as long as possible."

That was a good challenge for both of us, as I knew that we could both be having our orgasms within minutes. Sam thrust one more time to embed himself deeply within my core, and we held each other tightly. I felt Sam's erection throb within me. When the throbbing subsided, I moved my hips slowly and, using my vaginal muscles, drew Sam even further into me.

I breathed deeply of Sam's manly scent – his pheromones – as his tongue burned in my mouth, his lips joined mine with violent softness, and his hands pulled my head even closer to him. We had stopped thrusting again, but I knew we were both ready for fulfillment.

The last few strokes filled me with searing heat, and electric pulses traveled through my body and my soul, as our orgasms burst forth together, a million nerve endings suddenly flashing like twin rockets exploding fireworks, the multitude of sparks joining with a billion stars in the heavens above.

We lay there together, panting, our bodies spent, as the afterglow enveloped both of us. Sam kissed me lightly on the tip of my nose; then, again, our mouths joined, and we tasted each other's sweetness.

As I drifted off to sleep some minutes later, I realized that this had been the most 'ordinary' lovemaking we had done – very vanilla. But it had also been quite extraordinary: The intensity, the emotion, Sam's romanticism. Truly *making love*, not merely 'having sex'. My body was relaxed, and my mind contented, as I savored the feeling of Sam's warm body next to me. If there had been any doubt, it erased itself, my last thought being 'I love this man!' before I fell into a deep slumber.

CHAPTER 5: BIRTHDAY EVE

There was still quite a bit of work to finish the preparations for Kelly's birthday party. After a light breakfast, we updated the shopping list, and I checked my 'to do' list to make sure nothing had been forgotten. I reviewed the lunch and dinner menus with Kelly, to make sure they met with her satisfaction.

I had not planned a formal birthday lunch, but instead decided to make a variety of appetizers, including olive-dill vegetable dip, deviled eggs, cheese puffs made with Challah bread, guacamole and chips, wine crackers with cream cheese and jalapeno jelly, and mini hot-dogs in a barbeque sauce (a preview of the dinner), as well as a few frozen choices that had always worked out well.

In addition, I would make a large salad bowl with my signature green goddess dressing. I drew the line at homemade croutons, and had purchased a bag of some pre-made croutons that I knew were delicious.

We had a quick bite at the café in the market, and then headed to the specialty butcher shop, which had the ribs waiting for us. I had bought a few fresh salmon steaks at the market, just in case any of the girls didn't eat meat, or like ribs. Then, we stopped by the bakery, and picked up the birthday cake that had been made per my specifications.

Kelly was already a bit overwhelmed, and we hadn't even gotten started, yet. Next-door to the bakery was a sewing store, and I realized there was one more item that had not found itself onto my to do list. We went in, and I bought eight yards of pink satin ribbon; 24 feet seemed like a lot, but I hoped it would be enough. Kelly gave me a questioning look, and wasn't going to ask, but I volunteered, "This is for your corset." She just nodded.

Back home, we unpacked and put away the groceries, quickly filling my refrigerator. I would need to use the spare fridge in the garage for the dishes that we were making. We filled the lower half of the garage fridge with soft drinks and beers, and then I showed Kelly how I make my special sangria.

As usual, red wine and fruit – sliced apples, pears, oranges, lemons, and limes – went into the large Tupperware container, along with an inexpensive red wine that I liked. The *pièce de résistance* was the infusion of brandy into a measuring cup with sugar and fresh squeezed lemon juice; once this was dissolved, I poured it into the sangria and mixed everything with a long wooden spoon.

We put the sangria in the garage fridge and, as I was carrying the wooden spoon back to the sink to rinse it, I looked at Kelly with a smile. She arched her brows, looked down at the spoon, and then back up to my smiling face, which I nodded once.

Without any words being spoken, Kelly nodded, undid her pants, and pushed them down, along with her underwear. She bent over the kitchen table, her legs spread widely in a firm stance. I stood behind her, and placed the spoon on her right buttock, then asked, simply, "How many?"

With her chest pressed down to the kitchen table, and without looking up, she quickly replied, "Fifty, Sir." I suddenly had an erection that threatened to push through my pants. I bent down and kissed each side of Kelly's bottom. Then, I stood, placing the spoon against her soft tissues again, and applied 50 medium strokes of the wooden spoon, alternating sides, while Kelly held her position. When I finished, I put the spoon down on the table in front of Kelly. She turned her head back to me slightly, and said, "Thank you, Sir."

I undid my belt, and let my pants drop to the floor, along with my underwear. I pressed up against Kelly, my erection moving in the groove of her butt crack. Kelly quickly said, "Sir, there's a tampon still in me. I was still spotting this morning." I had forgotten.

"OK, Kelly, run into the pool room and take care of that. I'll expect you back here in two minutes." Kelly stood up and stepped out of her pants and underwear, which she put on one of the kitchen chairs. Then, she ran into the pool room. In less than a minute, Kelly was back, and bent over the kitchen table again.

I had gotten a little flaccid, so I rubbed myself on her again, until I was ready, and then let my hard member slide between Kelly's legs. Without lifting her chest off the table, Kelly reached under and put me inside her. I was immediately ready and, notwithstanding Kelly's needs, I thrusted less than a dozen times before coming, my front slapping against Kelly's thighs and hips, the kitchen table being pushed along the floor a few inches with each thrust.

I leaned over Kelly's back, still in her, as my body quaked a few more times. When I pulled out of her, Kelly stayed in position over the kitchen table. I pulled up my pants, and Kelly asked, "Is that all, Sir?"

I laughed, pulled her up, turned her around to face me, and hugged her tightly, "Yes, Kelly. Unless you would like a little attention, now. I would be happy to satisfy your every need."

Kelly laughed, "That's alright, Sir. Maybe later." I felt a little guilty getting off at her 'expense'; it was the first time I had ever satisfied my own needs while neglecting hers. But I was quite willing to make up for it, and Kelly knew it. Then, still laughing, Kelly asked, "Shall I wash the spoon now, Sir?" I hugged her again, and we went back to work.

We spent the rest of the afternoon cooking some dishes and preparing others that would be finished tomorrow, including my special potato salad recipe, and the barbeque sauce for the ribs. I pulled out a large can of baked beans, and told Kelly, "I make great baked beans – with green onions, some of the barbeque sauce with molasses and a touch of rum, and bacon on top. But if I serve it, we might have an 'openness challenge' at the slumber party ... like the scene in *Blazing Saddles*."

Kelly hadn't seen the movie – which dated me again – and I described the cowboys sitting around a campfire, eating their beans out of a can ... and then having a fart fest. Kelly laughed side-splittingly. Then I told her, "But I do have some 'Beano', in case anybody is worried. Let's just remember to pass them out *before* dinner."

As the sun set, and it got a little cooler outside, Kelly helped me put up the rest of the decorations for the party – more streamers, balloons, and a large 'Happy Birthday!' sign, that we taped to the eves of the house, outside the pool room.

I told Kelly that I hadn't planned to put her to work decorating her own party, but she wasn't bothered at all. "You've done all the work, so far. And it sounds like you've been working on this party for a couple of weeks. I'm not sure what all the preparations were, but it looks like we're ready for our guests, as far as I can see." I declined to explain the 'weeks of preparations'; she would find out soon enough.

We picked up a pizza from a take-out place, ready to bake, and when we returned home I added some of my own ingredients: Kalamata olives, sun dried tomatoes, and – since Kelly had done well with the Caesar salad – some anchovies, along with basil and oregano, fresh chopped Italian parsley, and a drizzle of extra virgin olive oil. While it was baking in the oven on a pizza stone, I opened a nice bottle of chianti.

We decided to eat on the patio table, to enjoy another evening; it looked like the weather would cooperate for Kelly's party tomorrow. Then I realized what else I had forgotten. After eating one slice of pizza, and leaving Kelly sitting at the patio table bewildered, I ran to the garage, climbed up on a ladder, and pulled down a couple of cardboard boxes, bringing them out to the patio, along with the ladder. "I forgot the lights," I informed Kelly.

"What lights?" was her obvious reply. Then, I started pulling things out of the boxes that had been labeled "XMAS". We had a dozen strands of white lights, some the 'dripping' type, and others with tiny bulbs that would twinkle in the branches of the trees. We finished our dinner, and I held off drinking more wine, not wanting to fall off a ladder on the eve of Kelly's birthday. Now *that* would put a dent on the celebration, if I broke my leg!

After stringing the lights around the eaves, I did a little tree climbing, Kelly throwing each strand of lights up to me, as I wove them through the branches. It would have been nice had I thought of this a week or two ago. We worked until it was dark outside, the only illumination coming from the patio lights and the nearly full moon rising over the house in the East.

Finally, I plugged in the multiple strands, and said, "Let there be light!" And there was light: Dripping from the eaves of the house all around the patio, and twinkling in several of the trees – at least as high up as I had been able to climb. It was starting to look festive out here!

I ran back into the garage, and emerged clutching half a dozen more tiki torches, which I set-up along the pathway in the backyard. I knew that at least one of these would need to be moved, when we dragged the 'pirate ship' over to the pool. I made sure all of the torches were filled with oil.

Kelly and I cleaned up the dinner, putting the leftover pizza in the garage fridge. Then, we retired to the playroom. Kelly's suitcases, tote, and a pile of clothes sat next to the desk in the office area, and I knew that her friends would also be bringing their things, so I suggested that we bring Kelly's stuff upstairs. I had a few things to do – without Kelly watching – so left her in the master closet to hang up her clothes, and organize the things she would need for tomorrow.

While Kelly was upstairs, I went into the pool room, and took down the background paper and tripods, putting everything back in the garage. I had left this up to hide the turntable – the 'Lazy Sam' – that was strapped vertically to the pool room wall.

It also prevented Kelly from opening the closet door, and seeing the pirate outfit. With her clothes upstairs, she would also hopefully not see the Victorian dress that was stuffed in the narrow closet in the downstairs bathroom.

I took some supplies from the exam room, put them in a nondescript cardboard box, and brought it up to the pool room, placing it under the massage table. I found the ribbon we had bought earlier, and dropped it into that box, also. Finally, I did a quick cleaning of the pool room bathroom, making sure that we had plenty of toilet paper, towels, and soap. Finally, I surveyed the pool room and the patio, making sure that everything was set for the party.

When I went back downstairs, Kelly was sitting on the couch, looking in a daze at the loveseat. "Still thinking about Julie's masturbation scene?"

Kelly looked up, surprised, as she hadn't heard me entering the room. "Yeah. I'm still impressed – and turned on – by her performance."

I nodded, "It was quite something. I think we'll find out tomorrow how open Linda and Kathy are." I didn't explain, but my mind was flooded with images: Of the girls on the turntable, their butts high in the air, playing 'spank poker'; of a 'pin the tail on the donkey' game that we would probably not play; and of the pirate scene, with Kelly lashed to the mast, getting flogged on some private parts of her anatomy.

Kelly, still unaware of most of my plans, was undoubtedly thinking about the 'skinny-dipping' part, and said, "I'm sure they'll do fine. I think you'll like Kathy." From what Kelly had told me about her, I was sure I would.

We decided to watch a movie, and I put on one of the newer on-demand films, *Blue Is the Warmest Color* – an incredibly sensual and erotic depiction of young lesbian love. Despite the nude lovemaking scenes, I excused myself for a few minutes to sit at my desk and go over my birthday party lists one more time.

I pulled out Kelly's birthday card from a desk drawer, signed it, and put it into an envelope. On the outside, I wrote in fancy script 'To Kelly – From Sir Sam' I sat back and remembered some of the humorous cards that I had seen. 'It took 25 years to look this good!', 'Mark this date: You are now officially old!', and 'Inside every old person is a young person, saying What the Hell Happened?' But I had gotten her a simple and serious card – 'Happy 25th Birthday ... to the one I love', with balloons on the front.

Going through the 'to do' list, it appeared that everything was checked off. That was good, as there wasn't much time to do anything else. Our guests would be arriving around 10AM. It promised to be an epic day.

I sat down on the couch next to Kelly, and we watched the rest of the movie. It was incredibly sensual, but also incredibly long, and near the end I offered to go down on Kelly. She smiled and yawned, suggesting that we go upstairs and make love. That was something I would not argue about. It wasn't yet midnight, so I would have to wait until morning to tell Kelly happy birthday.

We undressed as we walked up the stairs, dropping our clothes in the master bedroom closet. Kelly sat on the toilet and took out her tampon, announcing to me that her period was finally over. It was good timing, and I wondered whether any of her friends would be in the middle of their period tomorrow.

We made slow and purposeful love, both of us thinking unknowable thoughts. I could not help but realize that I was twice Kelly's age. But we felt perfectly suited for each other. I really did love this woman.

When I woke, Sam was spooning me. "Happy birthday!" Sam told me, as he lifted his head over me and kissed my cheek. I turned toward him, and we kissed properly. Sam chuckled, "So what would you like to do today?"

I laughed, "Make love to you?" We were joking around, but I realized that this might be the only time we would be able to make love, if we were with my friends all day, and having a 'slumber party' tonight.

Sam replied, "I think that can be arranged. Let me just make sure you're ready." Sam crawled under the sheets, and between my legs, which I let fall apart, giving him access.

As he expertly caressed and then licked my clit, I watched the sheet go up and down, as if I were pregnant, and the baby was trying to get out. I chuckled. What a strange thought that had been! I saw the sheet rise more, and Sam asked, "Am I tickling you?"

I laughed some more, and said, "No. Just something I was thinking."

Without missing a beat, Sam replied, "Well, if I'm not tickling your fancy, I should be." And with that, Sam began tickling me: My genitals and perineum, under my knees, blowing his breath under my hood, sucking my stomach and then making strange sounds that vibrated his lips against me.

Sam crawled his way up my body, tickling my breasts, and under my arms. When his head finally emerged from the sheet, he smiled and said, "I didn't know you were that ticklish."

Then, he continued – kissing my neck, chewing on an earlobe, and showering my face with little kisses, finally making canine sounds and lapping my entire face with his tongue. It was wet and sloppy. Then, Sam sat up, straddling my middle, putting his hands up like 'paws', and panting like a dog waiting for a treat.

"Good doggie," I said, as I 'shook' one of Sam's paws, and then surprised him by pulling him down onto me. I felt the warmth and the fullness, as he slid into me. Then he smiled, and gave me a slobbering lap on my lips. "OK, boy, now *roll over!*"

And, like the good dog that he was, Sam rolled us over, him inside me, our legs intertwined. I smiled at him, caressed his hair gently ... and then began roughly slobbering his face – lapping, like he had, and making occasional squeaks, like a small dog. We were laughing, but Sam was still thrusting into me.

Sam said, "OK, little puppy, if we're going to do this properly, I'll have to mount you from behind."

It was funny – and appropriate at any other time. But I frowned, "Sam, I'd rather make love this way today. It *is* my birthday, and it seems more loving, when we can look into each other's eyes." I hoped Sam would take my rejection of his 'doggy style' sex offer well.

Sam pulled my head to his, and gave me a deep kiss. "*Of course*, Kelly. Anything you want." He smiled and added, "Maybe someday, we can romp around like dogs, and I can chase you, and finally mount you like a proper dog." Then he barked a few times – loudly, and quite realistically. Unless you were a dog.

Sam lay passively – only occasionally thrusting his pelvis – as I took control. I felt power over this man, and liked the feeling; and I knew that Sam did, too. I imagined being Sam's slave, at his command, being punished mercilessly.

And then, after my training, Sam would be *my* slave. And he would face the consequences of his actions. I visualized Sam during our 'first experience' in the chair position, taking his punishment for mis-speaking to me about my age: Seeing him from behind, his package swinging, ass clenching, butt shaking after I had paddled him. I orgasmed over and over, Sam coming somewhere along the way, but continuing to move in me, as my body writhed in pleasure.

Julie may have shown animal passion when she masturbated for us, but no more than Kelly had just shown as we made love. I wondered what she had been fantasizing about over the past few minutes; I assumed it was related to her experience with Fiona, or her upcoming experience with Julie. Kelly seemed to find attachment to many of the sexual activities to which I had introduced her, and a few others, almost like a unique experience making a strong imprint on a child.

I had only been half joking when I had asked Kelly if I would lose her to a woman. I didn't think so – especially, if we were relaxed about her 'playing' with women alongside our relationship. But only time would tell.

After a bathroom break, I asked Kelly, "Would you please let me give you a couple of quick enemas, this morning?"

Kelly stared at me, "On my birthday?"

I shrugged, "I don't have anything specific planned, but would like you to be cleaned out, just in case."

Kelly shrugged, "I'll take one enema ... provided you do, too. I may think of some things to do with you, too."

The 'monster' had risen again, as I should have expected. But it was only fair, so I nodded, and we headed down to the exam room. On the stairs, Kelly informed me, "And you're going to get yours first."

That was OK: I'd just as soon get it over with. I had brought the usual enema equipment to the pool room (again, just in case), and decided it would be more expedient using the 200cc pressure syringe. We entered the exam room, and I took out the huge syringe, and mixed a gallon of saltwater. Neither of us had bothered getting dressed, yet.

I got up on the exam table, and into a knee-chest position. I still didn't like getting enemas, but was starting to get used to them. I didn't mind the feeling of the syringe tip in my anus, or the spraying of water into my rectum. But I didn't like the feeling in my abdomen when I was full of water. And, I *really* didn't like sitting on the toilet for ten minutes, flood after flood of water pouring out of me.

I heard Kelly behind me, and put my head into the pillow. Soon enough, I felt the tip of the syringe sitting in my anal canal, and water being squirted into me. Neither of us said anything, as Kelly proceeded to inject many syringes of saltwater into my bottom. I hadn't felt any cramping, but felt full, already.

Kelly said, "That's ten syringes. I think you made enough for about twelve each, so I'll give you another two." I managed not to groan, but remained silent, as Kelly pumped another two syringes of saltwater into me. I just hoped that she wouldn't ask me to do jumping jacks again! Fortunately, she didn't.

While I was in the bathroom, I wondered whether Kelly was in the playroom getting herself off again as she once again re-imagined Julie's masturbation scene. Whatever happened today, it should be interesting.

When I was finished, Kelly got up on the exam table, and I injected saltwater into her. She took it very well, and I felt a little bad that I had asked her to do this on her birthday; but we would both now be ready for whatever happened today. While she was on the toilet, I got into the shower; it was perhaps the first time I had showered without Kelly, while she had been at the house.

When I was finished, so was Kelly, and she got into the shower as I got out. I still had my fingers crossed that she wouldn't open the closet to get a robe, as she would see the Victorian dress hanging there. I decided to sit on the chaise in the shower area, watching Kelly bathe. When Kelly finished her shower, she sat, wrapped in her towel, on a chaise, and let me brush her hair, and put it in French Braids. Then, we went up to the master bedroom to get dressed for the party. Kelly put on a pair of shorts and a t-shirt, while I donned my usual running shorts and tank top.

Kelly brought her red bathing suit, and I brought a European men's thong, both dropped into her tote, down to the pool room. Upon seeing the huge circular wooden structure against the pool room wall, Kelly gave me a questioning look. I casually told her, "Just something I made ... that we might have a chance to use during the party."

I don't think Kelly could tell what it was, and she just shook her head, undoubtedly wondering what surprises were awaiting her today. I opened the pool room sliding doors to the patio, and moved the massage table into the opening at one end. It was a beautiful summer day, as we had hoped.

Kelly and I carried a small folding table from the garage to the patio, setting it next to the door to the kitchen, and I had Kelly set out piles of paper plates, plastic 'silverware', and plastic cups, while I brought a large cooler from the garage, and put it under the table.

I carried in most of the soft drinks and beers from the outside garage, and put them in the cooler, and dumped in a couple of bags of ice that we had picked up at the market yesterday. I also brought out five cardboard boxes of the type used to hold files, and lined those up against the pool room back wall, and labeled them with our names and those of each of our guests.

I spread a king size sheet on the lawn, next to the patio and pool, holding down the corners with smooth river stones that had decorated the edge of one of the planters in the back yard. This would give us another place to sit, in addition to the chaises lined up next to the pool, and chairs around the glass patio table.

Surveying the pool room, patio and backyard, it appeared that everything was ready for Kelly's birthday party. I cued up some music that we would play from the outdoor speakers, then sat at the patio table, amazed that all the preparations were now complete, and we were ready for our guests to arrive.

Kelly sat down next to me. It was the calm before the storm, as we were finally able to relax for a few minutes. It was nearly 10AM already. I asked Kelly, "Is there anything else that you can think of to get ready for the party? Or anything special we haven't talked about that you'd like to do during the party?"

Kelly chuckled, "All I'm expecting is to visit with my friends, go in the pool, and have lunch and dinner. I know you've planned a few things, but I don't know what – except for my 'birthday spanking'."

Then, Kelly looked down at her lap, and back up to me with a serious look, which broke into a smile. "And, I'll submit to anything you want to do to me today, Sir." Then, she added, "Even in front of my friends."

That was a good offer, one which certainly would be put to use, although most of my plans were meant for Kelly's enjoyment, as well as my own.

"Thank you, Kelly. We *will* be doing a few 'things' today ... but I'm hoping that you'll have fun with them. I'm not going to be hard on you today. I think you know most of what to expect." Of course, there would still be a few surprises ...

CHAPTER 6: GUESTS ARRIVE

Shortly after 10AM, Kelly's friends arrived, all together. We greeted them at the front door, and ushered them into the house.

I finally met Kathy who, as Kelly had said, was cute and had a very bright, enthusiastic personality, and a great smile. Her eyes were brown, her face smooth, and her teeth perfect. Kathy's hair was a light brown, streaked with blonde, and came down well below her shoulders in a multitude of waves. She was shorter than Julie and Kelly, roughly Linda's height, but had a very trim and athletic build. Kathy was well tanned, having just returned from a beach vacation with her parents on the Mexican Riviera.

Everyone hugged, and Kelly's friends wished her a happy birthday. All of the girls were wearing shorts and either a t-shirt or casual blouse. They each carried a beach tote and a wrapped present, and Kathy was carrying a large beach towel.

I had already piled a bunch of large towels in the pool room, and there were more downstairs, for use in the sauna, or drying off after a shower.

Julie pointed to her car, and said, "I have a trunk full of sleeping bags, in case we stay over tonight. We can bring them in later, if we need them." I hoped that the girls would be spending the night, as I had a few special things planned, including giving Julie and Kelly a chance to play together.

Kelly and I ushered everyone into the pool room, where they lined up their totes along the back wall, between my 'Lazy Sam' and the half-bath, in front of each of the labeled boxes. The girls looked around the mostly-empty room, and Kathy stepped out to the patio. "This is an awesome backyard!"

Kelly nodded, "You can see why I thought this would be a good place for my birthday party. Sam's done a lot of work, getting everything ready."

We all sat down at the patio table, the girls chit-chatting about their summer. Kelly asked Kathy, "So how was your Mexican vacation?"

Kathy shrugged, "It was OK. My parents rent a house every year on the coast between Mazatlan and Puerto Vallarta, and the nearby beach is very private. So I was able to work on my all-over tan. I guess it was a fun trip, but I would have preferred going with a boyfriend instead of my parents." Then, she added, "But they're pretty cool, though."

Kelly turned to me and said, unnecessarily, "Kathy's parents are the original 'hippies'. They are very open about nudity. Kathy's been going to nude beaches all her life." Kathy shrugged and nodded, having nothing to add to Kelly's matter-of-fact statement.

I thought this would be a good time to comment on today's activities. "I know that Kelly told you that I don't allow bathing suits in the pool ... and it would be more fun if we have a skinny-dipping birthday party; but I also hope that you're all comfortable, as well. If you want, we can start out with suits on, and hopefully by the time you're ready to use the pool, you'll be comfortable with them coming off."

Kathy laughed, "Well, I didn't even bring a suit. Why spoil the tan I've been working on for the past two weeks?"

The girls chuckled, but nobody seemed to have a problem with the plan.

I then gave Kelly's friends a little orientation. "You can use the 'pool room' for changing, and there's a half-bath when you need it." I pointed to the open room behind me. "We have a cooler with soft drinks and beers under that table," I pointed again, "and I also have a couple of wines in the fridge that will be nice on a hot day like this. We'll use plastic cups, as I don't want to take the chance of having any broken glass on the patio. If you want water, iced tea, fruit juice, or anything else, please ask me.

I outlined some of the plans. "I thought we could sit and talk, or lay in the sun, this morning, and use the pool and jacuzzi. I do have a few special activities planned that I think you'll find interesting." I glanced at Kelly, who gave me an almost imperceptible nod. "Especially, as Kelly has told me that she will be open with you guys, and share some of the sensual things we've been doing together."

Linda looked at Kathy and said, "Yeah, Sam likes to spank Kelly. And stick needles in her. When Julie and I came over last time, Sam forced me to take a 'birthday spanking'!" Everyone looked at Linda incredulously.

"Linda!" I said excitedly, "I didn't *force* you to do anything! And I seem to recall that you enjoyed the experience." I hoped Linda had been joking.

Linda smiled, "OK, I admit that I wasn't forced, and didn't put up a fight. It was an interesting experience." Then, she glanced at Julie, while still directing her comments to Kathy, "But the most interesting experience was watching Julie take a spanking ..." We knew what was coming. "... and then she masturbated in front of us. Lying across Sam's lap." Linda couldn't help but put her hands in front of her face; I could tell that she was blushing.

Kathy nodded, "Yes, Julie mentioned that." Kathy looked across the table at me, and stated, "But we're never surprised at what Julie does. She lives to challenge people around her with her directness, her openness." Today, I would be challenging Julie with some openness. Kathy added, "I think she does those things mainly for the shock value."

Julie looked at the sky, and then at Kathy, "Kathy, you weren't there. It was really hot – Sam lowering my underwear, and putting me across his lap; then spanking me. He knew that I was getting turned on, and offered to help me masturbate, but I decided to take things into my own hands, so to speak. If I had been going for 'shock value', I would have called his bluff, and let him 'do' me."

Julie didn't realize that would not have been 'calling my bluff'; I had sincerely offered, and half-expected Julie to allow me to satisfy her needs.

At that point, Kelly broke in, and suggested that we all get changed; it was already getting hot, and the pool would see some use soon. We went back into the pool room, and Kelly broke the ice by taking off her t-shirt; she was not wearing a bra. She put on the red bikini top, and then unbuttoned her shorts, and pushed them down, along with her underwear.

As she untangled them and dropped them into her storage box, Julie took off her blouse and shorts, and Linda stepped into the bathroom. Julie was wearing a Victoria's Secret bra and panty set. Nobody seemed to mind that I was standing in the room next to them, as we all got changed.

Kelly showed Julie her waxing, which now looked great, with only a hint of redness still left. Julie commented, "That looks really good. Maybe the social pressure will induce Linda to get waxed, too." Kelly put on the bright red Brazilian string bottom.

Linda came out of the bathroom, somewhat startled that we were all in various states of undress. I had taken my tank off, and now removed my shorts and picked up the tiny thong. The girls hardly seemed to notice that I was nude, before I pulled on the thong. *Then* a couple of them looked over and giggled.

Kathy had taken off her shorts, and was wearing bikini underwear – basic black, and rather a small cut, but otherwise undistinguished. Julie took off her bra, and put on a hot pink bikini top. She was relatively small on top – probably a B-cup – but still had shapely breasts. She pulled off her panties, and I saw that her dark pubic hair had been trimmed into a long, thin 'landing strip'.

Kathy pulled her t-shirt over her head. Standing there topless, only wearing her bikini panties, she said, "And, I didn't bring a bra, either. I guess I'll just start out like this." She looked fine: The underwear could just as well have been the bottom of a bikini bathing suit; and it wouldn't matter anyway, in a while, when everyone relaxed and decided to go nude.

Kathy's breasts were not very big, smaller than Julie's; and, like Julie's, they were shapely. Unlike Julie, Kathy had no tan lines.

Linda had taken off her shorts, already wearing tan-colored bikini bottoms that were perhaps a bit small for her generous bottom and hips. As Linda took off her t-shirt, Julie put on her pink bikini bottoms.

I handed a large towel to everyone, and we walked outside and sat in a circle on the large sheet on the grass area.

BIRTHDAY EXPERIENCE

CHAPTER 7: POOLSIDE CHAT

The five of us were a motley crew: Sam wearing that little thong, Kathy topless and in her underwear, me in a string bikini, Julie in hot pink, and Linda wearing her conservative tan bikini.

I explained to Kathy how we had come to this point. "I met Sam at a party my parents gave, and found that he had retired from a career in pharmaceutical development. I asked him to help me with my career planning, and we had a couple of lunches together. Along the way, we found that we had some similar fantasies, involving submission, and Sam invited me over here for a full day of experiences."

I continued, "Sam spanked me and, at some point, I started to get turned on. Then, over lunch, Sam made a comment about my age that I didn't like and, to make up, he let me spank him. That's when I started getting into it." Kathy was nodding.

"Sam continued to spank me in the afternoon, using many different 'implements', but was still very kind to me. He made sure I had plenty to eat and drink, and helped me come after some of the hardest spankings. But we didn't have sex."

Now Linda rolled her eyes, but I ignored her. "Sam wanted us to have our first experience without sex. But he defined sex as 'sharing of body fluids', so doing me with his fingers was allowed. Sam took me to dinner – that was on Linda's birthday, and we ended-up at the same fancy restaurant. I stayed over that night, and Sam was a perfect gentleman. Well, maybe not 'perfect', as I had been ready for sex. But Sam is a little 'old fashioned'."

I now saw Sam rolling his eyes, and I clarified, "I said 'old fashioned', not 'old'." He just nodded, and I wondered how uncomfortable he was about his age, in this setting with four much younger women.

Continuing my story, I told Kathy "Then, I stayed here over a long weekend, and Sam showed his romantic side: We made love passionately, but only after he had made a path of rose petals, lit the room with candlelight, and put on some sexy music." I wasn't sure if I had mentioned that to Julie and Linda.

I summarized my thoughts, "Sam really is a sweet guy," Out of the corner of my eye, I saw Sam rolling his eyes again. If he did that one more time, I might have to punish him. I finished my thoughts, "but he does get turned on by a few 'fetishes'. Such as spanking – or being spanked – and 'playing doctor'."

Kathy chuckled, "Playing doctor? It sounds like something a couple of grade-schoolers would do."

Now, I laughed, "Yes, Sam is turned on by some childish things. But his medical role-play is much more advanced than you can imagine: He has given me real shots and a full pelvic exam, and even stuck an endoscope up my butt." I saw Linda's mouth drop open; I guess we hadn't shared most of this with Julie or Linda.

"Sam is all about openness ... and submission. But I think these things are easier for the younger generation – like us – than it was in his day. For example, you guys aren't bothered by coming to a skinny-dipping birthday party, and both Julie and Linda have already let Sam spank them."

Linda asked, "Are you going to tell Kathy about getting stuck with needles?"

Well, now I guess I had to. "One of the things that turns Sam on is seeing how people react to things that might hurt or be embarrassing. He has a bunch of medical supplies, like long needles, that would frighten most people. In addition to giving shots, he has introduced me to 'needle play' – where needles are put through pinches of skin to make a decorative pattern."

Kathy looked at me curiously, so I elaborated, "We showed Julie and Linda a picture of a needle play 'artwork' that Sam did on my backside. I can show you that later." Then I looked around at my friends, "But I think Sam is planning a demonstration that will give you guys a better idea of what I'm talking about."

Linda piped up, "I hope that doesn't mean sticking needles in *our* bottoms!"

I laughed, but didn't really know all that Sam had planned. "The demonstration I'm talking about will be on me." I looked over at Sam, and he nodded. "He calls it a 'corset'." I couldn't help but chuckle, and told Linda, "But if you want Sam to try some needle art on you, I'm sure he would be happy to oblige you." Linda was shaking her head.

I decided to get a little more informal, and casually took off my top, putting it on the sheet beside me. It was already getting hot out here, and I was looking forward to going in the pool. Julie shrugged, and took off her top, also. Then, Kathy stood, looked down, and said, "These are silly," as she removed her underwear.

Kathy was a beautiful girl, perfectly proportioned, and in great physical shape. I noticed a tampon string, and realized that Kathy was already demonstrating her openness.

Then, Sam stood, and said, "I agree, it's silly wearing anything at all today." With that, he removed the thong.

I laughed, "Well, I think that thong is about the silliest thing any of us are wearing today." The girls laughed, slightly nervously, as Sam 'let it all hang out' for everyone to see. As he was already up, he offered, "Can I bring something to drink for any of you?" He listed the soft drinks and tropical juices we had in the cooler, and we all gave him our 'order'.

While Sam was getting our drinks, I told my friends, "I really don't know everything that Sam has planned for today. But let's all try to go with the flow; he really is a nice guy. And this may end up to be one of the more unusual birthday parties you guys have ever attended."

We were all laughing, as Sam returned, with two cans in each hand, and one more being held between them. He passed the drinks around and sat cross-legged on the sheet. As Kathy was already nude, I decided to take my bottoms off, also. They were cute, and sexy, but we were going for the 'natural' look today. I sat cross-legged next to Sam.

Then, Julie suddenly stood, and loudly proclaimed, "I know what Linda needs, to loosen her up enough to take her clothes off: A little grass." I closed my eyes, not knowing how Sam would take this. I wasn't surprised, having expected Julie and Linda – and probably Kathy – to want to get high. But I hadn't discussed this subject with Sam.

Julie picked up her top, and walked into the pool room. We saw her take off her bikini bottom, and drop the suit in a box, then rummage through her tote, pulling out her 'supplies'. She walked back to the sheet and sat down, four of us now nude, and Linda still wearing her suit.

Linda looked up at us, taking off her top, and said, "I don't need to smoke in order to get nude with you guys."

She dropped her top on the sheet, and added, "But getting high would be fun." Linda had large, full breasts that seemed appropriate to her overall body type – very curvy. She didn't seem embarrassed, although the entire scene was probably making her a little uncomfortable.

Julie got up and bent over the pool, filling a small plastic water pipe. When she sat back down on the sheet, she opened a small pill bottle, and poured some powdered marijuana into the bowl. Then, she took a small disposable lighter and lit up, taking a long drag on the end of the tiny tube that folded up from the side of the pipe.

She handed the pipe to Linda, who took a long puff and smiled, holding the smoke in as long as possible. Linda passed the pipe to Kathy, who took a puff, and then passed the pipe to Sam.

Sam looked at me and shrugged, taking a large puff himself, then leaning his head back and smiling. After he had exhaled, he said, "It's been a long time ..." The pipe came to me. I decided that getting stoned at my casual birthday party would be entirely appropriate, so I took a couple of hits.

By the time the pipe was back in Julie's hands, there was only one more puff left, which Julie took; then, she walked to the planter, dumped the small amount of water in the pipe, and refilled it from the pool. She loaded another bowl of grass, and we kept the pipe going around the circle.

After she'd had a second hit, Linda stood and pushed her bathing suit bottom down and stepped out of it. I hadn't seen Linda nude for a long time; she sported a neatly trimmed rectangular patch of dark pubic hair. We were all nude now, and the party had been going for only about 30 minutes. Everyone appeared to be comfortable;

perhaps more than comfortable, now that we were getting stoned.

I looked at Julie, and said, "Well, at least you didn't pass around tabs of acid."

Julie laughed, "I thought about it, but didn't want to be that far out of my mind at your party. I knew Linda would do it with me, but wasn't sure about the rest of you guys."

Sam spoke up, "That's where I would have drawn the line. I have no problem with grass, but I still have a lot to do today, so wouldn't have chanced taking LSD. I've never tried it before, but have heard a few horror stories about people who got crazy using it."

Julie said, "That can happen. It takes some getting used to."

The second pipe of grass made its way around the circle, and we were all feeling pretty mellow. Linda asked Kathy, "Did you have any grass in Mexico? Or did you get any down there?"

Kathy shook her head, "No, I don't have any safe way to buy grass there. I did bring some, of course. It was great lying on the beach, stoned, reading a book and getting my all-over tan. My parents still smoke, also."

Linda shook her head, "You're parents are pretty weird."

Kathy disagreed, "I think they're pretty cool. For older people." Kathy suddenly looked at Sam, and apologized, "Sorry, Sam."

Sam just shrugged. Then, he stood up, walked casually over to the pool, and dived in. We laughed, but I explained, "Sam is a little sensitive about his age. You can tell that he wants to be our age again. But he's pretty cool, also."

Julie nodded, "I wasn't sure how he would react to us smoking. But, if he's doing it too, I guess he's OK with it."

We all got up, and walked to the pool. Linda tested the water with a toe. "It feels perfect!" Then, she sat on the edge, and lowered herself into the water. Julie, Kathy and I followed, as Sam treaded water in the deep end, watching us.

When we were all in, we swam over to Sam. Kathy was almost bubbly, "The water feels great! What a nice day!" We all agreed: It was a nice day. Especially nice for a skinny-dipping birthday party.

I treaded water, as I watched the girls enter the pool, one by one. So far, the morning was working out well; everyone seemed comfortable without clothes. Julie had surprised me with the marijuana, but I took it in stride, just as the girls were not making a big deal about nudity.

It felt good to be stoned again, after so many years. I knew that it would wear off in a couple of hours – long before I had to cook dinner. It really was turning out to be an epic day, and the party had just begun.

Kelly swam over to me, and put her arms around me, her weight nearly pulling me under. But I treaded water faster, and kept our heads above the surface, as we kissed. "Your friends seem to be having a good time," I pointed out to Kelly.

She nodded, "Yeah, the party's been very nice, so far." Then, she added, "Thank you for not making a big deal about Julie getting us all high." Kelly let go of me, and treaded water next to me.

I shrugged, "It isn't a big deal. But I haven't gotten high for a few years, so I'm definitely feeling it." Kelly laughed, and swam over to her friends.

The pool felt good. And, looked good – the black bottom making it feel more like a lake than a pool. The waterfall was running, the sparkling water flowing over the rocks and cascading down to the dark water of the pool.

I had turned the valves so that the spa was not much warmer than the pool; I would need to remember to set them back to their normal positions in order to heat the jacuzzi to a proper temperature for this evening. I watched, as the girls frolicked in the cool water.

My only trepidation with the party was whether the pirate scene would come off as planned. We first had to drag my construction over to the pool, and lift it into the pipe I had placed in the ground; then, with the help of the girls, I would have to erect the mast (the *pirate ship* mast), cleat the stays to the house and the trees, and lower the sails. I would need to speak with the girls privately – i.e., without Kelly – at some point, to clue them in on the scene, and their responsibilities.

The pirate scene was intended to be a highlight of the day for Kelly, and I hoped it would fulfill her fantasy vision. The highlight of the day for me would undoubtedly be the girls playing 'spank poker' on the Lazy Sam ... if we got that far.

I got out of the water, grabbed my towel, and spread it on one of the chaises; then, I lay down on my stomach, my head near the pool, watching the girls, as the hot sun baked my backside. Kelly's friends were all very cute. Of course, what 25 year old girl *wasn't* cute to a 50 year old guy?

If I had to rate them, I would say that Kelly was still the most beautiful. Julie and Kathy were 'pretty'. And Linda was 'cute', with curves in all the right places, but a bit overweight. They all had great personalities, all very different.

Lying face down, with the pressure of my body pushing my front onto against the chaise, I felt my manhood throb. That wasn't good. I turned over on my back, putting my arms over my eyes to shield them from the bright sky.

A few minutes later, I opened my eyes and, to my right, I saw Julie lying on her stomach, in the chaise next to me. And, to my left, I saw Kathy, lying on her back, in the chaise on that side.

I looked up, and Kelly was over me, straddling the chaise, lowering herself. She held my cheeks in her hands, as she steadily, surely, lowered her head, joining her mouth to mine. When she came up for air, I stammered, "Kelly, I don't want to get turned on, in front of your friends."

Kelly laughed, a Cruella de Vil mock, "What? You're going to be *modest* in front of them?"

A monster. But one I loved. I knew she would submit to me. But could I ever allow myself to submit to her? Fully? The monster kissed me again, a cruel and loving fusion that had me thoroughly confused. Her friends were lying two feet from us. What did Kelly expect? What did she want?

A bit of sanity entered my mind, and I grabbed her head in my hands, briefly pushed her away – her eyes betraying a momentary look of terror – and then pulling her toward me, kissing her viciously – as she had done with me earlier. Then, I pushed her head away again, smiled at her sweetly ... and commanded, loudly, "Standing position, girl!"

There was a momentary flash of confusion in Kelly's eyes; it must have been mere milliseconds. Then, she pushed off me, and stood at the foot of the chaise, spreading her feet and putting her hands on her head, as she gazed forward – out towards the pool and the paths, the trees and flowers, and the forest, beyond. I sat up, seeing in my peripheral vision all three of Kelly's friends raise their heads, turn over, sit up, or otherwise notice.

I straddled the chaise, and stared at Kelly, "Are you ready for your corset, Miss?"

Kelly nodded, 'Yes, Sir. I'm ready. What would you like me to do?"

I smiled. I glanced to my far right, and saw Linda sitting up in her chaise, her mouth seemingly perpetually open, staring at Kelly.

"Before the main event, I think we should demonstrate a few things to your friends. Right here on the chaise would be fine." Kelly nodded. She knew exactly what I meant; and what was going to happen. I got up, and Kelly lay down on her stomach on the towel I had left on the chaise. Her friends were attentive, but silent, as I returned with a few supplies in my hands.

I addressed them, "Kelly's first 'gift' for the day will be needle art on her back: A corset. But first, I'll demonstrate a 'normal' needle insertion, versus needle play. Kelly let out her breath, as I swabbed her right hip. I uncapped the needle, and held it up for everyone to see; then I plunged it into Kelly; she was silent. I looked around, and all of her friends now had open mouths.

Julie asked, "Kelly, doesn't that hurt?"

Kelly, her eyes still closed, appearing very relaxed on the chaise, replied, "It doesn't feel that good. But it doesn't really hurt, either. Very minor."

I decided to 'make the point', and swabbed Kelly's left hip, inserting another needle on that side, to the astonishment of her friends. I explained, "It doesn't feel as bad as it looks. I'm using a very thin needle. But each needle releases endorphins, that dull most of the pain." Then, I looked up at Kelly's friends, and offered, "Perhaps you guys might want to see how this feels?" I didn't get any immediate 'takers'.

There was one more demonstration that might be interesting for everyone. "Kelly, I didn't bring a sharps container out here, so I'm going to have you get up and walk over to the massage table for me ... with those needles in you." Her friends' mouths were still hanging open. "And you may as well walk a lap around the pool."

Kelly sighed, and got herself up, gingerly, as the needles do hurt when moving around. Kelly slowly made her way around the pool, and over to the massage table, where I pulled the needles out and disposed of them.

"Are you ready for some needle play, now?"

Kelly looked at me, then leaned over and gave me a peck on the lips. "Yes, Sir. I'm ready."

"Good girl! Please get up on the massage table for me." I spread a clean beach towel over the massage table, and Kelly got up on it, lying face down.

CHAPTER 8: KELLY'S CORSET

As Kelly's friends lay on the chaises by the pool, talking, and getting their all-over tans, I pulled out the box from under the massage table. Using a ruler and marking pen, I put small dots on Kelly's back, starting just below her left shoulder blade, and continuing every inch to her upper buttocks. Being careful to align the dots, I marked another series on Kelly's right side, about five inches apart from the first set. When I was done, there were twin rows of tiny black dots, 15 on each side.

Next, I took a couple of alcohol swabs, and cleaned Kelly's back along the two rows of dots. Thankfully, the alcohol did not remove the dots; I had tried this earlier on my own skin. Then, I took out six packs of 25-gauge 1.5"-long needles, separating the five needles in each pack, and putting them into a small plastic bowl. I asked Kelly, "Would you like me to bring you a glass of wine, before we get started?"

Kelly, her head on the table and eyes closed, said, "No thanks. I'm still high from the grass, and pretty relaxed, already. I'll be fine."

I said, "OK. Then I'll start inserting the needles now." After putting an exam glove on my left hand, I peeled back the sterile wrapping of the first needle, uncapped it, and pinched the skin of Kelly's back, just below the first dot. Then, I smoothly slid the needle through, directly under the dot. I heard an 'Mmmm' from Kelly, her eyes still closed. I proceeded to insert the needles, one by one, down the row of dots on Kelly's right side, with the blue hubs of the needles on the outside, and the needle tips facing her spine.

When a dozen needles had been placed, I stopped, and walked around the massage table, putting my head down next to Kelly's. "How are you doing so far, Kelly?"

Kelly chortled, "I'm still here, aren't I?" She opened one eye to look at me, and said, "The needles hurt. But not that bad. I feel a line of pain down my back, but can't feel the individual needles. Those insertions hurt more than just sticking a needle in my butt." She closed her eye and sighed. "I guess you can continue, now."

I walked around to her other side, and began inserting needles in a line down the left side of her back, each needle paired with a needle I had inserted on her right side. On two or three of the insertions, Kelly let out a soft 'Ow'; I tried to push the needles through the pinches of skin quickly, but knew that they still hurt coming back out through her skin.

When a dozen needles were lined up going down her left side, I stood back and examined my work so far. The pairs of needles were lined up well, and made straight lines down each side of Kelly's back.

I decided to call Kelly's friends over to watch the last few needles being inserted, and the corset tied. When Linda saw Kelly's back, she gasped. "That *has* to hurt!" Julie just smiled. Kathy had a curious look on her face.

The girls stood across the table from me, as I pointed out the remaining three pairs of dots, on Kelly's lower back and upper hip. I opened a needle, uncapped it, and showed it to the girls at close range, hoping that none of them would faint. Linda had her hands in front of her face, and was shaking her head. Julie said, "That's a *long* needle!"

I pointed out that sticking a needle straight in results in breaking the skin only once, while needle play requires the needles to be inserted through the skin, and back out again, going through the skin twice. It was the needle coming back out through the skin that hurt the most.

I pinched the skin of Kelly's lower back using my gloved left hand, placed the needle against the pinch of skin, and pushed. The needle glided through the skin and back out. When I let go, the needle was sitting flat on her back, horizontally, in line with the needles above it. I continued inserting the last few needles, alternating sides, as the girls watched with rapt attention.

When all 30 needles had been placed, I reached into the box and pulled out the pink satin ribbon, which was about ½" wide. Holding the two ends in one hand, I managed to find the center of the ribbon, and positioned it between the two needles at the top of Kelly's back, the ribbon circling around the hubs of the needles. I then crossed the ribbon, and hooked it around the next two needles.

Continuing in this way, I crisscrossed the ribbon back and forth down Kelly's back, making turns around the next needles every inch down. Kelly whimpered a few times, as the ribbon pulled on the needles, but I tried to gently make a turn of the ribbon around each needle hub and keep the 'corset' tight, without pulling on the needles.

It took several minutes, but when the lacing of the ribbon was completed, Kelly had a 'corset' from shoulder blades to upper hips. I tied a pretty bow at the bottom of the corset using the remaining ribbon. I had estimated pretty well, but there was still a few feet of extra ribbon hanging down below the bow. I ran down to the office, and brought both a pair of scissors and my camera. When I returned to the pool room, Kelly was talking quietly with her friends. I cut the ribbon so that the 'tails' of the bow came down to the bottom of Kelly's butt.

I took a couple of snapshots of the corset while Kelly was on the table, and then helped her down. She made a lot of 'Ooohing' and 'Aaahing' sounds as she got off the table. "Shall we walk out to the backyard, so I can get some pictures of your corset in a more natural surrounding?"

Kelly smiled, "Sure. But first, can you help me get to the bathroom. I didn't think I needed to, before, but it seems that I need to pee now."

I helped Kelly walk over to the bathroom, and went in with her. I asked, "So how does that needle corset feel?"

Kelly looked up from the toilet and laughed, "I'll make a corset on *your* back next time, so you can feel what it's like." That wasn't exactly the answer I had been expecting, but knowing Kelly, I wasn't surprised to hear her response.

When Kelly was finished, we switched places, and I pee'd as she washed her hands. I wondered whether I should bring her downstairs, for some sensual pictures of her on the playroom bed, modeling her corset; but I decided to limit the amount of walking Kelly had to do with those needles in her.

We walked into the backyard and I took a few snapshots of Kelly hugging a tree, standing near the hedge and flower beds, and sitting on one of the boulders, facing away from the camera, her bottom at the edge of the huge slab of rock, the pink ribbon hanging down from the corset.

Finally, I walked her back to the chaises, turning one perpendicular to the others and sitting Kelly in the middle, facing her friends who were lying on the three parallel chaises. As I looked at the three clothes-free bodies lying next to each other, I visualized needles in each side of their butts. I might as well ask ...

"Would you guys like to have a quick 'needle experience' ... to see what it feels like? I could insert a couple of needles in each of your bottoms while you lie there ... or, you guys could sit up, and have me insert the needles in your hip as you watch me remove Kelly's corset." Linda was already shaking her head 'no'.

As a *pièce de résistance*, I asked Kelly if I could finish her needle play with decorations on her breasts. She shrugged, and said, "Yes, Sir. That would be OK." Her friends were shocked that there would be more which, I think, was Kelly's point. Julie and Linda didn't seem so 'adventurous' any more. I brought the box of needles and sharps container from the playroom to the chaises, and sat on the chaise with Kelly, turning her toward me.

As we had done during Kelly's first needle play experience, I made a 'rosette' of needles around each of her nipples, inserting the needles radially, each hub about an inch from Kelly's nipple, the needle extending outward, away from the nipple. Kelly sat there and smiled, as I proceeded to insert eight needles on each side.

Sitting cross-legged on the chaise, Kelly then turned to face her friends again. "Doesn't this look neat?" Kelly glanced at me, and continued, "I'm sure Sam could take some great photos, if we all had needle art around our breasts."

Linda was still shaking her head, and there was no response from Kathy. But, Julie sat up on her chaise, looked at me, and said, "I guess I could see what one needle feels like. Just one." I guess Julie really was adventurous. I sat on the edge of the chaise, and took out an alcohol swab and single needle.

Without asking Julie to pick a side, I quickly swabbed her left breast, just above her areola. Then, I uncapped a needle, took a pinch of skin, and said, "Here it is." With that, I slid the needle quickly through the pinch of skin, as Julie watched. She gasped slightly, then said, "Yes, it hurts." Kelly, Linda and Kathy were all watching, surprised first that Julie was game to try it, and surprised again that Julie didn't react much to the pain.

I explained, "As we said, Julie, sticking needles through a pinch of skin in needle play hurts more than just sticking a needle in your butt, as if you were getting a shot." Then I added hopefully, "But it's not *that* bad, is it?"

Julie shook her head, "I guess not. But I still can't imagine having nearly 50 needles in me, like Kelly has right now."

I laughed, "It *is* intimidating, isn't it? But Kelly is probably feeling it somewhat less due to the endorphins." I offered Julie, "Shall I take it back out, now?" She nodded.

I slowly pulled the needle out, as Julie winced, and I disposed of it in the sharps container. "Now that you've tried it the hard way, why don't you try a couple in your butt the normal way? Then, you can let me know what you think. I can do it with you sitting like this, or you might be more comfortable lying down for it."

Julie was uncertain she wanted to try any more needles, but Kelly nodded at her, and Julie finally said, "I guess I can let you do it. If it's OK, I'll just keep sitting here." Julie was sitting on the chaise, straddling it with her legs on the ground.

I took another alcohol swab and a couple of needles, and walked around behind Julie, straddling the chaise right behind her. "Which side do you want me to do, first?"

Julie chuckled, "I don't care. I'm not sure why I'm even doing this, but if Kelly can take it, so can I."

I swabbed Julie's left hip, and quickly inserted a needle; it glided smoothly into her flesh, leaving only the small blue hub sitting on her skin as evidence that there was an inch an a half of stainless steel in her. Then, without delay, I swabbed the other side, and inserted a needle there.

Linda and Kathy had sat up, leaning around to watch me insert the needles. This time, Linda wasn't hiding her eyes; she was actually watching the needle insertion, which indicated some progress in her acceptance of our needle play.

Julie didn't make a sound. I was surprised, and so was Julie. "Those really don't hurt much! Like you said, they were easier than the one you put in my breast."

"That's great." I said. "We'll just leave those in until I've finished removing all of Kelly's needles. As you probably noticed, they hurt being pulled out, also, so this will be a little challenging for Kelly." Julie nodded, as she looked around and leaned over to see the hub of the needle in her right hip.

I said, "Let me show you something ..." I pulled the needle out about ½", so Julie could see the steel shaft. Julie looked at the needle sticking out of her skin. "You can push it back in yourself, if you like." I wasn't sure Julie would do this, but she reached down, putting her finger on the hub ... and pushed. The needle slid back in to the hub, Julie emitting a quiet 'ow' as it went in.

I moved over to Kelly's chaise again, and began pulling out the needles around her breasts, depositing each one in the sharps container. Kelly winced a few times, but did very well. Then, I had her turn her back to her friends, and I began undoing the corset. First, I untied the bow. Then, I carefully took the ribbon out from around each needle hub, alternating sides, until only the lines of needles remained in her back.

I had Julie hold the end of the ribbon, and I walked into the pool room, pulling the ribbon taut, and reaching the back wall of the playroom. The girls were shocked to see that I had used more than twenty feet of ribbon for the corset. I rolled up the ribbon, and dropped it into the cardboard box by the massage table, and sat down next to Kelly again.

One by one, I slowly drew each needle out of Kelly's back, dropping it into the sharps container. Kelly emitted a few whines as the needles came out, but she had done very well. So had her friends: Nobody had fainted. And Julie was still sitting with a needle in each hip.

When all of the needles were out of Kelly, I got some Neosporin and a couple of 2x2" gauze pads from the box, and cleaned-up Kelly's back. Two lines of double needle pricks were clearly visible, and there were a few dots of blood. I quickly swabbed the lines with alcohol, and then dried Kelly's skin with a gauze pad. Then, I put some Neosporin on another pad, and wiped it down the twin lines of needle pricks, rubbing it in along the way.

Kelly sat on the chaise, her back to her friends, as I worked. When I was finished, Kelly turned around, smiled at her friends, and then at me, "Thank you, Sir. That was interesting." I leaned over and kissed her on the lips. Then she chuckled and said, "It *is* my birthday today, so I may have to demonstrate a few things on *you*, later."

I smiled, "Yes, dear. I fully expected that." Kelly just smiled and nodded.

Of course, I hadn't forgotten about the needles that were still in Julie's hips ... but I pretended I had. "Well, I guess that wraps up our needle play demonstration." I stood up, and Julie quickly said, "Haven't you forgotten something?"

I crossed my arms and held my chin in a hand, "Have I?" I smiled at Julie, and said, "I thought you might like to leave your needles in for a while."

Julie said indignantly, "I already have! Please take them out, now."

I nodded, "OK, of course. Would you like to walk a lap around the pool, first?"

Julie shook her head, and indignantly said, "No, thanks."

I sat behind Julie, and wiggled each of the needles. "I'm glad you didn't find them to be too uncomfortable." Then, I slowly pulled each needle out, dropping them into the sharps container, and wiping the two dots of blood with a 2x2" gauze pad, holding it on each side with pressure for a few seconds. Linda watched closely, but I noticed that Kathy was lying on her chaise, eyes closed. I doubted that she could have fallen asleep, and the message came through clearly: She wasn't interested in needles.

I put everything in the cardboard box, and left it in the playroom closet, next to the other boxes. In the kitchen, I prepared the vegetable dip by putting the already-cut vegetables in the small wells in the large smoked plastic tray, and the dill dip in a matching gray bowl in the center. We had carrots, celery, red and green peppers, broccoli, and zucchini.

I brought the tray and a few napkins outside, and over to the chaises, placing it in the middle of the cross-wise chaise, between Kelly and I. The girls sat on the ends of their chaises, as they tried a few of the vegetables and the thick olive-dill dip. I took everyone's drink orders, and went to the cooler to collect the soft drinks, bringing them back to the chaises, where we had a mid-morning picnic.

Since we – a least some of us – were on the subject of needles, I decided to open a related discussion. "Kelly and I had an interesting visitor who taught us a little about piercings ... including genital piercings. And tattoos. It seems strange that none of you got into that, with all your 'wildness'."

Linda shrugged, "We all have pierced ears." She glanced at Kathy, "How many do you have?"

Kathy said, "Three on each earlobe. But the third on each ear is going to close, unless I use it more." She looked at Kelly and I, "I've thought about getting a piercing – probably a nipple ring – but never did it. Maybe if I had a boyfriend who was interested ..."

Julie said, "*Genital* piercings? It seems like that would hurt."

Kelly related our experience with Fiona a little over a week ago. Linda winced, as Kelly described the vertical clit hood piercing that Fiona had shown us. Julie offered, "I would probably go for a piercing, if any of my friends were into it." The girls all laughed, and shook their heads.

Except Kelly, who replied, "Well, I'm considering it. Maybe we should have it done together?"

Julie snickered "I'll think about it." Then, she smiled at Kelly, "But I'd rather see you get yours first. If you don't scream too much, then I might do it." We all laughed.

Then, Kelly told her friends about the multiple frenum piercings that Fiona's boyfriend had. I shuddered, just thinking about it. Kelly, noticing my reaction, said brightly, "Now that I've let Sam do a corset on my back, I'm sure he would be happy to let me demonstrate a few needles through the skin under his dick."

I blanched. *No*, I was definitely not ready to offer myself for Kelly's demonstration. I gave Kelly a 'look', and she arched her eyebrows at me. Then, she leaned over and kissed me, "OK. I guess I can let you off the hook ... even though it's my birthday. Why don't you think about it. Maybe we can do it later."

Now, I would have a stomach ache the rest of the afternoon. Kelly knew that I wasn't afraid of needles per sé ... but I didn't like the thought of them *down there*! Of course, I would probably let Kelly have her way, if she insisted. But I hoped she didn't.

Kelly and I were sensitive to each other's boundaries, but still we pushed each other up to – and sometimes beyond – those limits. Although I might agree to my manhood being skewered by Kelly at some time, I didn't think that doing it in front of her friends would be a good idea. Especially, if I cried. Fortunately, Kelly moved on to other topics of conversation.

The subject of travel was brought up, partially in relation to Kathy's recent trip to Mexico, but also more generally. I found that Kelly's friends hadn't traveled much internationally.

It was something that I wanted to share with Kelly, and I had thought for the past few weeks about offering Kelly a 'birthday' trip. Not on her birthday, but an experience that I could give her as another birthday present. I was looking forward to visiting Henk and Zöe in The Netherlands, and sharing with Kelly some of the European viewpoints on nudity and openness. I decided to broach the idea with Kelly now.

"Kelly, I bought you a few small birthday presents, but I've been thinking about giving you something bigger, more significant. Something that will provide some new perspectives, and that will allow me to share some things with you that I have experienced." Kelly looked at me blankly, not having any idea of where I was going with this line of discussion.

"So, I just made the decision to offer you another birthday present; something that I think you'll appreciate. But we'll need to figure out the logistics and schedule – especially considering that school will be starting again very soon."

Kelly looked at me quizzically, and her three friends were sitting on the edge of their chaises, looking at us, and wondering what I was about to offer Kelly. I breathed deeply, knowing that this was something I wanted to do. And knowing that Kelly was the person I most wanted to do it with. In fact, she was the *only* person that I cared to do it with. It wasn't really a big deal, but would take some planning. I thought about the seasons, and how we would coordinate the timing.

I looked around at her friends, and then back to Kelly. I leaned over to kiss her, gently, on the lips. Her hazel eyes were bright and clear, but her eyelids were slightly closed, as Kelly squinted, trying unsuccessfully to see what was going through my mind. I sat cross-legged on the chaise, and took a sip of Diet Coke, keeping Kelly and her friends in suspense another moment, before continuing.

"Kelly, I would like to take you to Europe." Kelly's mouth dropped open, then closed, and then a broad smile formed on her beautiful face. Before Kelly could say anything, I added, "I have some friends there, and some favorite places I would like to share with you."

I thought a moment, and added, "We should take at least three weeks for the trip – it will only be an introduction, but give you a taste for European culture. The main issue will be the timing: Both to share with you certain things that depend on the weather, and to fit the trip into your school schedule."

Kelly put her arms around my neck and pulled me to her, giving me a languorous kiss that was perhaps too much, in front of her friends. Then, I realized that her friends were sitting in front of us, nude, and one of them had masturbated in front of us. And, I guess nothing was 'too much', when you were in love.

Julie, Linda and Kathy applauded, and congratulated Kelly on the upcoming trip. Kathy told us that she had been scheduled to go to Europe with her family just after graduating high school, but that she had come down with mono, and had to spend the month in bed, dreaming about the rest of her family on their European vacation.

Linda admitted that her secret dream was to go to Paris; it also, of course, included meeting a Parisian stud, and a 'happily ever after' ending.

Julie suggested opening champagne. Although I did have some in the bar fridge, I suggested that we save it for later. I asked the girls if we could start with a nice bottle of rosé; I reminded them that there was a lot of 'birthday party' left, and I didn't want us all to get drunk or fall asleep.

I went into the kitchen, and poured five plastic cups of the pink wine, bringing them to everyone on a tray. I thought about cooking the bready cheese puffs, but the girls assured me that the vegetable dip would satisfy their hunger for a while. We each made a toast to Kelly.

And then, Kelly toasted me. "Here's to Sam. My teacher, my protector, my dom, my friend ... and my lover." Kelly kissed me lightly as we held our wine glasses. Then she turned to her friends, "Sam really is the most considerate, caring, and loving man I know. The trip to Europe is a bit over-the-top, but just his preparing this party for us is amazing."

Julie lifted her wine glass, "Here's to Sam. Thank you for putting on Kelly's birthday party. It's great that we could meet you and get to know you a little."

I thought, 'you'll probably get to know me much better by the time we go to sleep tonight'. But I actually appreciated Julie's sentiments. It had been a lot of work, but the party was working out nicely, the girls were having fun, and I knew that Kelly appreciated my efforts. Little did she know what was coming up in just a little while!

CHAPTER 9: GROUP MASSAGE

Sam didn't realize it, but I was almost in tears. Of joy. I had never expected Sam to take me to Europe; especially not in the next few months. Sam was right that I would need to check with my advisor at the university, but as the semester was going to focus on my research – with just a few seminars to attend – I thought that time for the trip could be arranged. I was a little in shock. I drank the wine, which helped, and listened to Julie's nice toast.

When we had all finished our wine, Sam said, "I would like to suggest our next birthday 'experience'." We all looked at Sam expectantly; I had no idea what he had planned for the day.

He continued, "I have the temperature in the jacuzzi turned down, so it's warmer than the pool, but not hot; about body temperature. I'll turn the heat up this evening. What I suggest is that we all get in, and have a 'group massage'."

Before any of us could ask Sam what he meant, he explained, "We'll pick one person, who will float in the jacuzzi, with the other four of us supporting her, and also massaging her. We'll put a blindfold on her, so that she won't know who is massaging what parts. Just to clarify: I'm not talking about anything sexual, just sensual. It's a unique experience to have many sets of hands on your body."

It sounded interesting. Sam got up and went into the pool room to get the blindfold. At the same time, Kathy excused herself to use the bathroom. I looked at Linda, and she just shrugged. Then, Julie said, "It sounds like fun."

Sam returned with the blindfold; it was made of neoprene rubber, so that it could get wet without disintegrating. He bent down, looked closely at my breasts, and ran his fingers around my nipples, assessing the aftermath of the needle play experience. He also went behind me, and ran his fingers down the two lines where needles had been inserted for the corset.

I didn't feel any pain. I looked down at my breasts, and even tilted them so that I could see around my nipple area, but could not see any needle marks. I guess Sam wanted to make sure I was ready to go in the pool.

When Kathy returned, we all got in the spa, lowering ourselves into the lukewarm water. Sam held up the blindfold, and said, "I nominate Linda to be the first massaggee." Linda choked, but Julie and Kathy instantly voiced their agreement. I thought it was a good idea, also.

Linda reluctantly put on the blindfold, and lay back in the water. Eight arms and hands held her body at the surface of the water. Julie and I were on either side of Linda, Kathy next to Julie, and Sam at her feet. We held Linda, as he began massaging her feet and toes. Linda emitted a contented 'Mmmm'.

Julie and I realized that Linda was mostly floating, so it only took one arm from each of us to hold her up; thus freeing our other hand to do some massaging. I was further toward Linda's feet, and held her bottom, massaging the generous tissues of her butt. It felt very squishy and wobbly underwater.

Julie held Linda under the back with her left hand, and brought her right over Linda, running it lightly over Linda's chest, between her breasts, and over her stomach. Then, I brought my hand to Linda's stomach, continuing Julie's motions, as Julie's hand circled Linda's large breasts, which were floating, and also very wobbly.

In the meantime, Sam was doing long massage strokes up Linda's legs, and Kathy's hands were intertwined in ours, massaging Linda's breasts, stomach and hips.

Sam smiled at me, and nodded his head toward Linda's legs, and I brought both hands under Linda, moving down gradually from her hips to her knees. Sam put his hands under Linda's lower legs, parallel with mine. Then he winked at me, and moved around me so that I was holding Linda's legs, and Sam now had his left hand under Linda's butt. I held Linda up with both hands, giving Sam, Julie, and Kathy the chance to use both hands on Linda.

Julie massaged Linda's breasts, as Sam made long strokes between them and down across her stomach, while Kathy now held Linda under her waist and her bottom. Then, Sam moved up to Linda's head, while Julie ran her hands around Linda – her chest, breasts, stomach, and down to the dark patch of pubic hair.

After a few minutes, Kathy and Julie switched places, Kathy now fondling Linda's large breasts, as Julie kneaded Linda's hips. Sam took Linda's head in his hands, wrapping his thumbs around and massaging Linda's temples.

As my left arm held Linda under her knees, my right began stroking her thighs, wrapping around between her legs, and back to the sides. Slowly, I worked my way up to her crotch, massaging the insides of her legs, and up and over each hip, only grazing Linda's sensitive parts.

Sam moved next to me, and held Linda under her head with one hand, and upper back with the other. Julie had one hand under Linda's waist, and now used the other to move through Linda's bush and over her genitals. Linda flinched, but said nothing.

I thought that Julie was going to masturbate Linda – it would have been interesting to see if Linda would allow that – but she only ran her hand over Linda's tissues superficially, never focusing on her clit.

I wondered why Sam had made a point of the massage being 'sensual' and not 'sexual', although at the time, I thought it had been a good suggestion.

Sam nodded towards Linda's feet, and we switched positions again, now being nearly back to where we had started Linda's group massage, with only Kathy and Julie having switched positions. Sam signaled Julie, who moved down to Linda's feet, while I supported Linda under her waist.

Sam moved to the side opposite me, and put his hand between Linda's legs; I held my breath, wondering what he was going to do. His right arm was against Linda's genitals now, curled underneath her, and holding her bottom, while his left hand lightly skimmed Linda's stomach, and up between her breasts.

Finally, Sam took his arm back out from between Linda's legs, and moved down to her feet again, switching places with Julie. I leaned over to Linda, and whispered, "How are you doing, Linda?"

She smiled, and said, "This feels great!" She sighed, and then said, "I guess I should give somebody else a turn." We all laughed.

I took the blindfold off Linda, and she lifted her head, as we all supported her. She frowned, and said, "I couldn't tell whose hands were on my body." Then, she smiled at me, and said, "I assumed it was Sam massaging my breasts."

From Linda's feet, Sam laughed, and said, "Linda, I didn't touch your breasts."

I guess that was the idea: Without knowing who was touching you where, it was easy just to relax, and enjoy the feeling. It was clear that Linda would not have objected to Sam massaging her breasts – which was a surprise to me; I guess Linda was starting to relax a little.

Sam let go of Linda's feet, and we lowered her to a standing position in the spa. Linda had a broad smile; she looked down at the swirling water, and then at each of us, and said, "Thank you. That was really nice."

Sam said, "Who's next? Kathy? We may not have time to 'do' everyone now, but we can continue this evening, so nobody misses out on the experience."

Kathy looked around at Julie and I, "I'll volunteer, unless you guys want to go first." We both shook our heads, and I handed the blindfold to Kathy. She put it on, and lay back in the warm, frothy water, the other four of us 'catching' her, and supporting her near the surface of the water.

My hands were under her bottom; what a difference! In contrast to Linda, Kathy was athletic, muscular. Her bottom did not feel very wobbly at all, just a thin layer could be squished as my hand moved across it.

Again, Sam began with a foot massage, and Julie used her free hand to massage Kathy's small breasts. Linda stood for a moment, looking at Kathy's body, and finally began stroking her stomach and her hips.

We continued Kathy's group massage, similar to Linda's, as we switched positions, and each took turns massaging a different area of Kathy's body. This time, Sam did massage her breasts; then, he moved up to her chest, and to her neck. He cradled Kathy's head, and massaged her shoulders and neck, before briefly moving his fingers in a circular fashion over Kathy's temples, and across Kathy's forehead.

Julie and Linda switched positions, Linda now lightly touching Kathy's breasts, then running her hand around Kathy's nipples. Sam moved next to me, and Julie supported Kathy, so that both Sam and Linda could massage Kathy's breasts with both hands. Sam then did long strokes from Kathy's neck, between her breasts, over her stomach, and down through Kathy's thin, blonde pubic hair.

Then, he supported Kathy with both hands under her bottom, squeezing the firm tissue, and allowing Julie to use both hands on Kathy's front. As with Linda, Julie ran her hand over Kathy's genitals, but this time continued – between Kathy's legs, and under her, before stroking back up. Julie looked at me and smiled, then lightly rested her palm over Kathy's clit.

I expected a flinch, but just saw Kathy smile, below her blindfold. Again, I thought that Julie was going to masturbate Kathy, and again, it seemed that Kathy wouldn't have put up a fight. Julie continued moving her hands across Kathy's body – including over her clit and genitals, but kept her treatment of Kathy sensual, not sexual.

We spent several more minutes massaging Kathy, who probably would have let us keep going all day. Then, Julie surprised us: She bent down to Kathy, leaning across Linda, and whispered, "May we help you have an orgasm, now, Kathy?"

For a long moment, Kathy didn't respond. Then, she quietly said, "You can try."

Julie smiled, and put her hand over Kathy's clit again. Linda softly massaged Kathy's breasts, and my hands molded Kathy's bottom.

Sam stepped next to me, and ran his hands along Kathy's inner thigh, from her knees up to her groin. He did this several times, and then – on the last time – kept going, moving his hand along the groove of Kathy's labia, and back down. As Julie put her fingers on Kathy's clit hood, and squeezed together, while pressing down with a pulsing motion, Sam kept moving his hand up Kathy's leg, and over her labia.

I hoped that Sam had noticed that Kathy was wearing a tampon! Whether he did or not, he didn't attempt to put his fingers into Kathy, but moved back down to her legs, and used both hands – starting at the top of her thighs – to massage his way down her legs.

Kathy was starting to thrust her hips, as Julie continued the clit massage. Just as I wondered whether Julie would 'go down' on Kathy, my question was answered: She did! Now, I wondered whether Kathy knew whose tongue was lashing at her clit.

Julie's head hid Kathy's genitals from Sam and I, but she was working steadily, and Kathy was showing the result. Kathy let out a few squeaks, and panted, as she thrust her hips up, and Julie continued eating her. Finally, Kathy gasped, pushed her hips up one more time, and held them; After Julie licked a few more times, Kathy raised her head, and breathlessly screamed, "Yes!"

Julie leaned over Kathy, her breasts on Kathy's stomach, and her hands over Kathy's hips, holding her. Linda bent over and, holding Kathy under her head and back, pressed her large breasts against Kathy's smaller breasts. Then, I leaned over Kathy, putting my hands around her other hip, and pressing my own breasts against Kathy's genitals.

Not to be left out, Sam leaned over Kathy's legs, his hands around them, as his chest pressed down on top of them. Now, Kathy was covered by a 'blanket' of her friends. Within a minute or two, Kathy – still breathing heavily – reached up and took off her blindfold.

Eventually, we all realized this, and lifted our bodies off hers. Kathy looked down her body, seeing Linda and Julie on her right side, me on her left, and Sam holding her ankles. "Wow! That was interesting." She looked up at Julie, "I really didn't expect that to happen." We lowered her, and she stood in the shallow spa.

She took a couple of deep breaths, and said, "You know, I've never experienced a woman going down on me. And, I've never masturbated in front of a man." She turned to Julie, "Thank you. That was really nice." Then, she turned to Sam, "And I guess Sam is 'one of the girls', now." We all laughed.

It had already been a surprising day – the Europe trip being the biggest surprise. But Kathy allowing Julie to masturbate her, *in front of Sam*, was amazing. Of course, I knew that Kathy was very open, about her body and about sex. But I hadn't thought that Julie would make the offer, nor did I believe Kathy would have accepted.

Now, random thoughts were racing through my head. What if Sam had been masturbating Kathy? Could she have known the difference between a man and a woman, with no experience of a woman going down on her? What if Sam had been the one to ask her? Would she have still done it? I wondered ...

I saw Sam glance over at the clock on the exterior wall, near the kitchen door. He said, "I think we have time for one more ... if you guys are game." He looked up at Julie, gave her a strange smile, and said, "I believe it's Julie's turn."

Julie smiled back at Sam, and said to everyone, "Well, I think it's *Sam's* turn, now. He's arranged the party, and this group massage was his idea ... so at least he should have the benefit of it."

Sam shook his head, "Nonsense. I want to make you guys happy, and give you some new experiences. This party is for you guys."

Now, I had to speak up, "No, Sam. The party is for all of us, including you. I think Julie's idea is great: Let the four girls massage the only male at the party."

Sam reluctantly took the blindfold, still shaking his head, and asked me, "Are you sure *you* don't want to be next?" I helped him put on the blindfold, and held his shoulders, as he lay back into the water. Kathy and Julie were on Sam's right, and Linda and I were on his left side. We were experienced, now, so knew to put one hand under Sam for support, and use the other to massage him. Sam relaxed into our arms.

Julie massaged Sam's chest, tweaking his nipples a few times, while Kathy stroked his right leg, and Linda stroked his left. I massaged his bottom with both hands. Kathy's strokes began coming up higher on Sam's leg, his thigh, and his hips.

Kathy did long strokes, from Sam's knees up to his stomach, back and forth, along one side of his hips and then the other. Eventually, her strokes grazed Sam's penis, which was floating vertically whenever we lowered his middle into the water.

Linda massaged Sam's feet, as I continued to squeeze his buttocks. Watching Kathy stroking Sam, I moved my hand so that my pointer finger was pressed against Sam's anus. I didn't think I would be able to insert it without lube, so I held it there, pulsing against him.

Julie switched places with Kathy, and immediately took Sam's manhood in her hand, wrapping her fingers around it, and holding firmly, as the rest of us massaged him. Then, Julie pressed Sam's penis against his stomach, and held her hand over it, pressing down hard, but stroking only a short distance.

Sam tried to lift his head, blindfold still in place, and said, "Kelly, I don't want to get turned on in front of your friends. That wouldn't be very nice." He obviously assumed that I was the one stroking him.

I leaned over and told him, "Why not? They're being totally open with you. And they've seen a man with an erection, before."

Sam whined, "Kelly ... I thought this was going to be a sensual, *non-sexual*, experience with your friends."

I laughed, "Well, Kathy has already had an orgasm. So just relax." Then, I had to throw in, "If you're going to be uptight with my friends, I'm going to insist that we do the ring toss." Both Sam and I were laughing at our private joke, as my friends looked at me questioningly. Finally, Sam groaned, and laid his head back in Kathy's hand.

We continued massaging Sam, my finger still pressed against his anus, and Julie now stroking him with her flat hand, pushing his penis against his stomach. I glanced at Linda, amazed that she didn't already have her hands in front of her face.

As I was supporting Sam with both hands under his bottom, and Kathy holding his head and shoulders, Julie had both hands available. She caressed Sam's growing member with one hand, and cradled his balls in the other. I saw Sam's penis throb, as Sam's breathing became more rapid. Julie pointed to Linda, and then down to Sam.

I was sure that Linda wasn't going to help masturbate Sam, when she reached over, and took Sam in her hands, caressing him, and then using the 'OK' position of her fingers to surround Sam and slide down his length. Another surprise!

Julie, Kathy and I all watched, as Linda expertly handled Sam; it was obvious that Sam was now fully erect. She made a few more strokes, then curled her fingers around Sam at the base of his penis, and held it up straight, away from his body, and piercing the surface of the water.

I lifted Sam slightly, so that his pubic hair was at the surface of the water, and Sam's penis extended upwards; whether it was 6", 7" or 8", I couldn't estimate, but he looked big, and I'm sure my friends had to be impressed. I made a mental note to measure Sam sometime.

As she held his dick in a vertical position, Linda closed her other hand around its head, and she stroked down, first with one hand, and then with the other. I knew Sam wasn't going to last much longer.

I leaned over to Sam, and said, "We don't want to contaminate the spa water, so I'll take you in my mouth, now." I had little doubt that Julie would have done the honors; and we had agreed to allow oral sex, if it happened; but I decided to take matters into my own hands. Sam was still mine, and I intended to enjoy him; and to satisfy him.

My friends continued to massage Sam, Julie now putting her arms under him, and molding his bottom in her hands. I took the skin of Sam's frenum in my fingers, and moved them in the classic style of asking for a check from the waiter in a restaurant, as Sam had taught me. Then, I circled him, and gave a few more squeezing strokes, from the head to the base.

Finally, he was ready, and I took his length into my mouth, sucking, licking, and swirling my tongue around him. At the same time, I put my left hand between his legs, and pressed his perineum with my fingers, pulsing, poking, and massaging, as my mouth did its work.

It didn't take long: Sam thrust his hips and let out a satisfied 'Ahhhh' as he came in my mouth. As promised, no semen got into the spa, as I made sure to swallow it, continuing the licking and lapping, until Sam's motions calmed, and his body totally relaxed into Julie's, Kathy's, and Linda's arms.

I stood and smiled at my friends, who nodded and smiled back. Then we lowered Sam so that he could stand up and, before taking off his blindfold, I kissed him deeply.

Sam stood, uneasily, finally sitting down on the spa bench. He shook his head, as if trying to clear the cobwebs. "Well, that was interesting. You guys did a great job massaging me." Then, he looked up at me, "Thank you, Kelly. That was great." I bent down and kissed him again.

Then, Sam looked at my friends, moving from face to face, looking at them, before he explained, "I'm not embarrassed for you guys to see me – with an erection or not ... but I didn't want to do anything that would be inappropriate. As Kelly well knows, we can have a great – and sensual – time, without making it sexual."

He looked at me again, "Of course, sex is really nice, too. I just didn't want to make your friends uncomfortable."

I was sure my friends thought his comment crazy, as he had required them to attend the party nude, had stuck me with needles, and had massaged two of my friends in unknown places. Although, I could understand his point: Nudity, and even sensuality does not – necessarily – have to come with sex. Sam was being Sam. But he was a good boy, and had performed for my friends, as I had asked him.

I was sure that Kelly understood my thought process; sex was not a necessary ingredient of today's adventure. In fact, I did not expect it; now, two of us had orgasmed openly in front of the entire party. Again, I had to be careful what I wished for: The group massage had been my idea. But I had stipulated no sex, and didn't believe Kelly's friends would be that 'friendly' – at least, so early in the day. It had been an experience, being massaged by four beautiful women. I was certainly not regretful.

However, I was now quite concerned. I had planned Kelly's pirate role-play to be next ... and it was to end with me 'taking' Kelly over one of the boulders at the edge of the pool. Now, I had to 'recover', before that scenario could be realized. Of course, it would take some time to get everything set-up, while Kelly changed into her Victorian dress. But I wondered whether there would be sufficient time for me to perform when it counted – at the climax of Kelly's deepest fantasy.

I also had to get rid of Kelly. Well, not quite like that; but I needed time with her friends to arrange the pirate scene. If I sent Kelly downstairs to change, she would be back before we had everything set up. I realized I would need to instruct her to stay down there until someone came to get her. Although it wasn't time for lunch, yet, we had plenty of dishes prepared; so I decided to have Kelly make the cheese puffs. That would keep her in the kitchen long enough for me to clue in her friends.

We all got out of the spa, and her friends spread their towels on the chaises, and lay down. Again, I saw three beautiful butts lined up in a row. I wondered whether Kelly's friends would be up for a photo session sometime in the future.

"Kelly, could I ask a favor of you?" Then, under my breath "... on your birthday."

"Sure! What would you like me to do?"

"I think we should make the cheese puffs now. We've been out in the sun and the water, which creates an appetite; and we've had some wine. I'd like us to do one more thing before lunch, but I think we all need a little sustenance."

Kelly nodded, "That's not a problem. I know they're in the garage fridge, and they're cooked in the oven. Give me the details."

Now, I nodded, "That's the issue. They have to be cooked under the broiler; the top rack of the oven needs to be about 6" below the heat elements. The broiler needs to be turned on and the oven warmed up before putting the cookie sheet in. And once you put it in, there is no choice but to stand there and watch it."

I shook my head, hoping that Kelly wouldn't take her eyes off them. "I've tried timing it, but always burned them. And we don't have any extras – just the one sheet. They only take 3-4 minutes, but if you turn your back on them, they're 'toast' ... as they say."

Kelly said, "Sure, Sam. I'll keep an eye on them."

I finished the instructions, "You should take them out when they're getting brown on top ... but at the end they can go fast; they don't need to be too brown. Then, make sure you have mitts, and take the tray out of the oven, and put it on the stovetop. Then, you can turn off the oven, and transfer the cheese puffs to a large plate, which I've already taken out."

Kelly nodded, "No problem." As she skipped across the patio and opened the door to the kitchen, she said, "Have fun!"

CHAPTER 10: PIRATE SCENE

I intended to have some fun – with Kelly – after a bit of hard work. I sat on the cross-wise chaise, and asked Kelly's friends to turn over so I could tell them the plan. Julie already knew that I had something special planned for Kelly, and that I would need the help of all three girls. Now, I tried to ignore the six breasts lined up in a row, and looked into the eyes of Julie, Linda, and Kathy.

"I asked Kelly to do some work in the kitchen, so that I could talk privately with you guys. One of Kelly's fantasies – the one she shared with me during our second lunch together – is to be kidnapped from a luxury cruise by a pirate, who takes her on his ship, ties her to the mast, whips her breasts, and flogs her backside, finally breaking her; then taking her passionately."

Linda piped up, "That's a good fantasy!" Kathy nodded, and Julie chuckled.

"So I have built a 'pirate ship'." Now, the girls' eyes widened, and Linda's mouth dropped open. "I'll need your help to put up the mast and cleat the stays so that it doesn't fall over. The diving board will be the 'plank', and I may want her to 'walk the plank', before I give in and keep her ... and beat her into submission. You guys can yell to save her, and not make her walk the plank."

I coughed, and continued, "Now, I need to ask you something important: This is going to be a challenge for Kelly, doing this scene in front of you; so I would like to ask that you sit in the jacuzzi during the scene. I may blindfold Kelly so that she doesn't know where you guys are ... and we should keep it that way."

The girls nodded their understanding.

"I'm going to ask Kelly to go downstairs, where she will find an outfit that I've bought. And some accessories. As far as I'm aware, Kelly doesn't know what we're going to do – although she may have guessed. I'll ask her to stay down there, until someone comes to get her. Then, when we're ready, I'll send Julie down for her."

I smiled, envisioning the scene. "Julie can then make some offhand comments that will give Kelly the idea ... like 'this is really a nice head. The cabins are deluxe in this ship'. Or something like that. Then, when it dawns on Kelly, Julie can tell her 'we need to get on deck quickly – pirates have stormed the ship, and are rounding up all the passengers'."

The girls laughed. Linda – again – had her hands over her face, as she snorted.

I continued, "When we get Kelly up here, Julie will put some wrist- and ankle-cuffs on her; I'll leave the cuffs on the table for Julie. Then, I'll show up, and drag her off. At that point, you guys can get in the spa and watch our role-play. It may be a little intense. I want you to know that Kelly has a 'safeword' that she can use at any time to end the scene. And, although her bottom may get sore, I will not harm her."

Now, I had to tell them about the 'climax' of the scene. "At the end of the scene, I plan to bend Kelly over that rock," I pointed to the boulder at the edge of the pool. "and make love to her from behind. You guys shouldn't see anything from the jacuzzi. However, I may take off Kelly's blindfold, so that she is staring at you while I'm having my way with her. I'll have to play that by ear." In a manner of speaking.

I smiled at the girls, concluding, "And then we'll have lunch!"

Perfect timing, as Kelly was just bringing the plate of cheese puffs out to the patio. Kelly passed around small paper plates and napkins, and we all took a few of the cheese puffs. I offered, "Would anyone like something to drink? I could pour some iced tea. Or, we have soft drinks or beers in the cooler." Everyone decided that iced tea would be nice, so I went into the kitchen to pour cups for everyone.

When I returned to the chaises, the cheese puffs were nearly gone. I turned to Linda and asked her, "If Julie had offered, would you have let her masturbate you?"

Linda maintained her poise, although I could see her cheeks redden slightly. "Maybe." She popped another cheese puff in her mouth and thought a bit. "The blindfold somehow made it more impersonal – like my head was buried in the sand, and I could ignore you guys. And, the massage was making me very relaxed. I'm glad someone was holding my head above the water."

At this point, Linda was the only one of the four women I had not seen having an orgasm; I had a feeling that would be remedied by the end of the day.

"Kathy, you seemed to enjoy it."

Kathy shrugged, then nodded. She replied, "I didn't know that Julie was so talented." She smiled, "I don't think any of us has had much female-on-female experience." She looked around, and the girls were shaking their heads.

Then I asked Kathy, "Would it have been a problem if I had been the one masturbating you?"

Kathy said, "Not if I didn't know it was you." She chuckled, "And if you made me come." We all laughed. Then Kathy added, "But if you had asked me, I probably would have said no."

The girls talked about some of their dating experiences, as we finished the cheese puffs and our iced teas. It seemed that several of their hookups had gone down on them, many had fingered them, but none of the men had actually masturbated any of them. And only Julie had experienced being masturbated by another female.

I collected the paper plates and cups, putting them all on the serving plate, and brought everything inside. I went downstairs, and opened the exam room, then took the box of accessories for Kelly, and put it in the shower room on one of the chaises. Everything seemed to be ready for the pirate scene ... assuming that Kelly's friends and I could get the mast up. And, assuming that *I* could get it up.

When I sat back down on the chaise, the girls were still sharing experiences; it sounded like some real dating horror stories. When there was a break, I turned to Kelly, "Are you ready for one more activity – or experience – this morning?"

Kelly smiled, "Yes, Sir." She was already anticipating what kind of experience this would be. Little did she know. I hoped.

I hadn't really planned exactly what I was going to tell Kelly. So I winged it. "Kelly, I bought you a little something. Just a minor gift. I'd like you to go downstairs and try it on. You'll find it hanging with the robes in the bathroom, and there's a box in the shower room that has some accessories. If you wouldn't mind, please don't wear a bra or underwear." I thought, 'or I will have to cut them off of you'. That would have been fun, too.

Kelly was nodding, but looking a little perplexed. She said, "I knew you were planning something ... but I still don't know what it is."

I laughed, "You'll find out soon enough. Now go down and get dressed. And please stay down there until somebody comes and gets you."

Kelly nodded. She turned to her friends and shrugged, "Sam always has these crazy ideas. They're usually very creative; and sometimes romantic. But I can't imagine what he has planned." Her friends just smiled wanly at her, and Kelly shrugged again, turned, and went into the house.

I jumped up. "OK, ladies. We have some 'heavy lifting' to do." As I walked them around the back of the garage, I clarified, "Well, it's not that heavy; just bulky."

There were three loud gasps as we rounded the corner, and the girls saw my 'contraption'. It was huge, the mast being sixteen feet long, and having two cross booms with wrapped sails, that were lashed to the mast, but swung parallel to it. So it was just one long package to drag to the pool.

The four of us lifted it easily, and carried it to where I had put the pipe in the ground. We set it down, and I positioned the booms cross-wise to the mast, tightened the lashes, and lowered the sails. It was a good thing there was no wind today, or this flimsy assembly would undoubtedly come apart.

As I lifted the top of the mast, Julie guided the bottom into the pipe. The girls then held everything in place, until I could run one of the stays to the house. I stood on a chair, put it through a block that I had screwed into the eave, and pulled on the line. The mast slowly increased its angle, until it was standing vertically, the girls holding it in place, as I tied off the line.

Then, I did the same with two stays that I pulled to a couple of trees, ran the stays through blocks, pulled the line until it was taut, and cleated it off. I jiggled the mast, and it was relatively stable. I removed the bag of 'goodies' from where it was hooked to the bottom of the mast, and put it by the boulder. Then I took out the cuffs, and put them on the patio table.

Now, I had to get dressed in the pirate costume. I brought the girls into the pool room, and opened the closet. I took out the costume that was on a hanger, and put it on the massage table. Then, I put the box of accessories by the massage table. I put on the blousy shirt, and then the pants and belt, making sure the scabbard for the sword was threaded onto the belt.

I suggested to Julie that she could go downstairs to get Kelly, but to delay coming back up for at least five minutes. Kathy and Linda helped me with all of the accessories – bandana, boot covers, eye patch, a hook for my left hand, and even fake pirate dreads. Finally, the sash, vest, hat and sword. I was already getting overheated.

Sam was up to something – I knew it; I just didn't know *what* he was up to. I walked downstairs, stepped into the bathroom, and opened the narrow closet that was between the toilet/sink area and shower area. Hanging there were the robes that we had worn many times ... and a beautiful old-fashioned dress. I pulled it out, and examined the detailing.

Although it was cheaply made, it was still beautiful, with pale green calico cotton material printed with tiny roses, that came to points several inches up from the hem, which was lined with ruffled white material. The underskirt was white, and came down nearly to my ankles.

I checked the label, and found that it was my size; I remembered Sam taking notes during my first visit, including my dress size, pants size, bra and underwear sizes, and even shoe size. This was amazing!

I found the large cardboard box on one of the chaises in the shower room and opened it. There was a petticoat, boots, and gloves ... and a parasol was sitting on the chaise next to the box. It would be strange putting on this fancy outfit without wearing a bra or underwear, but I could imagine Sam's concept: He was obviously going to spank me.

I wondered if he might be planning an 'old-fashioned schoolgirl' role-play, but couldn't picture exactly where we would do this, and what the 'background story' would be. I couldn't be prepared with an explanation – for example, what I had done wrong to deserve a punishment – as he hadn't shared with me his concept for the scene.

As I stepped into the petticoat, and then wriggled the dress over my head, my mind was spinning. It wasn't even noon, yet, and we had all undressed together; sat around nude, talking; smoked some weed; made a needle play corset on my back ... Julie trying a needle through the skin of her breast, and allowing Sam to insert a needle in each of her hips, as she sat there watching him pull the needles out of me.

Then, there was the strange 'group massage' in the jacuzzi ... with Linda relaxing while we all massaged her ... and Kathy getting massaged, *and* masturbated by Julie; then, my friends and I massaging Sam ... Julie, Kathy, *and* Linda stroking him until he was turned-on, and my 'finishing' him with my mouth – all in front of my friends!

As usual, Sam had gone overboard in planning the party, and pushing my friends to participate in some rather strange party games. But Julie, Linda and Kathy had taken everything in stride; I was sure they were actually enjoying the experience with Sam.

All three of my friends had surprised me with their openness and enthusiasm in trying new things. Even Linda had relaxed, and not only seemed to be comfortable nude – in front of Sam – but also had enjoyed her multi-hand massage. My mind was a blur, and I couldn't imagine what else Sam had planned.

I shimmied the dress down my body, and over the petticoat; although it was the proper size, it was a bit tight in the waist and hips. I realized that the complete old-fashioned outfit would probably also include a corset; that would easily bring my waist down to size for the dress. But I was happy I didn't have to don a corset; I certainly would have needed help to lace it in back. Perhaps I would surprise Sam by getting a corset, and wearing it for him, someday.

I sat down on the chaise in the shower room, and tried to pull on the boots. As I was struggling with the first one, Julie walked into the bathroom, her eyes widening, and a broad smile appearing on her face. "That's a beautiful dress! Let me help you with those boots."

With both Julie and I working on them, I finally got the boots on, and stood. I would not be able to hike in these boots – or even walk very far – but they were fine for a short time. I walked back into the toilet room, swung the door partially closed, and looked at myself in the mirror. It really was a pretty dress.

Julie handed me the gloves, and then the parasol, which I put over my shoulder, feeling like one of the matrons strolling in the garden in an impressionist painting. I twirled the parasol, and looked at Julie; she smiled at me, as she sat down to pee. As she was washing her hands, she made some comments – about heads and cabins ... and then, she talked about 'pirates storming the ship', and 'making all the passengers – except the young women – walk the plank'.

Suddenly, I knew what Sam had planned: It was my pirate fantasy! I had mentioned this to Sam a few times, and now tried to recall what I had told him during our lunch together, when we had first shared fantasies with each other. My mind was muddled, but I didn't think I had gone into very much detail – other than being tied to the mast and whipped, and then being made love to.

Where would we do this? And where would my friends be? I knew that Sam would be spanking me today in front of my friends – if nothing else, there was my traditional 'birthday spanking'. But I wasn't sure I was prepared to have sex in front of my friends.

Then, I remembered that I had just 'forced' Sam to let my friends see him with an erection, and have an orgasm while they held him in the water. I realized that I would have no excuse – I would have to be open in front of my friends. A few months ago, I would have not even considered doing these things while my friends watched ... but they had shown their own openness. Two of them had already masturbated in front of Sam.

I thought about Linda's response to Sam's question of whether she would have let Julie masturbate her. At the time, I was surprised that Julie didn't just go ahead and do it; but I guess she was giving Linda some slack, as Linda was already being open with us about nudity, and with all of us – including Sam – touching her, on every part of her body.

I had told Sam that I didn't think my friends would 'play' with him – thinking about spankings, needles, and rectal insertions, but now I wasn't at all sure what to think. It seemed much more likely now that Sam would get his wish to play with my friends. I wondered again, what he had planned for the rest of the day.

Julie brought me upstairs and out to the patio. I saw Linda and Kathy sitting in the hot tub, talking. And *then*, I saw what must be Sam's 'pirate ship': It was really just a mast and what looked like sails, with a small flag waving from the cross-arm that showed a skull and crossbones.

But it was a *huge* structure, and I couldn't imagine how this had been assembled while I was downstairs getting dressed. Or, how Sam could have hidden this from me, as I had been over here several times in the past couple of weeks.

My memory flashed on our excursion to the pond, walking our bikes along the side of Sam's house; I remembered seeing some 'junk' lying there – a bunch of long pieces of wood, and some rope – and now realized that he had been building the pirate ship then.

Even though I had spent a lot of time with Sam over the past couple of months, I still couldn't imagine what Sam would come up with next. He had a very creative – and sex-oriented – mind, and had continued to surprise me; with more than I had ever expected. This was just one more example. I stood there, in the frilly dress, staring at the pirate ship, and I realized that now *I* was the one with a mouth that had fallen open.

I stood in the corner of the pool room, next to the massage table, and waited. Linda and Kathy got back into the spa. We all waited. It seemed like a long five minutes. Finally, I heard Kelly and Julie coming up the stairs, through the kitchen, and out to the patio. I picked up a remote control from the box at the foot of the massage table, and punched several keys. I hoped the video recorders were running.

Then I heard Kelly scream. I peaked around the corner and saw her standing by the patio table, staring at the pirate ship. "What!?!? I don't believe this!"

Then I heard squeals from Linda and Kathy. Linda exclaimed, "That's a beautiful dress!" Kelly was wearing the Victorian dress – calico and lace, flounced sleeves, and a scooped neck. She wore white boots, white gloves, and held a small parasol, which she twirled as she continued to stare at the mast, booms and sails. The dress really did look good on Kelly; presumably I had picked close to the correct size.

Julie explained that most of the passengers had been made to walk the plank. And there were hungry sharks waiting in the dark waters of the lagoon. But the pirate decided to pick one of the beautiful women to be his wench. He would either make her walk the plank, or beat her into submission. If she were to have a chance, she had to wear the cuffs, which Julie fastened around Kelly's wrists and ankles. Now, it was my turn.

I lifted my sword, swaggered around the corner, and yelled, "Well shiver me timbers! What 'a we got here? Another wench. This one's a purty one!" I really hammed it up.

Kelly was nearly apoplectic with laughter. Actually, I realized that everyone was laughing, now. To bring the mood back, I took Kelly by her French braids, and pulled her roughly around the pool to the mast, then past it, to the diving board. "Get up thar, wench!" Kelly stepped up onto the end of the board. She kept her hands behind her, even though I hadn't bound them.

I yelled to the girls in the spa, "Methinks this one'll walk the plank. Shark bait for Davy Jones' locker."

Right on cue, the girls yelled, "No! No! Please spare her!" It was great. We were having an audience-participation play right here in the backyard.

I pulled Kelly's hair, and she jumped off the board onto the aggregate deck, and we walked along the edge of the pool to the mast. I hooked the V-shaped halyard to the rings in Kelly's wrist cuffs, and hooked her ankle cuffs to a spreader bar at the bottom of the mast.

I hoisted her arms until they were above her head, but not stretched, or uncomfortable. Then, I paced back and forth in front of Kelly. Fortunately, I had memorized a few 'pirate' lines that I had found on the Internet. Let's see if Kelly could stop laughing.

Now, I was a stand-up comic. I spoke loudly, so Kelly's friends would be able to hear. As well as the recorders. "Avast, me beauty! A lubber ye are. But them scallywags want to save ya. A scrumpet! How'd you like to scrape the barnacles off me rudder? Arrrgh!"

I stepped up to Kelly, unbuttoned her dress, and pulled the front apart, so her breasts burst forth, the softness and sexiness of her bare skin against the old-fashioned dress. "That's some treasure chest, you have there, lassie." Kelly was hysterical again. It was difficult for me not to laugh also, but I tried to control myself.

I stomped over to the bag, and pulled out a flogger. Kelly had already felt this implement during her long weekend here. It comprised two dozen thin deer leather straps, braided into a nice handle. I stood in front of the wench and sneered.

Then, I swept the flogger across Kelly's chest, whipping her breasts. The tails of the flogger flew back and forth, until Kelly's breasts were nicely reddened. Kelly squealed a little, and I heard 'ow' a few times, but was moderating the intensity on Kelly's sensitive tissues. I reached over and pinched each nipple, twisting it roughly before I let go.

Kelly's mouth was hanging open. She was now half laughing, and half moaning – or groaning – due to the sting of her breasts. I then uncleated the halyard, and lowered Kelly's arms, which I put behind her, coupling the wrist cuff rings with a caribiner. Then, I took the clips on the ends of the halyard's V and attached them to Kelly's dress and petticoat.

I yelled, "Time for hoisting ye skirts, matey!" With one yank on the halyard, Kelly's dress and petticoat were raised in front of her face. She didn't need a blindfold, after all! Now, she was bare from the waist down, her legs spread widely, held by the ankle cuffs.

I took the flogger, and swung it vertically, coming up from under her, and lashing the insides of her legs; then up further, raining deer leather on Kelly's genitals. I had flogged Kelly's breasts lightly, and I was flogging her privates lightly; this *was* her birthday, after all!

I continued the flogging, sometimes reversing direction, and coming down across Kelly's pubes. As the tails of the flogger came up between Kelly's legs, and lashed her vulva, Kelly started whimpering, somewhere behind the skirts. I lightened my strokes, but continued for another couple of minutes. Now, Kelly looked like she had just been waxed – again.

I commanded, "Prepare to come about!" I uncleated the halyard, and lowered Kelly's skirts, unhooked her ankle cuffs, and spun her around, facing the mast. I brought her arms around the mast, hooking the wrist cuffs, so that Kelly could not move from the mast. I again spread her legs, and hooked the ankle cuffs. Then, I used the halyard again, this time raising the back hem of the dress and petticoat.

I walked back to the boulder, exchanging the flogger for a long leather strap, doubled over. This strap would sting, but was not a heavy implement like the tawse; the doubled construction, however, would result in a very loud slap sound when it was wielded.

Walking back to Kelly, I said, "Blimey! Sailed the seven seas, me have, and yer the sleekest schooner ever me sighted." Looking at her bottom, I added, "That's the finest pirate booty me's laid eyes on." Kelly laughed again. I lifted the strap, and held it against Kelly's bottom. "Prepare ye'self, wench!"

With that, I swung the strap hard, and it impacted Kelly's rear with a loud snapping sound. I heard an 'Ugggh' from Kelly. There was no question about Kelly holding her position, as she was trussed up and had very little freedom of motion. I swung the strap again. "Yer me property now, wench!" I continued to strap Kelly's bottom, one stroke coming every few seconds, until I had counted 36 strokes. Kelly whimpered a little, but maintained her composure; she now had a very red ass.

I stood directly behind Kelly, and rubbed her bottom. Leaning over, and around the raised skirts, I whispered, "Should I put a blindfold on you for the next part?"

Kelly didn't know what the next part was going to be, but answered, "Do with me what you will, bucko." I laughed, remembering the shortened term of 'buccaneer' from my Internet research. But I was surprised that Kelly knew this term.

I decided it would be more challenging for Kelly *without* the blindfold. Now it would be her turn to orgasm in front of her friends. I unclipped her wrist cuffs, and unhooked the ankle cuffs, then removed the clips that held Kelly's dress and petticoat up, letting them fall. I spun her around and, without warning, kissed her violently. Before she could react, I took her by the hair, and dragged her over to the boulder, pushing her over onto the towel that I had spread on it.

As I looked at the beautiful woman bent over the boulder, awaiting my attention, I realized that I would have no problem being turned on and coming again, even after the group massage 'happy ending' that Kelly had given me. I held Kelly's hips, and prepared myself for entry.

It was at this time that Kelly finally looked up ... directly into the faces of her three friends, across a short span of water, sitting in the jacuzzi. She started to raise up, but I put my hand on her back and, with only gentle pressure, she relaxed herself onto the boulder. I heard a small, high pitched, voice ask, "May I please have the blindfold now, Sir?"

Laughing, I replied, "As ye like, wench." I reached into the goody bag and pulled out the blindfold, carefully placing it over Kelly's eyes, the strap around the back of her head. I inquired, "How feels ye stern parts, wench?" as I undid the belt and dropped my pants.

Kelly laughed, "It feels like I've been keel hauled." Good response!

I rubbed myself along Kelly's butt crack until I was ready, then she guided me into the warm wetness between her legs. It didn't take long before I was pounding into her. I slowed, and put a hand under Kelly, sliding it up and over her hood. Making a V with my fingers, I kept my hand there, pressing against her, and feeling Kelly's hard button under the hood.

I thrusted forward, and Kelly pushed back, in perfect synchrony and, somehow, we came simultaneously. I was spent, and leaned over Kelly's back, pressing her down onto the boulder, kissing whatever parts of her I could reach.

I pulled up my pants, and re-buckled the belt. Kelly was still bent over the boulder, awaiting my command. Leaving her in position, I removed her blindfold; Kelly blinked a couple of times, and then focused on her friends. She gave them a thin smile, and then put her head back down.

I helped her up, and smoothed down her dress – making sure the points of light green calico material with little red roses and trimmed in ruffle lace were flat against the white underskirt. Then, I turned her toward me, carefully adjusted the dress on her shoulders, and re-buttoned the front. Finally, I took her in my arms, and held her tightly. We kissed long and hard, oblivious of Kelly's friends sitting nearby.

As far as I was concerned, the scene had worked; at least, the mast hadn't fallen down! Now, I was curious to find out what Kelly thought. She had only given me a few clues about her pirate fantasy, and I hoped that our role-play satisfied at least some of the elements about which she had fantasized.

The entire experience had gone quicker than I had imagined. I hadn't wanted to give Kelly too much pain on her birthday. And, maybe I could have teased her with more 'foreplay' while she was tied to the mast. I was now second-guessing what we could have done with the scene. But, overall, it was as I had visualized, when I had built the pirate ship, bought our costumes, and planned the experience.

Still holding Kelly, and looking into her eyes, I asked, "Did that bring to life some of your pirate fantasy?"

Kelly hugged me, "Yes. It was really special. I can't believe that you actually built all this, and got my friends to help ... and still kept it a secret."

Then, I inquired, "And how does your body feel? After your breasts and genitals have been flogged?"

Kelly shrugged, "I'm OK. The strapping is what hurt the most. I was surprised when you flogged my breasts ... but I remember telling you that was part of my fantasy. And I never imagined you would be flogging my private parts – that really stung. But I think the biggest turn-on was when you dragged me by my hair. That was the first time you really played 'rough' with me."

"Do you like the costumes I picked out? I'm glad the dress fit."

Kelly laughed, "Well, that's what took me so long getting ready. I had to take off some labels, and I wasn't sure how the outfit went together. I'm just glad that Julie came down to help me." Then, looking into my eyes, Kelly said, "It's a beautiful dress. Even when I saw it, I wasn't sure what you had planned. This was certainly the most interesting role play we've done."

I thought it was interesting, also, but not as much of a turn-on for me as either Schoolgirl Kelly, or Nurse Kelly. I was glad that Kelly had responded well, and found the experience interesting.

As we walked around the pool to the patio table, Kelly's friends got out of the spa, and walked over to us. They hugged Kelly, and Julie commented, "That was pretty hot! Sam told us what was going to happen, but I didn't expect such a fancy production." Julie looked into Kelly's eyes, and chuckled, "You were very open today, not only letting us watch Sam thrash your backside, but also make love to you ... right in front of us."

Linda pointed out, "We couldn't actually *see* anything, when you were over the boulder. But just watching the scene got me hot." She looked at me, while still talking to Kelly, "And you're right: Sam is very creative ..." Then, she added, "... in a perverted sort of way." Everyone laughed. The girls dried off, then put their towels on the patio chairs and sat down. Linda left her towel wrapped around her.

It was now time for lunch ... and the next small surprise.

CHAPTER 11: PAREO LUNCH

I announced to everyone, "You may have noticed those gift bags next to each of the boxes in the pool room. I got a few 'party favors' for everyone. If you don't mind getting up again, please go find your bag, pull out the top item, and come back here. I hope you like what I got, and it might be useful during our lunch break." The girls looked at me inquiringly, but got up and went into the pool room.

Kelly asked, "Do you want to help me get this dress off?" I usually don't turn down a beautiful woman's request to help her undress, so I followed Kelly into the pool room, and we stood next to the massage table, as I unbuttoned the dress, and helped Kelly out of it. She was now topless, but wearing a white ruffled petticoat.

I told her, "I was going to get a crinoline or a hoop with a bustle, but decided a regular petticoat would be more practical." Although I don't think anyone considered a petticoat to be 'regular' clothing. I helped Kelly pull off her white boots, and we put everything on the massage table. Then, I took off the pirate costume, putting it on the massage table with Kelly's outfit.

Julie was evidently in the bathroom, but the door was left open a crack. Kelly opened it a bit further and stood in the doorway talking to Julie in hushed tones. I heard the toilet flush, and Kelly went in to pee, still talking with Julie.

In the meantime, Kathy and Linda had pulled from their gift bags the amorphous items wrapped in colorful crinkled tissue paper. They didn't wait to open them and, as Julie and Kelly came out of the bathroom, Linda was squealing, and Kathy held up the colorful material for Julie to see.

I walked over to them, and explained, "These are pareos – a traditional Tahitian wrap-around skirt, similar to a Malaysian sarong. I thought you might want to wear these during lunch." Then, I chuckled, "But you don't have to 'dress' for lunch, if you don't want to."

The girls opened all of the packages, and compared the colorful patterns – mainly of leaves and flowers – on each of the pareos. I said, "I didn't know who would like which colors, so you guys can swap them, if you like."

Kelly hugged me, "These are very nice."

Then, Julie stepped up to me and gave me a sincere hug – not at all sexy or sensuous, but meaningful. "Thank you, Sam. I love it. You really are a considerate person." Kathy and Linda chimed in, thanking me for the gift. We went back outside to the patio table, and I opened the umbrella that rose through a small hole in the center of the glass.

The girls tried on their pareos: Linda wrapped herself, the thin material covering her from just above her breasts to just above her knees. Kathy folded the pareo over, and wrapped it around her waist. Kelly did the same. Julie wrapped her pareo around her waist without folding it, so that it came down to her ankles.

As the girls sat at the table chatting, I went into the kitchen and started readying the lunch. I brought several dishes from the fridge in the garage to the kitchen counter. I refilled the vegetables and olive-dill dip in the smoked gray plastic platter, and brought it out to the patio table, along with the deviled eggs, guacamole, and cream cheese-Jalapeño jelly plate.

I put a couple of the frozen items in the oven. These included mini-spanakopita, triangles of Greek pastry, filled with a spinach and feta cheese mixture; and pot stickers – for which I threw together a soy-mirin sauce. I heated the cocktail hot dogs in some of my special barbeque sauce in a pot on the stove, while I mixed the salad in a huge wooden bowl, and brought it out to the patio.

I realized that there were no place settings, so I brought out paper plates, napkins and silverware, handing everything to Kelly to distribute around the table. The oven dinged, and I took out the spanakopita and pot stickers, putting them on serving plates, and carried them out to the patio. Finally, I put the heated cocktail hot dogs and sauce into a ceramic fondue pot, and brought it to the table, which was now filled with dishes – and a lot of food.

As the girls started filling their plates, I took the drink orders. I was planning on having a beer, but Julie asked whether there was any more wine. So I opened the bottle of Chardonnay, and brought out a stack of cups. Then, I pulled a beer out of the cooler for myself. It looked like a feast ... and this was just our small lunch, to hold everyone until the barbeque tonight.

Kathy exclaimed, "This is yummy!" The other girls chimed in, each talking about a different dish that I had put out.

Kelly explained, "Sam is a really good cook. He made a great Italian dinner for me." Kelly gave a quick, enigmatic smile, and I knew that she was picturing me serving her, wearing nothing but a barbeque apron. And then spanking me.

I explained, "I love to eat ... and to cook. I've collected recipes from around the world for the past 25 years." I looked at Kelly, but didn't mention that I had been cooking since before she was born. From the look on Kelly's face, I didn't have to.

Then, I gave my disclaimers regarding the lunch. "Almost everything here was bought; tonight will be more of a production, but I wanted us to be able to 'graze', and provide enough dishes that you would all like at least something."

I looked around the table at the multitude of dishes. "The only things I prepared here are the olive-dill dip, the guacamole, the deviled eggs, and the salad dressing. And the barbeque sauce for the hot dogs is a preview of what we'll be having tonight."

The girls ate with gusto, finishing the eggs, most of the vegetable dip, and most of the salad. I got up and refilled the bowl of guacamole, and brought the bottle of wine to the table, pouring the rest for Kelly and her friends.

I stuck with my beer, and decided not to take a second one, lest I become too tired to orchestrate the rest of the party – which I still hoped would include the 'spank poker' game on the turntable I had built. Kelly's friends certainly seemed open enough, based on their comfort level this morning. We would just have to see ...

Julie got up and went into the pool room. When she came back to the patio table, she was pouring powdered marijuana from a small pill container into her plastic water pipe. She went to the pool to fill the pipe, but couldn't bend over, wearing the pareo down to her ankles. She took the pareo off, folded it, and then wrapped it around her waist again, as Kelly and Kathy had done. Then, she filled the pipe, lit up, and sat back down at the table, passing the pipe to Kelly.

The pipe came to me, next and, although I didn't feel compelled to smoke with the girls, it brought back memories, and I decided to indulge with them. As the pipe was passed around the table a second time, I got up and carried some of the dishes back to the kitchen.

When I got back to the table, the girls were talking about their skinny-dipping experience at Kelly's house, nearly ten years ago. I sat down as Kathy said, "I agree: It was Julie teasing your dad. She really made a scene."

Then, Julie broke in, "Well, it was Kelly's *step*-dad, anyway." I couldn't believe I had heard this from Julie. Linda and Kathy, in unison, said, "What!?!" as they stared at Kelly, then at Julie, and then back at Kelly.

Kelly was instantly furious, "JULIE!!" She looked away, shaking her head. When she turned back, her face was clouded, and I thought she might cry. She turned to Julie, angrily, and said, "That was something private that I shared with you!"

Linda put her hands over her face, obviously embarrassed for Kelly. She and Kathy looked at each other, wondering why they had been left in the dark.

The day had been going wonderfully, everyone being very open with each other. However, this was something that Kelly had considered private ... and should have stayed that way. Kelly was still working out her feelings – which might take forever; she hadn't been prepared to discuss this in detail with her friends. I gathered that Kelly had shared this secret with Julie during their recent lunch together, but Julie had had no right to share the sensitive information.

Julie apologized to Kelly, but it seemed half-hearted. It was clear that she'd had every intention of informing Linda and Kathy of Kelly's secret. I was now becoming very upset: As everyone knew, I was all about honesty; but I also very much valued *respect*.

Kelly had a right to keep her past a secret, and probably should have known better than to share it with

Julie. But Julie demonstrated a total lack of respect, when she blurted it out to Kelly's friends, after Kelly had asked her to keep it private.

I pushed my chair back abruptly, and stood up, everyone's eyes now on me. I looked at Julie, and commanded in a very stern voice, "Julie! Come with me!"

CHAPTER 12: JULIE'S PUNISHMENT

Julie looked surprised, and glanced around to the other girls, then shrugged and stood up next to me. I walked briskly into the house, through the kitchen, and down the stairs to the playroom, Julie following close behind. We walked to the desk, and I told Julie "Sit down, please!" I walked around the desk to the executive chair and sat, staring at Julie, who now had a guilty look on her face. I was very upset, and hardly knew where to start.

"Julie, I think you know that I love Kelly." She nodded uncertainly. "And I will do anything to make her happy. And, protect her." I stared at Julie, shaking my head slowly.

"Kelly has probably told you that I value honesty." Julie nodded again. "But what everyone values as the core of morality is *respect*. And *trust*."

I looked at Julie grimly, and said, "You've broken the trust. You did not respect Kelly's wishes to keep this private." I shook my head again. "And, on her birthday! I could see that Kelly feels hurt – deeply." I stared at my desk for a long moment.

Then, I softened a bit. "Julie, I think you're great. I respect you – for many things. Your ability to be open with us, your good nature, and your outrageous approach to things," Julie was looking down into her lap, but glanced up at me, "and your friendship with Kelly. I think you know that watching you masturbate was an incredible turn-on for Kelly; I've only been half-joking asking Kelly if she'll leave me for a woman." Julie started to laugh, but put her hand over her mouth, and quickly looked serious again.

I continued, "But I'm very disappointed in you. Everything was going so well." Then I thought for a moment, and said, "I don't even know why Kelly would share that with you ... after not telling her friends for the past decade."

I really was at a loss to understand why this had happened. I assumed that Kelly was explaining the details to Linda and Kathy out on the patio – and I had no doubt that she would have told them eventually. But Julie had no right to break her trusting relationship with Kelly in this way. On her birthday!

Julie looked up sheepishly, and quietly said, "Sam, I'm really sorry. And I'll apologize to Kelly, too." I gave her a disgusted look. Then she looked into my eyes, and tried to explain.

"Kelly was trying to explain her feelings for you." Now, I was caught off-guard. Julie continued, "She said that she had a very comfortable feeling being with you. The kind of feeling she remembers having with her natural parents. She had to explain her background to me, so that she could tell me about you."

Julie smiled and said, "This was sometime during our discussion of trying a little female-on-female action. I think you're safe – you're not going to lose Kelly to a woman." Well, that was something.

Julie concluded, "And Kelly did tell me that she was going to open up with Linda and Kathy." Then Julie looked at me sheepishly again, and back down to her lap, and added, "At the appropriate time." She exhaled deeply, "I know I should have let her do it when she was ready. It wasn't fair to blurt it out. I guess my mouth was going faster than my brain." She sat across the desk, looking at me. That was all she had to say.

"Julie, I think you should be punished for this. I know you'll apologize to Kelly, and hopefully, Kelly will recover, and we can have a nice afternoon and evening. But in my protectiveness of Kelly, I feel I have to make my point in a way you won't forget."

Julie gulped, probably knowing what was coming. "And how do you intend to make your point?"

I smiled, "On your bottom, of course! You've behaved like a schoolgirl, and should be punished like one. Something that you'll remember – and hopefully respect me for – but something that we can do in a few minutes and get back to the party." I stared at Julie, and she gulped again, and nodded her head very slowly.

Seeing that she was going to accept the punishment, I provided more details. "I don't think Kelly has told you this, but her punishments involve three elements: The punishment (sometimes after a warm-up), the corner time, and any corrective punishment that is needed." Julie's mouth predictably dropped open, as she continued to stare at me.

I wondered whether to share with her more unnecessary details, but I decided it would put her punishment in perspective. "The corner time is usually a rectal insertion – such as a butt plug – for five minutes. And the corrective punishment may be more of the original punishment, additional strokes with a more severe implement ... or some needles or shots." Now, Julie's eyes were downcast, and she slithered down in the chair.

Being somewhat soft on her, I suggested, "In this case, I'll agree that there won't be any corrective punishment, as long as you take the main punishment in full – holding your position for each stroke." Looking at the darkness that came over Julie's face, and her fidgeting, reminded me when I was going through the punishment agreement with Kelly. Julie no longer appeared to be the brash, aggressive girl that she had been a few minutes ago.

"But I will require the corner time." Julie glanced up at me and, almost imperceptibly, nodded once.

Now, for the final blow, "Since you have had experience with it, your punishment will be given with the school paddle – sometimes called a 'sorority' paddle." Julie gasped, but didn't object. "You will receive six medium- to hard-strokes on your bare bottom. The strokes will be repeated, if you get out of position."

Julie whined, "Sir, we never got more than two or three licks when we were in school."

I responded, "You're not in school any longer. You're a big girl – a woman. I'm upset with you, and want you to remember this; remember to respect Kelly." I reached into the credenza behind me, and pulled out the bumpy glass butt plug, holding it up for Julie to see.

"And this will be your corner time. I will insert it, play with it a little, then leave it in for five minutes. I'll put a timer in front of you, and allow you to take it out yourself – probably best done in the bathroom. Then, you can clean it up, wash yourself, and come back to the party."

Julie's mouth was open again, as she stared at the butt plug. I chuckled, "This is almost pure physical punishment, as I've already seen you undressed, already spanked you, and already inserted a butt plug into you. The swats will hurt a little, and will hopefully remind you to think before talking in the future. And the corner time will give your bottom time to recover, before you come up and join us."

I put the butt plug on the desk, swung the chair around and opened the credenza, and pulled out a paddle – about 18 inches long and 6 inches wide, with ten holes bored through the wood, so that the swing was not impeded by air pressure as the paddle strikes the bottom.

Julie appeared to be almost in tears; I had built enough tension. "Julie, do you accept this punishment for breaking the trust with Kelly?"

Julie nodded, and finally croaked, "Yes, Sir."

"Excellent. Stand up, please." Julie did so. "Spread your feet a little more than shoulder width, and put your hands on your head." Again, Julie did as I commanded. "I call this the 'standing position'. I'm going to administer your punishment with you in the 'chair position'; that's similar to a knee-chest position in the chair. Then, you can stay in that position for your corner time. If you insist, I'll allow you to take your swats bending over the desk ... and *then* get in the chair position for your corner time."

Julie was flustered, and said, "Whatever you tell me to do, Sir."

I nodded and walked around the desk, turning the chair around, and instructing Julie how to get into the chair position: Her knees against the sides of the chair about halfway back on the seat, and her head in her folded arms on the low back of the chair, her back arched, and bottom held high.

Julie took off the pareo, and dropped it on the adjacent chair, then got herself into position, as I had requested. I was now looking at Julie's privates from behind. Her labia were separated, and her anus was on display.

I had expected her to bend over the desk for the swats ... and I could have inserted the butt plug with her in that position. But the chair position would provide her a little more challenge, perhaps even a little embarrassment. However, I knew that Julie was already embarrassed about being in this situation, at all.

I moved the paddle, butt plug, and a small tube of KY from my desk drawer to the edge of the desk. I picked up the paddle, got into position – behind and just to the left of Julie, and placed the paddle across her bottom.

"Before we start, I want your agreement that you will hold your position. If you get out of position, you will instantly get back into position. And, if you move during or after a swat, that swat will be repeated, until you've taken the six swats while holding your position. Finally, after each stroke, you will give me the count, and a 'Thank you, Sir'. Do you understand, and agree to these conditions?"

I heard a faint, "Yes, Sir." from Julie. I hadn't offered her a trip to the bathroom – or my 'trick' of punishing her if she returned and didn't assume the standing position. If she had to go, I was sure she would have told me.

Raising my voice slightly, and speaking with authority, I asked, "Are you ready for your punishment, now, Julie?"

Again, a faint voice said, "Yes, Sir."

I brought the paddle back, and held it for a moment. Then, I swung it in an arc, the paddle moving upward, as it impacted Julie's butt. "Ow!!!" Julie cried. A moment later, she shouted, "One. Thank you, Sir!" She had held her position admirably.

Again, I brought the paddle back, this time swinging it immediately, and putting some force into the swat. And again, Julie shrieked, "God! That hurts!" And again, after a few moments, Julie cried, "Two. Thank you, Sir!" Julie's bottom swayed back and forth, and I waited until she settled down into a stable position.

The next swat was a zinger, impacting the lower part of Julie's bottom. "Aiyeee!" screamed Julie. She was now panting, and I heard a few whimpers before she said, "Three. Thank you, Sir."

The last three swats were applied very hard, I'm sure making an impression – in several ways – on Julie. She behaved very well, raising her head slightly on the last two strokes, and wagging her bottom in-between the swats, but counting them out between sobs.

I told her, "You will now stay in position, and not rub your bottom, as I begin your corner time. The back of the chair was next to the desk, so I took an old-fashioned stopwatch from a desk drawer and placed it on the edge of the desk, where Julie could easily see it. I then took my time lubing the glass butt plug, finally walking around behind Julie, and asking, "Are you ready for your corner time, now?"

Julie was still sobbing quietly, but managed to spit out, "Yes, Sir."

Julie's buttocks were already widely separated, her anus well exposed, due to being in the chair position. I placed the butt plug against her, and waited until she had flinched, then become used to the feeling of the smooth, cool surface against her anus. Then, I pushed gently, moving the plug in and out a fraction of an inch, then moving it farther into Julie, each time.

Julie gasped, and then groaned (or moaned?) a few times, as the bumps of the glass rod enlarged her anus, and then popped into her rectum. In less than two minutes, the butt plug was fully inserted, the narrow neck being held in place by Julie's anal muscles.

I stepped up to the desk, and started the stopwatch for five minutes. I told Julie, "Thank you for taking your punishment well. I hope you've learned a lesson today. I won't put up with anyone hurting Kelly."

Then I pleaded, "Julie, you are one of Kelly's best friends. Please try to act like one."

I knew I was coming across as an authority figure – perhaps as a parent disciplining his child. That's not how I wanted Julie to see me. I was really angry, and punishing Julie seemed appropriate to demonstrate my feelings. I might get turned on thinking about this later, but at the moment, I was certainly not turned on, just upset.

I warned Julie, "Don't even think about getting up before that timer rings." Then, I walked out of the playroom, climbed the stairs, and went out to the patio to join the party.

CHAPTER 13: HORSEPLAY, PONY PLAY

Kelly was sitting at the table with Linda and Kathy, having a quiet conversation. As I sat down, she gave me a knowing look, but did not smile. "I've explained everything to Linda and Kathy. I was, of course, going to share the information with them, but I just had lunch with Julie last weekend, and I hadn't planned on broaching the subject today."

Linda commented, "I can understand why Kelly didn't tell us when we were younger. It's quite a story. And sheds some light on a few things – like Kelly's relationship with her parents. I had assumed it was due to her jock father wanting another son, and only being interested in sports."

We were all quiet for a few minutes, and I got up to clear the table from our lunch, and put the remaining food in the fridge. On the way back, I decided to take another beer from the cooler. Kelly and Kathy were still sitting at the table top-free, while Linda had the pareo wrapped around her.

I suggested to Kelly, "If you want us to do something more physical, we could take your friends to the pond." There were not many advantages to that idea, except getting away from the house, going to a beautiful natural setting, and still being able to skinny-dip. But there would be more effort required. And, there was a possibility that there could be other people there.

Kelly responded, "We can do that another time. You don't have enough bikes for all of us, and it would be a long walk – and take up the rest of the day." Then, she casually looked around the backyard, and added, "And your backyard is so beautiful, we should take advantage of it." That was fine with me. I was already thinking about how I might introduce the idea of the 'spank poker' game to the girls.

Kathy asked me about the 'special places' in Europe that I had mentioned, and wanted to know where I might take Kelly. That was a good question, as I had not yet planned the trip, or even discussed the concept with Kelly. I tried to organize my thoughts, before laying out some ideas.

"There are really three types of things I would like to share with Kelly. First, there are some great cities – some of my favorites – that I would like Kelly to experience. We'll have to figure out how long Kelly can stay out of school, and that will undoubtedly limit how much we can see.

"But I would at least like to take her to Amsterdam, possibly Copenhagen, Berlin, and certainly Munich. Hopefully, we'll also have time for Switzerland – maybe Zurich. I don't know if we will get to Austria, but it would be great to see Vienna and Salzburg – and take Kelly through the salt mines, sliding down the old wooden chutes."

My mind whirled, as I thought of many other places I would like to share with Kelly. Cities like Prague, Stockholm and Oslo, and Barcelona; resort areas such as Sirmione in northern Italy, the Amalfi coast, and the French Riviera; and the countryside – such as along the Rhine river, the Dolomites, and central Switzerland.

I pictured Kelly and I standing on a deck outside our luxury villa in Zermatt, sipping wine and enjoying the splendor of the Matterhorn far above us.

"Then, there are my friends – especially a good friend in The Netherlands, Henk, and his partner, Zöe. They visited Sarah and I about five years ago, and we had planned to visit them ... until Sarah's accident. I haven't been back to Europe since then, but they would really like me to come for a visit."

I glanced at Kelly and smiled, "They even offered to bring us to some special clubs ... including a spanking club. Zöe is bi, and had offered to take Sarah to some of her clubs; thinking about it now, I'm sure Kelly would be interested to visit them. And I have friends in Italy, Germany, and Sweden – although we certainly won't have time to visit all of them."

I continued, "And finally, I would like Kelly to experience European culture – including music, art, and (especially) food. Europeans are not as hung-up about sex and nudity as Americans, so they have parks in the middle of big cities where people can sunbathe in the nude, and frolic in the small streams, everyone – dressed or not – having a fun time. And one of my favorite pastimes when I'm relaxing in Europe is to go to the saunas." I glanced over, and Linda was giving me a 'look'.

"The European saunas have nothing to do with sex. Some of them are almost like a high-class waterpark for adults – with multiple dry saunas, each at a different temperature; steam rooms; cold pools and regular swimming pools; waterfalls and misters; and beautiful grounds to explore." Linda was nodding.

I explained further, "And everyone is nude, and totally comfortable. Most have co-ed (or as they call it in Europe, 'mixed') dressing rooms. In a way, I guess it is similar to you guys coming over, all of us changing, and then spending they day together nude, enjoying the sun and the water, in a relaxing environment."

I looked at Kelly, "We'll have to discuss it. I haven't asked Kelly yet where *she* wants to visit." Kelly shrugged. "Depending on where we'll be going, we might have to fly between some cities ... but I hope that it will be mostly a driving trip."

Kelly beamed, "All that sounds great, to me."

Kathy concurred, "Yeah, it sounds like it will be a great trip. It's nice to know someone there. And it would be nice, if you guys can drive around on your own. My parents have done that several times, and they've always had a great time – and a few adventures, along the way."

Kelly was nodding, a broad smile on her already-beautiful face. Linda blurted, "I'd like to go to Paris." We all looked at her, and she explained. "The city of lights, Eiffel tower, shopping ..."

I laughed, "There are a lot of great – and historic – cities in Europe, and Paris is one of them. Even just to get a basic feeling for Paris would take a week or more." I laughed, thinking of one of my past trips, when I had a convention in Paris. "Especially, since the traffic is so bad. But between walking, and the Metro, most of Paris can be seen while avoiding the traffic jams."

There was so much that I wanted to share with Kelly. "Where we go, and what we do, will also depend on *when* we go: In the summer, there are beautiful parks, rivers, flower-covered mountains; even sailing on the lakes of Germany or Switzerland. In the winter, the saunas are all open." I remembered how I had several times gotten out of a 190-degree sauna in Zurich, then swam in the nearly-freezing lake.

"And, we could go skiing." Kelly was nodding, but I didn't know what kind of a skier she was – whether she stayed on *piste*, or off. The ski resorts, and nearby mountains, were huge, and back-country skiing was great; although you did need to watch out for crevasses and the edges of steep cliffs.

Linda said, brightly, "I love saunas. But the only ones I've been in are at our local health clubs." I remembered that we had briefly shown Linda and Julie the sauna downstairs, when they first visited; then, unbidden, my mind flashed on Linda's birthday spanking, and Julie's masturbation scene.

Kelly said, "We can use the sauna downstairs later this evening, if you like." Linda smiled and nodded excitedly.

Julie strolled out of the kitchen and onto the patio, wearing her pareo wrapped around her waist. Her face was freshly washed, and her countenance seemed upbeat, if not perky. She walked straight to the table, and stood between Kelly and I.

Glancing around the table, she said, contritely, "I would like to apologize to everyone." She looked down at Kelly, "And, especially to Kelly." Julie put her hands on Kelly shoulders, and Kelly looked up at her. "Kelly is my friend and, as Sam pointed out to me, I broke my trust with her. I respect you greatly, Kelly, and I had no right to divulge information that you shared with me privately."

Kelly stood, and she and Julie hugged. Although this was a serious occasion, I couldn't help notice the girls' breasts squished together, and Julie's hand caressing Kelly's head. Kelly let her hand drop, and held Julie's bottom. There was a slight flinch, and Kelly looked into Julie's eyes.

Julie nodded, "Yes, Kelly, Sam paddled me." I glanced over, and Kathy was smiling, while Linda's mouth dropped open, again. Julie continued, "And I deserved it." They hugged briefly again, and Kelly sat down, while Julie remained standing, holding the back of Kelly's chair.

Then, Julie added, "Kelly, you are one lucky woman to have Sam. He cares about you deeply, and is very protective of you. And I respect him greatly: You had told us about his high standards, and his sense of ethics and morality ... and I understand much better now what you meant. We were both nude, and other men might have tried to take advantage of the situation."

Julie looked down at me, "But, as you've told us, he was a perfect gentleman. Even though he spanked me hard."

Julie bent down, and kissed me on the cheek. "Thank you, Sam. I needed to be punished, and I appreciate your control, even though I know you were angry with me."

Then Julie straightened, and said, "But my bottom's going to be sore for a while. Maybe the pool will cool it off, a little?" Everyone laughed, but it was getting hot, and we were all ready for a refreshing dip. I wondered whether Julie would try to hide her reddened bottom, but she took off the pareo, folded it, and put it on the table, then walked casually to the pool, and entered via the ladder near the deep end.

We all watched as Julie walked to the pool, displaying her inflamed bottom. I did not feel sorry for her – she had deserved the spanking. In fact, I would have enjoyed spanking her myself, after what she did; but Sam was probably more controlled than I would have been.

Now that I had explained everything to Kathy and Linda, I was no longer as upset with Julie. But I was glad that Sam had taken matters into his own hands – in a manner of speaking; and Julie had obviously cooperated with him. Julie smiled at me from the pool, and I felt a stirring that caused me to squirm in the chair. The pool was a good idea. I stood up, took off my pareo, and walked to the edge of the deck. Then, I did a cannonball, landing a few feet from Julie.

Julie swam over to me, again apologizing for her *faux pas*, as Linda and Kathy walked over to the pool, both nude, and slipped into the cool, clear water. The black bottomed pool was a good substitute for the pond, although I knew I would have to bring my friends there, at some point. I floated on my back for a while, looking up at the deep blue sky; the weather was great, albeit a bit warm, but perfect for my party.

I thought about what Julie had said; she was beginning to understand Sam. I *was* a lucky woman to have met him ... or re-met him. I treaded water, while watching my friends float around the pool. Sam was busy pulling ropes on his pirate ship, and carrying things into the pool room. I still couldn't believe that he had built that contraption for our pirate role-play.

When Sam came out, he was carrying an armload of colorful plastic. Standing at the edge of the pool, he announced, "I thought you guys might like to play with these, for a while." Then, he tossed each of us a water gun. We all laughed, but Linda acted serious, and seriously excited, as she drew pool water into the gun, and started firing jets of water around the pool at all of us.

We hadn't done this in years, and we were all having a good time. It was only when I looked at Linda shooting water out of the long, thin tube that I flashed on me injecting water into Sam's ass, and realized that my perspective really had changed.

We all got into a water fight. A few minutes later, I saw Sam standing at the edge of the pool; his nude body looked tanned and I was proud of how fit he was ... for his age. He smiled at me, and dove in, easily swimming the length of the pool underwater, and coming up under Linda.

Suddenly, Linda's head disappeared, as she was dragged under the water. I saw some thrashing, and then calm, before both Linda and Sam rose to the surface. I thought Linda was going to scream at Sam, but she just coughed, ran her fingers through her hair, and smiled at him.

Sam was underwater again, swimming to Kathy, who tried to avoid him; but Sam kept cutting off the corners, and eventually I saw Kathy's head disappear beneath the water. More thrashing, and calm, again. The pair surfaced, and again there was no anger on Kathy's face, just a sweet smile at Sam.

When Sam slid beneath the water again, I saw Julie smile, and dive down, heading straight for Sam. They remained underwater for some time, but there was no thrashing. They surfaced together, and I could see that Julie's legs were wrapped around Sam's waist, and he was treading water furiously to keep their heads above the water.

Then Sam suddenly disappeared below Julie, surprising her with his swiftness and sudden moves, and he swam up to me. I let myself fall vertically, plunging in slow motion toward the bottom of the pool, exhaling. And then, opening my eyes to see Sam in front of my face, smiling. He hugged me, thrusting us sideways, and kissed me for as long as I could avoid breathing.

When we surfaced, Sam put his legs around *my* waist; but I didn't have the power to keep us up, and we slowly sank again, into the depths and blackness of the pool. Sam unwrapped his feet, and gave me the diver's 'OK' sign, and I returned it. Then, we swam to the ladder, and climbed out of the pool.

Julie, Linda, and Kathy followed us, as we walked to the jacuzzi, and slipped into the warm, bubbling water. We all sat there for a while, winded, and enjoying the relaxing flow of water, around our unclothed bodies. After a few minutes, or longer, Sam offered to get us some wine; I looked at my friends, thinking surely they would refuse ... but everyone nodded their assent. Sam got out of the spa, and disappeared into the kitchen.

I turned to Linda, glancing at Kathy, "I hope Sam wasn't bothering you in the pool." It was more of a question than a statement.

Linda smiled, "I was surprised when I was suddenly pulled under ... but Sam put his finger to his lips – to signal me to be silent – gave me an 'OK' signal, and then hugged me. He spun me around in the water until I was almost disoriented, but held me, as if protecting me. It was only a few seconds, but I got a very 'supportive' and comfortable feeling from him. He didn't try to kiss me, or touch me anywhere 'inappropriate'."

We all laughed; since we were totally nude, any hugging would obviously bring Sam's body into very close contact with any number of usually-private body parts. It didn't bother me in the least, and I was happy that Sam was having fun, while building trust with my friends.

Kathy was nodding, "Same with me. At first I thought he was just playing, and I was prepared to fight him ... but he really was sweet. He just wanted to hug. And he did it in a very sincere way; I didn't get any vibe of sexual intention from him."

I laughed, "Sam wouldn't have sex with any of you even if you asked. But, as you know, he's happy to see all of us nude, happy to touch you, and I'm sure would be happy to get you off, if that was something you wanted. But he doesn't want to force himself on you. As I said, he's basically a 'nice' guy. Just a perverted nice guy."

We all were laughing as Sam carried the lacquer tray with five plastic cups of white wine. I wondered whether any of us would make it to dinner.

I passed around the cups of chardonnay. We were all doing fine, and I didn't think less than six ounces of wine would adversely affect the girls. But it might loosen them up a bit; for the next birthday activities I had in mind.

As we sipped the wine, the bubbles still caressing our skin, I told everyone, "I've spent some time trying to think of some interesting and fun birthday party games." I looked around at everyone, "I know you guys can have fun by yourselves without playing games, but I was thinking of adult versions of some of the things we used to do when we were kids."

Julie, Kathy and Linda were listening intently, but Kelly was already shaking her head, wondering what my next 'surprise' would be.

I continued, "The horsing around in the pool reminded me of something we always did at birthday parties: Pin the tail on the donkey." It only took a few moments before Kelly blurted a fraction of a laugh, and Linda's hands went up to her face. I smiled, "Yes, I was thinking about the needles Kelly and I showed you. But I realized it would be too dangerous to do it blindfolded." I saw Kelly breath a sigh of relief. She didn't know what I was going to say next.

"Then, I thought of some old television dating shows, where they had a cut-out, and the husbands had to position themselves so their bottoms were showing through the cardboard ... and the wives had to pick out their husbands from their behinds." The girls laughed nervously, knowing that I had something planned.

"In this case, I envisioned Kelly, the birthday girl, trying to identify each of her friends, by your bottoms alone. But that wouldn't be very exciting." I sighed, "And then, I thought about Kelly 'doing' one or more of you, and you guys having to be silent, lest Kelly guess which one of you is which."

As it would be pretty easy to pick Linda out of the bunch, due to her size, I added, "And, Kelly could be blindfolded; I would lead her to each of you, and she would have to determine who it was by feel ... or your response to her fingering you." Now, all the girls were shaking their heads.

I smiled, "Yeah, I didn't think you guys would think much of that. So I scrapped the idea." After the girls enjoyed a few seconds of relief, I said, "The horseplay, and pinning the tail on the donkey, reminded me of another fetish. It seems like a really strange one, but I can see the potential of it." Now the girls were curious again. I got up and went into the pool room, and brought out a few things from the box in the closet. I also grabbed a folded towel, and then went back out to the edge of the jacuzzi.

"Kelly, will you submit to me, for a few minutes?"

Not knowing what was going to happen, Kelly smiled, stood on the shallow spa step, and got into the standing position. Then, she said, with mock meekness, "Yes, Sir. Of course!"

I put the towel down, and signaled Kelly to get out of the pool, and get onto 'all fours', on the towel. I showed her what I was going to do, and she giggled, and nodded her head. I quickly used the lube, and then held up the main item for Kelly's friends to see.

"Kelly and I haven't done this – yet – and I can only explain a little of it ... but this fetish is called 'pony play'." I turned to Kelly, separated her buttocks, and inserted the butt plug ... which had a long tail of horsehairs. I then put a leather bit in Kelly's mouth, bringing the reins back, and set them on her back.

I looked at Kelly's startled friends, "This fetish can get quite complex. The pony must be fully trained; to prance, and perform, based on signals from the reins." I glanced at Kelly, who had her head turned back to me; she whinnied.

"And, sometimes, a few good hard slaps of the crop on her rump." Kelly swallowed, undoubtedly wondering whether that meant I was going to crop her now. I had brought out the crop, and decided to give her one stroke, as a demonstration for her friends. Kelly, the pony, bucked and neighed.

"And, of course, the filly would need to get all her vaccinations." I poked the nail of my pointer finger into Kelly's bottom, and held it there, a poor simulation of giving her a shot.

Then, I unceremoniously took the bit out of Kelly's mouth, and the butt plug out of her rear. I wrapped the butt plug in tissue, and put everything back into the small box. "No, we're not going to do any 'pony play' today. But I may start Kelly's training process soon. She'll make a beautiful filly!"

I pulled Kelly up, and we hugged and I gave her a peck on the lips. Then, we got back into the jacuzzi.

Linda was shaking her head, "Where do you come up with all this, Sam?"

I laughed, "I've been exposed to a lot from various websites, and learned a lot from books I purchased. Each one of these fetishes is a whole field unto itself. I don't profess to be an expert on any of them. At this point, it's just an adventure for Kelly and I to try some new things."

I looked at Kelly, "And for me to try to convince Kelly that not all men are sexually boring, or inattentive to her needs. And some men are interested in foreplay ... and role play." The girls laughed. But they knew that I was serious.

I had to stay focused. Returning to the main subject, I said, "OK. I was telling you about my ideas for birthday party activities." Suddenly, the girls were attentive again. The cups of wine were empty, and we were all pretty mellow.

"The next thing I thought of was a type of 'Truth or Dare' game." Now, the girls' eyes lit up, and they smiled. Even Linda was nodding. "Of course, my version of it would have you guys talking about some intimate things ... or getting various types of spankings." Every 'round' of the game, you would need to tell even more intimate things ... or receive an even more serious spanking."

Linda was moaning, and Kathy was shaking her head, perhaps wondering what else I could possibly come up with. Julie sat there smiling; if I had to guess, I would bet that she was considering bringing the water pipe back over here and getting us stoned again.

I continued, "I actually came up with a different kind of game that I'll suggest in a few minutes. But, first, it might be interesting to do the 'Truth' part of the other game ... without the 'Dare'. I wonder how much detail you know about each other's sex lives? Your first times, your most interesting times, the times you did it in public ..." Linda and Kathy gasped in unison, as Julie cracked up. I stared at them, and then they stared at each other. Then I firmly said, "OK, Julie, you're first."

Julie blinked, looked away for a moment, and then began her story.

"I'm sure you guys are expecting me to share some of my 'wild' stories. Yes – I have had sex in public. I've masturbated during class in college. I've had several sexual experiences with other women. And you guys know about some of my hook-ups; I've been tied to a bed, role-played a rape fantasy, and even had two men at once."

Julie looked around at our startled faces. I tried to take this new information in stride, and keep a straight face. But, through my brain, flashed images of Julie in these situations.

I broke in, "Well, I guess we don't need anyone else to volunteer. Julie will keep us filled with stories for the rest of the afternoon."

Julie laughed, "I've had a few 'interesting' experiences." Then, she became serious, "But one of the most meaningful was when I lost my virginity ... to my cousin."

Linda's hands flew up to hide her face, and Kathy's mouth fell open. Kelly exclaimed, "But I thought you had sex first with that guy in high school; what was his name, Brad?" Now, Linda and Kathy were both nodding.

Julie sighed, "That was the first time with a 'regular' guy. I was sixteen and he was eighteen – a senior. I've told you guys all about that." Julie stood against the wall of the spa, over which there was a six-foot drop to the pool below.

"But I made it with my cousin Kenneth when I was barely fourteen years old. This was when we still lived in the South." I could see that the other girls were shocked to hear this.

Julie continued her story, "Kenny and I really liked each other. He lived in another state, and only visited us during the summer. He was 17 then, and I had just turned 14. But I was already mostly developed. We were left to play together most days, and we loved riding our bikes to the edge of town where there was a small lake. Before we left the house, we would get into our bathing suits. I'm not sure how it first happened, but Kenny would watch while I changed. Then, we would go to his room, and I would watch him; I had never seen a 'man' before, and he seemed so grown up and confident." We all listened with rapt attention.

"We were very comfortable with each other, and Kenny never tried to kiss me or force me to do anything. But whenever I would change, Kenny would watch, and sometimes ask if he could touch me – on my breasts, or feel my pubic hair. One time, I went to his room to watch him change, but the door was closed. I opened it, calling to him, and – when it swung open – Kenny was lying on his bed rubbing himself." Once again, Linda's hands flew up to her face.

Julie continued, "He jumped up, but that made his penis bob up and down, and he got really embarrassed. I had never seen an erection before; but for some reason, I wasn't scared or intimidated by it ... I was really curious how it could get so big and stiff. Kenny let me stay in the room while he put on his suit, but he was facing away from me, very self-conscious."

"We had a fun time at the lake. I don't know why, but we never thought of going skinny-dipping; I guess we didn't want to get caught being seen by other people. The next day, I asked Kenny to show me his dick, and he invited me into his room, and took off his pants and underwear. He let me touch it, and he showed me how to stroke it." We were all listening intently to Julie's story.

"It was probably another week, before I asked him if I could see him get big and stiff again. He lay on his bed, and let me stroke him, until he was hard. I remember seeing a drop of liquid on the tip of his dick, and said, 'I think you're leaking!'; I knew a little about sex, but not much about men's bodies, or the actual mechanics of sex. Kenny got embarrassed again, and asked me to leave his room."

Julie took a deep breath, "I think it was the next day when he nervously asked if I would like to watch him. I wasn't really sure what he meant, but he brought me into his bedroom, got undressed, and lay on the bed. I watched him stroke himself, get hard, and finally come; his breathing was heavy, and his motions violent, as he spurted cum over his stomach. When he was finished, he wiped himself with some tissues, and looked really embarrassed. I had enjoyed watching him, and told him so; I also told him that I was learning a lot about men."

"It was probably a few weeks before we did anything else. We still watched each other change, but he didn't get turned on. However, at some point, he asked if he could see my private parts. He had already seen me undressed, and he asked so nicely, that I lay down and let him examine me." Julie looked away for a moment, remembering.

"He poked me clumsily with his fingers, finally pushing one into me. It didn't hurt, but I didn't think it felt very good. Some time later, he actually let me stroke him, until he came. I thought that was pretty neat: I felt the power of being able to control his body, and see the look of satisfaction on his face when he finished."

"I wasn't ignorant of sex but, at that point, I don't think I really ever thought about having sex. Kenny and I enjoyed playing with each other, and before the end of the summer, he asked if I would want to see what it was like with him inside of me. I knew what he meant, but couldn't believe that his dick would fit inside me."

Julie smiled at each of us. "It was a Saturday morning, and my parents had gone into town, and Kenny and I were planning to go to the lake. But when I watched him get undressed, his dick was pointing to the ceiling. He said, 'Would you like to try it today?' I knew that I could get pregnant, and told him that I was worried about that. He pulled out a condom – the first time I had seen one – and he proceeded to open it and put it on."

"Then, I complained that it would hurt too much. He told me that he wouldn't force me, and if it hurt too much we could stop. I lay on his bed, and he climbed on top of me. He put his finger in me, and eventually figured out how to get his dick in me, as I just lay there, staring at the ceiling."

Julie looked up at us, "He was obviously still a virgin. He was careful with me, pushing himself into me slowly. It did hurt – I'm sure I must have been very dry – until he finally slid into me. Then, my muscles relaxed, I closed my eyes, and first experienced the glorious feeling of having a man inside me."

Julie chuckled, and looked at us from across the jacuzzi, "But the actual fucking didn't do much for me – he pounded his dick into me, and came within a couple of minutes."

"I haven't thought about that experience for ages. My feelings back then were mixed – I liked seeing Kenny undress, and I think I must have gotten a little turned-on by seeing his erection. And I really liked the feeling of him inside me. But I didn't particularly care for the rest of it."

Julie smiled at Linda, "I didn't have an orgasm until after we moved here – I must have been at least 17 or maybe 18 at the time. And it came from my own experimentation, not a guy. Kenny and I only did it that once, and then he left at the end of the summer. He graduated high school the next year, and spent the summer hitch-hiking around with some friends, and then went off to college. So we never had another close 'encounter'."

Julie explained, "I do see him from time to time, and we're still good friends. But we've never discussed what we did that summer, and he's never come on to me since then. Overall, I was very lucky: Fortunately he used a condom, so I didn't get pregnant – THAT would have been a disaster! And, he was very nice and gentle with me. He was just learning the ropes, also, so I never felt used. I looked at it as an educational experience."

Julie scanned our faces, "So that's my 'first time' story."

I applauded, and the girls followed. "That was a great story, Julie. I think it's terrific that you could share it." I thought about my first time, and hoped I wouldn't have to share it ... except with Kelly.

We all took different positions in the jacuzzi, and I looked around at everyone. It reminded me of a time in Amsterdam, when I had visited a sauna on a quiet afternoon. I had been sitting in the hot tub, when the doors from the changing room flew open, and a bevy of beautiful college-age girls walked out, casually carrying their towels in front of them. They decided to get in the hot tub, and walked toward me.

One by one, they hung up their towels, and walked down the ladder, nude, into the hot tub. Soon, the beauties surrounded me. I chit-chatted a few minutes with them, but had a dinner reservation at a fancy restaurant. So, despite the cute nude girls, I excused myself, and left to get dressed and go to dinner.

I chortled, "Can anybody top Julie's story?" I looked at each of the girls, in turn. "How about the most exciting or dangerous sex you've ever had? Linda?"

Linda shook her head, "I don't have any exciting sex stories to tell. I've never done it in public. I've had a few funny experiences doing it in a car, though ..."

Everyone laughed, but nobody wanted to volunteer to tell a story. So, I decided that it was time to introduce another 'main event' of the birthday party ... I hoped.

Starting right where I had left off, I said, "So after the 'Truth or Dare' spanking game idea, I came up with something I think you guys might like."

All eyes were on me, again. I suggested that we get out and sit at the table, and offered to get everyone a drink. The decision was iced tea, and Kelly went into the kitchen to bring the pitcher. Linda put the pareo around her waist, but Julie and Kathy just sat on their towels, totally comfortable with being nude at Kelly's birthday party.

CHAPTER 14: TURNTABLE TURNS

After Kelly had poured cups of iced tea for everyone and sat down at the patio table, I took a deep breath, and corralled my nerves. I hoped the girls would be 'game' for the game I had planned, even though it would require one more level of openness.

"You guys have been very open today: Skinny dipping," I glanced at Linda, "sitting around nude while we're talking," I glanced at Kathy, "having an orgasm in front of everyone," now I glanced at Kelly and Julie, "telling stories that your friends hadn't heard," I stared at Julie, "and even seeing what a couple of needles in the butt feels like." Everyone was nodding.

"You've watched Kelly and I role-play one of her fantasies, and make love. The game I'm going to suggest will require one more level of openness from you." I looked around at the girls, who were listening intently. I hoped what I was about to suggest wouldn't be a turn-off to them, or shock them ... too much.

"Kelly mentioned that you guys used to play poker when you were younger. For example, at your slumber parties."

The girls were nodding, and Linda had a big smile, "We loved to play poker." She looked at Julie and Kathy, and they nodded.

"I thought about poker and a party, and my first thought was 'strip poker' ... but that wouldn't work very well, as we're all nude already." The girls laughed.

"Of course, we could play 'dress poker', where we each have to put *on* a piece of clothing, each time we lose a hand." More laughing. Now was as good a time as there was going to be.

"Then, I thought about sharing some of the things I've exposed Kelly to ... and came up with 'spank poker'." Then Linda and Kathy groaned, but Kelly's eyes lit up, and Julie was nodding excitedly, if not enthusiastically.

"For each hand, there will be an ante – probably a spank on each side of your butt, using an implement chosen just for that hand. Then, one of you will deal the hand. Is 5-card stud poker OK?"

The girls nodded, and Kathy said, "That's what we usually played."

I nodded, "Then, you can do the first round of betting, and decide to keep or replace your cards – up to 3 – and we'll go around the table, back to the dealer. Then we'll have the second betting round. The person on her right will bet – either hold at the ante, or up the ante in units that I'll tell you for each hand." The girls looked confused.

"For example, if the spanks are by hand, you can raise in 6-spank increments. If the spanks are with the Ping Pong paddle, then you can raise in 2-spank increments. For harder implements, you can raise in 1-spank increments. Each time you raise, you will get that number of spanks. Then, the person to her right can either call, or raise again." Now, the girls were nodding, slowly.

"We'll go around the table this way, until there are no more raises. Then, everyone can show their hand. For each ante and raise, you'll throw chips into the center, and the winner will take those chips. For all hands except the first, you'll be allowed to 'fold'; if you decide to do that, then you will have a penalty. I'll describe that in a minute.

At the end, we'll add up the chips, and see who came in first, second, and so on. Then, tonight, we'll have the 'awards' ceremony." I glanced around the table, and finished the last of my iced tea. "How does that sound, so far?"

Linda looked at Kelly, and exclaimed, "He really is perverted, you know."

Kelly nodded, "I know." She looked at me, while she said to Linda, "And knowing Sam, I'm sure there's going to be more to this 'spank poker' than we've heard, already." Julie and Kathy were now staring at me. I had to fess up.

"The game – although I hope you'll have fun playing it – is about submission. There won't be that many spanks, unless you guys are 'high rollers'." I looked at Julie, wondering whether the girls would get high before this game. She smiled at me sweetly.

"And, the spanks won't be very hard. Just hard enough to appreciate what that implement can do." I was biding my time, but I really had to come clean. "The game will be played on a 'board'." I laughed, having not thought of this before, "So, I guess you could call it a 'board game'." I laughed again, but the girls looked confused again.

"Do you guys know what a 'Lazy Susan' is?"

Everyone nodded, and Linda piped up, "It's one of those turning platters that you see in the center of big round tables at Chinese restaurants."

I agreed, "Right. I thought about spanking you guys lined up ... but I would be going back and forth the entire game. I realized that it would be much easier just turning *you guys*. So I built a Lazy Susan – or, as I call it, a 'Lazy Sam'." The girls laughed.

Then, I challenged them, "To make the game fast – where the Lazy Sam can be turned, I give the spankings, and we move on – the only practical way is to have you guys in a knee-chest position." I held my breath, and looked around at everyone. I saw blank faces.

"You guys have been very open, and we've seen most of each other's bodies ... but to play this game (which *is*, after all, a game of submission), you'll have to be a little more open. Do you think that might be possible?"

Of course, there was no issue with Kelly; and I had already inserted a thermometer and butt plug into Julie. So, it was really down to the openness of Kathy and Linda. I wasn't worried so much about Kathy.

Kathy shrugged, "It's already been a bizarre day; but I've been having fun. I don't have a problem with you seeing my privates." Her gaze went from me to Kelly, "but maybe I'll let Kelly decide if this is something she thinks we should do."

Then, Kelly shrugged. "I know Sam pretty well, now. And I think you can expect a few things from him. First, I think we can trust him: He's not going to attack, or rape you ... in fact, I'm sure he would agree that he would not have intercourse with any of you, even if you begged him."

I was nodding, and Kelly smiled, "Of course, we've already seen that masturbation – either by ourselves, or at each other's hand (or Sam's hand) – isn't something that we consider 'sex'. Oral sex is on the border: Although Sam first considered oral contact to be sex – as STDs can be transmitted – that would preclude kissing, and even eating after each other."

Kelly looked at me, "So I think we've decided to allow consensual oral sex." Then, she added, "But I know Sam would never do anything that you didn't want."

Kelly took a deep breath, "Second, I know that Sam will be pushing us – *you* – all day, to do things that require openness, or give you new experiences, or are associated with submission or spanking. The openness is something that I'm getting used to, and I don't find it to be a big deal ... because Sam doesn't make a big deal about it. And as far as spanking, both Julie and Linda have gotten a taste of that ... and it seemed that they weren't bothered by it."

Kelly smiled broadly, first at Julie, and then at Linda, "And they might have even enjoyed it. Maybe not 'enjoyed' it, but gotten turned on by the idea of it." Then, she admitted, "And, to be honest, this stuff is something that I've wanted to share with you guys ... if you were interested."

Kelly turned to me, and said, "And now, I'm going to act like you, and ask Linda a very personal question." She turned to Linda, and asked, "Linda, have you – by any chance, since your birthday spanking – masturbated while thinking about Sam spanking you?" Julie and Kathy chuckled nervously, and looked at Linda.

Linda smiled peculiarly, and said, "Yes. I already told you that I like to fantasize about things like that. But it doesn't mean that I enjoy it at the time. And, actually, I've fantasized about Julie's spanking and masturbation scene much more than about getting spanked myself."

Kelly smiled, and nodded, "Me too." Now all eyes were on Julie.

Julie said, "I wasn't doing it for you guys. I was pretty turned on myself. And, yes, I've fantasized about it, also."

Kelly continued with her ideas about me, "And, finally, Sam has been very good about letting me – and maybe in this case *us* – have our way ... and making *him* submit. You guys might have fun spanking him."

Kelly looked at me with a big grin, and arched her brows. I arched my brows back at her, although I'm sure my grin wasn't quite as large. But, yes, if it would help get her friends interested in spanking and submission, I would let them top me, if they wanted.

Then, Linda blurted out, "In that case, let's see *him* get in a knee chest position for *us*." Kathy laughed, and Linda chuckled, while Kelly turned to me, and shrugged.

I looked at Linda, and asked, "Is that really something you want me to do? And, if I do it, will you play our 'spank poker' game?" Linda nodded. I immediately stood up, and started for the chaises, but Kelly grabbed my arm, and asked, "Will you go get a lubed thermometer, please?"

I smiled, and nodded. Everything was in the box next to the massage table, and as I walked over and got everything ready I thought 'Well, fair-is-fair: I plan to insert thermometers into their butts, so I can't deny them doing it to me'. And Kelly had requested it, undoubtedly to demonstrate my openness ... and, because she probably had guessed that it would be part of the spank poker scene.

I brought the thermometer to Kelly, and got into a knee-chest position on the cross-wise facing chaise. Linda turned her chair around, and gasped, as she saw me from behind – my anus relaxed and open, and my 'package' hanging down beneath me, swinging slightly. I closed my eyes and awaited Kelly's demonstration.

I felt Kelly's presence behind me, as she announced to her friends, "Sam is turned on by the idea of rectal insertions – whether it's me or him getting them. I think it's partly another way of demonstrating openness, and submission, and – for him – stimulation of his prostate."

I felt the tip of the thermometer against my anus, and consciously kept my anal muscles relaxed, as she pushed the thermometer into me. She moved it around, and I felt it being pulled out and pushed in several times, before Kelly left it in place – probably only an inch or so sticking out of me. I heard Kelly's steps, and the chair screeching on the stone of the patio.

Kelly was now talking with her friends. "Have you guys seen any good movies, lately?" The conversation ensued, while I was evidently being ignored. I knew better than to move or ask Kelly what was going on ... as she was now the domme, and I was submitting to her. I wondered whether she would also be spanking me, as I maintained this position in front of her friends?

I had to admit (to myself, if not to Kelly) that even after so much experience at nude beaches, with other women, and with Kelly, it was still a little embarrassing for me to be in a knee chest position, with a thermometer sticking out of my butt, as the girls watched me and casually discussed the weather.

I started to chuckle, but restrained myself: This was the first time Kathy and I had met! Well, I was trying to promote openness. And Kelly had become a monster.

Finally, I heard Kelly ask, "Shall I take the thermometer out of him? Is there any more you guys would like to see? Or any more challenges for Sam?"

I didn't hear any words, but there was a scuffling, another screech of the chair, and footsteps towards me. I felt the thermometer being wiggled around, and moved in and out of me slowly. It felt pretty good. Then, I heard Julie – *right behind me!* – saying "Yeah. This *is* fun!"

My anus involuntarily clenched, before I could will it to be relaxed, again. Julie laughed. Then, the thermometer was pulled out of me, and I heard Julie say, "Here, you can take this."

A moment later, Kelly sniggered, saying, "OK, Sam. You've been a good boy. You may get up, now." I got up, and took the thermometer from Kelly, bringing it into the pool room half bath, and washing and drying it, before putting it into the box near the massage table. Then, I returned to my seat at the patio table.

The girls looked at me, Linda trying not to laugh. "I admit, even with my experience, it *is* a bit embarrassing, because it's such a taboo, socially. But, from a scientific point of view, we're all basically the same – at least all men are the same, and all women are the same. Sure, there can be smaller and larger, fatter and thinner, or different colors, but once you've seen one, you've seen them all."

The girls laughed, and Linda said, "Well, we know you've seen at least one," she glanced at Kelly, "so there's no need to see the rest of us!" More laughter.

"Now that Kelly has done her rectal insertion demonstration, I'll tell you the rest of the spank poker rules."

Now, Kelly cracked up, "See! What did I tell you!"

I was nodding, "Kelly knows me pretty well, by now. Anyway, I'm looking forward to you guys betting, and raising – even though you may get a few spanks – but not giving up. So, the penalty for 'folding' a hand, will be to take a rectal insertion. I'll give you a little basket with some options, but you'll probably start with the smallest, and work up to larger ones, if you keep folding."

Now I heard groans from all the girls. Kathy was looking up at the sky, smiling but shaking her head. Linda was also shaking her head, and she said, "That's not very nice." Julie didn't react; she'd already had rectal insertions – earlier today, and when she came over with Linda a couple of weeks ago.

"Finally ..." I took a deep breath, "The first hand will be different. The ante will be insertion of the rectal thermometer, and the bets will be insertions of the 25-

gauge needles. And no folding will be allowed." I heard whines and 'Noooo's'. Then, I acquiesced – a little.

"OK. If you fold, you'll have to pick the next bigger rectal insertion. And we'll limit the betting to 3 needles on each side, no more." The whining stopped, and everyone was very quiet.

Kelly looked at me, and asked, reproachfully, "Sam ... is that *all*, now? The full disclosure for the 'spank poker' game?

I frowned, and looked at Kelly. "Well, there are a few things I hadn't decided, yet. Like how many hands should be played. We have about a dozen implements (including my hand and the needles) – so that's probably the maximum. Maybe 10 hands? And, then, what happens if somebody keeps folding, and uses up all the rectal insertions?" Kelly closed her eyes, knowing what I would say next.

"My thought was to do the injection enema – one syringe the first time, two, the next, and doubling each time after that. Finally, I'm not sure about the awards ceremony tonight – whether the 'awards' will be a carrot or a stick, in a manner of speaking. But I thought you and I could talk about that later."

Kelly was nodding, her friends just staring. Linda's mouth was hanging open, again, and she exclaimed, "What kind of bizarro birthday party is this, anyway?" We all laughed, and Kelly brought the pitcher of iced tea out to the table.

I admitted, "Kelly, there might be one or two more things, that I think we should play by ear." Kelly was shaking her head, as she poured some iced tea for herself.

Finally, Kelly coughed, and said, "OK. We can shoot for 10 hands, but we'll stop if we all vote to ... I mean us girls. I'm not sure about the enema idea, but hopefully none of us will have to fold that often. Maybe the game should end as soon as somebody takes the last butt plug? And we can talk later about whatever 'awards' you had in mind."

Then, Kelly looked into my eyes, and added, "And, if you're going to stick us with needles – *again* – I want you to let me give my friends a demonstration on *your* bottom. After our game." Then, Kelly had another thought, and stipulated, "And you can't use the cane on us!"

I nodded, "I can agree to all that. If everyone else does." Kelly's friends sat there dumbfounded. They had been listening to the conversation, and were now overwhelmed with thoughts of what was about to happen.

I was still holding my breath, waiting to hear whether they would agree to play this game. It really *was* asking a lot of them: A skinning-dipping party is one thing, but now they were being asked to take spankings, get rectal insertions, and be stuck with needles. I wondered how this would play out.

Kelly jumped in before anyone else had a chance to comment. "I think this could be fun; a really *different* kind of birthday party game. And I know that Sam has put a lot of work into this 'project', and won't abuse us." She looked at me, then around the table. "And, I will stop the game, if it gets too intense for everyone." I was happy Kelly had said 'everyone' and not 'anyone'.

Kelly then said, "We should all probably use the bathroom, first." Kelly got up, and so did Linda.

I turned to Julie, and asked, "May I please speak with Kathy privately, for a moment?" Julie looked at me, and there was a slight delay, but then she got up, and walked into the pool room. Kathy looked a little surprised that I needed to speak with her privately; she would understand soon enough.

"Kathy, I'm really proud of all of you, for being so open, and relaxed – with our skinny-dipping, and everything else we've done today. And I'm especially grateful to you for being here, participating with us, and being so open, despite the fact that you have your period."

Kathy shrugged, and said, "There's not much I can do about it."

I nodded, "I know. But you've still been very relaxed about going nude, with a string coming out of you. I realize it's not under your control – and I guess women get used to it – but it still seems unfair, especially, if you're going to play this game and get into a knee chest position." Kathy just shrugged, again.

"So, to even-up the game a little, I was thinking about making the other girls put in a tampon, so everyone will have a string hanging down."

Now, Kathy was laughing, "You really do come up with some strange things. Or maybe it's your strange logic?" She shook her head, "So what are you asking me? To provide some tampons?"

"No, Kelly has us stocked up. But my thought was to break this to everyone after you're all in position on the Lazy Sam. And have them insert the tampons while I watch from behind." Kathy was shaking her head and laughing at the same time.

"I will explain to them exactly what I told you – it's unfair for you to be the only one. But it would be difficult to ask them to do it while I watch ... unless *you* do it first. Then, they won't have any excuses. What do you think?"

Kathy was still shaking her head in disbelief, "I think that Linda's right: You're really perverted. Or, at least, you think of a lot of perverted things." I just stared at her, awaiting her answer. She looked at me, and said, "Yeah, I guess I could do that. Especially, if everyone else will. I'm probably more open than any of them; but it will be a little embarrassing for me, too."

I nodded, "Kathy, that's why I'm talking with you. I'm not going to force anyone to do anything. But your string will be showing, and it seems fair – or at least a good excuse – to ask the other girls to do the same. I guess if they all complain, I could let them get up and go into the bathroom to do it. Actually, all I have to do is spin the Lazy Sam around so they're on the other side from me. Then, I wouldn't see anything. But the whole idea is to provide another submission and openness challenge."

We went into the pool room, and Kathy went into the bathroom to remove her tampon. As the girls stood around talking, I unstrapped the Lazy Sam, and lowered it from the wall to the floor, then centered it in the room. The girls stared ... and stared; finally, Kelly cracked up, laughing riotously. When things calmed down, Kelly looked at me, and said, "Straps?"

I nodded, "First, the turntable needs to be balanced – I don't want it to break, and moving around on it might break it. Second, I don't want to deal with corrective punishment, if people don't hold their position. Third, it will speed-up the game, by ensuring that everyone is ready and in position when their turn comes." Kelly nodded, staring at the contraption I had built.

"If you guys are ready, let's get Kelly into position, first." I pointed to the knee pads, and told Kelly to position her knees there. As she did this, I separated her ankles, and wrapped the Velcro straps around them. Then, I wrapped the Velcro straps of the kneepads behind her knees. She got down on her forearms.

Then, I stood up, next to Kelly's friends, and pointed at Kelly's rear. "This is what I'll be seeing." I looked at them, as they stared at Kelly, "Do any of you think you look that much different? Maybe I should photograph your anogenital areas, and see if you guys can pick out which one is yours?" The girls shook their heads.

"OK, lets get Linda in place next, across from Kelly." Linda got down on her hands and knees on the carpet, and moved herself up and onto the turntable. I strapped her ankles and her knees. It looked like I had made the Lazy Sam just big enough, with about 18" between Kelly's hands and Linda's hands; barely room for the cards and poker chips.

I turned the Lazy Sam 90 degrees and Julie got herself into position. Once everyone knew what to do, it was fast. Then, I spun the Lazy Sam around, and let Kathy get into position. Leaving the turntable in that position, I addressed the girls, taking my time, as I surveyed the four naked bodies, asses up, and breasts hanging down to the turntable. This was going to be fun!

I decided to go one further step. "I'm sure you guys will behave yourselves. As Kelly well knows, the worst thing you can do is reach behind you to rub your bottom while I'm spanking you. As I've told her, what if you reached back while the paddle was coming down? It could break your hands. We don't want anything like that to happen." The girls were silent.

"But just in case one or more of you has a problem with that, I have these Velcro wrist straps. I'll show you what they're like, if I'm forced to use them." With that, I reached over the turntable and strapped the wrists of all the girls, turning the Lazy Sam between each one. Then, I stood up.

"OK, girls. First, I want to thank you for agreeing to play this 'spank poker' game. This will be new for all of us, but I hope you'll have some fun with it. Second, as Kelly pointed out, this is very much about *trust*. You guys are putting your trust into me; for example, so that I won't spank you too hard. But it's far more than that. What if I really were a lecherous old man (I don't consider myself 'old', and I'm certainly not lecherous), and I had tricked you into getting to this point?"

I smiled, "There would be nothing stopping me from having sex with you, even anal sex." The girls were wiggling, but the straps held them in position perfectly.

"Fortunately, I'm a nice person, and can be trusted, as Kelly has learned. It's much more important for me to have your friendship, openness, and trust than anything else, including sex. And, as Kelly told you, I am certainly not going to have sex with any of you; I'm true to Kelly and our relationship."

I was now serious, "And she's true to me. But it's nice that we can both 'play' with others in a sensual way. Perhaps, it's sexual, if you consider mutual masturbation 'sex'."

I turned the Lazy Sam again, reaching over and taking all of the wristbands off the girls. I was glad none of them slapped me, for having scared them for a moment. Now, it was time for the one remaining surprise – at least for most of them.

"Before we start, I do have one more request." Linda and Kelly groaned, and Kathy looked up at the ceiling – as best she could from that position. "You guys have been really great today, being open about nudity, watching my scene with Kelly, and even playing around a little. That was all I could really expect for the day."

I continued, "But I decided to build this thingamajig in the hopes that you might want to play more – and experience a few of the things that Kelly and I have done. I don't expect it to turn you on; in fact, it took Kelly more than half a day to get turned on by getting spanked. You're not going to get a hard enough spanking to really produce the endorphins you would need to 'enjoy' the feeling."

I explained, looking at each girl, in turn, "I'm impressed with all of you. But, in a way, I'm even more impressed with Kathy, who has been as open as any of you – going nude, being massaged, lying on the chaises – even though she is wearing a tampon. And whether or not it was visible before, it will certainly be visible during this game."

Linda snickered, and Julie chuckled. Kelly was staring at me, with a very perplexed look – having absolutely no idea where I was going with this.

"I'm a man, so may not understand ... but I feel sorry for Kathy having her period at this time, and forced to be more open than the rest of you; actually, it's very lucky that two or three of you aren't all at some point in your periods." The girls laughed uneasily. "So I thought it would be a good idea for all of you to wear tampons during this game."

Suddenly there was a howl from three of the girls, and Kathy was laughing. "I could have had you go into the bathroom and put a tampon in before getting you trussed-up on this turntable ... but I thought it would be more interesting – and open of you – if I had you put them in now." Another round of howls. Linda was squealing. Julie was laughing, but shaking her head.

"Then, I realized that it wouldn't be fair, making you put in tampons, while Kathy just left hers in. So I spoke with Kathy, and she agreed to take her tampon out, and put a new one in, also."

Kelly looked next to her, at Kathy, and yelled, "What?!?" Linda groaned loudly.

Kathy shrugged horizontally, and said, "I didn't think it would be fair making just you guys put yours in, in front of Sam, so I volunteered to do it, too." Kathy looked back at me with a very 'turned-on' smile, and said, "Sam's just trying to be fair!" I'm not sure if the girls were thinking about laughing or crying; they were silent, except Linda who was grumbling.

I said, "And Kathy has volunteered to go first." I pulled a tampon from the box, still in its wrapper, and handed it to Kathy. She ripped the wrapper, and took out the tampon, putting her hand under her, and smoothly inserting the device into her vagina, and making sure the string was hanging down, then pulling out the insertion tube.

"Very good!" I said, as Kathy handed me the wrapper and insertion device. I spun the Lazy Sam clockwise, until Kelly was in front of me; or, more precisely, her rear was in front of me. I handed a tampon to Kelly, and she proceeded to insert it.

"I forgot to tell you: Throughout this game, I'll be turning the Lazy Sam clockwise; so the order of the dealing and betting will be counterclockwise." I spun the Lazy Sam another 90 degrees, and Julie was in front of me. I handed her a tampon, and she inserted it quickly, without any fuss.

Finally, I spun the turntable until Linda was in front of me. She whined, "Do I have to?" The other three girls gave her a surprised look.

I responded, "No, Linda. I won't force you. Maybe, I should insert a speculum, and open it a bit, while you play the game?"

Linda shuddered and said "Ugggh!" Then she put her hand back, reaching for the tampon. She opened the package and gave a big sigh. The other girls were watching her, as she reached under, and inserted it. When her hand was in front of her again, she said softly, "Bizarro!"

I turned the Lazy Sam around to Kelly. I gave her the deck of cards, and counted out the chips, handing a stack to each of the girls. Then, I took out the baskets of butt plugs, and put them to the right of each girl. Finally, I took out the thermometers and KY, and announced, "Now, you'll ante up for the first hand. The ante this time will be the rectal thermometer. I'll start with Kelly." I lubed the first thermometer, and quickly inserted it into Kelly. I moved it around a little, while Kelly smiled at her friends.

Then, I turned to Julie, who took the thermometer without making a peep. I moved it around, and in and out for about 30 seconds before turning to Linda. When I touched the tip of the thermometer to Linda's anus, she clenched tightly; I held it there until she was able to relax herself sufficiently.

Then, I slowly pushed the thermometer in, moving it in wide circles, left-right, up-down, and finally slowly pulling it completely out before plunging it back in. Linda was cooperative, but she was groaning, her head on the turntable.

I said, "It doesn't hurt; you know it's not a big deal!"

Linda picked her head up off the board, and replied, "The big deal is picturing you back there, seeing what you're seeing, and inserting it." The other girls laughed.

I said, seriously, "Linda, I thought you would be pretty comfortable by now with me seeing your body." She didn't respond, just kept groaning. I followed-up, "At least, you don't have hemorrhoids!" Linda's groan turned into a gurgle, and the other girls laughed uproariously.

Finally, I turned the table to Kathy, who took the thermometer very well. I decided that it *would* be a good idea to photograph the girls – nothing recognizable, that was the point; just from their upper thighs to their waists, and including their hips on each side. I had stashed a small pocket digital camera in the box, and spun them around, snapping pictures of their rear ends. And their genitals.

With the turntable turned back to Kelly, I told everyone to put a chip on the table, and then I asked Kelly to deal the cards. I then gave everyone a 5-pack of needles, and told them to rip one off and hand it to me for each increase in the bet. Everyone looked at their card hands, I turned the table so that Julie was in front of me, and said, "Your bet, Julie."

Julie said, "I'll 'check' – won't increase the bet." I knew that could happen with the first person betting each hand. I turned to Linda.

"I call." I wasn't sure if that could be done, but a quick search on my tablet showed that everyone could 'check' on the first round ... but then, everyone would have to put up another ante. I informed the girls of this, and said the next ante would be a needle in each side.

That motivated some betting; when I turned to Kathy, she raised by one, tore off a needle, and handed it back to me. I swabbed her left hip, and inserted the needle quickly. Kathy emitted a quiet 'Ow', but didn't complain.

Then, I moved the table to Kelly. She looked at her hand, and said, "I'll raise by 2." I heard a groan from Linda. Kelly handed me three needles, and I inserted them, one by one, alternating sides. Then, I turned the table to Julie.

"Well, I guess I'll raise by one." She handed me four needles, and I inserted them. I didn't give any warning when I was going to insert a needle, and Julie was quiet throughout. When I was finished, Julie tilted her head back, and said, "Thank you, Sam." The girls were doing great.

I turned to Linda, and she groaned, "Should I call, or fold?" I told her to look in the small basket next to her.

When she had surveyed the range of butt plugs and vibrators, she groaned again, and said, "OK, I call." I swabbed both of her buttocks, and inserted the first needle on the left side. Linda emitted a brief squeal, and then groaned again. I inserted the other three needles, alternating sides, Linda groaning louder each time.

Finally, I was back to Kathy. She glanced to her left at Linda, and said, "I'll raise by 4." Linda howled like a wolf, Julie shook her head, and Kelly cracked up.

Then, Kathy said, "No. I guess I'll call." Now everyone was laughing. That was pretty good, considering that most of them had four needles in their butt. Kathy handed me three needles, and I inserted them quickly.

When I turned the table to Kelly, she was laughing as she said, "Well, giving consideration to Linda ... I'll call, also."

Now, the girls threw one to three cards onto the board, and Kelly dealt the new cards. I turned the table to Julie again. She smiled, and said, "I'll raise by one." I was surprised, but looking over Julie's shoulder, I could see that she had two pair. I inserted one more needle into her left hip.

I turned to Linda, and she quickly said, "Call." And, just as quickly, I inserted another needle in her bottom.

Turning to Kathy, she also quickly said, "I call." I inserted another needle, and turned to Kelly.

"I know you guys would like to get done with this round, so I'll call, also. Let's see everyone's cards." The girls put their cards on the table, Julie winning with her two pair. The girls had put up a chip to represent each needle, and Julie pulled the pile of chips to herself. I turned to her, and took out the needles, dropping them in a sharps container by my side. Quickly, I rotated the table, and pulled all the needles out of each girl in turn, ending with Kelly.

I said, "So that's the first round."

The girls were stirring, and Linda said, "Didn't you forget something?"

The girls laughed, and I said, "Oh! You want the thermometer out, too? OK." I pulled Kelly's thermometer out, putting it on a paper towel by my other side. Then, I turned the Lazy Sam, and wiggled each thermometer before taking it out.

Like a circus barker, I bellowed, "Next hand!" This time, the ante will be ten spanks with my hand. Each bet will be another six spanks. That should start getting your bottoms warmed up for the more serious implements." Kelly gave the deck of cards to Julie, and I turned the table to Linda. "Are you ready, Linda."

Unenthusiastically, Linda responded, "Yeah, I guess." I put my hand on her left buttock, then pulled it back, and began spanking her with medium strokes at about one per second, alternating sides. Other than a quick gasp after the first spank, Linda was silent. Her ante was up in ten seconds.

I turned the table to Kathy, and put my hand on her bottom. "Ready?"

Kathy quickly responded, "Yes, Sir." I administered her spanking, after which Kathy wiggled her bottom back and forth a few times. She was a cute girl; very enthusiastic, and as open as Kelly, Julie and Linda had said.

Finally, I turned to Kelly. I leaned over and whispered, "Yours will be a little harder." Then, I gave Kelly her spanking – more intense than the others, but not taking much longer, perhaps 15 seconds. Finally, I finished with Julie. Everyone put a chip on the table to match their ante.

Julie dealt the cards, and everyone looked at their hands. I said, "Linda, you have the first bet." Linda looked at her cards and smiled, "I guess I'll raise by two." The other girls looked up at her, wondering whether she had an incredible hand, or was trying to bluff. I reminded Linda that raising by two would mean another dozen spanks.

Linda said she understood. So I stood behind her, rubbed her bottom for a few seconds, and then proceeded to give her a dozen medium spanks. They probably took 30 seconds, and Linda rocked a little and groaned a couple of times, but behaved herself well. I turned the table to Kathy, and she said, "I call." When she was ready, I gave her twelve spanks.

Now, it was Kelly's turn. She smiled, and said, "I'll raise one." The other girls groaned. I told Kelly, "Please ask me for your spanking, when you're ready." I put my hand on her bottom.

A few seconds later, Kelly said, "I'm ready for my spanking, now, Sir."

I immediately began her spanking, giving her medium-hard swats, and taking nearly a minute to dole out the 18 spanks. Kelly grunted on a couple of the last spanks, but provided a great example to her friends.

Finally, I turned to Julie, who groaned, "I'm going to have to fold." Now all eyes were on her. July put her cards face down on the table. Now, she asked, "OK. What do I have to do?"

I smiled, "Pick out one of the devices in the basket. You'll find butt plugs of many shapes and sizes, and different materials, including glass. I suggest you start with the smallest sizes. Also in the basket are a couple of exam gloves. If you select one of those, I'll put it on, and lubricate your anus and rectum with my finger. It would be a good idea to choose that before trying any of the larger butt plugs. Whatever you select – except my finger – will stay in you until the hand is over."

Julie looked in the basket, and picked the smallest device, a bullet-shaped black butt plug that was only about ¾" in diameter, and six inches long. As with all the butt plugs, it tapered to a waist, where her anus would be located, and at the very end was a thin disk of polymer, about 1 ½" in diameter.

She handed it to me, and I lubed it, and pressed it against her anus. She flinched a little, but quickly relaxed her muscles, and the butt plug advanced into her, until the small waist passed through her anus, and the large disk was pressed against it. I pulled it out about half way, and moved it in and out a few more times, before pushing it all the way in. Julie did a good job of relaxing, as I was playing with the intruder in her rear.

Julie looked at her friends, and said, in an unnaturally high-pitched voice, "So, *what* did we do at Kelly's birthday party?!:!!?" Everyone laughed; it *was* funny.

I turned the table to Linda, "Next bet."

Linda looked at her cards and nodded her head, "I'll raise by one." Kathy was now the one who whined, "Linda!"

Linda smiled, and tilted her head back to me. "I'm ready, Sam." I gave her another six spanks – a little lighter than before. I was proud of Linda for being so open and so brave. Linda didn't make a sound as I spanked her, or afterward. She was looking to her right at Kathy, who now had to make a decision.

Kathy croaked, "Well, if it's only another six spanks, I guess I'll call." She looked at Kelly with a menacing glare and said, "But if Kelly raises, I'm going to have to fold."

I had a feeling that Kelly would be easy on her; she didn't want to be mean to her guests. And, by now, both Kelly and I had realized that there would likely be more opportunities to 'play' with her friends, now that we knew that they were open to the idea. Kathy said, "Ready." And I gave her six medium spanks very quickly. She squealed at the end, and wiggled her bottom, but didn't complain.

Now, I turned the table to Kelly. She looked at Kathy and said, "I'm sorry, Kathy. But Linda must have a good hand, and I want to see how far she'll go to bet it." Kathy dropped her head to the table. Linda was staring at Kelly.

Kelly laughed, and said, "OK, Linda. Instead of going round-and-round, let's make a deal. I'll let you win, but not until you take a lot more spanks. Because I have a good hand, too." Kelly looked into Linda's eyes, and said, "How many more spanks will you take to win this hand?"

Linda's mouth had dropped open, "That's not how you play poker!" She looked down, and then back up to Kelly, "How about another 30?" I think we were all dumbfounded.

But Kelly couldn't leave well enough alone: "We'll each take another forty, then Kathy can fold, then I'll fold." Kelly looked at Kathy, "At least the butt plugs won't be in long." That was true. But they probably weren't realizing that it would use up a size, and the next 'fold' would require using a bigger plug.

I smiled, "Does everyone agree? It *is* a strange way to play poker ... but I guess it's efficient." Everyone nodded, so I stood behind Kelly and said, "OK, young lady, you're going to get another forty spanks!" I spanked Kelly, alternating sides for about a minute, increasing the intensity towards the end. The last ten spanks or so were zingers. I should have remembered to wear a leather glove! But I liked the skin-on-skin feel of a good, old-fashioned, bare-bottom hand spanking.

The Lazy Sam rotated again, and now Linda's rear was facing me. She, somewhat dejectedly, said, "Ready." I spanked her exactly as I had spanked Kelly, even increasing the intensity at the end. There were several 'Oooo's' and 'Aaahh's', and Linda was actually whimpering at the end.

I leaned over her, and whispered in her ear, "Good job, Linda!"

Then, I turned the table again, and Kathy rummaged in the basked, pulling out the same type of butt plug as Julie had in her right now. Wordlessly, she handed it to me, and I lubed it. "I'm going to touch it to your anus now." and I did so, letting Kathy flinch, as anticipated.

"And now I'm going to move it slowly in and out, while you relax your muscles. When you're ready, say 'ready' and give a little push. Then, the butt plug will go in easier." I kept light pressure on the plug – and it slid in nearly an inch – until Kathy said 'ready', and I saw her anus dilate.

I pushed the butt plug, until the disk was against her. Kathy gasped, and I could hear her panting, but she didn't say a thing. As I had with the others, I pulled the plug out about halfway, and moved it slowly in and out a couple of inches, finally pushing it back into place.

As I rotated the table, Kelly put her cards on the table, and said, "I fold." Then, she smiled sweetly at me. My heart melted, again. I didn't want to show favoritism during the game, but leaned over, and kissed Kelly's cheek. Kelly handed me the same plug, and I went through the same procedure, Kelly taking it in stride, as expected.

Julie stammered, "OK, Linda, what do you have?"

Linda proudly displayed her cards, and said, "Full house! Queens over Jacks."

The girls shook their heads. I was surprised that nobody asked to see Kelly's hand, but they must have known that she wouldn't share it with them. I turned the Lazy Sam to Julie, and asked, unnecessarily, "Are you ready for the butt plug to come out, Julie?"

Julie snorted, "What do *you* think? Of course!" She looked up at her friends, "I don't mind the feel of anal, but it gets annoying, if it's in too long." Kelly, Linda, and Kathy laughed. I did, too. I asked her to give a little push, and I pulled the plug out, depositing it on the paper towel. Then, I rotated the table to Kathy.

"Well, Kathy, that was a pretty short rectal insertion. I'll have to play with it a little, before it comes out." Kathy groaned, but didn't argue. I asked her to give a push, and I pulled the plug nearly out, and then pushed it back in slowly, repeating this several times, before pulling it out entirely. I said, "You did very well, Kathy. It wasn't really so bad, was it?" Kathy just gave me a 'harrumph'.

Then, I rotated the Lazy Sam to Kelly, and as she pushed, I pulled the plug out. As with Kathy, I did a few in's-and-out's before taking it out completely. Then, I stood, surveying the four poker players, and said, "Next, the Ping Pong paddle. The ante is one on each side, and the minimum bet is one swat." The girls groaned again. I suggested, "I'm going to give you the ante's very quickly; you'll all be ante'd up in less than a minute. Prepare yourselves." Optimistic thinking.

I picked up the smooth Ping Pong paddle, and turned the table so that I was facing Kathy's rear. She flinched when she felt the paddle on her left butt cheek. I swung, and the paddle cracked against her skin. Kathy shrieked. Then, I put it against her right buttock, and swung again. It was as hard a swat, but this time, Kathy controlled herself, and just grunted. Then, she turned her head to me, and said, "That really hurts!"

I chuckled, "We're only on the third of ten implements. And they get much harder than this."

That was the breaking point. Both Kathy and Linda looked at Kelly, and pleaded, "Kelly!"

Kelly looked me and shrugged. She suggested, "How about if we only do one more implement?" She was looking around at her friends, who had broad smiles, and were nodding vigorously.

I sounded reluctant, when I said, "OK." But actually, I was amazed that the girls had done so well. I think they had gotten a little 'feeling' for what Kelly had experienced over the past couple of months.

In a serious and annoyed tone, I asked, "Can we continue your ante's, now?" The girls nodded, without enthusiasm, and I decided to finish up quickly. I rotated the table to Kelly, and quickly gave her a hard swat on each side. Then, the table turned to Julie, and she got the same – just as hard as Kelly's had been. She emitted a long 'Oooowoww', after receiving the second swat.

Then, the table turned to Linda. I took a little more time, but gave her swats that were nearly as hard as Julie's and Kelly's had been. She squeaked a short 'Ow!' after each stroke, but I was sure she could have taken much more.

Linda dealt the cards, and Kathy started the bidding, "I'll hold." She glanced up, and the other girls laughed.

I turned the table to Kelly, who smiled deviously, and said, "I'll raise by four!" I couldn't see her cards, but either she had a great hand, or she was a great bluffer. Knowing her, it could have been either. I stood behind her, and gave her four measured swats – two on each side – with the paddle, about one every five seconds. Then, I turned the table to Julie.

Julie looked at Kelly, and shook her head, "I guess I'll call." I gave Julie her four strokes of the paddle, and she was whining by the time the sound of the last swat died. Julie reached back with both hands, and rubbed her bottom, pulling her buttocks with each hand – which had the effect of separating them even more – and massaging them.

I turned the table to Linda. She coughed, put her cards face-down on the table, and said, "I fold." She rummaged in the basket, then whimpered a little. After a few long moments, she handed me the glove. I was surprised, as there was at least one more relatively small butt plug in the basket. But I didn't argue.

I pulled on the size 7 glove, a bit tight for my hands, and squeezed a dollop of KY onto the middle finger of my right hand. I leaned around Linda, and said quietly, "Are you ready, now?"

Linda nodded, "Yes, Sir." She wagged her bottom a tiny bit. At that moment, I noticed that her labia were glistening, and now separated, the white string of the unnecessary tampon still hanging down from her. I put my finger on her anus, not waiting for a flinch, but pushing it in to my first knuckle. Leaving it at that depth, I rotated my hand, feeling around just inside Linda's anus.

Then, I advanced it further, rotating, pushing, pulling back, and rotating the other way. After a minute or so, my finger was in her as far as it would go, my knuckles tight against her bottom. I moved my finger around inside her, angled my hand, so that pressure was put in different directions on her soft tissues, and moved in and out, sliding easily with both my finger and her rectum fully lubricated.

I tried to look around Linda, to see if her hands were in front of her face. I couldn't see, but when I glanced at Kelly, she closed her eyes, pointed at them, and then pointed at Linda. OK! Maybe Linda was actually enjoying the experience of my finger being in her.

I moved my finger slowly, sensually, through her rear passage, flicking the tip of my finger, rotating it, and finally taking it out, but teasing her rosebud; then – one more time – pushing it deeply into her. I asked Linda, "How does that feel?"

Linda seemed to be in another dimension, as she answered, almost dreamily, "It feels OK." Really? I looked closely, and she was now dripping; even the tampon string had a large drop ready to fall, as Linda feigned indifference to the feel of my finger. I leaned over Linda, and whispered, "May I?" I said this, as I reached underneath, cupping her vulva in my palm of my left hand, putting rhythmic and circular pressure on her clit hood.

Linda said, "Mmm hmm." I could tell that her eyes were still closed. I had been ready to take my finger out of her ... but she was actually enjoying it!

My right middle finger continued to move inside her, as my left hand morphed its motions ... very slowly ... fingers settling into the space between her labia; finger tips now under her hood, gracefully gliding along the sides of her clit; and the middle finger of my right hand deep inside her rectum, moving slowly, coordinated with the motions of my left hand.

Linda was swaying – very slowly, almost unnoticeably – and I knew she was enjoying the sensual feelings her body was receiving at that instant. I marveled that she could turn off the outside world, and get into herself, feeling the energy in her core, and appreciate the sensations of touch, if not sight, sound, or smell.

I wasn't sure how far to take it ... but I wasn't about to suddenly stop, unless Linda directed me to, or took over herself. But she seemed contented, just enjoying the feel. She must have been really wet for drops to be seen, even wearing a tampon. She was swaying gently, very little, really, but in a rhythmic pattern that mirrored the motions of my hands and fingers.

I realized that I hadn't looked up to see the reactions of the other girls ... and I decided not to look up now. Linda and I were – somehow – connecting, and she was being incredibly open. Something, I would not have expected, but had hoped for.

Kelly's friends were nice people. They were really trying hard, today. And Kelly and I weren't making it that easy on them. But this was going to be the last of the 'challenging' experiences. At least, as far as I had planned to this point.

Linda's motions increased, as I continued moving my distal appendages against her sensitive tissues. As I increased my pressure on her clit, now moving my fingers up and over, up and over, up and over ... I slowly pulled my finger out of her rear; almost out. And, finally, completely out, but moving against her anus, threatening a re-insertion, but teasing, tickling, and moving rhythmically in synchrony with the fingers of my left hand under her.

It seemed to be taking a long time – it was as if time were suspended. It probably *was* a good five minutes; which is an eternity, when people are holding their breath, watching a spectacle that they had never expected to witness.

Finally, Linda arched, she shook, and she tensed, as her pelvic muscles contracted. I knew not to over-stimulate her, and eased-off on the clitoral stimulation, but kept my right finger on her anus, occasionally pushing it into her up to my knuckle. Linda began, but then inhibited, a squeal, and her orgasm came in a series of grunts, and sounds that were close to purrs.

She calmed, and I released the pressure of my hand under her – but still kept my hand in intimate contact with her, and took the finger of my right hand off her anus. Linda sighed, and – I imagined – opened her eyes. I could see the other girls staring at her, open mouthed, perhaps holding their breaths: Stunned.

Finally, Julie spoke up, "That was really hot, Linda!" I think Julie was truly happy for her. Linda looked down to the table, saying nothing in response.

I took off the glove, putting it in the paper towel, and carried everything to the bathroom sink. I washed the thermometers and butt plugs, and disposed of the glove and paper towel. I put the cleaned items back in the box, and said, "Where were we? Oh, yes, Linda called." I looked at Kathy, "It's your turn now, Kathy." I heard a very quiet 'Great!'.

Finally, Kathy said, "OK ... I'll call."

I stood behind Kathy, and placed the Ping Pong paddle on her left buttock. I held it there. Kathy looked back, and I heard a very faint 'ready'. I gave Kathy four strokes – light strokes – alternating sides; but still, she shook, and I heard at least one 'Ugggh', a couple of "Oowww's", and an 'Aaaaahh!".

I knew that Kathy – her parents being hippies – had never been spanked at home. Of course, that subject was very controversial; I was glad my two sons were already grown! But Kathy's background showed, as she easily accepted normally embarrassing situations, but balked at a few swats with a thin paddle.

I rotated the table so that Kelly's butt was staring me in the face, and I said, loudly, "Next bet!"

Kelly laughed, and said, "I'll call." Then, Kelly looked back at me, and said, "Sam, even *I'm* getting a little bored with this." I nodded. Then, I gave Kelly four hard swats on her bottom, reddening both cheeks.

I turned to Julie, and she said, "I'll call." I could see that she had scrunched her face, her eyes tightly closed. I stood behind her, and gave her four solid swats.

Standing, I commanded, "Show your cards!" The girls put down their hands, and Kelly had won with three-of-a-kind, all Kings. I knew Kelly could have easily forced the other girls to take more swats on their bare bottom, or be subjected to an embarrassing rectal insertion.

The Lazy Sam turned, and I announced, "Well, I guess we're on the last hand, now. The implement will be the tawse ... and I'll give you light-to-medium strokes. Is everyone ready to ante up?" There was general grumbling, but the girls nodded.

I turned the table until Kelly was in front of me, then I stood and placed the tawse across her bottom. Kelly gave me a quiet 'ready', and I gave her two medium strokes of the tawse. She let out an 'Aaaahh' after the first stroke, and grunted after the second one.

I turned the table to Julie and, when she said 'ready', I gave her two strokes. She let out a loud 'Ow!' after each stroke, and then started laughing. "That thing *really* hurts!"

I agreed, "Yes, this can be a severe implement ... but I'm only giving you guys light strokes with it." Julie shook her head.

Then, I turned the table to Linda, and gave her two strokes of the tawse. She whined 'Oooowww' after each stroke. Finally, I turned to Kathy, who immediately said 'ready', and I quickly tawsed her bare bottom. After the first stroke, she yelled 'Aiyeeee!' and after the second stroke, she looked up at Kelly, and asked, "So you actually *like* to be spanked like this?"

Kelly laughed, "As Sam said, you guys aren't getting enough spanks to produce the endorphins that will dull the pain. And, yes, the spanks always hurt."

Now Kathy shook her head. Although they were very good sports playing the 'spank poker' game, the girls still wouldn't understand the potential 'turn on' of being spanked, except perhaps Linda.

Linda dealt the cards, and Kelly looked at her friends, and said, "I'll hold."

Julie's turn was next, but she kept looking at her cards. Finally, she tilted her head back, and said, "I'll raise by two." There was a gasp from Kathy. I gave Julie her two strokes, and turned the table to Linda.

Linda threw her cards down on the table, saying, "I fold!" I didn't say anything. Linda looked through the basket, and handed me a glass butt plug, one of the larger ones, with bumps along the sides. I lubed it, and pressed it against her anus. Linda sighed, and gave a push, allowing me to insert the plug; it repeatedly dilated her anus, as the bumps passed into her.

She didn't make a sound, but I could see that she was holding her hands in front of her face. When the plug was mostly inside her, I pulled it back out most of the way, and plunged it in again. After three ins-and-outs, I pushed the plug all the way in, and Linda gasped when it sucked in, placing the thin neck in position for her anal muscles to hold it.

I turned the table again, and Kathy also folded. I guess the tawse was just too scary for them; they had already been through a lot, but none of their bottoms were very red. I wondered which insertion Kathy would select, and was a little surprised when she handed me the latex glove.

I put it on, lubed the middle finger, and inserted it into Kathy's rectum unceremoniously. She gasped once, but remained calm, as I moved my finger around, and moved it in and out of her. My finger was in her less than a minute, when I decided to give her a break, and take it out. "That wasn't such a big deal, was it?"

Kathy sniffed a couple of times, and replied, "It reminds me why I don't like anal sex." The other girls laughed. Then they discarded their worst cards, and Kathy dealt replacements.

Kelly looked at her hand, and said, "I'll raise two more." I was a little surprised, but guessed that she was challenging Julie. I gave her two medium-hard strokes, and she dropped her head and groaned after the second one. Then, I rotated the Lazy Sam to Julie, who was shaking her head. Finally, she said, "OK. I'll call." I gave Julie two medium strokes of the tawse, and she was sniveling by the time the second one was finished.

Julie and Kelly showed their hands to each other: Julie exclaimed "Full house! Tens over eights."

Kelly laughed, and proudly announced, "I have four of a kind – sixes!" So Kelly took the pile of chips, and clapped her hands in victory.

I decided to offer one more possibility, "The game is over ... but if any of you want to earn more chips, you can volunteer to feel any of these other implements." I held up the hairbrush, the wooden spoon, and a thin switch. But before I could offer ten chips for trying any one of them, the girls were shaking their heads.

Kelly spoke up, "Sam, I think we're finished with this, now."

I nodded, "OK." I went to the closet and found a thin plastic bag, of the type markets use, and sat behind Kelly. Opening up the bag between her legs, and without warning, I pulled on the tampon string, the partially expanded device falling into the bag. Then I turned the table to Julie. She didn't comment, so I pulled her tampon out, also. She laughed nervously, "Well, that's the first time ... and probably the last time, that anyone has taken a tampon out of me!"

As I turned the table to Linda, she pleaded, "Sam, please let me take it out myself. In the bathroom."

The girls laughed, but I acquiesced, "Sure, Linda. You've done very well." I looked around the table, and said, "You've all been good sports. Sorry if the game turned out to not be very exciting for you." I began undoing the Velcro straps around the back of each girl's knees and ankles, turning the Lazy Sam, as each girl was released.

I suggested, "Let's have Kathy and Julie get off the turntable first." They awkwardly crawled backwards onto the carpet, and then stood up. Then, Linda and Kelly did the same. I lifted the Lazy Sam so it was vertical, against the wall again, and fastened the straps. Linda headed to the bathroom to take out her tampon.

I was about to put the box of supplies back in the closet, when Kelly announced, "Now, Sam is going to let us stick him with some needles." I had, unrealistically, hoped that perhaps Kelly would have forgotten about this part.

Looking at Kelly, I said, reluctantly, "OK. What do you want me to do?"

Kelly replied, "Get up on the massage table, please." She took the box from me, and we walked over to the massage table. I took the dress and pirate costume off the table, and dropped them underneath. Then, I climbed onto the table, lying on my stomach, and tried to relax.

Sam had really pushed my friends. And they had done very well – getting stuck with needles, taking rectal insertions, and being spanked with several implements. I was surprised they had made it that far; pushing them any more would not have been beneficial.

When Sam was in place on the massage table, I pulled two 5-packs of hypodermic needles from the box, along with a couple of alcohol swabs, and a gauze pad. I opened the swabs, and cleaned both of Sam's buttocks. Then, I opened two of the needles, as Julie, Linda and Kathy stepped up to the table, watching closely.

"I'm not going to actually teach you anything today; if you really want to do this safely, you'll have to learn how to find the injection site and, if you want to actually give injections, you'll need to learn how to assemble the shot, load the saline, and check for blood.

I looked at the two capped needles in my hand, and decided that Sam deserved to get a couple of injections, along with the needle sticks that my friends would be doing. I pulled out two 10cc syringes, attached the needles, and drew out 3cc of saline into each one. Then, I carefully re-capped the needles, and put them down on Sam's back.

It would also be easier for my friends to insert needles, if they were attached to syringes, so I unwrapped six small 3cc syringes, and attached the capped needles to them, lining them up along Sam's back.

Sam lifted his head, and asked, "What are you doing?"

I laughed, and told Sam to put his head back down, and trust me. Which I'm sure he did.

With Kathy next to me, and Julie and Linda on the other side of the table, I picked up one of the large shots, and uncapped the needle. Even though they had seen these needles earlier, Linda and Kathy both gasped; the needle really did look long, although it was the standard size for giving intramuscular injections.

I reached across Sam, and held the skin of his butt taut. Then, I explained, "The insertion is very easy: You just hold the needle an inch or two above his skin, hold the skin taut with your other hand, and then quickly dart the needle straight into Sam's butt." Without further ado, I inserted the needle, which slid in smoothly up to the hub. There were another couple of gasps, but Sam was silent.

I let go of the syringe, and let it stick out of Sam's butt by itself. I tapped the side of the syringe a couple of times, and it swayed back and forth. "See, it's easy. You don't want to 'poke' him, or pull the needle back out. Just take your time, and make sure the needle is pushed all the way in, like this." Julie and Linda were nodding.

I decided that a further demonstration would be appropriate. "Sam, I'm going to do a slow insertion on the other side." Sam started to whine, but quieted immediately, probably not wanting my friends to think he was a wuss.

I picked up the other shot, and uncapped the needle. Holding the skin of Sam's left buttock taut, I glanced up at my friends. "I want you guys to try to do a fast insertion, like I just did. But now, I'm going to show you what it looks like, if you push the needle in slowly. This will hurt Sam a little more. I lowered the needle until it was nearly touching Sam's butt, then slowly pushed.

Sam's skin indented before the needle popped through. Sam groaned. I let go of that syringe also, stepping back, and looking at the two large tubes standing nearly straight up from Sam's butt. Linda was shaking her head.

I told Sam, "I was going to let the girls try their hand at a couple of insertions, while these needles are in ... but I think I'm going to inject you now, and take these out to give them more room to play." I heard a tired, 'Ummm hmmm' from Sam.

Reaching over to the syringe sticking out of Sam's right butt, I pulled back on the plunger to check for blood, and then slowly injected the 3cc into his bottom. I looked at my friends and smiled, "That's all there is to it." Being nice to Sam, I pulled the needle out, and bent down to drop the whole thing in the sharps container. Then, I set the sharps box between Sam's legs.

Next, I injected Sam on the left side. When he was fully injected, but before I had taken out the needle, I asked, "Any questions?" The girls chuckled, but evidently there were no questions, so I pulled the needle out, and dumped the syringe in the sharps container. There was a small dot of blood where the second needle came out, so I opened the gauze pad, and held it on that area for a moment.

Looking at my friends, I said, "Now it's your turn! Each of you will insert two needles, one on Sam's left side and the other on the right. Take your time, and try to insert the needle all the way in one smooth motion. I've already swabbed his bottom, so there's nothing else to do.

I handed one of the syringe-needle sets to each of my friends. Linda's eyes were large, as she stared at the shot in her hand. I said, "Don't worry about each other; two of you can be inserting needles at the same time. And, here's how to uncap those needles safely."

I took one of the syringes from Kathy, and showed them how to hold the syringe while carefully putting pressure on the cap, until it slid off the needle. "If you get stuck by the needle, let me know, and we'll dispose it and get another one."

Julie didn't waste any time, as she uncapped the needle and leaned over Sam. I pointed out the area on each side where the needles should be inserted. Julie shrugged, and spread Sam's skin between the fingers of her left hand, while she held the shot with her right; it was shaking slightly. Finally, Julie took a deep breath, and plunged the needle into Sam's bottom; it went all the way in, and Julie looked up at me with a smile. "That wasn't so hard!"

I moved over, so Kathy had access to Sam's left butt. She slowly followed the steps, jabbing Sam with the needle. Sam emitted a quiet 'Ow'. The needle had only gone in about half way, so I told Kathy to push it the rest of the way in. Sam said 'Ow' again.

Now, it was Linda's turn. She picked a location about two inches from the shot that Julie had given, the small syringe still sticking out of Sam's butt. She looked serious, and concentrated, as she prepared to insert the needle. Finally, she darted it in perfectly. Now, Sam had three syringes sticking out of him.

I suggested that we all change sides, and then Julie picked up another syringe, and proceeded to uncap the needle, hold Sam's skin, and do the insertion, as if she had been doing it for years. Then, Kathy took her turn. She did much better the second time, with a more forceful insertion that went all the way in. Finally, Linda inserted the last needle into Sam's left side.

My friends stood there, all staring at Sam's butt, with the three syringes in each buttock looking like thin trees on a mountainside. I clapped, "Very good! Let's leave these in for a while." Sam predictably groaned, but didn't complain; he had left the needles in all of us for several minutes during our so-called 'spank poker' game.

I looked around at Julie, Linda, and Kathy, and asked, "So what do you think?"

Linda chuckled, and said, "I like giving shots a lot more than receiving them!" We all laughed. Even Sam. As he laughed, his bottom wiggled, and now it looked like the trees on the hillsides of his butt were bending to a high wind.

I decided to show them one more thing, and pulled each of the needles out about a quarter of an inch. The small syringes stayed vertical, but we could now see the gleaming stainless steel shaft of each needle, as it entered Sam's skin.

"OK, let's take them out, now. One by one." Kathy pulled one of the needles out, and I held the sharps container so that she could drop the syringe in. Taking turns, my friends pulled out all of the needles. I swabbed Sam's butt with alcohol again, and then rubbed it with the gauze pad. "OK, Sam, you're done." Sam sighed, as he rolled off the massage table, and stood next to us.

Sam looked around at us, and asked, "So was that interesting for you guys?"

The girls nodded, but Kathy said, "It was OK. But I didn't get turned on by it, in the least."

It was Linda who disagreed, "Well, I thought it was pretty hot. Just the fact that Sam submitted to us, and trusted us to not hurt him – too much – got me a little horny." Julie was shocked, "Again? You had an orgasm less than 30 minutes ago." Linda just shrugged.

Sam took the box of supplies, and stashed it in the pool room closet, and took out a step ladder, asking for our help to take down the 'pirate ship'. As three of us held the mast, Sam climbed up and uncleated the lines going to the house and the two trees. Then, he helped lift the mast out of the pipe, and we laid it carefully down on the grass.

Sam untied a few knots, and folded the booms along the mast, and then lashed them in place. We all lifted the contraption, and walked it behind the garage. As we walked back to the patio, Sam pulled me aside, and kissed me. Then, he suggested that we go in the sauna for a while, and get showered. While we girls dressed for dinner, Sam would start the barbeque.

We cleaned up the patio table, and dropped our pareos in the boxes Sam had set out for each of us in the pool room. Then, we all traipsed downstairs – five naked bodies in a row, and turned into the bathroom.

CHAPTER 15: HOT SAUNA, HOT WOMEN

We weren't all even in the bathroom yet, but Julie had already sat on the toilet. As Sam and I entered, she said, "I had to go." Sam continued into the shower room, and played with the sauna controls that were on the far wall, next to the smoked glass door.

I stepped under the shower, and started turning the faucets – for the huge rain shower, and for the various leg jets. Linda stood in the middle of the shower room, looking around, and commented, "This is a pretty neat set-up. I love saunas!"

Sam, Linda and I got under the rain jet, while Julie finished up, and Kathy sat down to take out her tampon. I soaped-up Sam, and then turned to Linda. She smiled, and turned around, as I washed her back.

As I was doing this, Sam picked up the soap and, standing in front of Linda, looked at her, held up the soap, and asked, "May I?" Linda nodded, and Sam soaped Linda's front as I worked on her back. He seemed to spend a long time washing Linda's large breasts, but apparently Linda didn't mind.

As I got down to Linda's bottom, I made a gesture to Sam, and he smiled and nodded. I slipped my soapy finger deep into Linda's rear. Linda jumped a little, and then chuckled. Then, Sam slipped a finger inside her, in front. We both did a few ins and outs, and then took our fingers out of her, continuing down her body; around her thighs, along her legs, and down to her feet. Sam washed Linda's feet, massaging her insole and each of her toes. Linda's eyes were closed, and she was nearly purring with contentment.

By this time, Julie and Kathy came into the shower room, and squeezed under the rain shower with us. I gave my soap to Linda, who began washing Julie, as Sam bathed Kathy. We all switched off, bathing each other, and Sam reminded us that this was just a pre-sauna 'rinse'; we would be taking real showers afterwards, before we dressed for dinner.

Sam stepped out of the shower, and watched the four girls bathing each other. We had never done this: Such a simple thing, but so intimate; and so much fun!

As we finished our 'quick' showers, Sam pulled five towels from the shelf, handing one to each of us. He asked, jovially, "Everybody ready for the sauna, now?" We all nodded, and Sam opened the glass door, and led us inside the warm, dark space, illuminated by a single red bulb.

He showed everyone how to lay out their towel, and pointed out the sand dials, and the wedge that would support the head of anyone lying down. There was some scuffling, as we all found our places. Sam sat in the corner cross-legged, watching with amusement, as my friends arranged their towels, and finally sat down. I glanced at the thermometer on the wall, and noted that the temperature was already 180 degrees.

We all sat quietly, letting the thick air envelop us. The sauna wasn't so large when there were five people inside. We all sat on the top bench, next to each other; there wasn't much room to move around. After a few minutes, Sam stepped down, and poured some water on the coals with the wooden ladle.

He looked at me, and said, "I need to refill this bucket, and I better get some icewater and cups for everyone. I'll set everything on the round table by the chaises." I nodded, and Sam left the sauna, pulling the door open only as far as necessary for him to squeeze through; then, he closed the door quickly, and it was now just us females in the sauna.

I looked at my friends, and said, apologetically, "I'm sorry, if Sam has been pushing you guys too hard. He loves to challenge people – especially with openness, pain, and new experiences – and see their reactions. You guys did very well with that crazy 'spank poker' game; I'm sure that Sam was impressed."

I looked at Linda, "He *does* think of some pretty perverted things! But you have to admit, they're also very creative." I smiled at her, "And sometimes they're a turn-on. It was too dark to tell if Linda was blushing.

My friends nodded, and Linda said, "The spanking was one thing. But to stick us with needles ... AND stick things up our butts ..." We all laughed, thinking of the scene that Sam had orchestrated.

Then, Linda added to Kathy's comments, "... AND make us put in tampons while he watched ..." Linda looked at me seriously, "Sam really is perverted, you know. How does he come up with all this stuff?" I reminded her that she had asked that before. We were all laughing, again.

I tried to answer Linda, "I don't know. Some of it comes from things he's seen on the Internet; and others come directly out of his perverted brain."

I took a deep breath, "And, now you can see how my visits here have gone: They've been a whirlwind of bizarre experiences, mixed in with some very nice experiences. By the end of each day, or weekend, I am amazed at all the things we've done."

Then, I decided that I had to provide a more balanced perspective, "But Sam is also a nice person, very gentle (except when he's spanking me), thoughtful and considerate. He's an interesting guy."

Kathy snorted, "That's an understatement."

Julie said, looking at all of us, "I think it's been an interesting day, so far." Obviously, none of us could deny that statement.

A moment later, Sam re-entered the sauna, and took his seat back in the corner of the top bench. He asked, "How's everyone doing?"

The girls nodded, and Julie offered, "We're OK." Sam could tell that something wasn't quite right.

He looked at me, and I shrugged. Glancing at my friends, I told him, "We were just talking about my birthday party, so far," I couldn't help but smile.

"Including everybody getting naked, massaging – and masturbating – each other in the hot tub, being tied to a mast, my private parts flogged, and then having sex with me, in front of my friends."

I took a big breath, "Then there was the needle play – with 30 needles through the skin of my back, making Julie sit with needles in her butt, asking Kathy to put her tampon in, while you watched – and then the *rest* of us having to put in a tampon.

"The spanking, and paddling and tawsing of our bottoms, putting more needles in us, and sticking all the butt plugs up our ass ..." I looked at my friends, trying to remember what else had transpired in the past six hours.

My friends were silent, Julie with her eyes closed, Linda with her mouth open, and Kathy looking up at the wood ceiling. I was on a roll, but I decided to praise him a little for the *good* things he'd done for us today.

"But ... I think we're all fine with partying with no clothes, changing in front of you, and even doing some massage in the jacuzzi."

I spread my hands, looking around the now small seeming sauna, and said, "And taking a sauna together, and bathing each other, and who knows what else you've got planned ... it's just been a lot.

"I'm getting used to it, I guess; but my friends have 'been through' a lot today. And they've been very open ... in many ways. They've really taken things in stride." I wasn't quite sure what message I was conveying to Sam.

Sam looked at each of us, giving a wan smile to my friends, and said, "I apologize if I've pushed you guys too hard today. To be honest, I really didn't expect so many things to happen – except for Kelly's pirate fantasy. But, I was prepared with a few things – mainly the 'Lazy Sam', and having the box of supplies ready."

Sam looked away, then back to us, closing his eyes for a few moments, and then opening them. "I guess my concept was to be ready with a range of interesting games we could play, things we could do ... and then play it by ear; see how you guys responded to each new experience, and tailor the party as we went."

"This morning, you guys could have shoo'ed me out of the pool room, while you got undressed, but you seemed very casual. We were all nude within fifteen minutes of going outside, and again you guys were great.

"As far as the massage in the spa, I had intended that only to be a sensual experience, not worrying about whether you're feeling male or female hands on parts of your body; but somehow it escalated into Julie masturbating Kathy ..."

I looked up at Kelly, "... and *you* masturbating me. Something that I would never have expected, or even offered."

A hazy thought flew through my brain; I couldn't quite pin it down. I closed my eyes. Oh my God! I suddenly looked into Kelly's eyes, "Kelly ... it *was* you, who was stroking me, wasn't it? Getting me hard, and getting me off? Going down on me?"

I had a cold feeling in my stomach, and held my breath, awaiting Kelly's response. Kelly looked at her friends, who were now all smiling; Linda put her hands over her face. Kathy and Julie were spellbound, waiting to see how this discussion would go.

I looked Sam in the eyes, and asked, "Does it *matter*?" He was about to say something, but I held up my hand; I decided that I would be in control, now.

"Sam, think about what you just said. The group massage was to be a sensual experience, with the blindfolded person able to relax, as she can't see if someone of the opposite sex is touching her in a sensitive place. So she's relaxed, and can enjoy the pure sensual feeling of eight hands on her body. Isn't that what you said?"

Sam nodded. "So why do you want to know now, hours later, who was doing the touching?" Sam looked at me with a blank expression.

I now addressed my friends, "Sam has preached to me, since we met, about openness. And he's explained to Julie and Linda his strange definition of 'sex'. Our first 'experience' together – which lasted 24 hours – wasn't intended to have any 'sex', per Sam's definition of 'body fluid transfer'."

I smiled at Sam, "Until we mixed up our glasses, and had 'sex' by drinking after each other. Then, at that French restaurant, we shared a gooey dessert together. More recently, we've relaxed the definition, and gone a lot further." All three of my friends' eyebrows went up.

"I admitted this to Julie when I had lunch with her last Saturday ... I made out with a woman – someone Sam and I had met at the nearby pond. Sam was not bothered by it, but it forced us to discuss how we would define sex, and what limits we would place on our activities, while we were together."

Linda had her hands covering the lower part of her face, wide eyes peaking out above them, and a rhythmic hacking motion that had to be laughter that she was trying to hold in. Julie's eyes were also wide, and she was grinning.

With mock indignance, I said, "You're not laughing at me, are you?" Julie, of course, knew that I was hoping to make out with her tonight.

Linda blurted, "Not laughing at you, just at the situation: We're all getting more open, and maybe more adventurous in our older age. And I thought that our ways had already been set. But even I've tried a few new things today ... and I actually enjoyed some of them." We all laughed.

Julie patted Linda on the back, then leaned over and kissed her on the cheek. "You've been great today, Linda, and surprised us with your openness, and willingness to try new things." It was true: None of us could have imagined Linda doing many of the things she had done today.

"So back to the subject of Sam's erection ..." Everyone laughed ... except Sam.

I stared at him, "Your whole philosophy is that people should be open and honest, try new things, and not get hung up by social or religious standards. And that human anatomy and physiology is basically the same for all of us, and there should be nothing to be embarrassed about." Sam was nodding, but the nodding was slowing down, as Sam realized that he was boxed in.

"And I *think* that you believe that you should follow your own philosophy, set an example?" Sam's head was moving slightly up and down, very slowly; barely a nod.

I went in for the kill, "So you were setting an example, in the hot tub: Being open about your body, and letting it respond to what was happening, not embarrassed, but enjoying your freedom, the sensuality and, finally, the resolution of your tensions ... in someone's mouth."

Sam looked startled. I had said that to put him a little off the track of finding out that Linda was stroking him until he was fully erect. But now Sam was imagining with whom he'd had oral sex ... if not me. I would let him stew about that, for a while.

Sam nodded, and quietly said, "Touché, Kelly. I deserved that. But I was hung up about getting an erection, no less having an orgasm, in front of your friends; I guess it is partially the social pressure, but mostly, I wanted us to have a fun, nude, day, without there being any pressure or worries regarding anything sexual."

Sam smiled, "Except having sex at the end of the pirate scene with you; but we were behind a rock, and I had told your friends to stay in the spa, so I don't think they saw much ... except the contorted expression on your blindfolded face, as you came."

I looked at my friends, and they laughed. Was it true? I could hardly remember, as my mind had been blank at that moment, in another world ... of ecstasy.

Sam continued, "I guess we've all had some new experiences today; been open about things that you might have thought yesterday that you would never do." I was looking at Sam, but saw Linda nodding her head in my peripheral vision.

He said, "Now, let me ask you guys a few questions ..."

I had to interrupt, "Sam could we get out of the sauna for a while? I think we're all getting pretty hot."

Sam smiled, as he got up, carrying his towel, "Of course! Let's get rinsed off." He held the door open for us, and we filed out of the sauna, and hung our towels on hooks in the shower room.

Sam got the shower going, and we all stood under the cool water, jostling each other for a more central position under the rain shower. Sam was gallant, and got out after he'd had a cursory rinse-off, and sat on his towel sideways on one of the chaises. He poured some water, and I think seeing that curtailed all of our showers, as we were getting dehydrated.

Eventually, we were all sitting on the chaises, facing each other, Sam pouring a cup of water for each of us. Most of the water had been drunk within a couple of minutes, and Sam offered to get us iced tea, coke, or anything else we could think of. We all declined, and I prompted Sam, "So what did you want to ask us?"

Sam finished his water and put his cup down on the table, chuckling – I presume – as he remembered the mix-up of our cups. Sam and I sat on one chaise, while Julie, Linda, and Kathy squeezed together on the other.

Sam looked at them, and asked, "Have you guys been OK – comfortable, and having fun – other than during the 'spank poker' game?" I looked at my friends, and they were all shrugging and nodding.

Julie said, "As Kelly said, I think we've been fine with going nude, playing around in the jacuzzi, watching you guys role play, going in the sauna. None of that is a big deal ... especially because you haven't made a big deal about it. And you have been a gentleman, and taken care of us. And I thought the 'spank poker' idea was pretty good – I didn't mind most of it. But I think we would have reacted better, if we hadn't been strapped down to that turntable – it was almost getting me dizzy."

Linda spoke up, "I didn't like the needles ... and I really didn't like putting in a tampon, while you watched from behind."

Sam shrugged, "I let you take it out yourself, in private."

Linda stuck out her tongue at Sam, "Thanks, a lot!"

Kathy finally got into the conversation, "I don't like getting spanked. I guess it never really hurt that much, but it seems degrading. Especially, since we were strapped down."

Kelly looked at me reproachfully, "Sam, I know you prefer people to voluntarily take their spankings, or whatever. I'm surprised you put straps on that stupid gizmo."

Sam laughed, "So now it's stupid? And, you're right – it would be more of a turn-on for me, if you guys were maintaining your positions by yourself ... but as this was your first time experiencing a lot of these things, I didn't want the game to be disrupted, and felt it would be more efficient – and you would take it more seriously – if you were kept in position throughout the game. I'm sorry."

Now, Sam looked at my friends, "But would you – could you – have stayed in position without the straps?"

Kathy nodded, "Of course! Once we agreed to play the game I think we would have followed any rules you gave us."

Julie was nodding, "I thought the 'bondage' was a turn-on, but if you had just asked us to stay in position, I think we would all have cooperated. And we would have felt more in control, less helpless. More dignified."

Sam was nodding, "Again, I apologize. I had tried to envision our games today, but really didn't know how you guys would react to any of it. But I'm glad that you've given me this feedback."

Kelly said, "Shall we go in the sauna for a few more minutes? Then, we can get showered and dressed for dinner." We all went back into the sauna, sitting quietly in the warmth, the heat, droplets of sweat appearing on all of us like the condensation on a bottle of Coke, right out of the freezer. Dripping down our bodies.

I looked at Sam: His eyes were closed. Linda was right that it had been a bizarre day ... but we had learned new things about each other, and about ourselves.

After ten minutes, we'd all had enough of the heat. We quietly exited the sauna, and started the shower, again.

Sam smiled, "I need to get out of here quickly, to get the fire started, and the meat smoking. Maybe you guys would like to bathe me, and then I'll go upstairs, and start cooking, and you can take your time showering and getting dressed for dinner?"

Sam was *still* pushing; although for nothing that we hadn't done, already. And we *had* said that we were all comfortable being nude, and touching each other.

The girls shrugged, and we all bathed Sam, as he closed his eyes, and slowly rotated his body under the rain shower. Julie washed his privates, and he didn't get turned on, or even open his eyes to see who was touching him. Finally, we were done washing Sam, and he went upstairs, leaving us girls to bathe ourselves. Or each other.

I left the girls in the shower, and ran up the stairs, up to the master bath, where I shaved, brushed my teeth, and combed my hair. I picked out an outfit – cargo shorts and a Hawaiian shirt in muted colors – and brought them down to the pool room, putting them on the massage table.

I opened a closet in the kitchen, and pulled out the BBQ apron, which I put on, tying it around the waist at the back. My front was entirely covered, and my backside was almost entirely uncovered. I would do the 'messy' part of the barbequing in this outfit, then dress for dinner. I pulled a beer out of the cooler and took a sip. Yes, the day had been very interesting. Kelly's friends really were open and adventurous.

CHAPTER 16: MOONLIGHT BARBEQUE

I pre-heated the oven, and put in the baked beans. Then, I went out to the barbeque, and got the fire started. Twenty minutes later, the fire was roaring; I had already made a salad, and the barbeque sauce, and prepared the ribs. I spread the fire and heated the grates – which I had cleaned last week, the first time in more than five years. I separated the coals into small bunches, and threw on some hickory that had been soaking since yesterday. Then I closed the top of the barbeque.

When I returned a few minutes later with the pan of ribs, smoke was billowing out of the air vents on the sides of the barbeque. I took a deep breath, opened the top, and placed the ribs on the grate, closing the top again so that a minimal amount of smoke was lost.

The ribs were already par-boiled, but would be smoked nearly an hour. Only in the last twenty minutes, would I slather on the sauce, glazing it onto the already-smoked ribs.

The girls came upstairs about half an hour after I had. They went into the pool room, and started taking clothes out of their totes. I took out the huge container of sangria, stirred the fruit around in the deep purple liquid, and ladled some into five cups, which I put on a lacquer tray.

I checked on the beans in the oven, and turned the heat down on the sauce, which was already boiling. Then, I carried the tray of sangrias into the pool room.

The girls were in various states of undress: Julie was wearing black thong underwear, and was putting on a black lace bra, as I entered. She looked up at me and smiled, as she clasped and adjusted her bra; Kathy was putting on pale blue bikini underwear.

Linda came out of the bathroom, still nude, rummaged in her tote, and pulled out a substantial bra that she put on, bending forward to adjust her breasts in the cups. Then, she rummaged more, and found a pair of generously-sized bikini underwear, which she slipped on.

Kelly walked up to me, still nude, and smiling, as she took a cup of sangria. She took a couple of sips, and said, "Yum! This is really good." She gave me a peck on the lips, and said, "I'm going upstairs to get dressed."

I nodded, and set the tray of sangrias on a roller stand – the one I had used to hold the electrical stimulation generator, when Kelly had come over for her first long weekend. Then, I rolled the tray over to the girls, leaving it near the wall between the stored turntable and the first boxes and tote bags.

Kathy, now just in her underwear, walked over and took a cup; she took a swallow, and had the same reaction as Kelly, "Wow! This is really good. Fruity ... tastes great, but I can tell there's alcohol in here."

I nodded, "Yes. Like Mai Tai's, this is a drink that goes down easily, but sneaks up on you. So please don't overdo it. I want everyone staying awake through dinner!" I took one more look at the girls, and walked back to the kitchen.

The bacon on the top of the beans was cooking nicely, and I put on a mitt and stirred the boiling mixture, then covered the ceramic dish, and turned down the oven. I went out to the barbeque, and added more hickory to the coals. The ribs were doing nicely, but weren't ready to turn, yet.

Julie walked out to the patio, carrying a cup of sangria, and wearing a black, sleeveless skater dress, with organza panels near the lower hem. I smiled at her and nodded, "You look beautiful!" She did.

Then, she spun around, and said, "Zip me, please." The zipper ran from below her waist, up to the scooped neck. I zipped her, and clasped the top. When she turned around again, she leaned over and kissed me on the cheek. "You really have been nice to us, Sam. Thank you for all the work you've done to prepare for this party."

She looked at the smoke pouring out of the barbeque, and exclaimed, "This is quite a production!" I explained that I considered 'barbeque' to be smoked meat, the sauce added only after the meat had been cooked long and slow. Ribs can be smoked for four hours or more, but I was doing a quick version for the party.

As Julie and I were talking, Kathy and Linda walked out of the pool room. Kathy was wearing palazzo pants with a floral print and a white bloused crop top with ruched neckline and ruffled mesh lace sleeves. Linda wore a sleeveless summer shift, navy blue, with large patches of colorful flowers in reds, pinks, and lavenders.

They looked fresh, and it was a treat seeing them in nice outfits; how ironic!

I told the girls that dinner would be ready in about half an hour, but I could take out the vegetable dip, and more guacamole and chips, if they wanted something sooner. They decided to wait for dinner, but were ready for more sangria. We went into the kitchen, and I ladled the sangria into their cups.

The girls chatted in the kitchen, while I brought the potato salad from the fridge in the garage. As I stepped into the garage, I heard them laughing uproariously; I wondered what the joke was. It was only after I had come back, and put the potato salad on the counter that they pointed ... and I remembered that I was half nude; the back half.

I had known I would get a laugh wearing just the apron, but had forgotten what I was wearing ... or not wearing, in this case. I opened olives and pickles, and put them in small bowls, and took out the silverware, and a stack of napkins.

Kelly came down the stairs and into the kitchen. She was radiantly beautiful, wearing a peach-colored ruffle-neck layered strapless dress. I ladled a cup of sangria for Kelly, and handed it to her, holding up my cup, and saying, "Here's to the birthday girl!" I refrained from adding 'now, a quarter of a century old'. I wasn't angling for punishment tonight.

I asked Kelly if she would prefer to eat in the dining room, but she was looking forward to having dinner on the patio. I handed the napkins and silverware to Julie, placemats to Linda, and the bowls of olives and pickles to Kathy, and they brought everything out to the patio table. I grabbed the pink tablecloth and ran ahead of them, first pulling out the umbrella, then throwing the tablecloth over the table with a flourish.

I handed Linda the matching pink napkins, and said, "Let's use these as our main napkins, and put the stack of paper napkins on the table, as we'll probably need them." The girls went to work setting the table, as I opened the barbeque, waved the smoke out of my eyes, and turned the ribs. They were doing very well. I dropped in a few more pieces of wet hickory, and closed the top of the barbeque.

Back in the kitchen, I found a liter wine carafe, and carefully poured the sangria into it, with about half still left in the large Tupperware container. I gave the carafe and a stack of cups to Kelly, and she brought them out to the table. Then, I pulled out a silver tray with three fat candles on it, which I put in the center of the patio table.

We would be starting to eat around 7:30PM, which was about twenty minutes before sunset. I decided to slow the dinner down, so that it was twilight before I served the main course. The ribs could smoke a while longer.

I went into the kitchen, and took the salad bowl from the fridge, shook the green goddess dressing, and tossed the salad. I brought it out to the patio, along with a stack of five salad plates. Fortunately, it had been a dry summer, and the insects were not bothering us.

Kelly served the salads, and I lit the candles. I suggested, "Let's have salad, and then we can take a short break before dinner. I'd like to serve the barbeque at just about sunset."

Linda laughed, "What? You don't want us seeing what we're eating?" There was snickering around the table.

"No, Linda. If you look over the roof of the pool room, you'll see that the moon is up, and it will be lighting our table by the time the sun sets. And, I've strung some lights, that I think will make this a more dramatic and festive setting."

Linda put her napkin in her lap, and picked up her fork. She gave me a sidelong glance, and shook her head.

I got compliments on the salad, but halfway through, I had to excuse myself and tend to the fire. I stood there – 'slaving over a hot stove', as they used to say – my bare backside facing the girls, as I turned over the slabs of ribs with a pair of tongs. I dropped more hickory on the fire, and closed the top again. The fire wasn't nearly as hot, now, so the timing would work out perfectly.

I went back to the table, and refilled everyone's cups of sangria. I sat down, and said, "I'll get dressed for the main part of the dinner; it's just the slathering of barbeque sauce on the ribs that can get messy." The girls just shrugged.

It was a pleasant evening, like many we'd had this summer. It was cooling off nicely, the air was clear, the sky blue, and now beginning to gradate to warmer colors toward the western horizon. The sun was already below the level of the trees in the forest behind the house; it would get much darker over the next thirty minutes.

The girls chatted about their outfits, other clothes they had bought during the summer, and plans for the fall season. When everyone was finished with salad, I collected the plates, and brought them into the kitchen, immediately rinsing them, and putting them in the dishwasher. Then, I brought the pot of sauce out to the barbeque.

I opened the top of the barbeque, and was blinded by smoke. When it finally cleared, I took the large brush, and slathered the ribs with the thick sauce. I put the top back on the saucepot, and put it on the barbeque side shelf, then closed the top again. I went into the kitchen, turned off the oven, and took out the beans, putting them on the stove. Then, I turned the oven to broil.

I cut a whole baguette on the bias, and quickly spread my special garlic butter on the bread, placing each slice on a metal tray. When all the bread was on the tray, I sprinkled freshly grated Parmesano-Reggiano cheese over the top; then, just a dash of paprika for color.

Of course, we didn't need the garlic bread, as we already had a lot of food prepared, but I didn't know what everyone liked, and wanted to have it available; also, it's great as a leftover. I put the bread in the broiler, and set the timer for 3 minutes.

I ran outside, and turned the ribs, saucing them generously. When I got back to the kitchen, the timer was buzzing ... but fortunately, the bread still needed another minute. When it was done, I stacked the slices on a plate, and brought it out to the table.

"We're going to have a lot of food tonight, but if the salad made you hungry, or the sangria is making you tipsy, you can have some of this." The girls each took a slice, and their eyes lit up.

That reminded me, "Kelly, were you going to remind me of something, before we started dinner?"

Kelly frowned, looked at me, and then grinned, "The Beano?" We laughed, and she went in to get it.

I asked the girls, "Have any of you seen the movie, '*Blazing Saddles*'?" I got only blank stares.

Then, Linda lit up, and asked, "I think I've heard of it. Was it with Mel Gibson?"

I laughed, "No, it was the comedian, Mel Brooks." Linda just nodded. Maybe I should let Kelly explain. Then, I thought I might as well.

"It was a hilarious western comedy. In one scene, a bunch of cowboys are finally having their dinner after a hard day – sitting on rocks around a campfire, and eating beans out of a can. Then, one of them farts. Then another. And, as they eat the beans, it's a chain reaction, until they all have to get up and walk away from the smelly fire." The girls laughed.

"Well, I've always made baked beans to go with barbeque; I make good baked beans, and Kelly asked for them. But then we realized that we're all going to be sleeping together ..." The girls gave me a look, and I gave them a look back, "Not in *that* way, you know that. Anyway, with five of us in the room, it could get pretty thick." The girls laughed even harder.

Kelly was walking out of the kitchen, carrying the small bottle. I finished, "So we decided that a prophylactic dose of Beano might be a good idea. It might not work perfectly, but we all might be more comfortable."

Kelly said, "I see you've already told them." I laughed, wondering whether Kelly had figured out how *she* was going to 'spill the beans', in a manner of speaking. She passed the bottle around, and we all took a couple of the tiny pills.

Now, I remembered that I had salmon steaks in the fridge, in case anybody didn't like barbeque. I asked the girls their preference, but they all chose the ribs. I guess Kelly and I would be having salmon tomorrow night for dinner.

It was time, and I went into the kitchen to bring out a large metal tray on which to put the ribs, as I took them out of the barbeque. The sauce, which contained black molasses, was glazed onto them, and they were just slightly charred on the tips. I brought the tray into the kitchen, along with the pot of sauce. I lined up all the dishes on the counter: Dinner plates, then ribs, potato salad, beans, and extra sauce.

I grabbed a handful of parsley, quickly washed it, then picked the 'flowers' off the branches, and put some around the potato salad, and at the corners of the rib tray. I put out tongs for the ribs, and spoons for everything else. I looked at the clock: It was five minutes before sunset.

I stepped out a few feet onto the patio, bowed formally, and said, "Dinnah is suhved, ladies." As Julie, Linda, and Kathy lined up and piled their plates with food, I hugged Kelly, and whispered, "Happy birthday! I love you!" We kissed, until Julie, carrying her plate of food, couldn't get by us.

We stepped aside, and Julie said, "There'll be plenty of time for that later."

I held the kitchen door open for Julie, and followed her out to the patio. After she had put her plate on the table, I whispered, "I just hope you don't steal her away from me. I would hate to lose her to another woman."

Julie loudly said, "Ha! I don't think that's going to happen. You don't have anything to worry about, Sam."

I patted Julie on the back, and went into the pool room; on the way, I turned on the strings of lights I had put in the trees, and also the pool lights. I left the patio lights off, hoping that we could eat by candlelight ... and moonlight.

I stood in the opening of the sliding door, next to the massage table, took off my BBQ apron, and got dressed. Looking at the backyard, I realized that I hadn't lit the Tiki torches, so I walked around the pool, and along the meandering path, lighting them. Then, I went into the kitchen for a plate of barbeque.

When we were finally all at the table with our food, I raised my glass, and toasted, "Here's to Kelly's 25th birthday!" We all sipped the sangria. Then, "And here's to all of you – for 'playing' with us today. Again, I apologize if I pushed a little too much," I grinned and looked around the table, "but I think you each probably got something out of the day. Anyway, thank you for coming to Kelly's birthday party, and being so open with us."

We sipped more sangria ... some sips bigger than others. Before I started eating, I got up, and refilled everyone's cups, and then went into the kitchen, and refilled the carafe. Finally, I dug in. As I held a sticky sauce-covered rib in my fingers, I noted that the table was quiet, except for munching sounds. Everyone seemed to be enjoying the dinner.

At some point, Kathy asked Kelly, "So where would you like to go, in Europe?"

Kelly stiffened, almost as if an electric current had passed through her. She exclaimed, "With everything we've been doing today, I forgot about the trip!" She looked at her half-eaten plate of food, then back at Kathy, "I haven't thought about it much. Maybe Italy, the French Riviera, Spain, ..."

I broke in, and suggested, "Kelly, can we possibly do those on the *next* trip? Unless you want to spend the semester abroad?"

Kelly smiled, "Sam, I'll be happy, wherever we go." She leaned over and kissed me. Now I felt like an electric current had passed through *my* body.

The girls talked about where they wanted to travel, mainly about places in Europe that they had dreamed about. They asked me to describe some of the bigger cities; I knew most of them quite well, having traveled throughout Europe on business for years. Oh, decades. Ouch!

I went into the house, and brought out the tray of ribs, going around the table. Julie and Linda actually took a second one; the ribs were large and, with all of the other dishes, I hadn't expected many of the ribs to get eaten. Then, I brought out the potato salad, and then the beans.

"Sam!" everyone cried. But I wasn't forcing them to take any. After I had passed the food around, I remembered to take Kelly's birthday cake out of the fridge in the garage. The whipped cream required refrigeration, but I wanted it to be closer to room temperature, by the time we ate it.

When I got back outside, I realized that it was already quite dark. I sat down, and ate a few more forkfuls of potato salad. I don't think anyone had noticed the lights, yet. I looked up, and – sure enough – the moon was nearly overhead. A full moon, that portended – I hoped – good things to come. My staring at the moon must have alerted the others, and soon there were a lot of Ooooh's and Aaaah's around the table. Then, I pointed to the backyard.

Linda turned, and gasped, "It's beautiful!" The pool lights were on, sparkling, and reflecting splatters of blue light on the trees. The small path lights meandered around the lawn and flowerbeds. And hundreds of tiny lights outlined the branches of the trees. Almost like Disneyland.

Kathy said, "Yeah. This really was a great place to have your party, Kelly." Then, Kathy turned to me, "Sam, I want to thank you for everything, too. I'm sorry if I complained; I've had a great time today."

She looked down and smiled, then looked up at me with her big brown eyes, "It was just that darn poker game." She looked at her friends, and said, "And I used to *like* to play poker." She chuckled, "But now I may never play another poker game in my life!"

I felt compelled to respond – a mistake, I knew, but one of my personality flaws. "Kathy! It wasn't really *that* bad, was it?"

She looked down, and quietly said, "I'll have to think about it." Then she looked at me, "But I think I'll probably have even worse feelings about it tomorrow."

I frowned. "Let me ask you, did the spanks really hurt? Your bottom wasn't very red at the end."

Now Kathy frowned, "Well, I guess they didn't hurt that much. I've never really been spanked before, so there was a psychological hurdle. A few of the spanks stung – especially with that strap. But there weren't that many of them." She looked at me, "It wasn't really the spanking part that bothered me."

I smiled, "And you seemed very relaxed about your body, and nudity, even being in a knee chest position. Were you embarrassed?"

Kathy shook her head, "Not really. I'm used to being nude with other people. And, sometimes, they see every part of me. Getting into that position was a little strange, but there was probably only a moment of embarrassment. Everyone else was in the same position."

She laughed, "And we had already seen *you* in a knee chest position. And, I offered to put in my tampon while you watched. I thought that was also pretty strange, but I was trying to be open; it's really not that big of a deal."

I asked, "What did you think about the rectal insertions?"

Kathy looked up at the moon, and back down to me, "I didn't like those, much. They didn't feel that bad, but they also didn't feel good. And, I guess it was one more element of embarrassment. I think you could have designed the game without those."

I laughed. "And what about the needles?"

Kathy shook her head, "I don't like the idea of that." She thought a minute, "Actually, they didn't hurt that much ... but it wasn't a good feeling. And it's psychologically frightening. I think it's lucky that none of us fainted, when you showed us the needles." Kathy was right: We had been lucky.

I deduced, "So, it comes down to that turntable?"

Kathy nodded, and looked at her friends. "I think that pushed me over the edge. If we had been in a knee chest position on the carpet, not bound, I think we would have been much more relaxed." Linda was nodding.

I stood, and pulled Kathy up, hugging her tightly. Then, we sat back down, and I said, sincerely, "Once again I'm really sorry. Everything you guys are saying makes sense. I just hadn't thought it out. I let my fantasies guide me, thinking optimistically about your reactions ... but not your feelings."

I glanced at Kelly, and then looked at her friends, "Well, I promise there will be no more needles tonight or tomorrow. And I won't be binding you in position again." Then I grinned, "Spankings ... I'm not sure about, yet." There was a chorus of mock groans from the girls, and I laughed.

The pace of our eating ground to a halt, as our stomachs became over-stuffed. I let Kelly chat with her friends, while I carried everything back into the kitchen. I washed the plates and silverware, threw away the cups and napkins, and put the pink napkins in the washing machine; only the tablecloth and candles remained on the patio table.

Then, I put Saran over all the dishes, and brought them out to the garage fridge. When I went back out to the patio, it was very dark, except for the moonlight and candlelight; and, of course, the pool lights, path lights, and the tiny bulbs in the trees.

"Kelly, would you mind if we delayed the cake for a while, so our stomachs can settle?"

Kelly laughed, "Of course, I was going to suggest that."

We sat at the patio table, contented after a long day and a big meal. And good friends all around. Literally.

I turned to Kelly, "Kelly, there are a few more things we'll be doing tonight – like opening your presents," she smiled, "and giving you your birthday spanking." She frowned, then, smiled at me. I continued, "I don't know if anybody is going to be up for going in the pool or jacuzzi again."

She shrugged, and I continued, "So, what would you think about us retiring to the playroom, and watching a movie? It will take about an hour and a half; at that point, we'll either be asleep, or have gotten our next wind. We can open the presents before or after the movie ... but if we're going to have the cake ... and Champagne, maybe we should wait for a while?"

Linda blurted, "Champagne? I love the bubbly!" The sangria had evidently not had that much effect on Linda. We'll see if she can stay awake during the movie.

"Actually, I had a movie in mind, but I'm open to your suggestions." I was now thinking that an action movie might be more appropriate.

Kelly asked, "What is it?"

I smiled, "I was thinking of the new Roman Polanski movie, *'Venus in Fur'*. It's a modern stage-play version of Sacher-Masoch's story of female domination and sadomasochism. It's in French, and subtitled."

Kelly scrunched her face, "I'm not sure we're up for a stage play. It sounds interesting, but maybe we can have a 'film night' with my friends, some other time, and show that. How about something more exciting? Like an adventure, or love story, or musical?"

I bellowed, "Musical?!?" My mind immediately thought of some of the older, classic musicals, like *'West Side Story'*, *'South Pacific'*, and *'The Sound of Music'*.

Kelly shook her head. "We could watch another *Indiana Jones* movie?"

Shrugging, I thought of some of my favorite foreign films, like *'Y Tu Mama Tambien'* and *'The Gods Must be Crazy'*, but realized that something lighter and fun – without subtitles – would be more appropriate.

I suggested one of the Star Wars series, or a James Bond film. I mentioned *'True Lies'*, *'Back to the Future'*, and a few other films to Kelly, even suggesting *'Blazing Saddles'*, which was in my collection. But I guess all of my films were from a long time ago – some before Kelly and her friends had been born. My age was showing again.

Julie had been listening to our discussion of movies, and suggested, "How about *'Hunger Games'* or one of the *'Twilight'* series movies?"

Linda spoke up, "Julie took me to the second *'Hunger Games'* movie on my birthday.

Kathy said, "I'm not sure if I ever saw the first *'Twilight'* film. That sounds good." Kelly was nodding enthusiastically, so it was decided. I had all the *'Twilight'* films on my media server, but hadn't watched any of them, yet.

I looked around the table, at everyone nicely dressed for a fancy night out, but perhaps overdressed for our new plans for the evening. The girls got started talking about films and television programs, and I was glad that we would be sitting out on the patio for a while longer. It was a beautiful night, and the backyard did look great – almost 'enchanting'. I glanced at my watch; it was already after 8PM.

I went back into the kitchen, and cleaned up most of the remaining mess – a couple of pots, trays, and serving platters. Then, I went down to the playroom, and set-up the video.

I closed the drapes that separated most of the room from the bed area, and pressed a button on the remote to lower the huge screen; then, I cued-up the movie, and adjusted the audio – as the IMAX people say, 'for maximum impact'. Then, I pivoted the love seat, until it was in line with the couch, facing the screen, and moved an end table next to the loveseat, so that we would all have a place to put a drink.

When I got back to the patio, the girls were still in a lively discussion – this time about vampires, relating the stories from some of the books they had recently read. I didn't really 'get' the current vampire craze. However, as I listened to the discussion and thought about it, I imagined some similarities between the bite of a vampire, and my submission fantasies. Well, I guess there was only a tenuous relationship ... but I had never considered it previously.

Kelly looked at me, and said, "Is everything ready, downstairs?" I flashed on how 'ready' I was for some things that we would not be doing – like showing the girls my exam room. "Yes, the movie is cued-up, and I changed the seating to a movie-watching configuration." I looked at Kelly, "I assumed we wouldn't worry about the Aero beds, until later." Kelly nodded.

Then, I decided that – with all the alcohol – I should give us all a good chance to stay awake through the movie, and actually get to Kelly's birthday presents ... and birthday spanking. I asked everyone, "Can I make some coffee, espresso, or cappuccino for anybody? It might help keep us awake." Julie and Kathy opted for espressos, and Linda licked her lips and requested a cappuccino.

I let the girls chat, while I made the coffees in the kitchen, bringing the demi tasses out on a small tray. We all enjoyed them, relaxing after the big dinner, as we looked out into the yard. It was a beautiful evening, and I breathed easily, knowing that most of the day had been a success. I had certainly given Kelly a 'unique' birthday party, with which to remember reaching the quarter-century mark.

I looked at Kelly's friends, "You guys look really beautiful in those outfits. Do you want to wear those during the movie, or get a little more comfortable?"

Kelly looked at me, questioningly, and Linda gave me a bit of a dirty look, wondering what else I could possibly have in mind, after our day of nudity. The girls shrugged, and Kelly said, "I wouldn't mind getting more comfortable." She looked around the table. The girls didn't say anything.

I asked, "Do you guys trust me?" That was a stupid question, after what we had done today, and all of our follow-up discussions.

Again, the girls shrugged, and Julie offered, "Sure, Sam."

I smiled, "Then come with me, please." The girls followed me into the pool room, where we stood in front of their totes and the boxes in which they had dropped the clothes they had been wearing this morning. They looked at me. I hoped that I wasn't pushing too hard again, but smiled, and asked nicely, "Please undress down to your bra and underwear."

Linda guffawed, and Kathy was shaking her head, but Julie turned her back to me, and said, "Zipper, please." I unzipped her, and the other girls began taking off their blouses, dresses and/or pants. Within a couple of minutes, there were four girls standing in their underwear. It was only fair ... so I took off my shorts and Hawaiian shirt, and stood next to them in my European underwear. Linda and Kathy giggled, and I knew they were all wondering what I would suggest next.

"It's time for me to give you guys your next 'party favor'." The girls looked even more nervous, as I pointed to the gift bags, and said, "Take out the next item, please." I quickly walked to the closet, and brought back two loosely-wrapped packages, one of which I handed to Kelly. The girls were squeezing the colorful tissue paper, now very curious as to what they were going to find inside.

Linda looked up, and said, "What? Another pareo?"

I laughed. That wasn't so far off the mark, but they would just have to find out. "Open them." I said.

It took only a moment to tear the paper, and find a pink t-shirt, nicely folded, inside. Julie held it up: It was an extra long shirt, suitable as a beach cover-up. On the front, was a small 'X' – comprised of the silhouettes of a riding crop and a tawse, crossing over each other.

Julie turned it around. On the back was a large circle, inside of which was a colorful graphic of a pirate ship, with a pirate waving his sword next to it, and coming out of the circle. Around the circle was stenciled, 'Kelly's 25th Birthday Party'.

The girls squealed, and Kelly smiled and hugged me. Braless, Kathy put the t-shirt over her head, and pulled it down; it came to mid-thigh. Julie took off her bra, and put on her shirt; hers came down to her upper thigh. She spun around, modeling it. "This is wonderful, Sam. Very thoughtful of you!"

Kelly also took off her bra, before putting on the shirt, but Linda put the tee on over her bra and underwear. Linda looked down at herself, and shook her head, "This is really nice; this soft fabric feels good." As she was saying that, I put my own tee on, our motley quintet now matching each other, all in pink.

Kelly put her arms over my shoulders, and kissed me. "Thank you, Sam." I was glad she liked it. This had been just one of the projects that had kept me busy over the past couple of weeks.

I grabbed my camera and the girls stood closely together, as I snapped a few images. They suggested that I get in the picture, so I set the camera on the massage table, and set the self-timer. It took a couple of shots to get us centered in the image, but the pictures looked good.

On a whim, I asked Kelly to lean over the massage table; the shirt just barely covered her underwear. Then, I asked her to bend over and hold her knees. About half her underwear was showing, but I was able to pull the end of the tee down, mostly covering them. Obviously, none of us were concerned with modesty by this point, but I was glad to see that the shirts provided some coverage, and were comfortable for the girls.

"Shall we go downstairs, now?" I inquired. Then I suggested, "You can bring down the presents for Kelly, if you like." The last party favors would be opened later, perhaps giving the girls the possibility of another new experience. They were in small rectangular boxes, which I had covered with the balloon-covered birthday wrapping paper.

Everything in hand, we all went down to the playroom. I had the girls put all the presents on one of the chairs in front of the desk, and then they all took places on the couch and loveseat.

I took the drink orders, and brought a tray of soft drinks (and a guava nectar for Kathy), and glasses with ice. Then, I pulled over a couple of ottomans on which to put our feet. When everyone was settled, I pushed a button on the remote, and the movie started playing.

It was an interesting and sensual movie, and I could understand why the girls would like it. There were no fangs; although Edward was 'strange', he was loving and protective of Bella. I couldn't help relating the movie to the relationship I had with Kelly: A relationship between an unlikely couple; submission, in the face of danger; and unconditional love.

I glanced at the girls, and they were enthralled with the story, and with the large screen and theater-quality surround sound system. It was better than seeing a movie in the theater.

In the middle of the movie, Julie got up to use the bathroom. I asked everyone if we should take a short intermission. Linda and Kathy shrugged, and Julie said, "You don't have to do that for me; I'll listen as I'm peeing." She went into the bathroom, leaving the door open to the hallway.

It was a good movie. I sat on the end of the loveseat, farthest from the couch, and snuggled with Kelly. In our t-shirts, the five of us were like little pink rabbits, huddled together in their hutch. When the movie ended, I hit the remote, and the screen silently raised into the ceiling. The drapes were still hiding the other end of the room, where the king size bed was located.

I turned off the video and sound systems, and set the lighting to the 'dim romantic' profile. Kelly helped me to swing the love seat back into position, making an 'L' with the couch, and move the small end-table to the corner between the couch and the loveseat.

I asked, "Is everyone ready for some dessert, now? And champagne? And opening the presents? ... And a birthday spanking?" The girls were wide awake, and tittering, as I asked this, but they all nodded.

I asked Julie to come upstairs and help me. When we were in the kitchen, I gave her a stack of five dessert plates, forks and napkins, and a tray to carry them. I put candles in the birthday cake, and set the lighter next to it.

Then, I went back downstairs, and took the champagne from the bar fridge, and lined up five fluted crystal glasses along the bar. I opened the sparkling wine (it actually being 'Champagne', since it was from Reims) with a flourish, the cork making a loud 'pop' as it came out of the bottle. I poured glasses of the bubbly liquid, leaving them on the bar, and placing the bottle on a trivet.

Then, I ran back upstairs and lit the candles on the birthday cake. Carefully carrying it down the stairs, along with the cake knife, I began singing 'Happy Birthday' as I entered the playroom.

The girls took up the chorus, as I walked to the coffee table, placing the cake down in front of Kelly. We finished singing, and Kelly looked at us with a broad smile; then, she blew out the candles.

It did take her two extra 'puffs', but we all clapped, and I leaned over and kissed Kelly, then handed her the wide, wedged knife. As she cut the cake, I brought the champagne glasses to the table, then made a second trip for the bottle and trivet. Linda was already sipping the pale, bubbly wine.

I sat down next to Kelly, and she passed me a plate of cake. I raised my champagne glass, again toasting to Kelly's birthday ... and again avoiding any reference to a fraction of a century. We tried the cake, and there were 'Yum!'s' all around.

It really was a delicious cake! I was glad that I had placed a custom order with the bakery, and not settled for a commercial cake from the market. The champagne went very well with the cake, and we were all enjoying our desserts, as evidenced by the lack of conversation, and only 'Mmmm' sounds from everyone.

Linda asked, "Sam, you didn't bake this yourself, did you?"

I chuckled, "Thanks for the great compliment, Linda. But no, I bought it at a local bakery. I had considered baking a cake myself, but knew I wouldn't be able to match their creations." I looked at Kelly, and added, "And, I had quite a few other projects to complete for the party."

I refilled everyone's champagne glass, and fetched the presents that had been brought by Kelly's friends, piling them on the table in front of Kelly. I also brought over my own bag of 'goodies'.

Kelly started opening the presents from her friends: Bath powders from Linda, and a book – *The Encyclopedia of BDSM* – from Kathy. Kelly started flipping through it, and Julie had to nudge her to put it down, and open the rest of the presents.

Kelly picked up Julie's gift, opening the small box, and pulling out a bracelet; she sat there staring at it, then gave Julie an inquisitive look. Julie just shrugged and gave Kelly a lascivious smile. Kelly hugged Julie.

When I finally got to see the bracelet, I noted the thin leather band, and a couple of charms – two female symbols. Julie had said that I had nothing to worry about, losing Kelly to a woman, but now, once again, I wasn't so sure. Kelly thanked everyone for the presents.

Now, it was my turn. I reached into the bag, and pulled out the first gift; it was a half-joke, and I wondered how Kelly would react when she opened it. Amazingly, it would be a pretty close match to the bracelet that Julie had given her. As with Julie's present, Kelly opened the small box, and pulled out the gift, staring at it for several moments, before cracking up. Then, she leaned over and kissed me on the nose.

Kathy and Linda simultaneously asked, "What is it?"

Kelly turned to them, and held up the present: It was a thick, but high quality leather collar, with a small key hanging from a large ring at the bottom of the collar. I helped Kelly put it on.

She exclaimed, "It's a 'slave' collar! I'm considering trying a new lifestyle for a month or two – as Sam's slave." Julie and Kathy involuntary belly laughed, as Linda covered her face, and shook her head. Kelly quickly expanded, "We haven't decided anything, yet, I'm just thinking about it."

I stood up, and said, "Well, that's everything." And, looking at Kelly, "Are you ready for your birthday spanking, now, young lady?" Kelly looked a bit confused, but nodded, her expression blank.

Then, I had my own belly laugh, and sat back down. As Steve Jobs did, during the Apple product introductions, I said, "I think there's just one more thing ..." I looked into the bag, and said, "Maybe more than one more thing." The girls were laughing, now. I pulled out the next gift, and handed it to Kelly.

Sam handed me the package, and all I could think was that he had gotten me another gag gift. Although I wasn't sure whether the collar was meant as a gag, or as the real thing. I could tell, when the first balloon-decorated wrapping paper came off that this box was from a major department store. I took off the top, and folded back the tissue. "Oh! This is beautiful, Sam." I held the satin negligee up for everyone to see, and my friends 'Ooooh'd' and 'Aaahh'd'.

It really was nice: A satin chemise night gown, actually more of a nightshirt. It wasn't especially sexy, but a comfortable style that I could actually wear. Sam had asked me about my preference in nightgowns, when I had first come over and modeled my PJs.

And, it was evident that he had listened. Although the straps were a little thin for my taste, it had no lace, ruffles, buttons, or other itchy things to bother me while I slept. It was very elegant – classy.

Now, Sam was reaching into the bag again, and pulled out another wrapped present, this time much smaller. I looked at him, and he explained, "I couldn't decide what to get you, so bought a couple of things," He smiled at me, and added, "hoping that you'll like at least one of them."

I laughed, and said, only half-jokingly, "But Sam, I liked the collar you bought me!"

Sam nodded, and said, "Yes, but that style may not go with all your outfits, so I decided to be safe and buy you another 'collar'." Now, I was confused. I took the box from Sam, and ripped off the wrapping paper. There was a small, flat box and, judging from the name on the front, appeared to have come from a top jewelry store in town.

I opened it, and nearly fainted: Sam had given me a beautiful pearl necklace. I didn't have anything like it, and had always dreamed of owning nice pearls ... but we had never discussed it. Somehow, Sam had read my mind, or at least had been on the same wavelength. I lifted the necklace, and Sam moved my hair aside, and clasped it for me. I would have to see myself in a mirror, but from the reaction of my friends, I knew it looked good.

Julie cried, "Kelly! That's gorgeous!" Kathy and Linda chimed in, and I scooted over on the couch to let them see it at closer range.

Sam explained, "These are cultured Akoya saltwater pearls from Japan, well-matched, and strung as a princess-length necklace. What I really liked about it, is the large pearl in the center, with graduations in size, slightly smaller, as you move away from the center. I thought this would look really good on you." Sam smiled, "And it does!"

I leaned over and kissed him again, this time a warm, wet, full-mouth kiss, our tongues entering each other and swirling, as I closed my eyes, and enjoyed the moment of intimacy with Sam. I fingered the pearls, and noticed that my friends were still staring at the necklace.

A tear came to my eye: Sam was really so sweet. Yes, he may be a bit perverted ... but aren't we all, if we admitted to it? But he was also so thoughtful, caring, and ... *sweet*. I know he wouldn't want to be described that way, but it was true. He really was the nicest man I had ever known. And I loved him deeply.

I looked at Sam warily, and said, "Is that everything, now, Sam?" It was really quite enough. *Especially* when the Europe trip was taken into account.

Sam looked into the bag, and coughed. He glanced at me with a fiendish smile. Oh, no! What now?

Sam pulled out a tissue-covered package, and put it into his lap, then looked around at all of us. He cleared his throat, and said, "Well, Kelly, the necklace was the last of your 'official' birthday presents. But I do have one more gift ... for everyone. It's the last 'party favor'."

He looked at Julie, Kathy and Linda, and said, "Each of you has one of these in your party bag, up in the pool room." Then, Sam said, huffily, "It's *not* meant to push you guys ... just to perhaps give you another new experience."

He looked around the couch, and laughed, "Maybe it's *not* new to you ... but I thought it was interesting. I had seen these in Amsterdam a long time ago, but found them on the Internet, and had to get one for each of you." He was really drawing this out, keeping us in suspense.

I took the package from Sam, and ripped off the paper. I giggled, but then had to stare, as I wasn't quite sure what it was. There was a thin cardboard box with clear plastic on the front, showing the device inside. I held it up for everyone to see, and read off the front of the box, "Triple Threat Rabbit Vibrating Dildo". My friends were hysterical. I passed it around.

Julie exclaimed, "Wow, I've never seen one of these, before." Then, under her breath, she admitted, "And I have quite a few vibrators."

At that, Linda looked up at Julie, staring at her, and shaking her head again. "Boy, we're sure learning a lot about each other today. And here, I thought during our decade of friendship we had shared everything with each other."

Julie said, quietly, "Not *quite* everything, Linda."

As I opened the box, and took out the Rube Goldberg-looking device, Sam was saying, "I got one for each of you, in different colors. Like the pareos, you're welcome to swap, if you don't like the color in your bag."

Linda said, sarcastically, "I don't think the color is going to matter much. I only masturbate in the dark."

Now, Julie looked over at Linda, with a crooked smile. "We sure *are* learning things about each other today!"

I held the mean-looking device, and flipped a switch on the vibrator; actually, there were several of them. As the thing buzzed in my hand, I turned it around, trying to figure out exactly how it was supposed to work. There was a large phallic-shaped central shaft, and a smaller curved portion that was evidently intended to be put in the butt. A third projection had several fine 'combs', which, I realized, were for clitoral stimulation. I had never seen anything like it.

Sam poured the remaining champagne into the beautiful crystal glasses in front of each of us. We had been drinking from plastic cups all day, so this cake and champagne celebration seemed particularly elegant.

As I sipped the luscious liquid, I closed my eyes, thinking about the day; it had been quite a party – both for my guests and for me. I realized that Sam would still be giving me a birthday spanking, but I wasn't concerned. A little pain, to make Sam happy, was not onerous; and perhaps it might even turn me on, a little.

CHAPTER 17: BIRTHDAY SPANKING

Sam turned to me, "Did you guys ever count the chips, at the end of the 'spank poker' game?"

"No, Sam. We stopped it in the middle, and I don't think any of us wanted an 'award'."

Sam laughed, "Too bad, I was going to give an airline ticket to anywhere the winner wanted to go." Now, *my* mouth was now hanging, open.

Then, Sam smiled, and I realized – fortunately – that he had been joking. Sam then said, quietly, "Actually, I was going to 'reward' the players with the school paddle: One swat for the winner, two for second place, and so on." He rolled his hands together, and gave a Frankenstein laugh. Or maybe it was Dracula.

My friends were sitting back casually, but watching us and, I'm sure, were listening to the discussion.

Sam said, "OK. How about this? You're going to need a good warm-up for your birthday spanking. Even if I leave off the extra three, it would be 25 swats with the school paddle. And," I bolted upright, "What?!?? The school paddle? Sam, I *will* submit to you, if you require it ... but I really don't feel like I need such a sore bottom, tonight. You *know* I'll be crying by the end."

Sam smiled sweetly, and took my hand. "I wouldn't have given you 25 'hard' swats." He glanced away, and then down. Quietly, he added, "That was just the start of my negotiating position." I shook my head; I really couldn't decipher Sam's intent at this moment.

Still holding my hands in his, Sam said, "When I started, I said you would need a good warm-up. And I was planning on using the school paddle." I waited to hear what he would say, but didn't like how he had started. Although I was certain that I would have a great orgasm by Sam's hand, afterward. Maybe, by Julie's hand. That was a thought! Sam was talking again ...

"Here's what I suggest. We'll get your friends involved." Uh oh. *Now*, what? Sam continued, "Each of them will give you 25 over-the-knee spanks – your birthday spanking from each of them. I'll give you 25 OTK – for an even 100 spanks, and then your 'main' birthday spanking of 25 with the smooth Ping Pong paddle. Then, you'll get the three extras with the school paddle."

Sam said sympathetically, "I'll heed your feedback; I don't want to hurt you. And it's not a challenge, just something to warm your butt before bedtime. So I'll reduce the intensity, if you tell me to."

That wasn't a bad offer. I knew I would get spanked tonight. And the idea of my friends spanking me was intriguing; I was already getting wet thinking about going over Julie's knee ...

Sam wasn't finished. "Maybe we can offer your friends something extra? They get to give you the first 25 spanks for 'free'. But if they want to give you more, they can 'buy' them. 25 more spanks for each swat with the school paddle?"

It was getting late, and I was now thinking that maybe Linda was right: Sam may not be a perverted person, but he sure had some perverted thoughts! But it *was* creative. And 25 spanks would be easy, even if my friends tried to spank hard.

"OK, Sam. We can suggest it to everyone. But I don't think you should expect them to take any swats with that big paddle."

Sam nodded, and looked at my friends, "I had thought about giving Kelly a challenging end to her birthday." I thought my 'end' is going to be challenged, all right. "But she has requested a lower intensity experience. Hopefully, it will still get her turned on." Sam turned to me, and whispered, "And if you want to have an orgasm, I know exactly how we'll do it." I couldn't tell if the others had heard Sam's offer. Or threat.

Sam said, "So here's what I suggest – and Kelly has agreed-to: She will go over each of your knees, for a bare-bottom hand spanking. This will actually just be the warm-up for the birthday spanking I'm going to give her. So I expect you to really spank her! If you don't spank hard enough, you will agree that I can put you over my knee, and show you how it should be done." I saw open mouths on all three of my friends.

Sam was very good at 'shock value', and had brought my friends' perception of themselves as 'wild' down a few notches. This was actually getting fun. I wasn't really worried about the spanking anymore. Now, thoughts fluttered through my mind about masturbating in front of my friends.

Continuing his instructions, Sam said, "You will have the opportunity to give Kelly 'more' for her birthday. For each swat you take on your bare bottom with the school paddle, you may give Kelly another 25 spanks. Any of those extra spanks can be done however you like – light, medium or hard.

"When all of you are finished with Kelly's warm-up, I will give her 25 spanks over my knee. Then, she will get in the 'chair' position (I pointed to the low-back chair on the side of the coffee table), and take her birthday spanking from me: 25 swats with the Ping Pong paddle. And then, the extra three will be medium swats with the school paddle."

Sam looked at each of my friends, "How does that sound?"

Julie was nodding slowly, a strange smile forming – and glanced quickly to me and back to Sam; Linda and Kathy were shrugging and nodding. Linda volunteered, "Yeah. I guess we can do that. But only if Kelly wants it." She looked at me. And I looked at Sam. He shrugged.

I sighed, and decided I was going to do this. Sam had been reasonable in compromising about my spanking. And I realized that this was his weakness. Sam really *wasn't* going to 'hurt' me, if I gave any indication that I didn't want to be hurt. My safeword had been in effect since my first experience here. I'd never needed to use it, yet.

And, I was still hopeful – given their reactions all day, and despite the stupid 'spank poker' game – that my friends might get more involved with Sam and I in terms of spanking and submission. A multi-person role-play could be fun.

But I wasn't as optimistic now, after everyone had balked at the game. Now that I thought about it again, they had said the biggest issue was being strapped down, and spun around; it wasn't so much about being spanked.

I don't even think they minded the rectal insertions much. But they weren't too happy about the needles; I would have to talk to Sam about controlling his urge to stick my friends in their butt with long needles.

Everyone was looking at me. I took a deep breath and stood up, moving to the side of the coffee table, facing everyone. I took off my underwear, wadded them, and put them on the coffee table. Then, I spread my feet, stood straight, and put my hands on my head. I looked forward, and addressed everyone.

"I agree with Sam's plan. I do want to be spanked and, of course, have been expecting my 'birthday spanking'. And I will proudly show you how Sam has taught me to take a spanking. Sam would like me to get turned on by the spanking, and knows that I undoubtedly would be turned on after 25 swats with the thick paddle. But I would also be crying and in real pain. And even have some bruising. I think I can get turned on without all that pain."

I smiled, and looked down at my friends, "Maybe I'll get turned on even easier by you guys spanking me ... not just Sam. And he's right: My bottom will need to be warmed-up, before I'll be able to take 25 swats, so you guys will be helping me, if you spank me hard. And, it's OK if you want to 'buy' more spanks from Sam." I smiled; that really was an interesting idea, even though my friends would never go for it.

I had to explain "And I want *all* of you to know," as I looked at Sam, "that I will submit to whatever Sam asks. Right now. And, once I've agreed to submit, I won't complain. But since Sam wants to be 'nice' to me on my birthday, he is agreeing to the limits I'm setting."

I quickly took the few steps to Sam, bent down, and kissed him on the lips, while keeping my hands on my head. Then, I immediately got back into the standing position at the side of the coffee table.

With my hands on my head, the t-shirt – as long as it was – was at the level of my crotch. I reached down, and rolled it up to my belly button, tucking it in so that it would hopefully stay that way for a while.

I faced forward, again, and said, forcefully, "I'm ready for my birthday spanking, now, Sir!"

Sam laughed. My friends were smiling, and Linda had a hand over her mouth. Sam then turned to my friends, and asked, "Would anybody like to buy some extra spanks for Kelly?" I held my breath, but couldn't imagine any of them accepting Sam's offer.

Linda scooted over to Julie, and whispered something in her ear. Julie was looking at me, nodding, then shrugged, then smiled. Linda moved back to her place.

Then, Julie said, "Linda and I will each buy another 50 spanks. I couldn't believe my ears! They were actually going to take *two* swats to be able to spank me more? I was dumbfounded. My brain quickly added up the spanks, 200 in total; a level-10 spanking.

Sam then turned to Kathy, and asked, "Would you like to buy any extra spanks, Kathy?" She quickly shook her head, "No, thanks."

Sam went to the desk area, and came back with the Ping Pong paddle, and the thick school paddle with the holes in it. He stood next to me, and asked, "Who would like to go first?"

Linda and Julie looked at each other. Then, Linda got up, and said, "I'll go first." Again, I was shocked. But we were finding that Linda really did get turned on by the idea – if not the act – of being spanked. Sam pointed to the chair, kitty-corner from where she sat on the couch.

Sam explained, "Put your knees against the sides of the chair, about halfway back on the seat, and bend and put your arms and head down on the back of the chair. Your back should be arched, and your butt high in the air."

Linda stepped over to the chair, then reached under her t-shirt, and took off her underwear, throwing them back to the couch where she had been sitting. She got up into the chair, positioning herself, her substantial bottom displayed for us.

Of course, we could also see between her legs, although she had not removed her hair in that area. I guess this is what Sam had been viewing throughout the 'spank poker' game.

Linda was much more 'open' than I had given her credit for; other than a few snide remarks, Linda had participated in everything we had done today. And it seemed like she had been having fun, at least most of the time.

Linda was finally in position, her bottom thrust up as Sam had asked. She turned her head slightly back to Sam, and said, "I'm ready for the paddle, Sir."

Sam smiled, and shook his head, as he took the few steps toward Linda. He bent over, and whispered to her ... and I realized he was asking her whether 'medium' swats would be OK, or whether she wanted lighter or heavier. I fully expected her to ask for lighter swats, when she said, "Medium is fine, Sir."

Any of my lingering doubts about Linda 'playing' with us in the future disappeared, as my mind struggled to assemble a new perspective of the friend I thought I had known.

Sam stood up, and placed the huge paddle against Linda's huge butt. Linda flinched slightly. Sam said nothing, but pulled the paddle back from Linda and then, in a fast, curving upward arc, swung the paddle against Linda's fleshy bottom. 'CRACK!'

The sound was much louder than everyone expected, and I saw Julie and Kathy jump slightly. Linda emitted a low grunt, but stayed perfectly still, as Sam held the paddle against her.

After a few seconds, Sam brought the paddle back again, and held it there for another few seconds. Then, he swung it again, in a duplicate arc, impacting Linda's ass with another 'CRACK!' This time, Linda was pushed forward, and I heard a quiet 'Oooohh!' Then, she quietly said, "Thank you, Sam."

I looked at Julie, and she sat there looking proud, as Linda took her spanking with complete dignity. Kathy had her hand on her forehead. I looked at Linda, who was staying perfectly in position, waiting for Sam to tell her to get up.

I *hoped* that Sam hadn't planned a 'corner time', as Julie and Linda were already submitting to a lot. I looked, but could not see any droplets in Linda's hairs, but wouldn't be at all surprised if she had been turned on even before she got into the chair.

Sam said, "And *that's* how a spanking should be taken. Please get up, Linda. You were fantastic!" When Linda extricated herself from the chair, and stood up, Sam hugged her firmly.

Then, he gave her a peck on the lips, and said, "Linda, I'm very proud of you; for participating all day, and for the way you took your spanking." Linda smiled demurely, and went back to the couch, putting on her underwear before she sat back down.

Sam didn't have to ask. Julie promptly stood, and walked over to the chair. She removed her underwear, and got into the chair position, without Sam having to provide any more instructions. Julie's labia were glistening.

I was getting turned on just looking at her: Private parts on display, butt proudly in the air, and awaiting a couple of swats that would certainly make her bottom red. In fact, her bottom already looked a bit red.

Sam waved the paddle, and announced, "For those of you who don't know, Julie has already received six swats with this paddle today. Hard ones."

When Linda and Kathy gave Sam questioning looks, he elucidated, "I brought Julie down here, after she had broken Kelly's trust by releasing the adoption information. We had a long talk, and Julie admitted that she had done something wrong; very wrong. It really wasn't fair to Kelly; especially on her birthday!

"So Julie agreed to let me punish her. The six swats I gave her were quite hard. But she was remorseful, and took her punishment well."

Sam looked back at me – I was still in the standing position, my hands now on my hips – and he added, "And I gave her a corner time, also." I wasn't surprised. And I still wasn't sorry for Julie – she really had hurt my feelings by releasing information I had shared with her in private.

Sam put the paddle across Julie's bottom; the paddle looked even bigger now, in relation to Julie's relatively small butt. Sam whispered to Julie, "You'll get the same 'medium' swats that I gave Linda." He moved the paddle back and forth on Julie's behind, finally pulling it back, and quickly swinging it – again in an upward curving arc – into Julie's bottom. 'SMACK!'

Like Linda before her, Julie maintained her position, and only emitted a slight grunt. Sam held the paddle against Julie's ass for another 15-20 seconds, finally pulling it back, and swinging it. It seemed harder this time, a loud 'CRACK!', like a gunshot reverberating around the playroom. Amazingly, Julie held her position, and was completely silent. After another 10-15 seconds, Julie looked back, and said, "Thank you, Sir, for the spanking."

Sam smiled, and helped Julie out of the chair. As with Linda, he hugged her, and gave her a peck on the mouth. I guess Sam was quickly accepting the idea of sharing saliva with other people. As they held each other, Julie looked into Sam's eyes, and kissed him on the cheek. Then, she grabbed her underwear, and returned to the couch.

Sam walked across the room, and pulled the small straight-backed chair from next to the side table to the side of the coffee table, where I was standing. Where everyone would have a good view. Sam sat down on the end of the loveseat, and looked at my friends. "Just to remind you, the first 25 spanks you give Kelly must be given good and hard ... or you will get over my lap and take 25 hard spanks from me."

Sam then looked directly at Kathy, and said, "Kathy, you're first." Kathy slowly rose, and walked to the backless chair. She sat down, and looked up at me.

I turned to her, leaned over, kissed her cheek, and whispered, "It's OK, Kathy. Please spank me as hard as you can. You don't want to have to get over Sam's knee and take a spanking from him."

Kathy gave me a thin smile, and I walked around to her right side, and positioned myself across her lap. Sam suggested that she straighten her right leg, and I moved myself forward, until I was over Kathy's left thigh, my hands on the floor, head down, and my legs straight, toes just touching the carpet.

Kathy put her hand on my bum, and moved it in a circular pattern, lightly grazing the surface of my buttocks. She asked me quietly, "Are you ready, Kelly?"

I promptly said, "Yes, Ma'am," and Kathy began spanking me. The first few spanks were tentative and, I'm sure, lighter than Sam would accept, but then Kathy began getting into it, and the spanks came harder and faster.

I made an effort, without difficulty, to remain motionless and quiet, so that Kathy did not feel that she was 'hurting' me. The spanking took less than a minute, and the last few spanks were harder, but still not a big deal or challenging for me.

After she had finished, and as she rubbed my bottom, I felt a stirring down below. I slightly altered my position, and made a small rocking motion, so that Kathy's thigh was putting pressure over my clit.

I was sure it hadn't been the spanking that turned me on, but perhaps it was the strange feeling that Kathy and I were 'submitting' to each other, even though, in fact, we were both submitting to Sam.

It was interesting that, in Kathy's case, a spanking didn't represent so much a physical experience, but a psychological one, as her family background had given her negative feelings about any sort of spanking.

When Sam told me I could get up, I slid off Kathy's thigh. I then straddled her, sitting on her lap, and took her head in my hands; when Kathy gave me a strange look, I smiled at her, and gave her a long and deep open-mouthed kiss.

Kathy resisted for an instant, but then relaxed, and allowed me to kiss her, although she remained mostly passive towards my advance. Still sitting on her lap, our breasts squished together, I hugged Kathy, and thanked her for the spanking.

She should certainly understand, by now, that I had wanted the spanking, and that she really hadn't 'hurt' me; I conveyed to her through my actions that even a short spanking was a turn on for me.

Finally, I got off Kathy's lap, and took the standing position, facing Linda and Julie. Kathy got up from the chair, and sat back down on the couch, and Sam said, "Now, it's Linda's turn."

Linda was smiling as she rose from the couch, and I could swear that she already looked a little 'turned on'.

While Linda was the most conservative and quiet of the bunch, I now knew that she was as 'sexual' a woman as any of us. Linda sat down on the straight-backed chair, and patted her thigh. I draped myself over Linda's leg, adjusting myself to maximize the contact between my pubic area and Linda's thigh.

I had barely gotten myself into position when Linda began spanking me – harder and faster than I had expected. In fact, she was only halfway through the first 25 spanks, as I realized that she was really spanking me hard; I felt an urge to kick my feet, and consciously pushed my toes into the carpet to hold myself still.

When the first 25 spanks had been given, Linda rubbed my bottom lightly, sensuously. I tilted my head back – getting a mouthful of hair – and mumbled, "Thank you, Linda."

Linda continued to rub me, as my head hung nearly down to the floor; it wasn't a comfortable position, but I was still being stimulated by Linda's leg – and by my own thoughts of Linda, now recalling the birthday spanking she had taken over Sam's lap. Linda's rubbing stopped, but her hand was still on my bottom. "Are you ready for the next 25 spanks, Kelly?"

Linda's question caused a clenching of my PC muscle, and I visualized how I must look to Julie, Kathy and Sam, as they watched me take my spanking from Linda.

It occurred to me that I was not in the least embarrassed doing this with, and in front of, my friends; we had come a long way, today, in terms of being open with each other – light years beyond what we had considered to be 'close' relationships, just a month ago.

I then pictured Linda in the chair position, voluntarily allowing Sam to paddle her; in fact, she had *asked* Sam to paddle her ... and *thanked* him, when he had finished. I clenched again, re-adjusted my position slightly, and told Linda, "Yes, I'm ready for the next 25 spanks, now, Linda."

I watched, as Linda rubbed Kelly's bottom, amazed at the hard spanking that she had just administered; it seemed that Kelly's friends were all getting into the scene, at least a little; perhaps more than a little. Linda looked up at me, and I nodded. Then, Linda began spanking Kelly, again giving her hard slaps on the butt – and now around her hips, and on her upper thighs.

Kelly was trying to hold herself in position, but was squirming on Linda's thigh, and occasionally kicking her feet. Kelly grunted a few times, but remained mostly silent. When the next 25 spanks were completed, Linda rubbed Kelly's bottom.

Then, Linda surprised all of us by putting her right hand under Kelly, sliding it up and back, then taking it out, and looking at it. She looked up at us, holding up her hand, and said, "She's wet, already!" Then, she put her hand back on Kelly's bottom, and announced, "And here are the last 25 spanks!"

Linda spanked Kelly again, this time not holding back, as she realized that Kelly really was getting turned on by the experience. Now, Kelly was bucking, her feet crossing and uncrossing. We heard a few quiet 'Ow's' from Kelly, as Linda reddened her bottom. I didn't realize how loud the spanks were, until it was over, and the room was silent, but for Kelly's heavy breathing.

Linda rubbed Kelly's bottom a while longer, then helped Kelly get off her leg. As with Kathy, Kelly straddled Linda, sitting on her lap, and gave her an open-mouth kiss. It didn't look like Linda put up a fight. The girls hugged, and Kelly stood and again assumed the standing position.

I looked at Linda, and she was smiling, but shaking her head. Eventually, she moved back to the couch, next to Julie. I announced, unnecessarily, "Julie's turn!"

Julie sat in the chair, and Kelly immediately got over her leg. Julie put her hand under Kelly, and held it there for a moment, Kelly flinching slightly, but then relaxing, her head hanging straight down, her hair hiding her face. Julie rubbed Kelly's back, and then her bottom, and the top of her thighs, which were red from Linda's slaps. Then, she bent over, and whispered, "Are you ready, now, Kelly?"

Kelly gurgled and spit out some hair, but managed to respond, "Yes, Ma'am."

Julie gave Kelly a solid, but not overly intense 25 spanks, alternating sides. I had to admit that all three of Kelly's friends had given her a 'respectable' spanking – not holding back ... and not risking getting a spanking from me.

I had planned to spank Kelly even harder than her friends had, but at this point decided to give her the same intensity spanking as she was now getting from Julie. Kelly was doing well and, we saw, even getting turned on. But she also had the Ping Pong paddle coming, as well as three swats with the school paddle.

Julie was now rubbing Kelly's bottom. She then leaned over Kelly and said, "Kelly, I know that you will be getting a hard spanking from Sam, and you've already taken a lot. I won't make you take the other 50 spanks, unless you want to.

Kelly turned her head under the cascade of hair, and said, "But, Julie, you already took two hard swats to 'buy' those spanks."

Julie chuckled, "That's OK. I didn't mind it. But I think you've taken a lot on your birthday."

The room was silent. Julie was right. Even if this were a turn on for Kelly, none of us wanted to overdo it. I made a spur-of-the-moment decision.

"Kelly, I'm going to make a suggestion: First, I will volunteer to take those spanks from Julie. And, second, I will forfeit giving you an OTK spanking. You've already taken 125 spanks – and your friends didn't hold back. I'll still give you your 'main' birthday spanking: 25 swats with the Ping Pong paddle ... *and* the three with the school paddle.

"But I think you're probably warmed up enough to skip the rest of the hand spankings. The girls have all had a chance to spank you, and I think that none of us would mind giving you a little break." I looked around at Kelly's friends, and they were nodding vigorously. Including Julie.

Kelly got off of Julie, and walked over to me. I stood, and we hugged and kissed – by now, a natural thing to do in front of her friends. Kelly said, "Thank you, Sam. My bottom doesn't hurt that much, but I know it will after the paddles."

Then, Kelly smiled at me, and glanced at her friends, "And I'm sure I'll be turned on enough for what I think you're planning afterward." I kissed her again, wondering if she had guessed how I wanted her to achieve her orgasm. She sat down on the loveseat, and I walked over to Julie, who looked up at me, smiled, and patted her thigh.

I reached under the long, pink t-shirt, and took off my underwear, putting them in a wad on the coffee table. None of the girls were laughing. Then, I got over Julie's left thigh, scooting up enough for my hands to reach the floor, and my legs to extend straight out, toes on the carpet. I continued to re-position myself, enjoying the feeling of my now-hardening penis being pressed between my stomach and Julie's thigh.

Julie gave me a hard slap on my right butt cheek, "That's enough moving. You're already getting me wet!" Now, the other girls laughed. I'm sure – even without Julie's comment – that it must have been a strange scene: A fifty year old man, taking an over-the-knee spanking from a cute 25 year old girl.

Julie's hand rested on my bottom, as I awaited my spanking. "Sam, I'm going to give you the full 50 spanks without stopping; as hard as what I would have given Kelly." I had known what to expect, when I volunteered to take Kelly's spanking.

"Yes, Miss, I understand. I'm ready for my spanking now, Miss."

I heard a stifled chuckle from Julie, but otherwise the room was silent. I let my head hang down, and tried to relax as much as I could. I was sure that my body still looked tense to the girls watching.

I felt Julie's hand leave my butt and, a moment later, it came down with a 'CRACK!' It stung, but before I could think about it, a second 'CRACK!' seared the other side. I again tried to relax, as the spanks rained down on my stinging buttocks, but I gave up, and just tried to hold my position.

Julie was giving me only about one spank every two seconds, but they were each quite hard; I was sure they were as hard as the hardest OTK spanks I had ever given to Kelly. By slowing the spanking down, Julie was drawing out my spanking to nearly two minutes.

It felt like it would never end. Even though she was using only her hand, and each individual spank should result in only a mild sting, the continuous hard spanks were making my bottom very sore; I had no doubt it would be bright red before Julie had finished. Ow! Julie didn't let up. I realized that my feet were off the floor, so I willed them back down into position. Ow!! I had stopped counting, but thought the spanking had to be over soon. Ow!!! I hoped...

Finally it was over; it had sure *felt* like more than 50 spanks! And, finally, I was actually able to relax, still across Julie's thigh. I heard myself panting. Julie was rubbing my bottom, and I rocked slightly, my hardness still pushing into Julie's leg.

My mind was in a whirl, and I was dimly aware of Kelly's legs, approaching Julie, and some motions above me. Then, I felt my buttocks being separated ... and, the rectal thermometer being inserted! I hadn't expected that.

I wondered if it was Julie or Kelly doing this, but my question was answered a moment later, when I saw Kelly's feet receding toward the loveseat. Julie spent several minutes moving the thermometer around in me, while holding my buttocks apart with her other hand. I relaxed my anal muscles, and tried to enjoy the feeling, despite – or maybe because of? – who was doing it.

I felt the thermometer being abruptly pulled out of my bottom, and heard Kelly command, "Get up, Sam! You now have the rest of your corner time coming!" I awkwardly climbed off of Julie, and got in the standing position, turning to face the couch. And now realized that I had a full-on erection! I looked down, and saw my pink t-shirt falling around my hard-on, with it sticking up in front.

Despite our earlier discussions, and my logical thinking, I still felt embarrassment, standing here like this in front of Kelly's friends. I looked, pleadingly, at Kelly.

"Good boy!" Kelly was smiling, and her friends were all smiling – although Linda's hands hid her smile;

however, they weren't sniggering or giggling at me, or my condition. She now asked, "Will you submit to me?"

I didn't understand. "Isn't that what I've been doing?"

Kelly shook her head, "No. You volunteered to take my spanking; which I appreciate. And you'll next be giving me a hard birthday spanking. Earlier, I was planning on letting my friends give *you* a good spanking, with all the implements that they've had to 'feel' today."

I quickly thought back: My hand, the Ping Pong paddle, the tawse, and the school paddle. I flashed again on how Kelly had become a monster; whatever challenge I thought of, it seemed that she could outdo it.

Now, Kelly continued, "But you preempted that by letting Julie spank you. And I don't think Kathy is interested in spanking you." She looked over at Kathy, who was shaking her head.

Then, Kelly really surprised me. "But I think Kathy wouldn't mind 'doing' you a little. I'd like to see that erection stay 'up' for a while." Kelly turned to Kathy, "Would you like to take 'first shift' in doing the honors?" I was again surprised, as Kathy smiled, and without saying a word, got up, sat down sideways in the straight backed spanking chair, and circled her fingers around my manhood, stroking slowly.

I was flustered, "Kelly!" But I knew that she wanted me to submit ... and overcome my embarrassment of being turned on in front of her friends. This situation was something I might have fantasized about ... and I *was* turned on ... but her friends stroking me in front of each other was beyond even my usual tolerance.

I closed my eyes. Kathy's hand did its magic, my erection now as big as it would get, my penis curving back toward me, and throbbing in Kathy's grip.

I heard a rustling, and opened my eyes. Kelly was walking to the couch and sitting down; then, she leaned over to Linda, and gave her something. Linda nodded, and stood up.

My hands were still on my head, my feet wide apart, in the 'standing' position, as Linda tapped Kathy on the shoulder, and Kathy went back to the couch. Taking me in her hand, Linda rolled a condom onto me, then started stroking me, using the 'OK' sign over my condom-covered maleness, and then her whole hand, as it slid down to the base. She held me at the base, gripping me tightly, as I throbbed.

Linda looked over her shoulder at Kelly, and said, "We could use some lotion." Kelly got up and ran to the bathroom, bringing back a small hotel-sample of body lotion. Linda let go of me long enough to open the bottle, and pour some of the thick, white fluid onto her hand. Then, she closed the bottle, and handed it back to Kelly, who sat down on the couch, while Linda began stroking me again. I closed my eyes; it felt wonderful.

Kelly then announced, "Sam, I would like one more thing from you: To take my corner time for me."

Another surprise! I hadn't even thought about the corner time I would give Kelly. Now that we were all being so open, and with Kelly's obvious intent to have me come in front of her friends, I didn't think it was such a bad idea. "Yes, dear," I replied, sheepishly.

Kelly got up, and a minute later came back with the small vibrator, lubed, and ready to go ... into my rear. She said, "OK, Sam, please get in the chair position for us."

Linda let go of me, and I promptly got into the low-backed chair that was kitty-corner to the couch. I separated my legs, put down my head, and thrust my bottom into the air. The girls had already seen me in this position, but it seemed a little more intimate now, with all of us around the coffee table in the playroom.

When I was in position, Linda continued to stroke me, standing to my left, as Kelly – on my right – inserted the vibrator. The one she had selected had a wood-grain exterior, and was about ¾" in diameter, and nearly eight inches long. I relaxed my anus, and gave a little push when I felt the tip of the vibrator against me. It slid in easily.

I closed my eyes again, the vibrator now stimulating my prostate on each stroke, and Linda still masturbating me. I heard Kathy's voice, "Now, I'm moving the vibrator, Sam. Just try to relax, and have fun."

I felt the vibrator moving side to side, up and down, and in wide circles, as Kathy manipulated it. Then, she grabbed my balls, and held them, as Linda continued to stroke me. It felt incredible!

Kathy released me, and I felt some movement, and then it was Julie's voice, over my right shoulder, saying, "It's my turn now, Sam." The vibrator moved in and out a few times, and then it was still, as Linda let go of me, and her hand was replaced by Julie's.

The vibrator slid out of me, and was pushed back in, repeatedly, as Julie stroked me in different ways, wrapping her hand around me, and moving down my shaft in a spiral motion. I was ready.

"May I come, now, Miss?" I squeaked, not knowing exactly who I was asking. A moment later, Kelly responded, "Yes, young man, you may."

My eyes closed, I rocked fore-and-aft, countering Julie's strokes, feeling the vibrator pulsing against my prostate, and focusing on my welcome task.

I heard myself make a few grunts, and my entire body spasmed, cum shooting into the condom, my anal muscles clenching the vibrator, my mind nearly a blank, as Julie continued to stroke me, finally holding as much of my length as her hands could curl around, and allowing me to contract and thrust repeatedly, squeezing out the last drops of my seed, and maintaining the glorious feeling of my orgasm for as long as possible.

Julie leaned over me, and whispered, "Good boy! That wasn't so hard, was it?" Well, I sure had been 'hard' a few moments before; but it had been a wonderful experience ... even now that I remembered that two other females whom I barely knew had not only been watching, but helping. One of those females, I had just met for the first time this morning!

I looked back slightly, and said, "Thank you, Julie. That was really great."

She pulled the butt plug out of me, and let go of my now-flagging erection. "You're welcome, Sam. I think that was fun for all of us."

Kelly said, "You may get up, now, Sam. I'm ready for my birthday spanking."

I got out of the chair, and stood next to Julie. Julie took my head in her hands, glanced at Kelly, and asked, "May I?" Kelly shrugged and nodded. Then, Julie gave me a slobbering wet, full-on, open-mouth kiss. She pulled my head toward her, and our tongues met. I returned her kiss, but pulled away from her. Then I hugged her, her breasts pressed up against my chest through our t-shirts, and our cheeks together.

When we released each other, Julie looked sincerely into my eyes, and said, "Thank you, Sam." I wasn't quite sure if she was thanking me for the hug, for the French kiss, or for allowing her to masturbate me. It didn't matter.

Sam quickly walked to the bathroom to remove the condom, and Julie sat down on the couch. I was surprised, but not bothered, by Julie kissing Sam. They had done some intimate things together over the past 15 minutes.

And Sam had performed for us, despite his obvious embarrassment. Sam, the openness guru! Well, we had all been very open with each other today, and I knew that I would be getting one more turn at openness in a few minutes.

I looked at my friends, "Thank you guys for 'playing along' with Sam and I. As you can see, Sam professes to be so open ... but is still embarrassed by many things. I'm trying to loosen him up, and help him get over his hang-ups."

Then I had to clarify, "If we had invited you guys over for sex – a 'ménage a cinq', then I don't think Sam would be embarrassed to be turned on in front of you. But Sam's idea of this party was a social gathering, albeit a nude one, and maybe sharing some things like spanks or needles, but *not* doing anything sexual with you guys.

"And, a few weeks ago, he would never have let Julie kiss him. He didn't even want *us* to kiss the first time I came over, even though he masturbated me many times. Now, we're finding our way, exploring the limits."

I scanned the faces of my friends, and added, "You guys were very open about helping him masturbate; that was really nice of you. Now, he won't pester me about who touched him in the jacuzzi."

Everyone was laughing, as Sam walked back into the playroom. He walked to the corner of the coffee table, picked up his black bikini European underwear and put them on, pulling down the pink t-shirt, and sat down next to me on the loveseat.

We all looked at him. He shrugged, "Well, that was interesting! I offered to take a short spanking from Julie, and somehow I ended-up in the chair, with you guys moving the vibrator in my rear, and masturbating me." It *was* pretty funny, and we all laughed.

I said, "Well, Sam, I'm glad you're beginning to relax around my friends."

He gave me a funny look. He had been 'relaxed' all day – going nude with us, and not getting turned on. I clarified, by whispering to him, "I meant ... 'relaxing your anus'." It was obviously loud enough for my friends to hear, and they cracked up. Sam laughed too.

I stood, picked up the Ping Pong paddle from the loveseat, and took the standing position on the side of the coffee table, holding the paddle out on my palms-up hands. Sam moved the straight backed chair back to the side table near the opposite wall, and approached me, taking the paddle from my hands.

As I stood there, Sam addressed me. "Kelly, I love you. And I hope you've had a nice birthday, today. I know that the party wasn't perfect, but I hope you enjoyed it." At that point, I broke protocol, turned, and hugged Sam. We kissed, taking our time, and savoring every moment of our joined mouths. Then, I got back into the standing position, facing straight ahead, again.

Sam continued, "And now, I would like to give you your birthday spanking." Sam laughed, "You don't have to be in the standing position, Kelly. This isn't a punishment, or a challenge. Just some loving 'contact' from me to you. And, as I told you before, you may ask that I give you lighter spanks, anytime you want. I won't hold it against you in any way. I'd like to give you something to get turned on by."

That triggered something in my brain, and I turned and whispered something in Sam's ear; this time, a *real* whisper that my friends couldn't hear. Sam smiled, and nodded. I asked, "In the exam room?" Sam nodded again.

I ran to the exam room, pressed the key combination, and opened the door. I found what I was looking for, and did what I needed – wanted – to do. Then, I returned to the playroom and took the standing position again, next to the coffee table. I smiled at Sam, and he smiled back; there would be at least one more surprise for my friends.

Sam said, in a sweet voice, rather than as a command, "You may get into the chair, now, Kelly." It was time. I sighed, and walked the few steps to the chair that Sam had been in, just a few minutes ago. I took the chair position, reaching under and separating my labia, as well as making another adjustment underneath. Then, I put my head down, and announced, "I'm ready for my birthday spanking, now, Sam." I would normally have used 'Sir', but Sam wanted to do this informally.

Sam stepped behind me, and put the paddle on my left butt cheek. "I would like you to count out," And I finished the sentence for him in my mind, 'the strokes ...', but Sam had another idea "the years, Kelly. Starting with your 1st birthday – 1990." That was different. Then, Sam asked, "Should I wait after each stroke for your 'ready', or just give them to you at the pace I want?" I trusted Sam. He wouldn't rush the spanking, if he knew that I needed to recover from a hard stroke.

"You may give the spanking at whatever pace you think is right, Sam."

Then, I heard, "Prepare yourself!"

The first swat stung my bottom, but I remembered to give the count: "1990, Sir." Immediately, I felt the second swat searing my right cheek. "1991, Sir." Then, Sam slowed down, waiting a few seconds between each swat. My bottom burned, but it actually felt good. Perhaps it was the champagne, still relaxing me?

Sam continued the paddling, allowing several seconds after I counted the years, before he again applied the paddle to my bum. By the time we'd reached the millennium, my butt was ablaze. Sam slowed the pace again, waiting perhaps 10 seconds between each swat. I dutifully counted the years. Sam increased the intensity of the last four swats, giving me two on the left side, and then two on the right side.

Had Sam given me this paddling the first day I had visited, it would have been a major challenge; but now – as I was used to the feeling, and trusted Sam implicitly, I was able to take the stinging without making a fuss or getting out of position.

Sam rubbed my bottom, "You did very well, Kelly. Happy 25th!" But I knew it wasn't over, yet. Sam walked back to the loveseat, exchanging the Ping Pong paddle for the school paddle, and positioned himself behind me, again. He gently said, "Kelly, when you're ready, you can call out the three 'extra' spanks."

I swallowed, and wondered how it was going to feel, getting wacked with that huge paddle ... considering what was inside me. I wiggled my bottom, and readjusted my head on the back of the chair.

Then, I closed my eyes, and said loudly, "One for good health!" A moment later, there was a loud 'THWACK!', and my bottom was on fire!

I waited a while, and finally said, "One for good wealth!" 'WHACK!' My bottom felt like hot lava, about to melt off my body. I involuntarily whimpered once, before getting control of myself.

I waited even longer, this time. I took a deep breath and released it. "And one for long life!" 'SMACK!'

It was over, my bottom now throbbing. I spit hair out of my mouth, and turned my head back towards Sam. "Thank you very much for my birthday spanking, Sir." Then I added, "Those last three were challenging." I chuckled, and only Sam knew what was about to transpire.

"Would you please rub my bottom for me, now?" I felt Sam's hand lightly sliding over my butt, and after a minute or two, the pain dulled, and I realized that I was getting horny again. As Sam rubbed my bum, I felt his fingers briefly under me, flicking between my labia. I said, "Thank you, Sir. That feels good."

Sam stepped back, allowing my friends to see me fully. Sam said, "I took your corner time for you, so your birthday spanking is now over." Now, he was chuckling.

Suddenly, Linda blurted, "Kelly! Are you wearing a tampon?" I knew that Kathy and Julie were now staring between my legs, wondering he same thing.

Sam played it well. "What?" I knew he was bending down, closely examining my genitals. Then, he said, "What do we have here?" I felt him pulling the string and, one after the other, several large stainless steel balls came popping out of my vagina. I heard all the girls gasp.

Julie said, "What is *that*?" Sam continued to pull the string and a few more balls came out. I turned my head, and saw my friends staring at the string of 'anal beads' that I had stuffed into myself in the exam room. Sam was holding the loop at the end of the string, and the gleaming, now slightly wet, balls were hanging down in a line.

Sam laughed, and said, "*This* was Kelly's idea. They're anal beads, but I guess Kelly preferred them in front. If I hadn't taken Kelly's corner time, I probably would have inserted these in her rear."

The girls were apoplectic, and Linda was shaking her head again, hands in front of her face. Sam told me I could get up, and I stood, hugging him, and kissing him lightly on the lips. "Thank you, Sam. That was a nice birthday spanking." Then, I had a second thought, "Maybe, we could forget about those 'extra three' on my birthdays after this?" Sam laughed, as did my friends.

I turned my head as much as I could, and looked at my butt: It was very red, as I had expected. I felt a stirring, and realized that I was getting more turned on, as I stood here. I turned to Sam, "I thought you might diddle my clit, and pull those out as I came?" I had expected Sam to masturbate me, while I was still in the chair position; now I wondered whether he had forgotten.

Sam laughed, and said, "Actually, I had a different idea for easing your tension." He looked into my eyes, "And, demonstrate your openness." Uh oh. *Now* what?

I returned Sam's look, and asked, "And what might that be?" I wasn't sure I wanted to hear the answer.

Sam laughed again, and hugged me quickly, before stepping back and pointing, "I thought you might want to try out ... and demonstrate ... the party favor that I got for everyone." I looked toward the loveseat, and saw the 'triple threat' vibrator sitting on the table, where I had left it. Oh! That's what Sam had in mind.

I felt a twinge of embarrassment, but quickly realized that we'd all masturbated in front of each other, already. I had 'forced' Sam, in the jacuzzi, and lectured him about it in the sauna. I accepted that I was going to masturbate for everyone in the next few minutes.

Sam set a small tube of KY on the coffee table, and got into the loveseat, partly sitting and partly laying back against the armrest nearest me. He spread his legs, and I walked between the loveseat and coffee table, over his left leg, and sat between his legs, lying back, my head on his chest, and my back on his stomach and crotch – with only one large 'hard spot', that I positioned vertically in the center of my back.

I reached over and picked up the vibrator and KY from the coffee table, and took my time lubing the strange-looking device. On one side of the package it said 'Triple Threat', and on the other, it said 'Triple Treat'. I was afraid it might be the first, but hoped it would be the second.

With supreme openness, I asked my friends to sit at the end of the couch, only a few feet from my genitals, and had them turn on the light on the corner table. I was a little amazed that Sam was happy with me lying on him, precluding his viewing of my first masturbation using his gift.

I lifted my head, and looked down at the triple-headed vibrator, which was purple with pink trim. I reached over and picked up the box again, to see what the controls were for, and realized it had *three* separate motors, and there were speed controls for each.

I threw the box back onto the coffee table, and turned the vibrator around in my hands, then the other way, then reversed, in mock-confusion over how it might fit into me. I glanced over at my friends, and they were chuckling, but enthralled by the scene before them.

I lay back on Sam, and lifted my legs to my chest, Sam holding them in position for me, as I reached down with the vibrator. It was actually pretty simple: Like a keyed electrical plug, the thick center vaginal portion went in first, and then the device could be rotated slightly to 'fine tune' the position so that the anal/rectal portion could be inserted. The rectal insertion was smaller in diameter than my little finger, but it was nearly six inches long.

I was plenty wet, and the penis-shaped vaginal projection slid in easily. I felt for the rectal arm, and positioned its lubricated tip on my anus. I pushed slowly, advancing both the vaginal and anal portions into me.

Incredibly, the clitoral stimulator actually reached my clit. It wasn't as soft and flexible as I would have liked, but it slipped under my hood, and felt good, as I clenched and relaxed my muscles, alternately pulling the central portion in and pushing it out. It took only a fraction of an inch of travel for the clit stimulator to perform its magic.

I found that I didn't even have to touch the device with my hands, but could move it, and stimulate myself, through my own muscular control. I lay back on Sam with my eyes closed, Sam's hands still holding my legs. I tried turning on one motor then another, feeling the various ways this device could become the instrument of my pleasure.

I took the vibrator in my hand, and rocked it, then inserted it further, pressing the clit stimulator against me. Now, I could just hold it in place, the motors vibrating with a low hum, and thrust my pelvis at the device to get myself off.

My bottom still stung a little, but it only served to remind me of going over Kathy's lap, and Linda's and Julie's, as they spanked me. Then I visualized Sam over Julie's lap, his body tensing as Julie spanked him hard on his bare bottom.

Then, my mind's eye saw Sam standing in front of us in his cute tee, with a huge erection pointing to the crossed tawse and crop on his chest; Kathy stroking him, then Linda stroking him and putting on the condom.

And, I saw Sam in the chair position, my friends moving a vibrator in and out of him, and stroking him.

Finally, an image formed of Julie, one hand moving the vibrator, and the other stroking Sam, as he came.

My orgasm burst forth, as I continued thrusting against the triple treat vibrator. I had barely touched myself, but I came as hard as any time I had masturbated previously. I heard myself breathing, and emitting strange noises, little yelps, that I hadn't known I was making until that point.

I pushed Sam's hands off my thighs, and put my feet down on the loveseat, my legs falling outward. My eyes were still closed, and the room was silent; I felt like I could fall asleep very easily, right here, just like this. Sam held me, and I could feel his stirrings down my spine – literally.

Finally, I opened my eyes, and reached down, pulling out the weird but wonderful device. Sam helped me sit up, and I saw the faces of my friends, smiling, curious, incredulous.

Julie nodded at me, and smiled. Kathy said, "Kelly, that looked hot!" Linda just nodded, unable to say anything.

CHAPTER 18: SLUMBER PARTY

Kelly's masturbation scene with the triple vibrator *was* hot. I had decided to be 'supportive' – literally – and give her friends a chance to watch at close range. Kelly had been very open to do this in the harsh light of the corner table and her friends sitting only a few feet away.

I wondered what Kelly had been fantasizing, when she came? My bet would be that she had been thinking of her upcoming girl-on-girl experience with Julie. I knew how I wanted to orchestrate this, but it would depend on whether the girls agreed.

Kelly went into the bathroom to clean herself and the vibrator. I wondered if she had read the cleaning instructions, so as not to damage the electronics? And I wondered what her friends had thought of Kelly's performance. So I decided to ask them.

"What did you guys think about Kelly's demonstration of the triple treat vibrator?"

All three girls were nodding their heads, just at different speeds. Julie was the most enthusiastic, as usual. "Kelly gave a *great* demonstration! And I'm looking forward to trying mine. That thing looks pretty strange – and I never would have believed it would actually fit in the right places – but I guess Kelly liked it."

Kathy said, "I would try it. I don't usually get turned on by mechanical devices ... but it looks like fun. Something you might try once, maybe as a joke."

Linda said, seriously, "Kathy, that didn't look like a joke, to me." Linda looked at Julie, "Unless Kelly's a much better actor than we thought." Julie was shaking her head.

I said, "It was real. Kelly wasn't faking it." I thought again: I just didn't know what she was *thinking*. What was *actually* turning her on.

I got up, and cleared the coffee table, setting everything on the bar. Then I sat down on the loveseat, and addressed the girls. "We have enough beds and bedrooms that you could each have a room, if you want to sleep separately." I glanced at each of Kelly's friends.

"But, in the spirit of the old 'slumber party', we bought Aero beds for everyone. I thought you could put your sleeping bags on those. We'll supply the pillows, and we also have sheets, if you'd like to open your sleeping bag, and use it on the bottom, and a sheet on top. Kelly thought it would be fun, with all of us sleeping in here ... or talking through the night ... whatever girls do at slumber parties." The girls laughed.

Linda blurted, "We usually play poker!" Now we were all hysterical.

Kathy offered, "I think it would be more fun sleeping together in this room. That's what Kelly had suggested to us." Everyone nodded.

I got up, and said, "Then would you girls please help me? We need to open the beds, and get them pumped up." I walked past the bar, pointing at the five boxes lined up vertically along the back wall of the playroom. I went to my desk, and handed Kathy a couple of pairs of scissors, and a couple of box knives. "Just be careful with those knives – we don't want to damage the beds. I'm going to the garage to get the air pump."

I took the birthday cake from the bar top, bringing it back to the kitchen and putting it in the fridge. I couldn't resist going to the cooler outside, and grabbing another beer. We'd drunk a lot, but I'd still performed for Kelly and her friends.

As embarrassed as I was, initially, I guess I would have been more embarrassed, if I *couldn't* get it up! I didn't think I would need to get it up again tonight, so I took a few swigs of my favorite IPA. It was only about 7% alcohol – about half that of wine.

We'd had a lot of wine today. The girls hadn't seemed to be affected by it much, and had enjoyed the sangria ... and champagne ... even after our white and rosé wines. I realized I might be a bad influence on these young women, and maybe on myself. My mind spun as I quickly calculated ... about 20 ounces of wine each. That was a lot. But that was over the past 12 hours. They'd probably only had half that in the 3 hours since we started dinner.

I put the beer down on the kitchen counter, as I went into the garage to find the air pump. I hadn't worried about finding it, until we were sure that we'd be using the Aero beds. Now, I was scrambling to find it. Although, I think the beds came with a foot pump, which we could use, if necessary.

When I got back to the playroom, all the boxes had been opened, and the beds removed. The girls were working with focus, two of them inflating beds with the foot pumps. I plugged in the air pump, and began inflating the beds and, with everyone working together, they were ready in no time.

We lined up the boxes on the back wall again, and put all the miscellaneous stuff in a small box. I moved the side table and straight-backed chair to the back of the room, and we lined up the beds along the wall across from my office and the coffee table. From the door to the curtain, we could only fit four beds, with a couple of feet between each one. Like a dormitory.

Kelly frowned, "Well, it's my birthday, and I take the prerogative to sleep in the big bed, tonight!" Under her breath, we all heard her say, "With whomever I want." Well, at least her English was proper. The girls laughed, but I hoped that I would be the one actually sleeping in that bed.

I had an idea for one more activity before sleep, and hoped that the girls would go along, as this was the way I was going to get Julie and Kelly together with a modicum of privacy. I did not suggest to them that they 'perform' in front of all of us; I knew that Kelly looked at her time with Julie in a much more important way. But she had insisted on trying for the hook-up on her birthday. And there wasn't much birthday time left.

I asked Julie to help me upstairs, and we brought in the cooler, and unloaded scores of drinks into the fridge. While I was with her, I informed her of my idea for the evening. She chuckled, and said, 'Good luck!' But she agreed to help. Julie would take the Aero bed closest to the big bed. I would be 'imposing' on the girls once again. But imposing in only a minor way; unless they wanted more.

When we finished with the cooler, we went out to Julie's car, and each carried in an armload of sleeping bags. I realized we probably had enough sheets and blankets to have made up 'real' beds for the girls, but this might seem more authentic, a reminder of their youth. That reminded *me* of their 'youth'. I coughed.

It took the girls half an hour to make their beds, and get cleaned up to retire for the night. But Julie looked across the room at Kelly, and yelled, "Anybody for the hot tub?" The girls laughed.

Kelly yelled back, "We're getting tired, and we want to talk a while. Why don't you and Sam use the pool and jacuzzi?" I was surprised to hear that, but then realized that they were trying to get rid of me – so they could 'talk'. Interesting that they didn't ask just me to leave, and Julie to stay.

I went into the shower room to grab a couple of towels and robes. When I turned around, Julie was sitting on the toilet, looking up at me and smiling. I sat down on the chaise while she finished, and then she came in, bent down, and kissed me on the cheek.

I suggested, "Why don't we get undressed here, and wear robes upstairs?"

Julie shrugged, and pulled the pink t-shirt over her head. She had very nice breasts – not large, but well rounded, and firm. As she took off her bikini underwear, she asked, "Why do we even need robes?"

I shrugged, "You don't have to wear one; but it might be chilly outside. And, they're comfortable." Julie shrugged and put on the robe, leaving it untied in front. I put mine on the same way. I pulled some sandals from the shoe rack, and we walked upstairs.

On the way out to the patio, I picked up the now-warm beer that I had left on the counter. I held the door for Julie, and followed her outside. All the lights were still on, and the Tiki torches were still burning; I had forgotten to extinguish them.

I headed to the patio table, to leave my robe, but Julie took my hand, and pulled me back toward her. She held me at the waist, and looked into my eyes. "Sam, you don't have to apologize about the birthday party: I thought it was great. I'm beginning to understand why Kelly keeps talking about your kindness ... and your creativity."

She chuckled, "But you *are* one intense guy! I think it's been challenging for Linda and Kathy … but Linda has really surprised me with her openness today."

Julie thought a moment, and chuckled again, "And we really did learn some interesting things about each other."

Then she put her head down, finally bringing it up searchingly, "And, Sam, I really am sorry for what I did earlier, and I do apologize. I'll make sure Kelly knows that, also."

Julie looked around, now staring at the barbeque, smoke still rising in wisps from the vents. "And you made a great dinner! It was all good." Then, she made a quick fart, shrugged, and smiled at me. "I guess the Beano didn't work perfectly. I was glad to come outside for a while." I laughed, and Julie farted again. I had to appreciate that she was being very open.

Then, she stepped toward me, and we hugged, our robes still open in the front. Julie kissed me on the lips, but neither of us deigned to go further. We took off our robes, and walked to the pool, then I dived in. When I came up, Julie smiled, and dived in surprisingly well.

As we talked, treading water, she told me she had been on her high school swim team. We raced two lengths of the pool, and were neck-and-neck, although I don't think either of us was energetic enough for a 'real' swim. I got out, and made a quick detour to turn off the pool lights.

When I joined Julie back in the pool, she said, "That's incredible!" I noticed that she was looking at the full moon, now over the trees in the west, a great viewing angle from the pool and jacuzzi.

I said, "That is beautiful, but the bright moonlight doesn't help to see the stars – and the Milky Way. Let's let our eyes get a little more dark-adapted. I want to do a little casual 'star gazing'." I flipped onto my back, and floated, motionless, looking up at the sky. There were no clouds, and the atmosphere was clear, but with the moon so bright, it wasn't as impressive as it could be. Then, we saw a bright meteor, crossing much of the sky.

"Did you see that?" Julie exclaimed.

"Yes – a meteor. Then, I pointed out two satellites – pinpoints of light crossing above, moving slowly through the stars.

I asked Julie, "How are you feeling?"

Julie said, "I'm getting a little chilled." We got out and walked around to the spa, lowering ourselves into the now-hot water. It felt great; very relaxing.

After we had mellowed a few minutes more, I decided to show Julie one of the 'features' of the jacuzzi. I positioned her near the wall, in front of the main hot water jet, and maneuvered her until the jet was focused where it would do the most good. And, I wasn't talking about sore muscles.

I pressed my chest to her back, and reached around with both hands, holding her labia to each side, and allowing the jet of water to massage Julie, flowing upward, and vibrating her clit hood, until it broke up into bubbles that rose to the surface. Julie giggled, but got the idea, and began positioning herself for maximum pleasure.

I retreated, and sat on the bench, as Julie closed her eyes, and enjoyed the feeling of the water on her sensitive tissues for several minutes. I put my head back on the edge of the spa, and looked up at the stars. I wondered what was 'in the stars' for Kelly and I.

Julie eventually broke herself away from the jet, and moved over to me, sitting on my lap, and wrapping her legs around me. I could see that she really liked playing the 'vixen' role. But she knew that I may enjoy her advances but would shun her, if she tried to get more intimate. At this point, the only 'intimate' thing we hadn't done was having intercourse. And that wasn't going to happen.

But Julie was just being close, holding me, her eyes closed, rocking. Her legs still around me, our bodies in close contact, she opened her eyes and smiled. "You guys were impressed with my masturbation scene when Linda and I came over ... but just think of all the scenes from today!

"Just my doing Kathy right here, in front of everyone, was incredible. I can't imagine that ever happening had we not come to Kelly's birthday party. And then there was Linda having an orgasm, with your finger in her rear, during the so-called spank poker game.

"And there was you, in the chair, with your ass up, coming as I rubbed your dick and moved that thing around in you. And there was Kelly, masturbating a few feet from us, trying out that purple vibrator thingy."

I tried to think back through all of the events of the party; had Julie masturbated, or had an orgasm today? I looked at Julie: She had an inquisitive look, but didn't appear to be upset. "Julie, did we neglect you, today? I can't remember you having an orgasm."

What a strange question, and strange thing to say! I had to remember how much our perspectives had changed over the past couple of months, in our quest for openness.

Julie looked at me sweetly, and gave me a peck on the lips. "I don't feel neglected, at all. And I'm hoping to have some fun with Kelly in a little while; I'm sure we'll get each other off. And, you can get me turned on, as a warm-up act for Kelly." That was nice of Julie – a bone thrown to the dog, perhaps.

Then, she looked into my eyes seriously, and said, "Sam, thank you for giving me time with Kelly tonight. I'll give her back to you when I'm finished with her." Then, she cackled, "But she might be a little tired."

I laughed, "I haven't worried about drinking more, tonight, as I was sure I wouldn't have to 'get it up'. But you guys surprised me in the playroom."

Now Julie laughed, "But you didn't seem to have any problem, in that department! I think we were all impressed." I knew that Julie was just saying this to make me feel good. Julie continued, "And despite Kelly teasing you about your insecurities, we were impressed that *you* were so open with us. It was your openness and your casual attitude, not paying attention to us when we were undressing, or sitting together nude ... just like now."

I cocked my head, and she explained, "We're in a hot tub together, in the dark, romantic lights around us, and the moon above. And, I have my legs around you, our bodies together. You're holding me so that I won't fall backward into the water ... but not fondling me, or trying to kiss me, or being threatening, in any way."

Then, she added, "You're not even turned on!" She put her hand down between us, and felt me. "Well, maybe a little." We laughed.

"Julie, that's the whole point: Trust!" The alcohol was finally hitting me, "And, I've already fondled you, you've kissed me, and strapping you guys down on a turntable seemed pretty threatening to Linda and Kathy." Julie hooted.

I hugged her briefly, and said, "And, I've already told you: I would much rather have you as a friend, than as a lover. Kelly does just fine, in that department!" We laughed again, but I was serious, and Julie knew it.

We had been out here quite a while, and I looked over at the clock outside the kitchen door, squinting to make out the hands. It looked like it was close to midnight. I guess I *wouldn't* be making love to Kelly again on her birthday. I suggested to Julie that we should go back downstairs, and we got out, dried off, and put on our robes. I remembered to extinguish the Tiki torches, and turn off all the outdoor lights.

Julie and I walked down the stairs, and stopped in the bathroom to hang the robes and put on our t-shirts. We both left our underwear off.

When we entered the playroom, Kathy, Linda and Kelly were talking quietly. Kelly was lying on the big bed, on her stomach, her head rising above the foot of the bed, facing the wall of Aero beds, where Kathy and Linda casually lay on open sleeping bags, on their sides, facing Kelly. Julie went over to the Aero bed closest to Kelly, and I sat down on the Aero bed closest to the door and hallway.

When there was a lull in the conversation, Kelly looked up at me, giving me a chance to suggest the next step. I had briefly discussed this with Kelly earlier, not going into great detail, but letting her know that I could get her and Julie together in a non-obvious way. Of course, all they had to do, was walk up to the master bedroom. That was still a possibility, if my plan didn't work. I cleared my throat.

"You guys missed a great night out there: The full moon was beautiful, and we even saw a meteor and two satellites!" The girls nodded, unenthusiastically.

Julie added, "And the pool and hot tub were great! We turned off the lights, so we could see the stars." Linda shook her head, and Kathy looked up at the ceiling.

They didn't believe her! But we *had* looked up at the stars. And Julie hadn't even wanted me to help her masturbate, while we were in the spa. I knew that she was 'saving herself' for Kelly. It was time to set the stage for the next 'act' of the birthday party.

I started, "Before we go to sleep – or even talk a while – I want to make sure everybody is happy and safe tonight. When we're ready to go to sleep, I'm going to turn off all the lights, except for the nightlight in the bathroom; that will be bright enough for you to get there and avoid tripping over the beds. Hopefully."

I smiled at the girls, and they smiled back at me. "Second, please tell me what I can get you to drink – for example, a bottle of water to keep by your bed; or a can of something. The girls agreed that a bottle of water would be nice, so I got up and walked across to the bar.

As I was handing out cold bottles of Evian, Linda giggled, and pointed. I looked down, and realized that the t-shirt didn't really go down far enough. Not much of me was 'peaking' under the tee, but enough – from Linda's perspective.

It was interesting that she would do that, even though she had seen me nude all day. Again, it was the taboo, the forbidden fruit, that most interested people. I tugged the t-shirt down a little, before I realized that Linda was just teasing me. I handed Kelly a drink for herself and one for me; she put them on 'our' sides of the bed.

Then, I got the remote, and one more drink – in case I slept on the Aero bed – and sat back down on the squishy surface that Kelly had covered with a blanket. The girls were uncapping their waters and taking a swig, then putting things they needed by the side of their beds.

"Finally, I would like to suggest *just one more thing* for the evening. It's not a game, but I will ask you for a small favor." Linda shook her head, but the other girls were quiet. "I'm going to put some light music on; not very loud. And then I will make it pitch black in here."

Linda went 'wooooohhh!' as in a scary Halloween movie. Everyone laughed quietly. "And I would like to 'visit' each of you, in a random order. Ending, of course, with Kelly." The girls still weren't groaning, and I took that as a good sign.

I continued, "I would like to spend five or ten minutes with each of you. The 'favor' I would like to ask, is to allow me to lie with you, maybe snuggle a little bit, if that would be OK. But I'll respect your limits."

I gulped, and went straight into my next offer. "Now, I think it would be great if I could help you get off. Or maybe lie with you, as you get yourself off." I laughed, "Kelly once blindfolded me, faced me down on the bed, and masturbated on top of me. It was one of the hottest experiences we've had."

Kelly concurred, and Kathy, in the bed next to mine, smiled more than I had seen earlier in the day, "Wow! That *is* hot!" She was sitting cross-legged, and her hands were in her lap. And they were not still.

I continued, "If you would like me to 'do' you, just ask me. It would really be an honor to be allowed, no less asked, to give something back to Kelly's good friends. You guys have stood by her, and you were really good sports with her 'experimental' birthday party." I laughed, and had to say it, "Even if we didn't get to play 'pin the donkey' today."

Now, the girls boo'd, and I was surprised they weren't throwing things at me. I had to bring this back for the 'close'. "But, seriously, I would very much like to be with you while you get off." I looked at the four beauties in the room, each different, unique; each beautiful in her own way, both in body and spirit.

"When I change the music to Indian sitar and tabla, and turn on the nightlight, you will know that I have 'made my rounds', and you guys can 'visit' each other. Or, I can turn off the music, so you guys can talk again. If nobody asks me to turn off the music, I'll set it for 15 minutes, and it will turn itself off. Is that OK with everybody?" The girls nodded, the detail perhaps overwhelming them.

I warned, "The lights are probably going to be off for 30 minutes or more ... so does anybody want to use the bathroom, now?" Nobody needed to go.

I thought I should make another point. "If any of you have an orgasm, others might – despite the music – hear you. But, hopefully, you've learned today that you're all sexual women. You all masturbate. You all have orgasms. You all fantasize, and have your own needs.

"So you may hear your bedmate, but please respect her right to get off without judgment, without making her worry what her best friends think. Is that too much to ask?" I thought it was a good speech, but I only saw blank faces staring at me.

Just for good measure, I added, "And if you *do* have to go to the bathroom, please walk carefully; by the time you're at my bed, you'll see the nightlight. Please leave the bathroom light off – preferably, or, close the door before you turn on the light. Does anybody have any questions?"

Nobody said a word. The girls lay back in their beds; most of them staring up at the ceiling. I hit a button on the remote, and the room dimmed to the minimum setting; that would be my 'last' setting, in case I needed to turn the lights on. Then, I hit a button, and the music started: Soft jazz. Finally, I hit 'all off', and we were plunged into blackness.

I immediately stood and, using the bearings I had memorized when the lights were on, I tiptoed down the row of Aero beds until I felt the large bed, and left the remote on the dresser. Then I turned, backtracked a few feet, and found Julie's bed. I lay next to Julie, my front pressing her side, and my arm around her waist. I leaned forward, and kissed the air, until my lips made contact with Julie's cheek. She turned her head, and kissed me on the lips.

"Good job, Sam! I'm surprised Kathy and Linda went for it." She turned onto her side, and put her arm around my waist. "I could use some of your attention, now, Sam." I reached down, until my fingers slid over her labia. I pulled my fingers back slowly, and left my hand on her, putting periodic pressure over her clit hood.

Julie suddenly turned over. I moved down a few inches, and put my hand under her, sliding it up and over her hood, back down; up and pushing her hood back, as my fingers squeezed her clit, and her whole body shuddered. Then, two of my fingers entered her. This was not the ideal position, and I pulled my fingers out, and ran my hand over her clit again, settling my hand over her hood, pressing in an arrhythmic pattern.

Julie responded with her motions, somehow focused but muted, thrusting against my palm. Too soon, she rolled onto her side, facing me, and whispered, "I think you've done enough, big boy. I'm ready for Kelly, now." Julie and I pressed together, both of us on our sides. Then, Julie turned onto her back. "Sam," she whispered, "would you please get on top of me, so I can give you a proper kiss?"

I smiled inwardly (as outwardly, there was nothing but absolute blackness). I crawled over Julie, and on top of her. I had expected her legs to be together, but they were separated. I positioned myself between her legs, and lowered myself onto her, my chest pressing against her breasts, my head lowering, and our mouths joining.

Julie took the dominant role, and kissed me desperately. It felt like all of her emotions had come out, as if she were about to die, and was compelled to expose her feelings. I kissed her back. I decided that I really liked Julie. I whispered in her ear, "Have fun with Kelly!"

Julie and I rose together – she taking the few steps to the big bed, where Kelly waited; and me, carefully walking the line, trying not to trip over anyone's bed, as I swung my right toe, measuring when it hit an Aero bed, and gauging my steps.

I got down on all fours, and crawled on the carpet next to Kathy's bed. I whispered, "May I get in bed with you?" Kathy giggled, and said, "Yes, Sam." I lay on Kathy's bed on my back, next to her. Turning my head toward her, I whispered, "Are you OK, Kathy?"

Kathy rolled onto her side, and put her arm around my waist. "I'm fine, Sam. Thank you for the nice day, and the dinner." Then, she chuckled, "And for all the interesting experiences."

I put my arm around her waist. "Kathy, I'm really sorry you didn't like the 'spank poker' game. I haven't done any of this stuff before, and am 'flying by the seat of my pants'. Or, I guess I was high, mostly *without* my pants." Kathy laughed, and rolled over onto her back.

I scooted over, and lay on my side, against Kathy, my arm across her, and occasionally moving my hand over her far breast, grazing her nipple, as we talked. I was not getting that good of a vibe, but ventured, "Kathy, would you allow me to help you get off?"

Kathy surprised me by saying, "Yes. Sam, I would like to do as you suggested, and let me masturbate on top of you." I was surprised, but not shocked. Kathy continued, "You may lie face-up, but I don't want you to touch me down there, unless I tell you to. Is that acceptable?"

I whispered in her ear, "Yes. That sounds fine. Just let me know, if you'd like me to help." That was optimistic, as I knew that Kathy would get herself off, without my help. Kathy moved over, and I lay on my back in the center of the Aero bed, my legs together. I felt Kathy taking off her underwear, as she bumped against me on the edge of the bed. Which surprised me: I'd expected her to leave them on.

Kathy straddled me, and lowered herself, her breasts squashed against my stomach, and her head on my chest. Then, Kathy's hands squeezed between our bodies, reaching down under herself. Interestingly, her arms grazed my flaccid penis, but she seemed unbothered by this, as she began tending to her own needs.

I held Kathy's bottom in my hands, firmly, but just holding her – not massaging, kneading or rubbing. As my eyes looked into the blackness above me, Kathy did her thing. Initially, I felt very little, as she used only her fingers, but within a couple of minutes, her arms were moving slightly. My hands were still on Kathy's bottom, maintaining a firm hold, but not moving.

A few minutes later, Kathy's body was rocking and her breathing was faster, breaths coming more urgently. Kathy's body was tensing and relaxing, and she made some grunting and moaning sounds, as her motions became more erratic. Suddenly, her motions stopped, and she farted; her cheek still on my chest, Kathy murmured, "Excuse me, Sam."

I said nothing, but expected giggling from Linda, who was only a few feet away in the next-door Aero bed. I heard nothing, until a few moments later, when there was a fart from her bed. As Kathy started moving again, I wondered if we really would have a 'Blazing Saddles' slumber party.

Kathy moaned a few more times, and then her entire body tensed, and she emitted a long 'Aaaaaaahhh', as she came. Her motions continued for a few moments, and then Kathy relaxed completely, her entire weight now on me. My arms circled her back, and I pulled her tightly to me and held her.

Eventually, Kathy pulled her hands out from between us, and she pushed herself up my body, until her head hovered over mine; I felt her hot breath on my face, as she said, "Thank you, Sam." She tried to kiss me, but missed, her mouth landing on the side of my nose, before she corrected her position and kissed my cheek.

As she slid off my body, and lay on her side next to me on the edge of the Aero bed, I chuckled, and whispered, "What for? I didn't do anything." I moved over so that Kathy would have more room. She scooted over, but was still on her side, pressed up against me, her arm across my chest.

Kathy stifled a laugh, and whispered, "That's the point!"

I half-expected Kathy to 'reward' me by offering her 'hand' ... but she didn't, and I was not going to suggest it. Tonight was for the girls; I hadn't even gotten an erection during Kathy's masturbation on top of me, although my mind was plenty turned on. Perhaps it was the alcohol, catching up with me, or perhaps it was my exhaustion after the big day.

My thoughts had focused on Kathy, and not my own body. I felt very relaxed, and was glad to provide her a new experience, without pushing her, or doing anything sexual that might be threatening to her. I was still trying to gain the trust of Kelly's friends. As I always would be.

I said good night to Kathy, and crawled off the bed, moving again on all fours between her bed and mine. I decided to wash my hands before visiting Linda, so got up, and carefully navigated to the bathroom. It was totally black in the playroom, but looking up the stairs, I could see a faint glow of moonlight on the wall. I left the bathroom door open, as I pee'd and then washed my hands with hot water. Then, I walked back into the playroom, and made my way to Linda's bed. Again, I crawled between the beds, and whispered, "May I get in bed with you, Linda?"

Linda moved over, giving me room to lie next to her. I lay on my side, my body against hers, and put my arm across her, over the t-shirt, and under her full breasts. She was no longer wearing a bra under her tee. I asked, "How are *you* doing, Linda?"

Linda turned her head toward me, and whispered, "I'm fine, Sam. It was a really nice birthday party. I enjoyed all the food and wine ... and especially the champagne." Then, she added, "And that was a great cake!" Her chuckle was louder than a whisper.

I cupped Linda's left breast in my hand, but kept my hand motionless. I wasn't going to push Linda, but she whispered, "Sam, I wouldn't mind, if you want to help me 'get off'." I was surprised, but pleased. Again.

Our heads must have been less than a foot apart, but I could see only black. I whispered, "You 'wouldn't mind', or you would actually 'like' me to get you off?"

Linda chortled, "I would like that. If you want to."

"Of course!" I realized my voice was too loud, as I had spoken during a soft passage of the music. I whispered, "Linda, it would be my pleasure to do that for you." And, of course, I meant it. I awkwardly moved myself down toward the foot of the bed, and held the waistband of Linda's underwear in both hands, then slowly pulled them down, as Linda bent her legs, and held them up, allowing me to take her panties off her.

I handed them to her, so that she would know where they were later. Before she put her legs back down, I held her ankles, separated them, and sat in the center of the bed, near the foot, my legs along each side of her; then, I draped her legs over my thighs. She rolled her knees outward, her legs circling around each side of my waist. Our genitals were only a few inches apart, but not touching.

Had the lights been on, this would have been a very revealing position; I imagined us in this position, as I waxed Linda's pubes. But it was pitch black, only the feeling of Linda's legs around my waist confirming that she was actually lying in front of me. I visualized her body, gaining a degree of proprioception of our linked forms.

I leaned forward, my hands grasping Linda's hips, massaging and then sliding up the sides of her body as far as I could reach. I held her breasts in my hands, lightly cupping them, and grazing over her nipples several times with my thumbs. I then lightly pinched both her nipples, and ran my palms over them, in circular motions.

My hands slid down Linda's body, alongside her patch of pubic hair, and continued along the insides of her thighs. Linda moaned softly, and I wondered whether Kathy could hear us. Or whether Linda cared.

My hands lightly followed Linda's contours, moving up the insides of her thighs, and across her mons. Then, they moved slowly downwards, on either side of her clit, my thumbs separating her labia. I rested my left hand in her folds, moving infinitesimally, my middle finger sliding along her lips, and eventually settling within them.

My right hand moved up, my palm now applying pressure over her hood. I slightly increased the pressure of both hands against her body, my left middle finger settling farther into her womanly folds, while my right hand began making tiny circular movements while maintaining the position and pressure of my palm over her hood.

Linda was now slowly thrusting her pelvis, as my minimal motions and gradually increasing pressure began to have an effect on her. I could feel her clit under my palm, and I slid my hand up, so that the heel of my hand was now doing the stimulating, Linda's patch of pubic hair now in my palm. I kept up the circular motion, and added a rocking motion, using Linda's hard button as a fulcrum. Linda's motions increased, correspondingly.

I considered going down on Linda, and using my tongue on her clit, but decided – as she seemed to be doing very well – to keep my contact 'non-sexual'; at least using our original definition of sex as 'body fluid transfer'; now, excluding oral-oral contact.

Of course, I knew that Kelly and Julie were probably having oral-genital contact at this moment. I hoped that Kelly was finding the experience to be as much of a turn on as Julie's masturbation scene had been. I also couldn't help wondering how different Kelly would find her 'play' with Julie to be, compared to that with Fiona.

My circular motions over Linda's sensitive tissues quickened, and the middle finger of my left hand bent slightly, and then advanced halfway into her. Linda was becoming nicely aroused, and was now sufficiently lubricated so I slowly pulled my finger back ... and inserted two fingers, slowly advancing until they were deeply inside her.

Linda's vaginal muscles tightened around my fingers, clenching and unclenching, as I slid them slightly in and out. Linda's breathing was becoming ragged, and I pushed my two fingers against her anterior vaginal wall, adjusting the position very slightly, until Linda drew in her breath. I held my fingers there, pulsing the pressure both inside with my fingers, and outside with the heel of my right hand.

I very slowly rubbed my fingers against the wall of Linda's vagina, moving no more than half an inch in any direction, but gradually increasing the pressure. I wondered whether she might actually achieve a 'squirting' orgasm ... which might require re-making her bed with fresh linens.

As I held my fingers inside her, I made a 'V' with my right hand (remembering my earlier thought of the Vulcan greeting), positioning my fingers on either side of her clit, still over her hood. Linda thrusted more, and finally emitted a squeal that she was quick to quench ... but not quick enough, as I heard Kathy chuckle in the next bed.

Linda's orgasm continued to build, as she thrust her hips, clenched her muscles, and creamed my fingers with her thick secretions. I held my fingers perfectly still, while applying gentle pressure to her G-spot. My right hand remained in position, and I moved my fingers as if playing a trill on the piano. Linda continued thrusting, her legs squeezing my waist, and her butt lifting off the bed. She was now moaning, evidently unaware of or uncaring about the others in the blackened room. The soft music continued, only partially masking Linda's moans.

I pulled my fingers out of her, and slowly released the pressure of my fingers on either side of her clit. I wiped my left hand on the bottom of my t-shirt, and fell forward onto Linda, taking her shoulders in my hands, and slowly lowering my head, until I found her mouth. I gave her a full-on kiss, which she returned, with feeling.

I managed to straighten my legs, and was now lying on top of Linda, her feet still around my waist. We hugged, and I held her for several minutes, while she calmed. I realized that Linda was exhibiting ultimate trust, as I was now between her legs, her vagina fully lubricated and ready to accept whatever was inserted.

But I was still flaccid, and had no intention of doing anything else with Linda. Eventually, Linda released my waist, and put her feet down on the bed, on either side of me. My mouth to her ear, I whispered, "Was that OK for you, m'lady?" Linda giggled, and whispered, "It was wonderful. Thank you."

I pushed myself up, and crawled down her body and between her legs, until I was at the foot of the bed. Then, on all-fours again, I crawled on the carpet back to the head of Linda's bed, and leaned over her. I kissed her on the nose, in the blackness, and said, "You're very welcome. Thank you again, for being so open with us today."

Then, I crawled backwards on the carpet, until I reached the foot of her bed, turned, and continued crawling until I reached the foot of Julie's bed. I lay down, staring up into the blackness, thinking about the two girls next to me, who had been open and relaxed enough to have – and enjoy – an orgasm in my presence and, in Linda's case, by my hand.

I listened, but could not hear any sounds from Kelly and Julie – at least sounds loud enough to discern over the music. I thought about climbing into bed with them, and lying on the edge, while they finished whatever they were doing, but decided that would be too intrusive. Kelly had asked for some time alone with Julie on her birthday, and I was going to honor her request.

However, that did not stop my mind from carrying the scenario forward, with Kelly, Julie and I having a *ménage à trois*. Now *that* would be hot! I had never really thought about a ménage, since well before my wife passed; she had never wanted to do it, and over the past five years, it had been hard enough to find one female at a time, let alone two.

I closed my eyes, and drifted into a light sleep. At some point, Julie was shaking me, and I woke, lifting my head, disoriented, as the room was still black. I moved over, and Julie climbed into her bed, lying next to me. She whispered, "Thank you again, Sam. Kelly and I had fun." She put her hand casually on my chest, twirling my hairs in her fingers.

After a few moments, she reached down, and put her hand over my penis, lightly pressing it down onto my stomach. Julie put her mouth to my ear, and whispered, "I would be happy to get you ready for Kelly, if you like?" She held my flaccidity in her curled fingers, and squeezed gently.

I smiled an invisible smile, and replied, "That's a great offer, Julie. But, if you don't mind, I think I'll decline this time. I'm not even sure if Kelly will be 'in the mood', and I don't want to put any pressure on her."

Julie let go of my manhood, and kissed me on the cheek. "OK, Sam. Thank you again for everything you did for us today." Then, she chuckled, "And *to* us."

I crawled off the bed, and whispered, "Good night, Julie." I continued crawling, around Julie's bed, and then stood, feeling for the big bed. When I found it, I leaned over, trying to sense Kelly's presence. I whispered, "Are you asleep?"

Kelly's hand reached out and touched my face, then caressed it. "No. But I'm pretty tired. Get in bed, and let's snuggle."

I asked Kelly to wait a moment, and made my way carefully down the length of the room, and into the bathroom. As I passed Linda and Kathy, I could hear light snores coming from each of their beds. I washed my hands, and turned on the nightlight.

As I had thought, there was enough light now – and our eyes were dark-adapted sufficiently – to make out the larger items in the playroom, including the four Aero beds. I tiptoed back to the big bed, and pushed the remote, turning off the music. Then, I climbed into bed with Kelly.

I put my arm around Kelly's waist, and said, "One last 'happy birthday', although it's not your birthday anymore." Kelly turned her head to me, and we kissed; it was passionate, but brief. I could tell that Kelly was really tired. She should be, after the big day we'd had. And, undoubtedly, the big time she'd had with Julie.

Kelly ran her hand through my hair, and said, "Sam, I'm sorry. I planned for us to make love ... but I'm really tired now. Would it be OK, if we just went to sleep?"

Smiling, I said, "Of course, Kelly." I'd half expected this; actually, more than half. I had no doubt that Kelly and Julie had satisfied each other's needs, and everyone was tired. I heard Julie breathing regularly in the bed below us.

Kelly turned onto her side, and I spooned her, my arm around her, and under her breasts, and my crotch against her bottom. Within a minute or two, Kelly was asleep. It didn't take me long to join her, slumbering at the slumber party.

CHAPTER 19: HAPPY ENDING

When I woke, the room was quiet and dark, except for a sliver of light coming from under the bathroom door. Next to me, Sam was snoring softly. He was still wearing his pink tee; he had evidently come to bed so tired, that he didn't even realize he was wearing it. My tee was on the dresser.

I stared at the ceiling, as I thought about the birthday party that Sam had given me yesterday. And all the things we had done with my friends. I sat up, and looked at the clock; it was nearly 8AM!

I heard a 'Pssst', and looked down to see Julie sitting on her Aero bed, smiling at me. Now, a flood of memories flowed through my brain, reminding me of the incredible experience I'd had with Julie last night.

Sam had kept his word: He had not only figured out how to get us together, right under the noses of Linda and Kathy, but he'd also had left us alone to do our thing, uninterrupted. I had actually expected him to join us; at least at the end of the half-hour that he had said the music would play. But he had respected my time with Julie, and hadn't intruded.

Julie stood, smiled, and took off her tee. Then, she crawled into bed on the other side of Sam. It was clear that Julie could be turned on by both of us, which opened the possibility of a threesome, sometime in the future. The bathroom light went off, and the door opened. I sat up, and saw Linda tiptoeing to her bed. I waved, and she looked up and smiled at me.

Then, she must have seen Julie in bed with us, and her hands went up to her face. She cocked her head, and I signaled her to come over. Julie lifted her head, and smiled at Linda, then sat up, and whispered something to us; we agreed, and Linda walked back to her bed, and took off her tee and her underwear.

Kathy was now stirring – lifting her head and yawning, as she watched Linda undress. Linda bent down, and whispered to her, and Kathy nodded. Linda quietly climbed into bed with us, while Kathy went into the bathroom to pee, not bothering to close the door or turn on the light.

As she walked back into the playroom, she took off her tee and her underwear, throwing them onto her bed, and climbed into bed with us. We surrounded Sam, who slept like a baby. The girls whispered quietly, and Sam stirred. I put my face in front of his, our noses rubbing.

Sam's eyes opened, and I smiled at him, and kissed his nose, then his lips. "Good morning, sleepyhead." Sam closed his eyes again, and I asked, "Are you ready for a 'Sam sandwich'?"

Sam squinted, and yawned, turning over onto his back, and stretching his arms. As he was about to ask, 'A what?', his right arm hit Julie, and he flinched, and suddenly raised his head. I hoped he wouldn't have a heart attack.

Julie leaned over and kissed Sam on the lips. Then, Linda and Kathy lifted their heads so that Sam could see them, leaned over Julie and I, and kissed Sam on the lips, also. Sam was now awake. "What!??!"

I repeated, "We decided to make a 'Sam sandwich' for breakfast." My friends laughed. I announced to them, "I'm going to want Sam for myself in a few minutes. But, I have to use the toilet, first."

As I got out of bed, I added, "You guys can prepare him." I walked around to Sam's side of the bed, and found the button on the remote that said 'Lights'; I hadn't learned the ins-and-outs of Sam's electronics, yet, but the lights came on, the room now dimly lit, as it had been last night.

I walked to the bathroom, hearing tittering, twittering and sniggering behind me, as the girls realized what I was asking.

I must be in heaven. Three beautiful, nude women surrounded me, and helped me sit up; then, they pulled off the pink t-shirt that I had forgotten to take off last night. Had I been THAT tired ... or drunk?

As I tried to clear my head, the girls laid me back on the pillow, and started caressing me. Kathy put her hands on my chest, while Linda ran her hands through my hair. Julie began stroking me. Wow! What a way to wake up!

And I was waking up quickly, as the girls moved to my middle, and took turns holding and stroking me, until I was hard. Kelly returned, and the girls looked up, Julie asking, "Kelly, may we?" She had her hand wrapped around the base of my erection, holding me and making lapping motions in the air with her tongue, as if licking a lollipop.

Kelly laughed, "As long as he doesn't come. I'll give you a few minutes; then, I want my turn with him." I was lying on my back, nude, being stroked by three nude women, hearing everyone talk about me, as if I weren't here. I guess I had no say in the matter.

Up to this point, I'd had only oral-oral contact with Kelly's friends, and I wasn't sure it should be taken any farther. But I now felt Julie's lips close over my manhood, her tongue swirling around me, her head bobbing up and down, as she took me deeply into her mouth.

Then, I was 'handed off' (in a manner of speaking) to Kathy, my maleness glistening with Julie's saliva, as Kathy put me into her mouth. This was incredible! There was nothing I could do but lay back, close my eyes, and enjoy the feeling of having three girls 'prepare' me for Kelly. When I opened my eyes, Linda now had me in her mouth. I could take this all day!

As much as I hated to spoil the fun, I told the girls that I was ready for Kelly. They sat up, and Kelly climbed onto the bed, and took me in her mouth. After a moment, Kelly held me vertically, examining my purple and throbbing cock, as her friends looked on.

"I think he's ready for me, now." Kelly laughed, and her friends got off the bed. Kelly added, "I'd like to have 15 minutes alone with him, now." The girls nodded, picked up their underwear and t-shirts from their beds, and walked out of the room.

Kelly reached over and handed me the remote, and said, "Drapes." I pushed the appropriate button, and the drapes closed silently, enclosing us in our own small, private space. Then, Kelly climbed on top of me, straddling my thighs, and put me in her. She fell forward on top of me, and we made love – slowly, passionately, and meaningfully.

As we lay together afterwards, Kelly's muscles clenching to hold me in her, Kelly held my head, and said, "Sam, thank you again for the birthday party. We all had a great time." My mind was muddled, so I just nodded, and smiled.

I finally slipped out of Kelly, and we lay on our backs next to each other, looking at the ceiling. I turned my head to her, and asked, "Did you have fun after we turned off the lights, last night?"

Kelly arched her brows, and asked, "Did *you*?" We laughed, but were both nodding, in response to each other's question.

We slipped on our t-shirts, and walked upstairs. We found Kelly's friends out on the patio, talking quietly; they were all wearing the pink t-shirts. Julie had a box in her hands that I recognized as one of the triple-threat vibrators. "Are you going to try it, Julie?"

The girls looked up at us and smiled. Julie replied, "Of course. Just not now." We all laughed.

I started, "I'll make breakfast for everyone."

I was about to suggest the menu options, but Kelly broke in, "After we go upstairs, and take a shower." Kelly pulled my hand, and I shrugged at her friends. Then, we went upstairs to the master bath, took off our tees and stepped into the shower together.

When we got back downstairs, fresh and ready for the day, Linda and Kathy were in the jacuzzi talking, while Julie swam laps in the pool, all of them nude. I looked at Kelly, and said, "I guess they just can't keep their clothes on!"

Kelly laughed, "But you told them that they weren't allowed to wear suits in the pool. And Kathy didn't even bring a bathing suit." I went out and confirmed the menu with everyone, and then Kelly and I prepared breakfast. Kelly cut up fresh melons, and put them in a large bowl with strawberries and blueberries, as I cooked bacon and started making waffles.

When the aroma of bacon wafted outside, the girls got out of the pool, dried off, and went into the pool room. I assumed they were going to get dressed. But when we started bringing everything outside to the patio table, they were sitting there, all three top-free, wearing pareos around their waists. Kelly and I were wearing shorts and regular t-shirts. We sat around the table, enjoying our Sunday breakfast; it was another beautiful blue-sky day. With four beautiful women.

Most of our breakfast conversation focused on the girls' plans for the day, and the coming week. But during a lull, I exclaimed, "Well, that was sure a nice way to wake up, this morning! I thought I must have died and gone to heaven!" The girls laughed.

Julie spoke up. "Sam, we all appreciated how considerate you were last night, with all of us." She glanced at Linda and Kathy, who smiled, and nodded. "You put our needs before your own. And you were especially nice to give Kelly and I some time to ourselves." I gathered that Julie must have told Kathy and Linda what had transpired when the lights were out.

Julie continued, "We've gotten to know you a lot better over the past 24 hours." Now, everyone cracked up, thinking of *how* much better we knew each other. Julie continued, "And we wanted to do something nice for you this morning." All the girls were nodding.

I hardly knew what to say. "It *was* really nice. Thank you. But, you guys already did something 'nice' for me by coming to Kelly's party, going skinny dipping with us, and trying a lot of new things – some of which I realize you didn't like much."

There wasn't much else I could say. It had been an incredible day, and Kelly's friends had been much more open with us, and receptive to what I had planned, than we had ever expected, or could have imagined. As the girls said, we had all learned a lot about each other over the past 24 hours.

After breakfast, while Kelly and I cleaned up, the girls went downstairs to take a shower. I wondered whether they would bathe each other, but didn't bother them by going into the shower room to find out.

I did go downstairs, however, and sat at my computer, uploading images from my small camera, and doing some minimal Photoshopping. Then, I fired up the photo printer, and brought the results upstairs.

A while later, the girls came upstairs, and walked through the kitchen nude, folding their pareos, as they carried them. We all went into the pool room, and talked, as the girls got dressed. They packed their things in the totes, and put their party favors back in the fancy gift bags.

I handed them each one more memento of the party to drop into their bags: A glossy photo of the five of us, wearing our pink tees. The girls gushed, and hugged me, thanking me again for everything I had done to make the party a success.

Then, we all went downstairs, and rolled up the sleeping bags, carrying them out to Julie's car, and stuffing them into the trunk. We went back to the playroom, and retrieved the totes and gift bags, and walked with the girls back out to the car.

Kelly's friends gave her a big hug, and wished her happy birthday again, and then hugged me, and thanked me again for everything. I thanked *them* for everything, and they all piled into Julie's car. There were lots of waves and smiles, as Julie drove off. Then Kelly and I went back into the house.

We deflated the Aero beds, folded the blankets, and put the sheets and pillowcases in the washing machine. I decided to leave the lights in the trees and Tiki torches out, and would clean the barbeque later. I hugged Kelly, and we sat at the patio table, thinking about the whirlwind 24 hours we had just spent with her friends.

I knew we would spend the rest of the day relaxing; and, talking about all the experiences we had shared with Kelly's friends. But as we sat there, in our own thoughts, we realized that we were both shaking our heads slowly, in disbelief at all that had happened. We smiled at each other and laughed.

Kelly told me about the experience she'd had with Julie last night, and I informed Kelly of what I'd done with Kathy and Linda. We were both convinced that her friends would 'play' with us again.

In fact, Kelly let me know that Julie had suggested a threesome with Kelly and I. Julie was really something – open, adventurous, and wild; but also a very nice girl, sweet, and a good friend to Kelly; despite releasing the adoption information to Linda and Kathy.

Each of Kelly's friends was unique; they were all interesting and, we had learned, very sexual women. And, more open than Kelly or I could have imagined.

When we had reviewed some of the things we had all done together, and how her friends had responded to our 'play' scenarios, Kelly smiled at me, and said, "It will be fun to get together with them again ... together, or separately." She thought for a moment, and looked at the forest, beyond the backyard. Then, she chuckled, and said, "There are a lot of possibilities."

Yes, I thought. It was impossible to know what the future might hold for our relationship with Kelly's friends. But there were many interesting possibilities.

###

HAPPY ENDING

Thank you for reading Book 4 of the Experiences series. If you enjoyed it, please take a moment to leave a review at your favorite retailer. And, if you liked this story, you'll LOVE the continuation in Book 5: European Experience!

- Simone Freier

Discover other titles by Simone Freier

Experiences Series Book 1: Origins of a Fetish

Experiences Series Book 2: First Experience

Experiences Series Book 3: Weekend Experience

Experiences Series Book 4: Birthday Experience

Experiences Series Book 5: European Experience

Experiences Series Book 6: Friends' Experience

Experiences Series Book 7: Island Experience

Experiences Series Book 8: Domme Experience

Connect with the Author

Follow me on Twitter: http://twitter.com/SimoneFreier

Friend me on Facebook: http://facebook.com/SimoneFreierAuthor

Subscribe to my blog: http://SimoneFreier.com

Favorite me at Smashwords: http://smashwords.com/SimoneFreier

www.ingramcontent.com/pod-product-compliance
Lightning Source LLC
Chambersburg PA
CBHW050917250626
47155CB00001B/266